MW00754228

Praise for Barbara Dawson Smith and her novels

With All My Heart

"Barbara Dawson Smith is a masterful storyteller of complex plotting and three-dimensional characters, making *With All My Heart* a delightful romance . . . fabulous . . . one marvelous read." —*Romantic Times* Top Pick

"A well-fleshed-out page-turner! . . . Ms. Smith is such a good writer." —*Old Book Barn Gazette*

Tempt Me Twice

"A fabulous hero who has finally met his match—the tension sizzles." —Christina Dodd

"A delectable, fast-paced tale with charming characters . . . great dialogue and heart-melting love scenes make this a book you don't want to miss." —*The Oakland Press*

"Another keeper from Barbara Dawson Smith . . . a wonderful mix of mystery, humor, and romance."

—*Heartland Critiques*

"Capturing both the era and the essence of suspense, Ms. Smith draws readers into her web and spins a tale that holds their attention and wins their praise."

—*Romantic Times Magazine*

"With Barbara Dawson Smith's deserved reputation for strong novels, Regency romantic suspense fans will not need a second temptation to read her latest tale . . . the story line is exciting, loaded with intrigue, and never slows down for a breather as the plot spins to a fabulous climax. Smith goes to the bestseller lists as usual."

—*Reviewer's Book Watch*

ST. MARTIN'S PAPERBACKS TITLES
BY BARBARA DAWSON SMITH

One Wild Night

With All My Heart

Tempt Me Twice

Romancing the Rogue

Seduced by a Scoundrel

Too Wicked to Love

Once Upon a Scandal

Never a Lady

A Glimpse of Heaven

THE *Wedding* NIGHT

Barbara Dawson Smith

St. Martin's Paperbacks

THE WEDDING NIGHT

ISBN: 0-312-98230-5
EAN: 80312-98230-0

Printed in the United States of America

St. Martin's Paperbacks edition / April 2004

St. Martin's Paperbacks are published by St. Martin's Press, 175 Fifth Avenue, New York, NY 10010.

10 9 8 7 6 5 4 3 2

THE *Wedding* NIGHT

The Rosebuds
Line of Descent

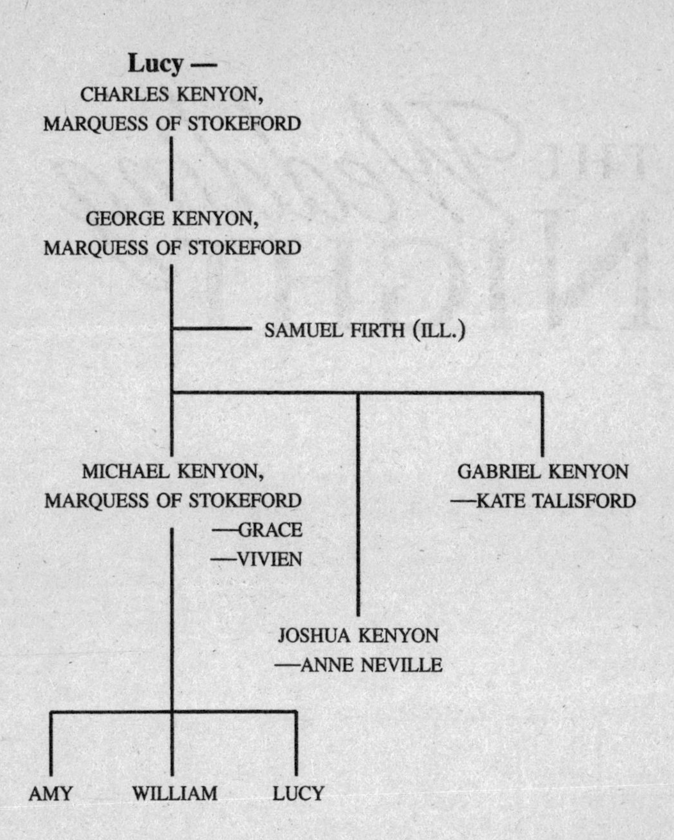

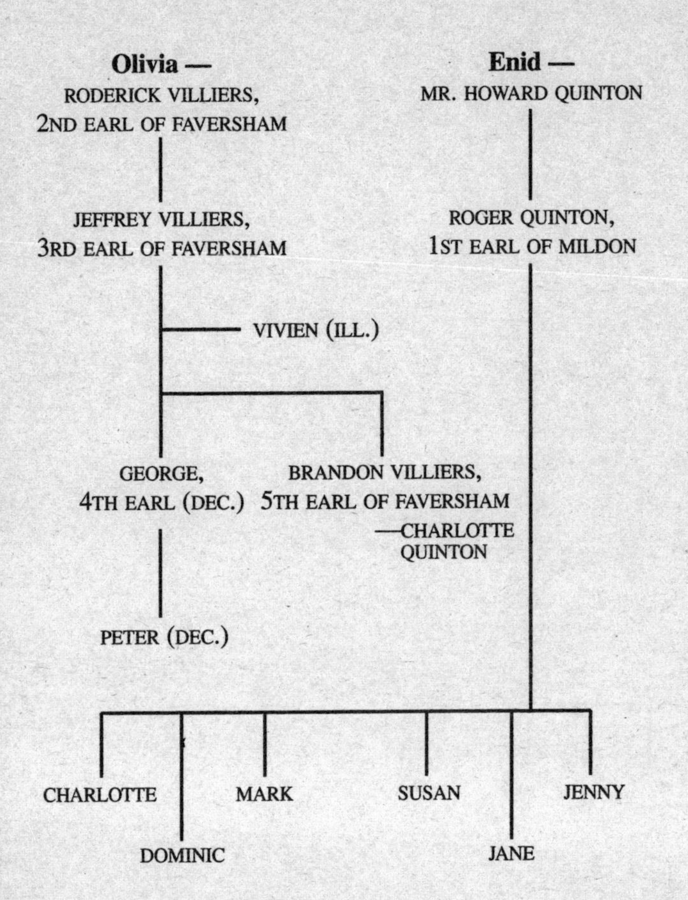

Olivia —
RODERICK VILLIERS,
2ND EARL OF FAVERSHAM
Enid —
MR. HOWARD QUINTON
JEFFREY VILLIERS,
3RD EARL OF FAVERSHAM
ROGER QUINTON,
1ST EARL OF MILDON
VIVIEN (ILL.)
GEORGE,
4TH EARL (DEC.)
BRANDON VILLIERS,
5TH EARL OF FAVERSHAM
—CHARLOTTE QUINTON
PETER (DEC.)
CHARLOTTE
DOMINIC
MARK
SUSAN
JANE
JENNY

Prologue

20th February 1816
London

Dear Diary,
Tonight is my wedding night, on what was to have been the happiest day of my life. But I have known the most wretched, mortifying turn of events. Oh, how foolish and naïve I have been about the ways of men!

Only a week ago, I was sitting at a dull geography lesson in Chiltern Palace when the letter arrived from my father. He had arranged a marriage for me and commanded my presence in London at once. The news stunned me, yet I reveled at the prospect of leaving the schoolroom and setting off on an exciting adventure. Had I but known what lay in store for me, I should have run far, far away instead!

I spent the long journey from Lancashire lost in imaginings of my mysterious bridegroom. He would be a gallant hero who would sweep me away on his white steed. We would fall madly in love and live happily ever after.

Those wildly romantic notions did not prepare me for the tall, darkly handsome older man I met only yesterday. Mr. Samuel Firth was aloof and forbidding, and I was too awed to utter a single word. My father explained that Mr. Firth is a wealthy merchant who would pay off our considerable debts in exchange for my hand. The cold bargain daunted me, yet I was certain that marriage would soften my husband's stern countenance and reveal the compassionate man beneath the cold mask.

How wrong I was! How I misjudged his character! Mr. Firth is neither kind nor considerate—and certainly no gentleman!

I found out that truth when he entered my bedchamber this evening, clad in his dressing gown. His presence startled me, setting my heart aflutter. I thought—I hoped!—he would take me in his arms and bestow a gentle kiss upon my lips, as he bade me good night. Instead, he made indecent advances on my person! When I shied away, he told me of my duties in the marriage bed. The shock of it caused me to burst into a torrent of weeping.

All the while, he watched me with those icy blue eyes, never once attempting to console me. Then he announced his intention to depart on a long journey around the world. He withdrew from my chamber before I could so much as dry my tears or gather my composure.

I must confess, I am as much appalled by his expectations of a wife as I am by the thought of being abandoned so swiftly. Oh, why did I ever consent to this dreadful marriage?

—from the diary of Lady Cassandra, daughter of the Duke of Chiltern

The golden light of a hundred candles lit the ballroom, and the lovely music of a waltz drifted through the air. The guests in their evening finery looked like butterflies flitting to and fro. But I could not be happy in their midst, for my guardian, Victor Montcliff, was nowhere to be seen.

—The Black Swan

Chapter 1

THE SECRET MESSAGE

March 1820 (four years later)

Lady Cassandra Firth was dressing for the theater when the letter arrived in the evening post.

Cassie was in a mad rush, having been at her desk, engrossed in her writings, all afternoon. The footman had delivered the mail a few moments ago, and she could see the letters from the doorway of the dressing room, sitting in a tantalizing pile atop her desk. She did so hope to find a message from her publisher with news on when her first book, *The Black Swan,* would be printed.

Ruefully, she regarded the ink that smudged the fingers of her right hand. "These stains are quite hopeless," she told her abigail, a thin, birdlike woman with kind brown eyes and a brusque manner. "I did scrub them."

"A good soak in lemon water should do the trick," Gladys said. "I'll nip down to the kitchen and fetch it."

"I'm afraid there's no time. Walt will be arriving at any moment, and you know how he dislikes being kept waiting."

Picking up a white glove from the dressing table, Cassie wriggled her fingers into the tight fabric.

Gladys clucked her tongue. "Do have a care, dear. And turn around lest you go off with your buttons undone like a hoyden."

Cassie dutifully swiveled and presented her back to the maid. While Gladys fastened the blue muslin gown, Cassie stepped into the matching slippers that Gladys had laid out for her. She glanced at the ormolu clock atop the mahogany chest of drawers. Maybe she'd have a few minutes in which to read over her daily pages. And to look through those letters . . .

Someone rapped on the outer door, and Cassie sighed. "There's the footman announcing Walt. Oh, why is my cousin never late?"

"Promptness is a virtue," Gladys said, a severe look on her plain sparrow face. "One you would do well to learn."

Cassie opened her mouth to grumble, but the maidservant had already left the dressing room. She returned in a moment with the news that His Grace was indeed waiting downstairs.

While Gladys went to the wardrobe to fetch a pelisse, Cassie stole out into the bedchamber and glanced furtively through the letters. No one but her closest friend Flora knew about her recent literary sale, not even Gladys, who had served Cassie these past four years.

To her disappointment, though, most of the mail appeared to be invitations that she would politely decline. The daughter of a duke, Cassie was invariably asked to the best parties, yet she seldom attended, having little desire to make stilted conversation with strangers. She had never felt comfortable in the exclusive world of the *ton,* where fashion and frivolity ruled, where women were expected to be pretty ornaments who flirted and flattered men. Cassie had more important things to do with her life.

Then the letter on the bottom of the stack caught her

attention. She might have set it aside with the others if not for two facts. First, it was printed in block letters rather than handwritten. Second, it bore an outmoded form of address: "Lady Cassandra Grey."

Cassie hadn't used the name Grey since her marriage four years ago to a man she hadn't seen since their wedding night. She stared down at the letter clutched in her gloved hands. Though she had come to terms with her husband's absence, a painful longing wrenched her. If only she could be Lady Cassandra Grey again. If only she could return to the innocent girl she had once been.

Senseless, impossible thought.

She broke the wafer that sealed the note, unfolded the paper, and saw that the brief message also was printed rather than penned in cursive.

My dearest Lady Cassandra,

No longer am I able to keep silent the love that burns in my heart. Pray know that you are held in the highest esteem by one who adores you. Whatever may happen, I shall always watch over you.

A chill touched Cassie, raising gooseflesh on her arms. There was no signature. Who had sent the note?

Though the firm, neat letters appeared to have been written by an educated man, she recognized nothing familiar about the penmanship. Nor was there anything distinctive about the white paper, which could have been purchased at any stationer's shop. Had the sender printed the words because he was someone she knew, someone who was anxious to disguise his identity? But surely no one in her close circle of friends would write such an unorthodox message rather than confess the truth to her face.

Perhaps a stranger was watching her. Perhaps she was being observed as she went about her errands, walking to the lending library or taking her daily constitutional. Although the notion made her uneasy, something about it also appealed to the romantic in her.

Was it possible that an unknown gentleman had fallen in love with her from afar? That he knew she was out of his reach? That he merely wished to pour out his deepest feelings to her? Perhaps he longed for her in daytime and dreamed of her at night . . .

Cassie curbed her runaway imagination. She couldn't fathom why such a man would address a letter to her as if she were an unmarried lady. Could he be someone from her distant past? Someone who knew her from Lancashire where she had grown up? On their infrequent visits, her parents had often brought guests from London.

"M'lady? Is aught amiss?"

Gladys regarded her with sharp eyes, so Cassie summoned a smile. "A letter from an old acquaintance," she fibbed. "It's of no consequence."

Most likely, it was a prank played by Walt or Philip or Bertie. In the past, she had learned the value of ignoring their tricks.

Folding the note, she turned her mind to the evening ahead. The unwanted invitations she tossed atop the clutter of quills and papers on her desk. After a moment's hesitation, she placed the mysterious letter inside the drawer of her bedside table.

Yet as she headed downstairs, she couldn't help but puzzle over the message. The words had been intensely passionate, tenderly romantic.

"Pray know that you are held in the highest esteem by one who adores you."

Upon learning of my mother's untimely death, he pressed my hands between his and uttered in an anguished tone, "My poor Belinda, I should have been there."

" 'Twas no fault of yours!" I assured him. "You were tending to your estates and could not have known of her illness."

"Nevertheless I have failed in my duty as your guardian."

I lapsed into silence at that, for I so yearned to be more than a duty to the Honorable Victor Montcliff, the devoted son and heir of Baron S——.

—The Black Swan

Chapter 2

A Chance Meeting

Within moments of entering the private box at the theater, Samuel Firth noticed the woman.

He was late, and that fact irritated him. The crush of traffic outside the theater had tried his patience. After four years abroad, he had forgotten the difficulties of negotiating the crowded streets of London. But he hadn't forgotten the glittering allure of the *ton.*

Giving a nod of greeting to Ellis MacDermot, he took a seat beside his business acquaintance in the front row and scanned the packed theater. Women in fancy gowns and sparkling gemstones sat with gentlemen in tailored coats and elaborate cravats. Chandeliers lit the red and gilt décor of the vast room with its high domed ceiling. In addition to the central seating on the main floor, three tiers of box seats hugged the walls, topped by another two rows of balcony for those of lesser stature. The orchestra in the pit played softly to underscore the booming voices of the actors on stage. Footlights cast a flickering glow over the scene with its backdrop depicting a drawing room.

Samuel settled back to watch the drama. Not even the Kabuki shows of Japan or the sari dancers of India could compare to good English theater. A stab of nostalgia took him unawares. Few knew that he had grown up in the world of the theater in Brighton. He had read lines with the actors, run errands for the director, hauled trunks of costumes in and out of storage. It had been hard work for a child, but he had enjoyed the excitement of the stage. That happy phase of his life had come to an abrupt end at the age of twelve with the untimely death of his mother and the words she had spoken before breathing her last.

His gut twisted at the memory. He had always known he was a bastard, but not that his father was George Kenyon, the Marquess of Stokeford, or that he had three legitimate half brothers. His mother had confessed to writing to Lord Stokeford numerous times, begging him to acknowledge her son, but her letters had never been answered. In broken gasps, she had pleaded with Samuel to go to Devonshire and approach the marquess himself.

He had never gone, of course. His insides had burned with pain and grief and anger. He refused to push himself on the haughty man who had rejected his unwanted bastard son. Spurred by cold hatred, Samuel had set out to make his fortune. He had sworn to avenge the wrong done to him and his mother by becoming the equal of the Kenyons.

Even now, a knot of ruthless resolve tightened inside him. With his innate skill in business, he had achieved wealth to rival that of the richest aristocrats. But money wasn't enough. He was so close now. So very close to achieving his revenge by founding his own dynasty.

A disturbance directly across the theater distracted Samuel.

Three gentlemen in a private box scuffled over something

on the floor. Their brief battle for possession created a stir in the audience and a chorus of hissing. Then one of the toffs straightened up and victoriously waved a program. With a bow and a flourish, he handed it to the lady sitting in their midst. She afforded the fellow a nod of thanks and returned her gaze to the stage.

Beautiful.

Samuel forgot the actors reciting their lines. Carnal interest stirred in him as he stared intently at the woman. Fair and delicate, she was the epitome of the aristocratic lady. Her face bore the fine features of a cameo, a testament to her noble breeding. Her sole adornment was a spray of pink rosebuds tucked into her golden hair. If not for her air of regal confidence, he might have thought her a debutante in her first season.

But she was no maiden fresh from the schoolroom. The maturity of a woman radiated from her. He could imagine all that soft blond hair spread over a pillow—his pillow. He could imagine himself lying over her, pressing himself into the cradle of her slim thighs . . .

The image was so vivid, so carnal, he had to restrain himself from going to her at once. He knew nothing of her, least of all her marital status. But with several men sniffing around her, she must be unattached—or had a fool for a husband. Who was she? For once, Samuel regretted his lack of a quizzing glass used by so many of the fops here. He wanted to take a closer look at her.

He forced his gaze back to the stage. But his attention returned to her from time to time, and he willed her to glance his way so that he might somehow catch her eye. The play, however, absorbed her completely. Not once did she scan the audience as did so many others who considered attendance at the theater a social affair.

A few minutes prior to the interlude, one of the men in her entourage leaned over to whisper in her ear. She smiled and nodded, and the gentleman scuttled out the back door of the box, presumably to fetch a refreshment for her. The other two men in her party looked disgruntled at the missed opportunity.

But she took no notice of them. She leaned forward slightly to watch the closing moments of the act. The audience laughed at some tidbit of dialogue on stage, and so did she. The glimmer of animation on her face transfixed Samuel.

That smile. Where had he seen it before?

As the crimson curtain descended, and people left their seats to stroll in the lobby, a gruff voice with an Irish lilt muttered, "See someone you know, Firth?"

Samuel glanced at the affable features of Ellis MacDermot. With his curly ginger hair and ready smile, the fashionable coat and perfectly tied cravat, he appeared more a gentleman about town than a canny businessman. But like Samuel, MacDermot had earned his considerable riches through hard labor. He owned several textile mills and often used Samuel's ships to send his wares to the far reaches of the globe.

"I don't know a soul besides you," Samuel replied. "I may be somewhat tolerated in Brighton society, but not here in London."

"Yet you're staring at someone. A lady, I'll wager."

"Several have caught my eye." Samuel deliberately kept his gaze on MacDermot. Having never been one to share his women, he had no wish to point her out. Not even to an old friend.

MacDermot peered across the theater. "One in particular, I'd say. The lass with the golden hair, directly across from us. Ah, she's a choice one."

Samuel made no reply. He knew better than to encourage MacDermot.

Nevertheless, the Irishman went on. "Looks like you've

competition, eh? They're gathered like stallions guarding their favorite mare."

Samuel let himself look at her again. She had arisen from her chair and stood conversing with her admirers. A filmy blue gown skimmed her shapely form. The bodice was cut fashionably low, giving him a glimpse of a fine bosom. His pulse quickened. Even from across the crowded theater, the sight of her exquisite beauty stirred his blood.

It had been many weeks since he'd had a woman. The only females aboard the ship from India had been the elderly wife of a colonel and a young girl of perhaps seven in the company of her dour, middle-aged nanny. Over the past four years, he had traveled to his far-flung holdings all over the world. A sugarcane plantation in the West Indies. A gold mine in Africa. A tea estate in Ceylon. Almost constantly on the move, he had eased his physical needs in occasional discreet encounters with local women.

But he had no intention of taking a mistress while here in London. He had too much at stake, a plan that was vital to his scheme of revenge. A plan he intended to set in motion on the morrow.

So why was he even considering a visit to the box across the stage?

"What business matter did you wish to discuss?" he asked MacDermot. "You said it was urgent."

His reddish brows lowering, MacDermot appeared loath to change the subject. He folded his long fingers over his dark green waistcoat. "It concerns a bank draft I sent to your purser a fortnight ago. Your man swears it never arrived, yet my records show the bill was paid in full."

Samuel frowned. In his absence, other funds had gone missing from the London office. "An oversight, perhaps. I'll look into the matter. Was it Babbage who handled it?"

"I spoke with him personally, of course. Humorless fellow. Didn't crack a smile at any of my jests."

"Not everyone appreciates your ribald stories."

"Have I told you the one about the nun and the Peeping Tom?" MacDermot's teeth flashed in a grin, then he sobered, though his brown eyes still gleamed. "Never mind, I'm prattling. You've enough on your mind, considering the situation with your wife."

Samuel tensed. His expression turned icy, though inside his emotions churned. Guilt for the way he had reordered her life. Shame for the botch he'd made of their wedding night. And anger—nay, *fury*—that anyone would pry into his personal affairs. But he should have known rumors would circulate. She was, after all, the only child of the Duke of Chiltern. "What about my wife?"

"Gossip has it she moved out of your town house months ago. It can't have been a pleasant discovery."

"I knew. I've been in correspondence with Andrew Jamison, my solicitor." The most recent report had enclosed a document that still had the power to make Samuel clench his teeth. It had caused him to book passage on the fastest ship home.

"Have you called on her yet?" MacDermot asked.

"No." His tone curt, Samuel made it clear that he would not discuss his wife. He hadn't seen Cassie in four years, so one more day wouldn't matter. It was for her sake as well as his that he resolve their estrangement with as little fuss as possible. He must proceed carefully and without giving vent to his rage. His wife was a shy girl, easily influenced, and he had no wish to frighten her any more than he already had done on their wedding night.

Unwilling to revisit that memory, Samuel focused on the present. He would let himself think only of punishing those who had undoubtedly persuaded her to take this disastrous course of action.

MacDermot eyed him thoughtfully, then glanced over at the blonde. "You're free tonight, perhaps your last night of freedom for a while. You oughtn't waste it on me."

Samuel said nothing, though awareness of the woman burned in him. He craved a diversion—he craved *her*. She appeared to have the sensuality and experience he preferred in a bed partner, qualities his wife would learn in time. However, he wanted a woman *now*. His body ached with the need for physical release. It was distracting him from his purpose in returning to London.

And that he wouldn't tolerate.

"Go on," MacDermot said with an encouraging wave of his hand. "Unless you doubt your ability to fight off her throng of admirers."

A hint of deviltry touched the Irishman's eyes, but Samuel didn't bother to question it. He was well aware of being manipulated. MacDermot claimed a place on the fringes of polite society by virtue of his relation to Irish nobility. Perhaps he knew the lady to be a predator of men or a notable ice queen. But whoever she was, Samuel made up his mind to have her.

Rising from his chair, he said, "Don't wait for me after the performance."

MacDermot chuckled. "The best of luck to you, old fellow."

Samuel left through the rear door of the private box. Ladies and gentlemen thronged the passageway and the ornate lobby. Some bore champagne flutes, others crystal glasses of punch. He cut a path through the crowd, eliciting a few curious glances from the other theatergoers. He doubted anyone here would recognize him. These noble folk knew him solely by hearsay.

All that would change in the weeks to come.

Then he could think only of *her*. As he made his way toward the opposite passageway, he felt a lusty excitement. Despite his confidence, he couldn't be certain of persuading her. Ladies often required a period of courtship, and he had no time for such nonsense. Much would depend upon her nature, whether she was warm or cool.

He would wager on the latter. *Yes*. Eminently more challenging, yet all the more satisfying in her ultimate surrender.

He neared the end of the corridor closest to the stage. The door to her private box stood ajar, and the rumble of male voices emanated from within, followed by a throaty feminine laugh that caused his loins to tighten.

Samuel stepped into the shadowed enclosure. Another lady, somewhat homely and in her thirties, hovered on the fringe of the group. The obligatory chaperone.

His eyes focused on the object of his interest. A glass of punch in her hand, she stood by the railing in the center of a group of three gentlemen. He could see only her golden hair, a glimpse of fair features.

"You must look beyond mere words," she said to one of the men. "That discourse had more to do with the character's grief over losing her father than proving her to be a shrew. She was hurting inside, grieving. If her betrothed had offered her comfort, tragedy could have been averted."

Her melodious voice sparked a restlessness inside Samuel that had nothing to do with desire. Again he had that vague sense of recognition. Was she someone he'd met in Brighton society? No, surely he would have remembered a woman so utterly entrancing.

One of her harem spied Samuel and came forward to intercept him. A mere youngster in the tailored garb of a nobleman, he had sandy hair and skin marred by red carbuncles. "You there," he said imperiously. "I'm afraid you've wandered into the wrong box."

"I'd like a word with the lady."

That spotted face took Samuel's measure. "Is she acquainted with you?"

"That's for her to decide."

Although his hazel eyes wavered under Samuel's

intimidating stare, the young pup stubbornly held his place. Whoever she was, she inspired loyalty in her following. "Tell me your name," the fellow said grudgingly. "I'll see if she'll receive you."

"I'll do the honors myself."

Before her champion could object, Samuel stepped past him, past a row of gilt chairs and to her side. Convention dictated that an intermediary perform the introductions. But the petty rules of society had never stopped him.

She had turned away to speak to one of the other gentlemen. Samuel stood close enough to touch the slender curves of her body, close enough to detect her faint perfume, close enough to stroke the fine golden wisps at the nape of her neck. He kept his hands to himself. Curbing his impatience, he waited for her to finish speaking to a young man whose sullenly handsome face was framed by an artistic disarray of brown curls.

She placed her white-gloved hand on the sleeve of his pale yellow coat. "Now don't pout, dear Philip. We women are mysterious creatures. No man can be expected to understand us completely."

The flirtatious tone of her voice took the sting out of her words. Dear Philip gazed at her with the moody intensity of those who delude themselves into mistaking lust for love. He snatched up her gloved hand and kissed the back. "I concede your point, my lady. Though perhaps we should resume our discussion after we view the second act of the play."

"I always knew you were a clever man." Smiling, she turned back to the others.

Samuel was prepared to lure her with every trick in his considerable repertoire. But his witty overture died on his tongue.

She was even more heart-stoppingly lovely from close up. Spun-gold hair framed the delicate face of an angel. High cheekbones and an inbred refinement testified to her noble blood. Her eyes were a deep sapphire blue . . . eyes so familiar that he felt as if he'd been punched in the stomach . . . eyes that had once regarded him with fear and loathing and utter disillusionment.

Shock robbed him of breath. His vision narrowed on her. He was aware of no one but the two of them. Yet still he doubted his own perceptions. Disbelief gripped him, the inability to accept the identity of the woman standing in front of him. *"Cassie?"*

Her smile froze in place, then slowly vanished. One of her eyebrows arched slightly in disdain. Her steady, fathomless gaze regarded him as she would an uninvited guest. Or a total stranger.

But they were *not* strangers. She was Lady Cassandra, the girl who had been brought to London from the country to be his bride. The girl whom he had first glimpsed from a window of her father's town house on a cold January morning, lying in the snowy garden on her back and making an angel. It had been the day before their wedding . . .

Damn MacDermot! He must have recognized her and thought it great sport to send Samuel here unawares. And damn Andrew Jamison for not mentioning her transformation in his monthly reports.

She wasn't the gawky, timid, awestruck girl Samuel remembered. Yet he could see in her the innocent face of his fifteen-year-old bride.

Nineteen, he reminded himself. She was nineteen years old now, a woman of remarkable poise and beauty. Even as he struggled to grasp that truth, her attraction struck him with the force of a velvet hammer.

"Cassie," he said again, his voice hoarse.

Her lips parted. Sensual lips, naturally rosy. "Ah," she said calmly. "So you've come back."

"I've made arrangements for you to stay the summer at my estate in Northumberland, chaperoned by my aunt," he said. "I will join you there in a fortnight."

My heart swelled with joy. Although we would be separated for a short time, I would soon spend my days in the company of my dear Mr. Montcliff.

—The Black Swan

Chapter 3

INTO THE NIGHT

Cassie feared the quaking of her knees might cause her to collapse. The erratic thrumming of her heart made her feel in danger of swooning for the first time in her life. Steeling her spine, she held herself upright by force of will. She refused to appear anything but serene and unruffled.

Samuel Firth meant nothing to her. Nothing at all.

But her worst nightmare had come true. Dear God, he must have received that letter and headed straight home.

She had envisioned this moment countless times over the past four years. The moment of coming face to face with the man who had bought and abandoned her. In her favorite fantasy, Mr. Firth had sunk to the floor to beg her forgiveness, and she had turned on her heel and walked away.

He wasn't groveling now, though. Nor would he.

Cassie had half-convinced herself it was only the tender age she had been at her wedding that had made him appear so tall and fearsome. But in truth, he was even more arrogant and imposing than memory served.

His vibrant presence overshadowed the other men. The burnished teak of his skin contrasted with the white cravat at his throat. His black hair was in need of trimming, and the strong lines of his face held a harshness that bordered on cruelty. Beneath the charcoal gray coat and tailored black breeches of a gentleman, he had the fit, muscled form of a common laborer. And judging by his glares at Walt and Bertie and Philip, Mr. Firth was prepared to trounce all three of her male companions.

The sight of Walt's pinched lips and furious hazel eyes cut through her paralysis. "Walt," she said belatedly, "may I present my husband. Mr. Firth, my cousin, Walter, the Duke of Chiltern."

Her husband inclined his head in a cool nod that bordered on contempt. "A pleasure to meet you at last, Your Grace. A pity you were away at school at the time of my marriage."

"So you're the bastard moneylender who purchased Cassie," Walt said, his upper lip curled in his most haughty expression. "Wed in haste for fear that someone would stop you from robbing the cradle."

"I'll assume you were too young to have heard the whole story," Mr. Firth said coldly. "We married with her father's full consent—the previous duke. And, I might add, Lady Cassandra offered no objection to the match."

Cassie hoped no one noticed the heat of shame in her cheeks. Yes, she had been a foolish girl with romantic notions, imagining the aloof Mr. Firth to be a knight rescuing her from a lonely life.

"You bought up my uncle's gaming debts," Walt accused. "If he hadn't given you Cassie as repayment, you'd have ruined him."

Mr. Firth had the audacity to laugh. "Alas, one cannot

ruin a duke of the realm. Nor can he be imprisoned for debt. As I'm sure you know, rank provides immunity from prosecution."

Walt flushed, his mottled cheeks turning a uniform red. "You used my uncle's weakness for cards to press your advantage. By gad, I shall call you out for that."

Horrified to see her cousin peel off one of his white kid gloves, Cassie stepped between the two men before he could slap Mr. Firth's cheek. "Don't, Walt. I forbid you!"

"As head of the family, I must defend our honor. Step aside, now, there's a good girl."

Her heart racing, Cassie maintained her desperate stance between them. Out of the corner of her eye, she could see people returning to their seats on the floor of the theater, chatting and laughing, unaware of the sordid drama taking place in this private box. The orchestra launched into a dramatic tune that signaled the imminent start of second act. "I won't tolerate fighting," she said sternly. "It won't solve anything."

"An admirable sentiment, darling," Mr. Firth murmured in her ear. His warm breath sent a strange prickling over her skin, and before she could so much as flinch, his strong hands encircled her waist from behind. "But if the pup wants a duel, then so be it."

He tried to thrust her aside, but she held on to the back of a chair and stood firm, her legs braced. She had no doubt he could have lifted her with ease, but apparently he was reluctant to create a spectacle in full view of the audience. Cassie banked upon that slight advantage. Walt was only eighteen, a year her junior. Whether with swords or pistols, he was no match for a mature man of experience.

Her stomach clenched. She knew honor had nothing to do with her husband's willingness to fight. This quarrel was about possession, his determination to stake his claim on her. With sudden, hideous certainty she feared that Samuel Firth would kill Walt—or any man who stood in his way.

"There will be no challenge," she said in a penetrating whisper. "Is that clear to both of you?"

"But the blackguard cannot be allowed to stroll back into your life—" Walt protested.

"He is my husband." The words soured her tongue, and only years of training in ladylike behavior enabled Cassie to speak calmly. "I'll see him alone. The rest of you shall remain here and enjoy the second half of the performance."

On cue, the curtain lifted and a hush fell over the audience. The voices of the actors rang out into the theater.

Mr. Firth took hold of her arm. The gentlemanly gesture was perfectly proper, yet she stiffened at the shock of his fingers on the bare flesh of her arm. With effort, she kept her expression serene. It wouldn't do to alarm her friends. They watched in concern, bless them, Philip Uppingham, Bertie Gunther, Walt, and dear Flora, who had once been her governess. Cassie knew that if she gave any indication of distress, they would rush to her rescue en masse.

She refused to appeal for help. It wasn't fair to embroil them in her marital woes. Besides, she was no longer a cowardly, misguided girl. Now she knew exactly what she wanted from life—and Samuel Firth had no part in her plans.

Keeping a watchful eye on him, Flora sidled forward and spoke to Cassie in a whisper. "Shall I go with you?"

Cassie's heart warmed. She knew how much courage the offer had cost Flora, and she squeezed her friend's hand reassuringly. "Thank you, but no. I'll be fine."

Mr. Firth drew her out of the private box. The ornate corridor was deserted except for a liveried footman with a tray of empty glasses heading toward the lobby. Their footsteps were muffled by the gold-patterned crimson carpet. Cassie concentrated on maintaining an expression of pleasant serenity. They might have been a happily married couple going for a stroll.

Nothing could be further from the truth.

Her mind went blank to all but the awareness of *him*. The rock-hard strength of his muscled arm. The intimidating brush of his leg against hers. The unfair legal power he wielded over her.

Andrew Jamison had warned her that Mr. Firth would likely return to England upon receiving the deed. She had been foolish to hope otherwise, to let herself be lulled into thinking her husband might stay abroad forever.

If only Mr. Jamison were here tonight, she thought in fierce longing. But he'd had a dinner engagement this evening. There was no one who could help her, no one but herself.

Dear God. How was she to mollify this dangerous stranger?

Cassie warded off panic by taking steady breaths. Mr. Firth could scarcely do harm to her in the midst of servants clearing away the glassware and punchbowls. Besides, she was no longer a starry-eyed child whose scant knowledge of men had come from heroic tales. In the past few years, she had learned much about the male of the species. They could be managed by a woman of shrewd wit.

Nevertheless, Cassie felt another lurch of alarm as they reached the front doors of the theater. She looked up into her husband's keen blue eyes and said, "I thought we would talk right here."

"What we say will be said in private."

"There's no one of consequence listening. Everyone is watching the play."

"This is London. The walls have ears."

He opened the door and propelled her out into the cold starry night. A line of carriages waited alongside the curbstone, the drivers and footmen conversing in small groups. Their laughter sounded hollow to her ears, as if a glass wall separated her from all that was normal and familiar.

A shiver chilled her to the bone. It had been a mistake to

come with him unchaperoned. She knew him to be callous and unforgiving, a man who had married her solely for the purpose of revenge. Having lived apart from him for so long, she had almost forgotten that he had the right to arrange her life as he pleased. To do with her as he willed . . .

"Cold?"

That voice. Its silken depths could lull a woman into believing he truly cared for her comfort. Cassie made a show of rubbing her bare arms. "I left my pelisse behind. I'll have to go back and fetch it."

"That won't be necessary." He shrugged off his coat and draped it over her shoulders. Then he moved his hand to the back of her waist and applied pressure. The deceptively gentle push increased her inner agitation.

The heat of his body clung to his garment, warming her like an embrace. She could smell his faint scent of sandalwood: dark, exotic, uncivilized. Instinct urged her to bolt as far and as fast as she could go.

But God help her, she would *not* run away. She would *not* be a coward. She would settle their differences on her own terms.

Cassie stopped, wheeling around to face him in the gloom beneath a towering oak tree. They stood in a deserted spot halfway between the carriages and the gas-lit entrance to the theater. Keeping her voice low, she asked, "Where are you taking me?"

"Home. *Our* home."

The inflection in his voice held the sharp edge of wrath. Of course, he had discovered she'd vacated that echoing, sterile, magnificent mansion on Berkeley Square. She couldn't—wouldn't—set foot there ever again. "We'll speak right here. It's private enough."

He glanced impatiently at the servants a short distance away. "You know as well as I that we can't air our disagreements in public."

"Then you may call on me tomorrow afternoon."

"At the Stokeford town house? Under the scrutiny of his lordship and his grandmother? I think not."

His sneering tone roused her ire. Cassie had heard the story of his past from the dowager Lady Stokeford. Samuel Firth was her bastard grandson, although the family hadn't known of his existence for some thirty years. It had been one of her legitimate grandsons, Joshua, who had uncovered the stunning truth nearly five years ago. Since then, Mr. Firth had rejected the dowager's efforts to draw him into the bosom of the family.

The elderly Lady Stokeford had warned Cassie of his hatred of them and begged her to have patience with his cold nature, for in time he could change. But Cassie could feel no charity toward the man towering over her. He must have a marble heart to have shunned the dear, sweet dowager.

"They are *your* brother and *your* grandmother," she corrected. "They are presently in Devon, along with your other two brothers. Michael's wife gave birth to a baby girl last month—"

"Spare me the family anecdotes. I've no interest in them." His grip firmed around her arm. "Come along now. I won't publish our affairs to the world."

Cassie wrenched away. "I shan't go anywhere with you, sir. If you try to force me, I shall scream to high heaven. A score of servants will come running to my aid. Will that make matters public enough for you?"

Darkness masked his features. She braced herself lest he seize her up and carry her to his coach, fighting off a dozen burly coachmen in the process. If indeed they bothered to stop him once he'd told them she was his rebellious wife . . .

"Well, well," he said softly, reaching out to touch her cheek in a tingling caress. "At one time you were so shy you could scarcely string two words together."

She angled her face away. "You'll find I'm quite different now. I'm not so easily maneuvered."

"Yet I do believe you're afraid of me."

"*You* taught me to be cautious of men."

He made no instant response, and Cassie wondered if he was recalling their wedding night. Heaven help her, she didn't want to even think of that awkward, shocking intimacy.

"I mean you no harm," he said in a silken tone that caused a peculiar disturbance inside her. "I give you my word on that."

"Your word means nothing." Although she lowered her voice, she couldn't keep out the resentment. "You return without warning after four years abroad, take me away from my friends, and demand that I go off alone with you. Any woman of sense would be alarmed."

"Without warning?" The words stabbed through the darkness, as sharp as the cold gust of wind that blew through the streets. He stood looking at her, too close for comfort. "You knew I'd come back, Cassie. It isn't often a man receives a deed of private separation from his wife."

So he would get straight to the heart of the matter. She could do no less. Huddled inside his coat, she said, "It isn't often a wife is wed and abandoned on the same day. I merely seek to make the fact of our separation legal."

"Why?"

"I should think that's clear. Our marriage was a mistake. You must realize that, since you've stayed away for so many years. It's only logical for us to continue to go our separate ways."

He stood quietly for a moment, and she wondered feverishly what he was thinking. Could she persuade him to sign the document? She must. The loss of her freedom would mean the loss of all that was dear to her. She couldn't bear the thought of being under the strict command of this man.

If he were to claim his marital rights . . .

Unexpectedly, his hand flashed out to encircle her wrist, holding it possessively. "Tell me the real reason," he snapped. "Which one of those young pups in there do you fancy? Is it your cousin Walt? Or dear Philip?"

His lewd assumption sickened her. The grip of his fingers felt like a shackle, entrapping her. Dry-mouthed, she summoned her iciest tone, and said, "Unhand me. At once."

Menace emanated from him in waves, and the faint glitter of his eyes pierced her. He brought her hand to his mouth and pressed a stirring kiss to the back of her glove. Only then did he release her. "Or you shall scream?" he mocked. "Kindly save your breath. I've no wish to draw undue attention."

His desire for privacy was a weapon in her meager arsenal. "You will not make false accusations against my friends," she said in a fierce whisper. "My decision to seek a separation has naught to do with any of them."

"That remains to be seen. I may be forced to bring a suit of criminal conduct against one or more of them in a court of law. Any man who has cuckolded me will pay dearly for his mistake."

Cassie blanched. Such suits were rare, sought in cases where the wife had been unfaithful. "You wouldn't dare!"

"I would dare much where you're concerned, Cassie." He stepped closer, crowding her, his tone smooth and frightening. "If necessary, I'll publicly humiliate your lover in court and force him to pay me a huge fine. I'll ruin him."

It horrified Cassie to think of Mr. Firth prosecuting her friends unfairly. And dragging her own good name through the dirt of public opinion. "You won't prove anything," she said tightly. "My friends have treated me with complete respect. If you had been here these past four years, you would know so."

"If I'd been here, you wouldn't have your stable of suitors."

"They aren't suitors, they're my dearest *friends*. We discuss books and plays and essays. It's all very proper."

He gave a harsh laugh. "Men and women can't simply be friends. There's always an element of physical attraction."

His suggestive tone hinted at secrets she would never know. Cassie felt flushed and disoriented, intensely aware of his masculinity. He stood so close she drew in his disturbing scent with every breath. "That may be so for men who see women as objects to be used and discarded," she said frostily. "As for myself, I cannot understand it. My friends are not at all like that."

He chuckled again. "Then you don't know them very well."

Out of the blue, Cassie remembered that mysterious note. Could Walt or Philip or Bertie have sent it? Did one of them harbor a secret passion for her? She didn't know, didn't care about anything but winning her freedom from this hostile, frustrating, disquieting stranger who was her husband.

"Think what you will," she said. "I know only that our marriage cannot continue as it is."

Leaning over her, he pressed a hand to the tree trunk, his face in dense shadow and his pose that of a man in control of his world. "You're quite right," he mused. "Things *will* have to change."

"I'm glad you understand that. If you'll sign the legal papers—"

"A deed of separation won't dissolve our marriage. We will still be husband and wife." He watched her closely. "However, if I can prove your adultery, then I can petition Parliament to issue a bill of divorcement."

She stiffened, everything in her rebelling at the prospect of notoriety. Growing up, she had witnessed enough scandalous behavior in her parents. "There has been no adultery," she said again. "And a divorce isn't necessary. I'm content simply to live apart from you."

"But *I'm* not content. I won't have a wife who is not truly a wife."

"You've had one for the past four years." Awareness of his power stirred up the old feelings of confusion and inadequacy in her. But she would *not* let him make her feel helpless. "Perhaps it's you who should be sued, Mr. Firth. I've heard gossip of your many mistresses. No doubt you've had numerous affairs during your travels."

His white teeth flashed in the darkness. "Men are free to spread their seed far and wide. That's the way of the world."

Cassie's cheeks felt hot. The arrogant rascal didn't even bother to deny his philandering. "Your lack of propriety is precisely why you and I will never suit," she said, removing his coat and thrusting it at him. "There is no point to this discussion. I'm going back inside to rejoin my friends."

"As you wish." Like a man stroking a treasured possession, he let his fingertips drift down her cheek. "But know this, my lady. I paid a steep price for you. I've every intention of reaping certain dividends on my investment."

My maid fell into a slumber as our coach travelled o'er the lonely road that ran along the deserted seashore. I was content to gaze out the window, admiring the wild scenery of crashing waves and wheeling seagulls. Little did I know, my musings were soon to be ended.

Outside, a sudden commotion of shouting caused the horses to rear and plunge. A gunshot exploded into the air. As the coach rocked, I clung to the seat in desperation. We were beset by bandits!

—The Black Swan

Chapter 4
The Best of Plans

Hector Babbage sat in Samuel's office, a ledger book spread out before him. The rain-muted light from the tall window glistened on the chief accountant's balding pate. Adjusting his gold-rimmed spectacles, the pudgy man peered down at the open page, slid a fearful glance at the window, then at Samuel.

"I'm afraid there is no record of a payment from Mr. MacDermot last month. I can't imagine why he would say such a thing . . ."

"His records show the bank draft was issued and paid."

Babbage shifted his bulk in the chair. "Pardon me, sir, but I take especial care with all the receipts. And I convey all the deposits to the bank myself."

"Perhaps this particular one was lost."

Babbage cast another glance at the window. "I—I scarcely know what to say. Not a single pence has ever gone unaccounted for under my stewardship."

Samuel regarded the man, wondering if his nervousness was due only to his fear of heights. For the chief accountant to venture up even one flight of stairs to this office required great effort. It was the only flaw in an otherwise exemplary employee.

Babbage labored for long hours without complaint and exhibited his loyalty in other ways, turning down offers for employment from rival companies. Yet perhaps he was too meticulous to see the larger picture. Unlike Samuel, who for some time had had a suspicion that other funds had gone missing.

During his absence, the ledgers had been copied faithfully and sent to him for approval, wherever he happened to be in the world. The profits over the past year had risen only slightly despite the proportionately larger increase in business. Granted, there had been expansions made in the office, ships to build, salaries to meet, and other expenditures. Yet Samuel had a sharp eye for the bottom line and a nagging hunch that something was amiss.

How far could he trust Babbage? It was time to find out.

"I want a thorough audit," he told Babbage. "Down to every last nail and board in the building. I'll expect the report on my desk within the fortnight."

Babbage's eyes rounded, magnified by his thick glasses. His face looked pasty gray. "Audit, sir? But there's all my other work . . ."

"Postpone everything nonessential. I'm sure you can handle the matter."

"Yes, sir. Straightaway, sir." His brow furrowed, the accountant picked up the ledger, glanced at the window again, and sidled out the door.

No sooner had he gone than Samuel's secretary stepped inside. The sober, unobtrusive Rochester intoned, "Mr. Jamison has arrived."

"Send him in."

Rising, Samuel rounded the desk as Andrew Jamison entered the office. A handsome man in his early fifties, the solicitor looked fit and vigorous in a dark brown coat with biscuit breeches. Threads of silver in his brown hair lent him a distinguished air. The second son of a viscount, Jamison had defied his family's wishes and followed his passion for the law. Samuel had considered him a highly valued employee—until that infuriating letter he had written on Cassie's behalf.

The letter that had included the deed of separation.

A reserved smile lit Jamison's well-bred features. "Welcome home, Mr. Firth. I came the moment I received your summons."

Samuel shook the man's proferred hand and directed him to a pair of chairs by the hearth. "I was sorry to hear about your wife."

"It's been three years since her passing, but thank you." Jamison turned the topic from his wife's death. "What kept you away so long?"

Cassie.

Samuel set his jaw. He'd wanted to give his child bride the chance to grow up, to forget the unfortunate start to their marriage. But he'd never anticipated so complete a metamorphosis. Her rare beauty had knocked him off kilter, and he still felt as if he couldn't quite catch his breath. Since encountering her at the theater the previous night, he'd thought of little else. He'd sat up late, drinking brandy and pondering the best way to proceed.

She wasn't the malleable girl he'd married. Her quick intelligence and strong will made her a formidable opponent. No, not formidable—just feisty enough to make his seduction of her an exhilarating prospect. He found himself looking forward to the task.

But first he had a score to settle.

Samuel perched on the edge of his desk, crossed his

arms, and aimed a hard stare at the solicitor. "I'm sure you know why I came back."

Jamison's gray eyes were steady. "The deed of separation, of course. Have you called on Lady Cassandra yet?"

Samuel shook his head. He wasn't yet ready to offer the information that he'd encountered Cassie at the theater. "I wanted to speak to you first. To find out why you drew up the deed on behalf of my wife. Correct me if I'm wrong, but you're in *my* employ, not hers."

"Quite. However, you appointed me Lady Cassandra's guardian in your absence. I was to see to her needs and her education with all the care of a father. Those were your exact words."

Spoken in a fit of remorse. But Jamison didn't know about Samuel's moment of truth, the galling self-revelation of the knave he had become through blind ambition.

With effort, he focused on his anger. "So you took that as permission to undermine my marriage?"

"Allow me to explain—"

"Yes, do. I'd especially like to know who else influenced her to make such a decision."

Jamison looked crisp and calm, as if he'd come prepared for this very discussion. He folded his hands in his lap and regarded Samuel. "As you know, I've kept a close watch over Lady Cassandra these past four years. I've seen to it that she has had the best tutors, an irreproachable chaperone, and an ample allowance. However, unlike other ladies her age, your wife has little interest in shopping or social events. She prefers literary pursuits and is a patron of the Hampton Lending Library."

"I know all that," Samuel said testily. "But you said nothing in your monthly reports about her being dissatisfied with her life."

Jamison glanced down at his elegant hands. "It came as

somewhat of a surprise to myself, too. She is the perfect lady, never laying her complaints on anyone else."

"Complaints?" Samuel prowled back and forth in front of the desk. "What the devil does she have to complain about? Her pin money has been more than generous. Was there something she lacked, something I can purchase for her?"

Jamison gravely shook his head. "Only her freedom, I fear. She has come to treasure her independence."

"Dammit, I've given her all the comforts—and far too *much* freedom." Furious at Cassie, at Jamison, and at himself for not returning sooner, Samuel stalked to the window. On the street below, traffic jammed the Strand with drays and cabs and carriages. The cold rain pelting the glass seemed a portent after four years in sunny climes. Annoyed with the fanciful thought, he turned sharply to Jamison. "What the hell were you thinking, to prepare that deed? You should have discouraged her from this foolishness."

"The lady has a strong will, as I'm sure you'll discover. Had I not complied with her wishes, she would have gone to another solicitor, someone who might well have spread gossip about your marriage. I thought it best to write the deed myself, then you could handle the matter as you saw fit."

The explanation was perfectly logical, yet Samuel had to probe deeper. "Cassie's led a sheltered life. Who put such an idea into her head?"

"She's remarkably well read for a young lady. Or perhaps she heard talk from one in her circle of friends."

Samuel didn't doubt that dear Philip or Cousin Walt could have advised her to get the deed of separation. But there were others he suspected more likely to seek a rift in his marriage. The mere thought of his estranged family set his teeth on edge. "Or perhaps Lord Stokeford and his grandmother," he said darkly. "I suspect you've permitted her to associate with them. Against my express wishes."

Jamison shifted in his chair, his first sign of uneasiness. "I assure you, there have been only letters and the occasional visit. The dowager Lady Stokeford can be quite overpowering. She said it was her duty to bring the wife of her grandson into the family."

"And what of *your* duty to me, dammit? I gave orders that Cassie was to be cut off from them. Instead, I return to England to find her living in Stokeford's own town house. Will you tell me you couldn't stop that, either?"

Jamison didn't flinch. Rather, he frowned at Samuel in an accusatory manner. "Short of locking your wife in her chambers, no, I couldn't stop her. She regards your grandmother with great affection."

"Bloody hell," Samuel muttered under his breath. Old Lady Stokeford clearly hoped to use his wife as a means of dragging him into the midst of her adoring grandsons. So why would she now press for a separation? "I'll put a stop to that association at once."

Jamison leaned forward in his chair. "Pray consider that Lady Cassandra has no family outside of her cousin, the present duke. Since the death of her father two years ago, she's been lonely."

Loath to reveal the extent of his hatred for the Stokefords, Samuel vented his wrath on the previous Duke of Chiltern. "He was no one to mourn."

"He was her father. She cared for him in his last illness, as was proper. I admired her devotion."

"Better she had stabbed the old goat in the heart."

Samuel swung back toward the window. He couldn't imagine why Cassie would have nursed a wily wastrel who had squandered an immense fortune at the gaming tables. All that had been left was the crumbling ducal palace in Lancashire and his adolescent daughter. In the end, the wretch had sold her, too, the gold crown in a life of dissipation.

The duke's loss had been Samuel's gain. Ambitious to

start a dynasty to rival that of his half brothers, Samuel had fixed on Lady Cassandra as the most blue-blooded maiden in the land. He had paid off the duke's massive debts in return for the hand of his fifteen-year-old daughter in marriage. Intent on his scheme, he hadn't bothered to get to know his shy, gawky bride. It wasn't until the wedding night that he'd realized just how young she was. He had departed the following morning on a trip to his holdings around the world.

Samuel avoided the black pit of guilt. He wouldn't wallow in worthless sentiment. She had been a child, and he had given her time to grow up. She should be thankful for that courtesy.

Abruptly, he said, "I spoke with Cassie last night at the theater."

"But . . . you said you hadn't seen her yet."

"I said I hadn't gone to visit her." In a deliberate show of arrogance, Samuel walked forward and stared down at the solicitor. "I informed her that I have no intention of letting her go."

A frown darkened Jamison's face. He looked like a father prepared to defend his cub. "She deserves the chance to make her own life. The two of you haven't spent a single day of married life together. You're from completely different worlds, and it's doubtful you could ever understand—"

"Enough," Samuel snapped. "When I want your advice, I'll ask for it."

"It is indeed my concern," the solicitor continued doggedly. "This guardianship has required me to spend a good deal of time in her ladyship's company. She's a fine, virtuous woman, and I won't see her come to harm."

Moodily, Samuel observed the way Jamison gripped the arms of the chair, his knuckles white. "So you're her champion, too. She certainly inspires loyalty in her followers."

"I must caution you not to do anything rash, sir. It can't

be to your liking to have an unwilling wife. If you'll stop to consider, the deed of separation may be in your best interest. The matter can be handled with tact and delicacy. As your solicitor—"

"No longer." He made the decision coldly.

"I beg your pardon?"

"I'm letting you go. My wife doesn't require a guardian now that I'm back in England. I'll have no further need of your services."

Jamison tensed visibly. "You can't be serious."

"I assure you, I am." A strange tension burned inside Samuel. Jealousy, he realized. He was jealous of Jamison and all the other men who adored his wife. It chafed him to imagine her smiling at them, enjoying their company, flirting with them. Men born to her exalted social class.

Ever the gentleman, Jamison stood up and bowed. "It shall be as you wish," he said in a stiff tone. "But allow me to speak one last time on your wife's behalf. She had no choice in making the marriage. At least give her a voice in its dissolution."

"Dissolution be damned. Now get out."

Samuel stalked to the door and yanked it open. As the solicitor left the office, only strength of will kept Samuel from taking a swing at him. How he wanted to punish the man for his ineffectual handling of Cassie! Couldn't Jamison have maintained control of one young woman?

Closing the door, Samuel gripped the handle for a few moments until the heat of his rage had passed and he could think clearly again. Cassie was his, whether she liked it or not. Now that she had attained womanhood, he had every intention of keeping her all to himself. It was time for her to fulfill her role as his wife, to accept him into her bed and to give him children.

The memory of her beauty filled him with fire. If he could believe her protestations of innocence, she had never known the joys of the bedchamber. On their disastrous wedding night, he had neglected to take her youth into account or to consider that she might be ignorant about marital relations.

But that mistake lay in the past. She was ready for him now, and he had considerable skills to overcome her aversion.

Samuel relished the heat of anticipation. Once his wife experienced the pleasures of lovemaking, she would forget all about that deed of separation. He would make certain of it.

My wrists secured, I found myself taken to a small cabin on board a ship named The Black Swan. *My captor was a fierce, tall man with black hair and ocean-blue eyes. He swaggered before me as one who is proud of his criminal exploits. His features were even, almost handsome, but his manners were crude as he tossed me onto a chair.*

"This is an outrage!" I cried. "Release me at once."

"All in due time," the pirate said with a sneer. "Your guardian must first pay your ransom."

—The Black Swan

Chapter 5

The Waiting Game

"Order, ladies and gentlemen." With his flare for drama, Philip Uppingham rapped the gavel on the table in Cassie's library. "Especially you, Your Grace. We cannot conclude this meeting without keeping to the course of discussion."

As Cassie watched, Walt wiped the grin from his face. He managed to appear almost angelic, although a moment ago he had been relating a juicy tidbit of gossip. Now, a faint red flush tinged his mottled skin, and she felt a moment's sympathy. For all his exalted rank and hot-headed nature, her cousin was young and easily embarrassed.

A hush fell over the gathering of two women and three men. Philip Uppingham and Walt occupied opposite ends of the oak table, with Bertie Gunther and Flora Woodruff on one side, facing Cassie on the other.

Two branches of candles augmented the light of a rainy afternoon. The rich scent of book bindings and the hiss of the fire created a cozy aura. The library at the Stokeford town house was Cassie's favorite chamber because the tall shelves of volumes provided an endless array of fascinating topics.

For the past two years, the Mayfair Literary Society had met once a week for lively discussions of books, poems, and essays. The members had become fast friends, supporting one another through thick and thin, the tragic death of Bertie's young wife, the rejections of Philip's poetry by publishers, and Flora's escape from an abusive husband. Cassie had fallen into the role of confidante, for she had a sympathetic ear and a tender heart. She knew each person at this table better than she knew her own husband.

Her heart faltered over a beat. She had tried to block Samuel Firth from her mind, to go on with her normal daily activities. Yet an uneasy tension had plagued her nonetheless. All day, he had loomed like a dark cloud on the horizon. When would he come to call on her? She despised waiting on pins and needles, no longer certain about her future.

At this time yesterday afternoon, she had been blithely at work at her desk upstairs, unaware of his return. She had gone to the theater and enjoyed the first half of the play in blissful ignorance. She would never forget the moment of turning around and spying his tall, overtly masculine presence. His fury over the deed of separation had been daunting.

I paid a steep price for you. I've every intention of reaping certain dividends on my investment.

By law, a husband had complete control of his wife. He could force her to live with him, to devote herself to pleasing him. And he could take her to his bed. The prospect made her feel dizzy and distracted.

But she was determined not to let him change her life.

She focused her gaze on Philip Uppingham. Nattily dressed in an aqua-blue coat and yellow breeches, he held a gold-rimmed quizzing glass to his eye and squinted at his notes. With his tumult of brown curls, he looked the part of the brooding poet he fancied himself to be. "Now, then. The last item on our agenda is selecting a work for our next meeting. I would suggest Dante's *Purgatory* and *Paradise.* There's a new translation just published."

"Too somber," Walt declared. "We get enough fire and brimstone in church on Sunday."

"Perhaps we need something more adventuresome," Bertie said. He was a rather shy man, tall and thin, with big ears and nondescript brown hair.

"I have it," Walt said, snapping his fingers. "*Don Juan.* The first two cantos are smashing good fun."

Cassie exchanged a glance with Flora, who looked dismayed. "As much as I admire Lord Byron's work," Cassie said, "that poem is an epic of one man's imprudent behavior with women."

"What would you suggest, then?" Philip said, his fervid brown eyes focusing on Cassie.

She rose and went to one of the shelves, plucking out a thin volume. "This one. Miss Austen's final book, *Northanger Abbey.*"

Protests came from the gentlemen.

Philip clutched his middle, mimicking illness. "Lud, that's a gothic tale for the ladies."

"The Regent himself was a patron of Miss Austen," Cassie pointed out. "You ought not criticize until you've read some of her books."

"*I* tried, remember?" Walt said with a look of disgust. "*Pride and Prejudice* is about a family of girls looking for husbands. Tolerably written, but dull as dust."

"Dull!" Flora objected. "Why, it's . . . it's exceedingly clever. And Mr. Darcy is so wonderfully heroic." Blushing, she ducked her chin and lapsed into silence.

"But . . . a romantic tale?" Bertie said, stifling a yawn. "We'd as well study *The Mysteries of Udolophant.*"

"Mrs. Radcliffe's novel is called *The Mysteries of Udolpho*," Cassie corrected. "And it's quite good, although Miss Austen is undoubtedly the more accomplished author."

Philip waved his gavel. "Lurid tales, all of 'em. My mother used to read that silly rubbish."

"So did mine," Cassie retorted, replacing the book and sitting back down at the table. "She enjoyed it very much. I can't see that it did her any harm."

Walt stretched out his legs beneath the table. "Pray don't be offended, but Aunt Helen was hardly the intellectual. She preferred balls to academic debates."

Cassie couldn't quarrel with that. Loathing the shabby ducal palace in Lancashire, the duchess had spent most of her time in London. Cassie had seen her parents only twice a year, at Christmas and for a short time during the summer. One of her most vivid memories was of her glamorous mother lounging on a chaise, paging through a stack of the latest novels. The moment her parents returned to the city, Cassie would secretly gather the books that the duchess had left behind and hide them in the attic. Then she would curl up on a pile of old cushions for hours, lost in another time and place. In those pages, she had discovered a world rich in melodrama, of crashing waves beneath castles on cliffs, of villains and heroes engaged in swordfights, of long-lost heirs and kidnapped ladies.

Except for Flora, none here knew of Cassie's love for romantic novels. Heaven help her if Bertie or Walt or Philip ever found out she had written one herself—and sold it to a publisher recently.

Cassie had arranged for her book to be published under a pen name. She had sworn the publisher to absolute secrecy. No one must guess that the author of *The Black Swan* was the daughter of the late Duke of Chiltern and cousin to the present duke.

And certainly no one would ever know that Cassie had

put her estranged husband in the book, thinly disguised as the pirate villain.

Her stomach lurched. Mr. Firth deserved the role, yet now she regretted her imprudence. If anyone realized the truth, she would become the object of jests, the talk of the *ton*. People would stare at her and speculate on the state of her marriage. She'd had enough of scandal after being sold into marriage and abandoned less than twenty-four hours later.

Her only consolation was that she kept away from the sharp eyes of society. It wasn't as if anyone would connect *her* with an obscure novel, let alone recognize the true identity of the evil pirate.

The group bandied about several more possibilities for next week's selection before finally settling on an old favorite, *Gulliver's Travels*. The meeting drew to a close, and Flora went off to check on dinner arrangements. As the others left the library, Walt took Cassie by the hand and led her to the chaise by the fire.

"You can't fool me with that bright smile," he said, gazing askance at her. "You're looking far too down in the dumps today. What you need is a glass of sherry."

Before he could tug the bellrope, she stopped him with a touch of her hand. "It's quite all right. My head aches a bit, that's all."

"It's because of that devil Firth, ain't it? You've scarce spoken a word about the bounder. I wish you'd tell me what he said to you last night."

"There's little to report. Except that he intends to call on me today." Walt didn't know about the deed of separation or Mr. Firth's refusal to sign it. Cassie thought it best not to add fuel to the fire of her cousin's resentment. He would only try to help, bless him, and she didn't need his intervention, however well meaning it might be.

"This marriage must be annulled," Walt said, pacing.

"That's the ticket, I'll hire the best lawyer in London to handle the case."

"Annulment is impossible, you know that. Lord Stokeford looked into the matter right after the wedding. Besides, what of the vast amount Mr. Firth paid to Papa? The money's gone to cover debts, and neither you nor I can ever replace it."

Walt slapped his palm against the white mantelpiece, rattling the pair of china dogs displayed there. "Blast him! The fellow's a knave for buying you like a . . . a prime mare."

"If it hadn't been Mr. Firth, it would have been some other man," Cassie reminded him. "Either that, or total poverty."

"Dash it all. I still wish I could right matters."

His loyal support made Cassie's eyes prickle. Determined not to dissolve into tears, she went to the window to gaze out on the rear garden. Rain sluiced down the glass panes, lending a hazy quality to the view of early springtime. A mist of green covered the winter-bare earth. Buds dotted the tree branches, and violets formed nests of purple in the flower beds.

If only she could revel in the beauty of the season.

His expression disgruntled, Walt appeared beside her. "Firth looked deuced shocked to see you last night. I'll wager he didn't know it was you at first."

Her heart beat a little faster as she remembered his bold stare. "Of course he didn't. I'm not a child anymore."

"That's just it. I'm saying he didn't come to our private box to visit his *wife*."

"Pardon?"

"The scoundrel spied a pretty woman and came to seduce her, that's what. Instead he found you."

Cassie laughed. "That's too incredulous a notion. It's far more likely that someone told him I was there at the theater. He wouldn't mistake me for . . . his sort of woman."

Although she shunned society, over the years Cassie had heard bits and pieces of gossip about her husband's exploits. On one memorable occasion, while visiting a bookstore shortly after her marriage, she had overheard two ladies whispering about the scandal. They had roundly condemned Mr. Firth for his many mistresses and had gone on to express pity for his naïve child bride, thrust into marriage with a common blackguard. At the time, Cassie had been so mortified that she'd slunk away. Now, however, she had perfected a cool glare that silenced any tongue-waggers.

An earnest intensity showed on Walt's face. "No, you're *not* his sort, dash it. Not at all. But you're vastly pretty, Cass. You've only to gaze into any mirror to see that."

She dipped an exaggerated curtsy. "I thank you for the compliment, Your Grace."

"For pity's sake, don't make your bows to *me*." Looking embarrassed, Walt pulled her to her feet. "There ain't a lady in society half as lovely as you are. If you went to balls and such, the fellows would gather like flies round a honeypot."

"It's comforting to know that I can attract flies."

"Hah. You wouldn't be jesting if you'd noticed how Firth was looking at you last night."

Cassie *had* noticed—but she had thought it due to her husband's shock at the change in her. That he'd believed her to be a stranger was too great a coincidence to be credited. She certainly didn't consider herself any more attractive than many other women.

Yet she pictured him in the moment when she had turned around to see him for the first time in four years. For a second, there had been a flirtatious smile on his tanned features, an interest that was swiftly replaced by blank incredulity.

Walt was right.

Cassie sank down onto the cushioned ledge of the window. She stared at the carpet, seeing not the blue-and-gold scrollwork but that flash of charm on her husband's face. On the one hand, it was perversely gratifying to know that he considered her beautiful. On the other, the rascal had been intent on securing a liaison in full view of the *ton*.

"Drat him," she muttered under her breath.

"He deserves a good drubbing, that's what."

Her gaze flew to her cousin. "You do, and I'll box your ears! I thought we'd settled that last night."

His expression sulky, Walt flopped down beside her and propped his booted heels on the arm of a nearby chair. "You can't tell me what to do anymore. I'm eighteen and old enough to make up my own mind."

She pushed his feet off the fine blue upholstery. "Then show some sense, for heaven's sake. I won't have you risking your life on my behalf."

"It's my duty to look out for you."

"It's also your duty to behave in a respectable manner. And that means controlling your temper."

"You probably think I can't best the rogue," Walt said crossly. "Dash it all, I've a fine right hook, and I'm even better with a pistol. Me and the fellows, we practice twice a week." He pointed an imaginary gun at the wall. His lanky form and blemished face made him appear more like an overgrown schoolboy than a duke of the realm.

Fear for him rose in her. It was on the tip of her tongue to say that Mr. Firth had power, cunning, and experience on his side. But if she stung her cousin's pride, Walt might be goaded into proving himself a man. "You know how I loathe scandal," she said with feeling. "I beg you, please, give me your promise that you won't fight my husband."

Walt scowled, his hazel eyes stubborn. But in a moment his expression softened and he huffed out a breath. "Oh, all right, have it your way. But if ever he lifts a finger to harm you, the bargain is off."

"I very much doubt it will come to that." In an effort to distract her cousin, she gently grasped his chin and turned his head to the side. "Have you been using the new skin potion I gave you?"

"The stuff stinks to high heaven." Grimacing, Walt pushed her hand away. "But don't try to divert my attention, Cass. And don't underestimate Firth. He'll try to keep you from your friends. He'll want you all to himself."

"I shouldn't expect he'll bother much with me. He's certainly paid no heed to me these past four years."

"He'll bother, all right. He'll want you to live with him."

The thought of being in Mr. Firth's presence every day made her distinctly queasy. "He didn't suggest any such thing to me."

"But he will," her cousin said ominously. "There's no two ways about it. You'll have to come live under my protection, and that's that."

"Don't be ridiculous. Your bachelor's lodgings are far too small. And it wouldn't be respectable, either."

His lips pursed, Walt drummed his fingers on the cushion. "I have it! I'll air out the old manse on Grosvenor Square, hire servants to dust off the furniture and polish the brasswork. That's what I should've done months ago, so's you wouldn't have to live here at Stokeford's place."

Touched by his eagerness to help her, Cassie took his hands and held tightly, taking comfort from his warmth. For so many years, *she* had been the one to watch over *him.* "That's very kind of you, darling, but you know you can't afford the expense of keeping a big house. I'll be fine here." At least until she could afford a cottage in the country where she could concentrate on her writing.

"Firth'll take you back to his house, you mark my words," Walt said glumly.

"He most certainly will not. Nor will he want to join me in this house. He despises the Stokefords."

"Then mayhap he'll spirit you away to Brighton. That's where he hails from, ain't it?"

She squeezed his hands. "Do stop worrying. I've no intention of moving anywhere—"

"That remains to be seen." The deep male voice struck like a blow from the other end of the library.

Her heart leaping, Cassie looked across the chamber. In the doorway, his black hair slick with rain and his face thunderous, loomed the tall form of her husband.

"I sent your guardian a message. He is to deliver the ransom himself." The pirate looked like a devil with black hair and piercing blue eyes. He ran his thumb along the wickedly sharp edge of his knife. "Then I shall kill him."

My blood ran cold with fear. "You must not!" I cried. "You have no reason to harm Mr. Montcliff."

"Perhaps you'll understand when I introduce myself." Sheathing his blade, my captor swept a courtly bow. "I am Percival Cranditch, the baseborn son of Lord S——."

I gasped. "That means . . ."

"Aye, m'lady. The Honorable Victor Montcliff is my half brother."

—The Black Swan

Chapter 6
The Bargain

Samuel had come determined to charm his wife. After leaving his office, he had stopped at home to change into a burgundy coat with buff breeches. He had mastered his aversion to entering the Stokeford town house, the lair of his eldest half brother and his grandmother. He had even put aside his fury over the deed of separation.

But a resurgence of wrath struck him upon seeing Cassie sitting on the window seat with her cousin Walt. They were holding hands, discussing where she would live, by God. As if her husband had no say in the matter.

Cassie's thick-lashed blue eyes revealed a flicker of emotion. Guilt? Was she having an affair with her own cousin? Did she prefer that aristocratic pup to an experienced man?

Samuel warned himself not to make rash assumptions. It was far more likely that she merely resented his presence. All that would soon change, of course. But not if he knocked her cousin bleeding to the floor.

Striding forward, he studied his wife. Cassie was even more beautiful by daylight. And so very different from their wedding night four years ago when she'd worn a cap tied beneath her chin and a gown buttoned to her throat. Now, her blond hair was swept up in a sleek style that made him crave to unpin it. In a gown of bronze muslin that skimmed a curvaceous form, she looked positively ravishing.

No one was allowed to ravish her but him.

"Take your hands off my wife," he said, keeping his voice pleasant.

Walt scrambled to his feet, his spotty face sour with resentment. "The devil! You can't order me—"

Cassie shushed him with a gesture, all the while keeping her eyes on Samuel as if he were a tiger on the prowl. "Good afternoon, Mr. Firth," she said with chilly politeness. "I'm surprised the footman didn't announce you."

"I let myself in."

"This is an outrage," her cousin snapped. "You can't walk into private homes uninvited."

"Allow me to handle the matter," Cassie said sharply. She sent Samuel a quelling stare. "I'm sure Mr. Firth will follow the rules next time."

"So you'll excuse the blackguard?" Walt said huffily. "I've a mind to toss him out on his ear."

"Go ahead and try," Samuel taunted. "If you've more guts than brains."

Walt lunged, but Cassie latched on to her cousin's arm and clung fiercely. "Stop, both of you. Walt, I must ask you to go. At once."

"And leave you alone with this scapegrace? You need a protector."

"There are servants nearby. I'll speak with my husband now. You may call on me tomorrow afternoon."

Walt continued to protest, but she propelled him toward the door like a mother disciplining a rebellious child. Over his shoulder, he called to Samuel, "Treat her well, or you'll answer to me."

Cassie escorted her cousin out into the corridor and shut the door behind him. Then she turned around and walked briskly back to Samuel.

He wondered if she had any idea how delectably her hips swayed, giving him a glimpse of curves that had been far less developed four years ago. Her lips were compressed in a way that made him want to soften them with a kiss.

"You needn't gloat," she said, one eyebrow elevated in well-bred disdain. "You behaved as badly as he did."

Samuel hadn't even realized he was smiling. "But I won the prize."

"You've won nothing, sir, but my contempt. It's no fair sport to antagonize a man who is far younger and less worldly than you are."

"I apologize for offending you, then."

That haughty eyebrow arched higher. Quite clearly, she doubted his sincerity. Little did she know, Samuel meant what he'd said. He hadn't come here to antagonize her, but to melt the ice of her reserve.

He added smoothly, "I'm pleased you see the sense in talking to me. You'll find me very interested in resolving our differences to our mutual satisfaction."

Cassie stopped a short distance from him and clasped her hands primly at her waist. "I suggest we postpone this discussion. It would be more appropriate for us to meet at the offices of Mr. Jamison. I'll send a letter to him requesting an appointment at eleven o'clock tomorrow morning."

Samuel had to admire her mettle. "Don't bother yourself. I let Jamison go this afternoon."

"Pardon?"

"Since you no longer need a guardian, I released him from my employ. And you may be certain I'll not write him a letter of reference. I was less than pleased with his performance of his duties."

An utter stillness descended on Cassie. Her blue eyes flashing, she gripped her hands together as if to prevent herself from flying at him in a rage. "How dare you? Mr. Jamison has always behaved with the utmost courtesy. He's the perfect gentleman and undeserving of your ill opinion."

"He disobeyed my orders. That's something I won't tolerate in an employee."

"He cared for me like a father these past four years. He offered comfort and advice during my own father's illness and death. For shame, to treat a good man with so little regard."

Her heated defense revealed a passion that Samuel craved all for himself. He was jealous of her affection for a mere servant and annoyed that she would question his perfectly logical action. "The matter is over with and done. You will not be seeing Jamison again."

He walked to a cabinet that held a row of crystal decanters. Taking up a glass, he poured himself a brandy. The pungent liquor slid down his throat and gave him a perverse satisfaction. Drinking from Stokeford's private store served as a reminder that nothing mattered but vengeance. And Cassie was a prime element in his plan.

When he turned back around, he found her standing behind him, her arms crossed beneath her fine bosom. The cut of her bodice allowed him an enticing glimpse of her breasts. He would soon feel their weight filling his palms; he would soon have her in his bed . . .

"Dismiss Mr. Jamison if you like," she said. "However, I intend to retain him as my solicitor."

Samuel nearly choked on a swallow of brandy. "The devil you will. I'll refuse the bill."

"Our marriage contract guarantees me a quarterly allowance for my personal use. I shall apply those funds to the expense."

Funds that came out of *his* pocket. Samuel held tight rein to his temper. It was time to set the trap. "You've no need of a solicitor. I'll handle any necessary legal matters. Including the deed of separation."

She went for the bait. Her eyes alight, she took a step toward him. "Does that mean you'll sign it?"

Idly swirling the liquid in his glass, he studied his wife. The glimmer of hope on her beautiful face was an emotion he intended to exploit. "Perhaps," he said, deliberately cryptic. "If you meet my conditions."

"What do you mean?"

"I'd like to place a proposition before you. Come, we'll discuss the matter."

He reached for her arm, intending to lead her to the blue chaise, where he could begin her seduction. But Cassie marched to an oak table and seated herself at one end like a queen taking her throne. She gave an imperious wave toward the opposite end of the table. "Do sit down, Mr. Firth. I trust you've brought the deed with you."

He took the chair directly beside her. "Call me Samuel."

Her unflinching gaze met his. "You're a stranger to me, Mr. Firth. Quite frankly, there is no point to such an informality."

"We won't be strangers for long. Not if you agree to my conditions."

"Kindly explain yourself."

He was struck anew by the change in Cassie. No longer was she the shy, skittish adolescent who had made him feel as if he were robbing the cradle. As her twig-thin form had blossomed into the lush curves of a woman, so had her naïve nature matured into the keen perceptions of an adult.

It wouldn't be easy to win her cooperation. Yet that made him savor the task all the more.

Samuel leaned back in his chair. "I married you for a reason, Cassie. I wish to be accepted into London society. And until I accomplish that purpose, there'll be no signing of any documents."

She didn't speak for a moment. The coal fire hissed into the silence of the library, and rain pattered against the windowpanes. Then she said, "Are you suggesting . . . that if I assist you in the matter, you'll sign the deed? You'll grant me my freedom?"

"Yes."

It wasn't precisely a lie. By the time he had seduced her, his wife would no longer crave independence. She would be as soft and malleable as melted wax. And most likely, increasing with his child.

The prospect made him burn with impatience. He wanted to found a dynasty to rival the Stokefords. He wanted to conquer this woman, to learn her innermost secrets. He desired her as much as he desired revenge.

Giving her time to mull over the offer, he sipped his brandy. Cassie sat with her hands folded on the table and her posture straight. Unlike most women, she didn't try to maneuver him with crocodile tears or saucy smiles. Whatever thoughts lurked behind the cameo perfection of her face remained a mystery to him.

Had he miscalculated?

Abruptly, she spoke. "I seldom go into society."

"Surely you must receive invitations."

"Yes, but I've no interest in attending fancy parties. Or in making conversation with strangers."

"You call me a stranger," he observed. "Yet you don't seem to have any trouble talking to *me*."

"Only on the topic of our marriage. But I'll hardly speak of *that* in public."

Was it the legacy of childhood timidity that kept her from leaping to the lure? He reminded himself that Cassie wasn't like his other women, demanding attention, desiring to occupy center stage, easily placated by money and promises.

Nevertheless, she *was* a woman, and all women had their weaknesses.

"Surely you can overcome your reservations for a short time," he coaxed. "It's a simple contract. You'll introduce me to society in exchange for your independence."

"How do I know you'll keep to the bargain?"

"I give you my word. Shall we shake on it?"

Without waiting for her consent, he placed his hand over hers, relishing the feel of delicate, supple skin. Her eyes widened and she tugged at his grip, but Samuel maintained his hold on her.

"We've no agreement yet," she said stiffly. "Tell me, why should I trust a man who purchased me like a slave?"

His gaze trapping hers, he rubbed his thumb over her dainty fingers. "I repaid your father's considerable debts. I've given you every comfort and asked nothing of you in return—until now."

"And *I* didn't ask to be sold into marriage." Cassie gave another yank, and this time, he let her go. She thrust her hands beneath the table and glared at him. "You haven't told me all the particulars of what you would expect of me."

Samuel could smell the faint flowery fragrance of her skin. He could sense the awareness in her, as well as the uncertainty. "It's quite simple," he said. "You'll accompany me to society events. You'll introduce me to all the lords and their ladies. The task will occupy you for the entire season, two months perhaps."

"You've been abroad for four years. You can know nothing of dancing and manners."

"Then you'll have to teach me." He could think of quite a lot he'd teach her in return.

"Society holds no interest for me. Nor should it for you—unless you enjoy parading in the latest fashions and exchanging polite trivialities." Her gaze sharpened on him. "But then, that isn't your real purpose, is it, Mr. Firth?"

Had she guessed that he planned to seduce her? "My purpose is to become a full-fledged member of the upper crust."

"You wish to raise yourself to the level of the Kenyons. That's why you married me. Not because you love me, but because you hate *them*."

Her blunt words struck Samuel like a sword thrust. He should be satisfied that she believed him motivated solely by a desire for revenge. Yet he resented the censure in her voice. What did she know of his hardscrabble childhood, or his mother's dying plea?

No one knew the gut-wrenching agony he'd endured, being asked to go crawling to the noble father who had rejected him. Samuel had grown up in that pivotal moment, his pain turning to fury at George Kenyon, the Marquess of Stokeford, for misusing a vulnerable woman and then abandoning his own son.

"Never mind the Kenyons," he said coldly. "They've nothing to do with us."

"But they *do*. The dowager Lady Stokeford has let it be known that you're her grandson. When you go into society, people will talk."

Samuel was shaken by that news. He hadn't considered that anyone outside of the family knew of the relationship. But he hid his shock behind a cool mask. "Your only concern should be getting my signature on the deed of separation. I'll sign it in return for your help in getting me accepted by society. Will you agree to the bargain or not?"

With genteel aloofness, his wife rose gracefully from her chair and strolled to the nearest shelf of books. In any other woman he would have known it for an artifice designed to make him notice her exceptional figure. But with Cassie, her actions could have signified anything from boredom to a discomfort with his closeness.

He'd cast his vote on the latter. And if he made her edgy, that proved her vulnerable to him. He would have his way with her. No matter how strong she was, he was stronger.

Seemingly at random, she plucked out a book and idly turned the pages. Her attention flitted from the volume to him. "You said there were *conditions*. What else would you require of me?"

"There's the matter of appearances." Samuel paused before adding the coup de grâce. "For the next two months, we'll have to live under one roof."

She clapped the book shut. "*No.* If I agree to this scheme of yours—and I haven't yet, mind—you can fetch me from this house before any party or ball."

"People will talk if we keep separate homes. They'll say it isn't a true reconciliation." The gossips could go to hell for all he cared, but Cassie needn't know that. When she opened her mouth to argue, he held up his hand. "Yes, scandal already taints my reputation. But that only makes the ruse all the more important. The nobility will be more amenable to accepting me into their fold if they believe our marriage is solid."

"For a callous man, you're absurdly concerned with the opinions of others."

"Rather, I recognize the standards to which the aristocracy will hold me. I'll be scrutinized and judged before being deemed acceptable."

"If we're careful, no one need find out we're living apart." But her voice lacked conviction.

Rising, he removed the book from her unresisting hands and slid it back into its slot on the shelf. "I'm afraid we can't take the chance," he said firmly but gently. "You'll have to move back into my house."

She stiffened. "Absolutely not."

"Now who's being absurd? I'll be gone during the day. You'll have the place all to yourself. Surely you can tolerate my presence in the evenings. That is, if you truly want that legal separation."

She did, he could see it in her eyes. Yet she stated, "I won't inconvenience myself. I'm quite settled where I am."

"There are servants to pack your things. You needn't lift one of these beautiful fingers." Taking her hand again, he drew it to his mouth and kissed each dainty finger in turn. There were dark spots on several of them, and suspicion struck him. "These ink stains. You've been writing recently, haven't you?"

Her eyes grew larger and she pulled her hand away, retreating a step so that her spine met the bookshelf. She glanced down at her fingers as she curled them into her palm. "What matter is it to you? My time is my own."

"Not if you're writing letters to old Lady Stokeford, asking her to intervene for you."

Cassie blinked. "Intervene? You're mistaken. I wouldn't dream of upsetting her with the news of her grandson's return."

Her indignant tone reassured Samuel. The last thing he wanted was interference from that officious old matriarch. Upon learning of his existence nearly five years ago, Lady Stokeford had made a belated attempt to draw him into the bosom of her exalted family. She had viewed him as a charity case, no doubt. He'd burn in hell before he became another of her adoring grandsons. "Very well, then. You may write to whomever else you please—so long as you do it in my home."

Cassie shook her head. "If you insist on sharing a household, you'll have to move in here."

Live in Stokeford's domain? Samuel gritted his teeth against an explosive denial. "It's *your* insistence I find intolerable," he said tightly. "A wife belongs in her husband's house."

"I won't return there, not ever. Your house is far too cold."

Of all the reasons she could have given, this one astonished him. "Didn't the servants keep the fires lit?"

"You mistake me. Your house isn't a home, it's a mausoleum. I never felt at ease reading or writing"—her gaze flicked down to her entwined hands—"writing letters as I like to do. The fact of the matter is, I despised living there."

She might as well have slapped him. His London residence was the epitome of stylish perfection. Before the wedding, he'd had it completely redecorated to suit the refined tastes of a noble bride. Why the hell would she prefer to remain in the dated elegance of the Stokeford town house?

He glanced moodily around the library. The place had the aura of entrenched aristocracy. The upholstery showed signs of wear and the chair cushions sagged. The musty scent of old books reminded him of costumes stored too long in a trunk. He ground out, "And *this* is more to your liking?"

"*This* is a home." With a twitch of her skirts, Cassie walked to a small writing desk and picked up a framed picture. "Here's a sketch done by your brother Michael's daughter Amy. She's quite accomplished at art. And this"—Cassie stooped down to pluck a scraggly stuffed dog from a basket by the fire—"this belongs to Lucy, another of Michael's children. It's her favorite playmate when the family comes to town. She says that Spotty likes this room the best."

"Good God. If you want knickknacks, then buy whatever you like."

"It's more than that." Cassie cuddled the stuffed animal to her bosom, stroking its tattered brown fur. "These things have a sentimental value that can't be purchased. This house feels warm . . . comfortable . . . *happy*. Exactly as I've always imagined a family dwelling should be."

She had grown up in a dilapidated relic of a palace. He had meant to dazzle her with his wealth, to cosset his young bride by surrounding her in opulence. Instead, she'd disdained his offering. She had chosen to live in the house of his sworn enemy.

Michael Kenyon, the Marquess of Stokeford. His half brother.

The icy knot of rage tightened in Samuel. He wanted to surge forward, toss her over his shoulder, and carry her back to his house where she belonged. But she would kick and scream and cause a scandal, and then where would he be?

He would have won the battle, but lost the war.

Realizing he was gripping his fists, he forced his fingers to relax. Heated emotions had no place in any negotiation. He mustn't allow his personal hatred to get in the way of his ultimate plan. It was just a damned house, anyway.

Her chin elevated and her posture perfect, Cassie watched him. Her patrician dignity made him aware of the gulf between them. A gulf he intended to bridge—with soft seduction and iron willpower.

"All right, then," he said in a clipped voice. "We have a bargain. I'll move in here at once."

For the next three days, the pirate ship remained anchored some distance from a stretch of lonely beach. I was imprisoned in a private cabin, left alone save for the meals brought to me by a cabin boy. I attempted to enlist his aid in fleeing, but he dashed my hopes by stoutly declaring his loyalty to the evil Captain Cranditch. How I despaired of my helplessness! Even if I were to escape the confines of my cell, how was I to reach the shore? I could only pass the time by praying for deliverance and worrying that my dear Mr. Montcliff would come to harm at the hands of his deceitful half brother.

Then, on the eve of the fourth day, I was summoned above deck by none other than Percival Cranditch.

—The Black Swan

Chapter 7

Thwarting Mr. Firth

Cassie clung to her composure until she reached her chambers. As she'd hoped, the room was deserted. Gladys did her chores early in the day, under strict orders not to disturb Cassie in the afternoons. At this hour, Cassie was usually writing at her desk, lost in the fantasy world of her characters.

Instead, she felt caught in a nightmare of reality.

Samuel Firth intended to live here in this house. At this very moment, he was on his way home to order his belongings packed. By dinnertime, he would be ensconced in a nearby bedchamber.

Her heart jumped. Never had she dreamed he would agree to her ultimatum and move into the home of his enemy. But he had made the conditions of the bargain clear. If she wanted his signature on the deed of separation, she must pretend for a time that he was her beloved husband.

Blast him! Why could he not be maneuvered like the people in her novels? If only she could write him out of her life!

Cassie snatched up an embroidered pillow from the chaise and hurled it at the bed. The dainty square of yellow silk bounced off and landed on the patterned blue carpet, an ineffectual release for her roiling emotions.

Collapsing into a chair by the unlit fireplace, she discharged a huff of breath. She buried her face in her hands and tried to unravel the tangle of her emotions. She felt anger at his high-handed arrogance in disrupting her life. Frustration at her inability to persuade him to sign the deed. Alarm at his relentlessly seductive manner, for she suspected he had more in mind than a simple introduction to society.

She was afraid he wanted *her*.

Unable to sit still, Cassie sprang to her feet and paced the chamber. Her restless steps carried her to the window, where rain sluiced down the glass in monotonous rivulets. The damp cold weather matched her mood, and she shivered from a draft of chilly air. Rubbing her arms, she faced a deeper fear.

She feared her own response to him.

Despite her lack of experience, she had the sense to recognize the source of her excitable tension whenever he was near. Samuel Firth stirred her womanly passions. She had experienced the unique sensation the previous night at the theater, and today in the library when he had stood beside her and kissed her hand. No other man had ever kindled such warmth inside her.

Not a warmth of the heart, but of the body.

It was a perfectly natural response, she assured herself. The dowager Lady Stokeford had explained all that happened between a husband and wife. The frank discussion had been enlightening, although at the time Cassie couldn't imagine being a willing participant in so shameful an act.

Now, however, she had an inkling of understanding. In her husband's presence, she felt unsettled and distracted. She had found herself wondering what it would be like to feel his arms around her and his hands caressing her. Even now, the thought stirred her deeply. But it would be folly to indulge her curiosity. Samuel Firth was a dangerous man, a man who would use her for his nefarious purposes.

Or at least he would *try* to do so.

Never again would she be so horribly naïve as she had been on her wedding night. The nuptials had been hurried, a sparsely attended ceremony by special license at St. George's in Mayfair. Her father had smelled of brandy and had refused to meet her eyes. Her mother had died nearly two years previous, and there had been no one to prepare Cassie but a haughty French maidservant provided by Mr. Firth.

Cassie herself had been lost in tongue-tied wonder. She had fancied Samuel Firth to be a dashing hero who had fallen madly in love with her from afar. Her vision of marriage had been cozy chats by the fireside and a few chaste kisses before retiring to their separate rooms. Married couples, after all, slept apart.

His entry into her bedchamber on the night of their wedding had startled and mortified her. What he had done next still had the power to make her blush. As if it were yesterday, she could see him standing beside her bed, untying his robe, the garment falling open to reveal the full spendor of his muscular form . . .

Someone tapped on the door. Cassie jumped and spun around. Her cheeks felt flushed. Had Mr. Firth returned already? Would he guess that she had been remembering their wedding night? Then the rapping came again, and she recognized Flora's hesitant knock.

For an instant, Cassie was tempted to pretend she wasn't

there. But her friend needed to be warned. Heaven only knew how Flora would react to having a man living in the house.

Especially an aggressive, seductive, manipulative man like Samuel Firth.

Taking several deep breaths to steady herself, Cassie went to the door and opened it. Flora hovered in the corridor, her embroidery clutched in her hands. Clad in nut brown with her equally brown hair scraped into a bun, she looked rather like a fluttering wren. The distress on her pale face made it clear she had already heard about the visit.

Her worried brown eyes scanned Cassie as if searching for bruises. "Oh, my lady. Are you all right? The footman said that your husband just left."

"Yes, and I'm perfectly fine. There's no need to upset yourself. Come, sit down."

Determined to soothe Flora, Cassie brought her inside and then fetched a glass of water from the fresh pitcher on the writing desk. Poor Flora. Few knew the true circumstances of her escape from a cruel husband.

Flora had been Cassie's governess. After Cassie's marriage to Samuel Firth, Flora had wed the vicar of St. Edmund's Church near Chiltern Palace in Lancashire. It had seemed a brilliant match. At least until Flora had arrived on Cassie's doorstep a year ago with a broken arm and haunted eyes.

Horrified, Cassie had summoned a doctor and then enlisted the help of Andrew Jamison to obtain a private deed of separation for Flora. As the younger son of a baron, the Reverend Norman Woodruff knew the value of a man's reputation. He had signed the document on the threat that if he did not comply, Cassie would expose his abusive nature to his congregation. No one but Cassie and Mr. Jamison knew the truth.

Her friend's situation satisfactorily resolved, Cassie had

decided to obtain her own deed of separation. She had found the courage to move out of her husband's house and take up residence here. Who would have thought the aloof Mr. Firth would prove more difficult to maneuver than a hypocritical wife-beater?

Flora sank into one of the blue-and-yellow-striped chairs by the fireplace. Cassie handed her the glass of water, but she refused it with an anxious shake of her head. "Did Mr. Firth sign the deed, then?" she asked.

Taking the opposite chair, Cassie shook her head. She touched the water glass to her warm cheek and relished its coolness. "I'm afraid not. Although he promised to do so if I'll introduce him to society."

Flora's frown deepened. "Men promise all sorts of nonsense. You told me so yourself. You mustn't trust him."

"I've no other choice." Sipping the water and tasting her own bitterness, Cassie considered ways to soften the news, then decided on the bald truth. "There's more. I'm afraid he's going to stay here with us for a few weeks. He'll join us for dinner tonight."

Gasping, Flora sprang to her feet. Her embroidery hoop fell unheeded to the carpet. "Dinner? *Here?* I must tell Cook at once."

Cassie set down the water glass and retrieved the hoop, which had rolled against the fireplace grate. Brushing it off, she handed it back. "Please don't," she said quickly. "It's a simple matter to have the footman set another place. Or if you don't wish to join us, I'll certainly understand."

"That's not what I mean. Mr. Firth will be vexed that we're only having a small joint of lamb with spring peas. Norman always fussed if there wasn't enough food on the table."

Cassie pressed her back into the chair. "Lamb will do admirably. If Mr. Firth is displeased, then he can return to his house to eat."

Flora cast her a doubtful look. "But aren't you afraid he'll be angry?"

"Frankly, no. If he's going to live here, he'll have to conform to our habits." Mr. Firth used more subtle means of control with women than his fists. Cassie didn't want to think about that, so she focused her attention on Flora. "I see you're embroidering another pillow cover."

"Oh . . . yes. Indeed. It's for the morning room." Flora's face brightened, but only for a moment. As she caught up the dangling thread and needle and held it poised over the hoop, her troubled gaze remained on Cassie. "Will Mr. Firth . . . share your bedchamber?"

"Certainly not!" The very thought discomfited Cassie. "That isn't part of our bargain."

"But you and I occupy the only two spare bedchambers. Where will you put him, then?"

"Out in the carriage house with the groom and coachman."

Flora blinked. "You wouldn't!"

Laughing, Cassie shook her head. "But I would *like* to do so. I'd like to make him bed down in a filthy stall with manure as his pillow. Didn't you ever envision ways to punish *your* husband?"

Flora's cheeks reddened and she glanced down at her sewing. But when she lifted her head, there was an impish glint in her brown eyes that lent a girlish prettiness to her plain features. "It's terribly irreverent . . ."

"That makes me all the more interested."

"I wanted to loosen the seams on his trousers so they would fall down while he stood before the congregation."

Cassie giggled. "How inspired. As for Mr. Firth, perhaps I shall relent and let him stay inside the house."

"Surely not in the dowager's frilly bedchamber. Or in Lord Stokeford's. You did say he hates his half brothers."

"There's the nursery. Wouldn't that be fine? His feet would hang off those short beds."

They shared another laugh, and the very fact that Flora could enjoy a jest over a man filled Cassie with thankfulness. Over the past year, Flora had blossomed, once again becoming a happy, content companion. Cassie could only hope that she soon would see her own situation resolved so satisfactorily.

Leaving her chair, she wandered the room that had been her home for the past six months. The lovely chamber with its pale blue draperies and the four-poster bed had been a welcome haven. She owed a debt of gratitude to Michael Kenyon, Lord Stokeford, for allowing her to live here temporarily. The Kenyon family had invited her to stay at Stokeford Abbey in Devon, but Cassie feared she'd be tempted never to leave their happy home. She was determined to make her own way in the world. The sale of her book had buoyed her confidence that it was only a matter of time before she could afford to purchase a cottage in the country.

Her book. Feeling a twinge of misgiving, she picked up a quill pen from her desk and absently ruffled the feather. Would she repay the kindness of the Stokefords by creating a scandal?

"I must do something about *The Black Swan,*" she mused aloud.

Flora looked up from her sewing. "Do? It's a marvelous story, and all the ladies shall read it. You'll be hugely popular and make pots of money."

"That's exactly what I'm afraid of—the popularity, I mean."

"But . . . you're using an assumed name, are you not? No one will know the author is *you,* my lady."

"I wish I could believe that." Fidgety, Cassie walked back and forth, twirling the quill in her fingers. "But if I go into society as Mr. Firth wishes, someone is bound to put two and two together."

"How so?"

Imagining Mr. Firth in the guise of a pirate, Cassie felt her heart stumble. "It's the way I described the villain. Percival Cranditch with his piercing blue eyes and black hair."

Flora drew in a sharp breath. "I *knew* Mr. Firth reminded me of someone when I first saw him at the theater."

"See? *You* noticed." Cassie's stomach churned with anxiety. "What's worse, my husband is the baseborn son of the previous Lord Stokeford. Oh, whatever possessed me to make Percival Cranditch the baseborn son of Lord S——?"

"It's only a minor detail," her friend said comfortingly. "What seems obvious to us won't be so to your readers."

"I would agree if not for Mr. Firth's scheme to enter society. The *ton* will be agog over the news that he and I have reconciled. The gossipy hens will be clucking. We'll be highly visible, and I don't care to think what may happen if someone makes the connection."

"Bless me, I see what you mean," Flora said, her teeth worrying her lip. "Mr. Firth will be furious. It will make him the object of ridicule."

"Bah, I don't care a snap for *his* reputation." Cassie flung the quill down onto the desk. "It's the Stokefords who concern me. They've been so kind, and I won't have them embarrassed as a result of my folly."

"Oh, dear. When is the book to go on sale?"

The publisher, a brusque businessman named Mr. Quinnell, had been very enthusiastic over the novel and had promised to get it into print as soon as possible. "I intend to find out first thing tomorrow. And I must persuade Mr. Quinnell to allow me to alter the manuscript."

"An excellent notion," Flora concurred. "If Mr. Firth becomes a laughingstock, it will quite ruin him in the eyes of society. And then he may well refuse to sign the deed of separation."

That unwelcome thought had occurred to Cassie, too. She couldn't keep the bitterness from her voice. "Yes, my freedom hinges upon my success in introducing him to a flock of empty-headed, self-righteous geese. How I shall despise the task."

Flora attended to her embroidery, deftly drawing the blue-threaded needle in and out of the white fabric. "In a way, perhaps I was fortunate. Odd to think so, isn't it? But at least *I* had a means to secure Norman's cooperation."

The comment sparked an inspiration in Cassie. "That's it!" She threw her arms around her friend in an impulsive hug, causing her to drop the needlework. "Oh, Flora, you're brilliant. Simply brilliant!"

"What—what did I say?"

"You gave me an idea, that's what. All I need is another *means* to convince my husband to sign the document."

An aghast expression widened Flora's eyes. "Oh, dear me. Surely you won't encourage him to *strike* you?"

"No, no, of course not." Her mind leaping, Cassie refined her clever plan. It would work, it *had* to work. "The dowager Lady Stokeford once told me that Mr. Firth engages in shady business dealings. If I can find proof that he's committed a crime, then I can force him to give me my freedom."

I was taken to the top deck, where to my great surprise, a lavish dinner had been set on a linen-draped table. A cool breeze blew and an awning of canvas sail provided shade from the lowering sun. In dapper attire for so rough a character, Percival Cranditch held out a chair for me.

"Do join me for dinner," he said.

"I would sooner sup with Satan."

"Your wish is granted," he said, a devilish glint in his blue eyes. "Sit now. My brother—your guardian—will be expecting to see you."

My revulsion vanished under a wave of hope. "Mr. Montcliff is here?"

The pirate gave a raspy chuckle. "Nay, m'lady. But he will be soon."

—The Black Swan

Chapter 8

TOOTH OF THE TIGER

The evening began badly. Arriving early, Mr. Firth had the temerity to step into Cassie's chamber while Gladys was buttoning her gown. He looked sinfully handsome in a dark blue coat that deepened the blue of his eyes. He proceeded to bewitch stuffy Gladys with a kiss on the hand for her excellent service to his wife during his four-year absence. Then downstairs, he took Cassie's place at the head of the dining table, directing Flora to his left and relegating his wife to his right.

Although Cassie had resolved to afford him no special favors, the servants apparently saw otherwise. The table had been set with polished silver and fine crystal as if he were the lord and master. Dinner was served on the best gold-rimmed china plates, rather than the everyday crockery that Cassie preferred to use. Unbidden, Cook had prepared a bounty of food. Courses of leek soup and stuffed trout preceded the lamb and peas, followed by a fruit tart and a selection of cheeses.

The servants must have heard the gossip that her husband had abandoned his young bride for reasons unknown. Perhaps they hoped to facilitate a reconciliation.

The notion appalled her, and she consoled herself by thinking about her plan. If everything went well, it was only a matter of time before she saw the last of Mr. Samuel Firth.

All throughout dinner, Cassie had kept a sharp ear open for any information about Mr. Firth's business enterprises. It was imperative that she learn as much as possible about him in order to investigate his criminal deeds. But he'd parried her questions with the saber of charm. Seemingly determined to speak of lighter matters, he'd regaled her and Flora with colorful stories about his travels throughout the world.

To Cassie's dismay, even her friend had fallen victim to his venomous charisma.

"I've a cousin in India," Flora said shyly as the footman bore away the remains of dessert. A blush lent color to her pale cheeks. "Will you tell us more about that country? That is, sir, if you don't mind my inquisition."

Wine glass in hand, Mr. Firth settled back in his chair. "I'll be happy to oblige. So long as I'm not boring my wife."

My wife.

The possessive phrase resonated in Cassie, spreading a telltale warmth through her. The gleam in his eyes irked her as did her involuntary reaction to it. Oh, yes, she could understand his power over women. But awareness was its own defense. "Please go on," she said with chilly politeness.

"Well, Mrs. Woodruff," he said, returning his attention to Flora, "what interests you about India? The odd customs of the people, the wild beasts, or perhaps the unusual scenery?"

"Everything," Flora said fervently.

With a laugh, he proceeded to describe sandbanks shimmering in the heat, white temples bathed in moonlight, enormous rivers teeming with crocodiles. Fascinated in spite of herself, Cassie listened in rapt attention as he painted word pictures of young women wrapped in vivid saris and old crones weighed down by necklaces of barbaric splendor. Sacred cows wearing marigold garlands roamed the dusty villages, while dense jungles abounded with exotic wildlife: elephants, sloth bears, poisonous cobras.

"And tigers?" Flora asked breathily, looking for all the world like a bright-eyed child instead of a mature woman of three-and-thirty. "Did you ever encounter any tigers in India?"

Mr. Firth inclined his head in a nod. "As a matter of fact, I did. Perhaps you'd like to hear about the time I plucked a tooth from a live tiger."

Flora gasped. "Truly?"

Cassie rolled her eyes. "Do tell."

He smiled faintly at her. "In Kashmir, I was invited to spend a week at the palace of the maharajah. It was a massive, sprawling place built of polished marble, and he kept a menagerie for his private entertainment. There was one tiger in particular whom he had raised from an orphaned cub and he was very fond of it. Baba, he called it, meaning 'baby.'"

"Ah," Cassie said dryly. "You pulled a baby tooth."

"Quite the contrary. The tiger was in his prime, a full-grown male, twice as long as I am. From the nose to the end of the tail, he measured thirteen feet. Baba often was allowed to hunt prey within an enclosed atrium while the maharajah and his court watched. But on the last day of my stay there, Baba refused to hunt. His handlers suspected a rotted tooth, but no one dared to look into his mouth."

"Except for you, of course," Cassie mocked, though secretly taken by the story. Flora was more openly enthralled, as was the footman who stood with his mouth agape by the door.

Mr. Firth chuckled. "Yes, it's true," he said without a shred of humility. "However, I first took the precaution of asking the handler to add a lavish amount of poppy juice to Baba's water bowl. Once the tiger fell into a stupor, the handlers pried open his mouth and located the bad tooth. They allowed me the honor of pulling it out with gold pliers. The maharajah was so overjoyed he gave me a priceless gift."

"What was it?" Flora asked, her eyes wide. "Did he shower you with rubies and emeralds?"

"No," Mr. Firth said, sliding a sly glance at Cassie. "He awarded me his daughter's hand in marriage. A rather nubile princess, I might add. I refused, of course."

Cassie gritted her teeth at the picture of him being offered a dark, sloe-eyed beauty. Did he regret turning down the outrageous gift? And why did she wonder, anyway?

"So in other parts of the world," she said tartly, "men also treat women as property to be given away or sold to the highest bidder."

His eyes sparkled with amusement as he regarded her over the rim of his wine glass. "The princess seemed vastly disappointed to lose me. However, if it disturbs you, I'll remember to censor the rest of my stories accordingly."

"There's more?" Though faintly shocked at her scathing discourtesy, Cassie couldn't stop herself from adding, "I find it difficult to believe that one man could have as many adventures as you've related this evening."

"Such things happen in books," Flora piped up, looking distraught by the undercurrents. "You should know . . ." Her voice trailed off when Cassie shot her a swift frown.

But Mr. Firth didn't appear to notice Flora's reference to Cassie's secret vocation as a novelist. He was reaching into an inside pocket of his coat.

"Since you require proof," he said easily, "have a look

at this. I keep it with me as a good-luck charm of sorts."

He leaned across the table, turned over Cassie's hand, and dropped something into her palm. Dumbstruck, she stared down in utter astonishment. In her hand lay a long, wickedly curved tooth. The blackened base indicated where it had rotted.

A tiger's tooth.

Unbidden, her imagination conjured up a scene wherein the hero of her novel-in-progress appeared out of the jungle in the nick of time to save the heroine from an attack by a vicious tiger. But somehow the flaxen-haired Sir Dudley took on the dark features of Samuel Firth.

Nonsense. Mr. Firth was better cast as the villainous Percival Cranditch in *The Black Swan.*

"Bless me!" Flora exclaimed, half rising out of her chair and craning her neck. "May I see?" Cassie passed the tooth to her, and her friend gingerly touched it as if fearing it might spring to life and bite her. "I never imagined that a tiger's tooth could be so large. Only think, Mr. Firth, you plucked it out yourself."

"I'm sure my wife will say I purchased it in a bazaar or perhaps found it lying on a jungle pathway."

Cassie flushed under his scrutiny, for she had been thinking just that. "Actually, I was about to propose that we retire for the evening. It's been a long day, and I've quite a lot to do tomorrow."

As they rose from the table, Mr. Firth pocketed the tiger's tooth, then offered an arm to each woman and escorted them out into the corridor. His keen eyes bored into Cassie. In a low-pitched voice, he said, "And what, may I ask, occupies your time on the morrow?"

A visit to my publisher. And an investigation into your criminal vices. "I'm going out to select some books for the Hampton Lending Library," she fibbed. "It's quite an involved task, so I'll be busy most of the day."

Thankfully, he didn't question the explanation. He turned to Flora and flashed her a charming smile. "I've enjoyed your company, Mrs. Woodruff. I'm glad to know that my wife has had such a good companion in my absence."

Pinkness suffused Flora's face. "The pleasure is mine, sir."

Mr. Firth believed Flora to be a widow, and Cassie hadn't corrected the assumption. He wouldn't be pleased to learn that Flora had been involved in scandal, that she too had taken the unusual step of obtaining a deed of separation. But Cassie felt no temptation to reveal the truth. She was committed to protecting Flora's privacy.

Belatedly, she noticed that her friend was already heading toward the stairway. Leaving Cassie alone with Mr. Firth.

"Good night," she said quickly.

Mr. Firth maintained his hold on her arm. "Not yet, dear wife. I'd like a word with you before we go to bed."

His caressing tone made the remark sound like an indecent proposal. Her heart commenced an unnaturally fast pace. Again, she was aware of that vulnerable warmth deep within her. "We've spoken enough for one day," she said. "I'm quite weary—"

"Surely you can spare a few moments," he cajoled. "It's only nine o'clock. You shouldn't leave your guest alone so early."

"You're hardly a normal guest."

"Yes, I'm your husband. And if ever you hope to be shed of me, you'd do well to keep me in a good humor."

Was that a threat or a jest? He was needling her, she decided. The twinkle in his eyes had a disconcerting effect on her. It scattered her thoughts and melted her resistance. Within moments, she found herself seated beside him on a chaise in the cozy sitting room, where a fire danced in the grate and several branches of lighted candles created a soft, romantic aura.

It had all the hallmarks of preparation.

Eyeing him suspiciously, Cassie sat up straight with her hands clasped in her lap. "The fire in this room is never lit in the evenings. That can only mean you gave the order before dinner."

He flashed a shameless grin. "I confess, I was hoping we could have a private chat in here."

What else did he want from her?

Seeing that he'd shut the door, she felt her wariness increase. She was alone with an uncivilized adventurer clad in the garb of a gentleman. With every breath, she drew in the spicy scent of his cologne; with every glance, she noticed the span of his shoulders and the chiseled masculinity of his features. If he planned to force his attentions on her . . .

Dread and desire knotted her insides. Perhaps her best defense was to direct the conversation. "This is the younger Lady Stokeford's favorite chamber," she said. "Whenever they're in town, she and Lord Stokeford sit here in the evenings."

As Mr. Firth glanced over the comfortable furnishings with their green-and-yellow upholstery, a shadow flitted across his face. Or was it merely a trick of the light? When he spoke, he made no reference to his half brother. "You like it here, too," he said. "There's a stack of your books over there on the table by the window."

"How do you know they don't belong to your brother?"

"They're ladies' novels, are they not?" he countered. "I had a glance at them earlier."

"Perhaps your sister-in-law Vivien left them here. She loves to read, you know. It's a family joke that the tip of her nose should be black because it's so often stuck in a book."

He raised a sardonic eyebrow. "There's a card bearing your name inside the top volume. I must add, you have me wondering why you don't want me to know they're yours."

Her stomach lurched. "You mistake me. I prefer to speak of your family."

"A topic far less interesting than you, Cassie. I find it especially fascinating to discover that you enjoy tales of derring-do. It shows that we share a common fondness for adventure."

Had he leaned closer, or was it her imagination? And how had he managed to learn so much about her already? Steering him away from the dangerous topic of romantic books, Cassie stated, "We're not alike in the least. Especially not in the matter of your family. I love them dearly, yet you've spent your life despising them."

His eyelids lowered slightly, giving him a hooded look that concealed his thoughts. "They've nothing to do with us. Forget about them."

But she couldn't forget. After the wedding, the dowager Lady Stokeford had taken Cassie under her wing, fetching her from Chiltern Palace in Lancashire, where Cassie had sought refuge. She had been frightened of the dowager at first. But she'd soon realized that the brusque old woman was kind and fiercely loyal to her family. From her, Cassie had learned how to comport herself in society and to gain the confidence to overcome her shyness.

And she had learned much about Mr. Firth. The unfortunate circumstances of his birth. The resentment he held toward the Kenyons. The reason he had pulled himself up out of poverty—as a means of attaining revenge on them by becoming their social equal. She might have felt compassion for him had he not blamed the entire family for his father's rejection of him. But it chafed her to know that he had married her solely on the basis of her impeccable lineage.

So many unanswered questions remained. Questions that made Cassie curious in spite of her resolve to remain aloof. Since he was being evasive, she would get straight to the point. "How can you hold your family to blame when the dowager was unaware of your existence until you were a man of one-and-thirty? How can you shun them now? If you'd set aside your hatred, you'd find out how very generous and loving they can be."

In the firelight, his face appeared cast in bronze. "Let me make this clear," he said with studied calm. "I will not speak of Stokeford or the dowager or any other of the Kenyons."

"Why not?" Cassie wanted to understand him as well as she did the characters in her novels, to delve beneath his coldness in the hopes of finding a scrap of humanity. For the dowager's sake, not her own. "You have three married brothers, and between them all, twelve nieces and nephews. They're wonderful, loving people. Do you resent them because the circumstances of your birth makes you their inferior? I assure you, bloodlines don't matter to them."

His lips firmed into a tight line. "Enough. They're dead to me, and I'll hear no more about them."

His callousness disturbed her in a way she couldn't explain. Perhaps it was her regret over not making peace with her own father until he lay on his deathbed. She stopped herself from putting her hand on Mr. Firth's arm in supplication. "But they're your only living relations. You're making a dreadful mistake in rejecting them. Nothing is more important than family."

His darkened gaze flitted to her lips. "There's the deed of separation. If you wish me to sign it, you'll have to play this game by my rules. Do we understand one another?"

Cassie had an instantaneous awareness of his proximity. His arm rested directly behind her on the back of the chaise. At some point, he had turned toward her, and she was acutely conscious of his knee pressing lightly against her thigh.

All of her frustrations about his family vanished beneath the heat of forbidden attraction. His concentrated stare made her feel pinned in place, unable to think or move. In a throaty voice, she said, "Our agreement is not a game but a business deal, Mr. Firth. I'll warn you to keep your distance."

"It's time you accustom yourself to calling me Samuel. The *ton* must be convinced that we're devoted to one another."

Cassie shifted slightly, but she was trapped between him and the upholstered arm of the chaise. Her skin tingled from the brush of his fingers against her shoulder. "We'll be parting in two months, *Mr. Firth.* If you overplay this ruse, you'll only appear the cad later."

"An excellent point," he murmured. "But the fact remains, you're far too formal with me. I want to hear my name on your lips."

Samuel.

To refuse him seemed stubborn and unreasonable, yet Cassie couldn't bring herself to speak. Agreeing to his request implied an intimacy reserved for close friends and family.

And for lovers.

His direct gaze held an air of confidence that she found dangerously attractive. "Cassie," he chided, his voice low and raspy. "Is it so difficult for you to forget your pride? Perhaps it's time to take drastic measures."

"Drastic—"

"Since you refuse to comply, I'll have to use another method to lower the barriers between us." Before Cassie perceived his purpose, he bent his head and placed his mouth on hers.

The caress of his lips kindled all of her senses. In a state of stunned awareness, she drew in the spicy scent of his skin and the heady taste of his mouth. Her eyes closed of their own accord, and the departure of rational thought left her floundering in a sea of excitement. Never before had she felt so alive, as if she'd been slumbering until awakened by the elixir of his kiss.

Samuel.

His palm cradled her cheek, his fingers lightly tracing the

shape of her face, as if she were precious to him. The turmoil evoked by his touch swept downward, tingling through her bosom and settling in her hidden depths. It seemed only natural to press herself to him, to slide her hands over his broad chest and into the thickness of his hair.

His breathing quickened and his arms tightened, drawing her flush against his muscled form. She felt the nudge of his tongue, and like a lock responding to a key, her lips opened to a new and shockingly enjoyable intimacy. At the same moment, his hands moved downward to cup her breasts over the fabric of her bodice. The sinful pleasure made her ache to be unclothed, to feel him stroke her bare flesh.

An echo of alarm came from her beleaguered conscience. She was kissing *Samuel.* Her *husband.* It was *his* hands and mouth that stirred a storm of passion in her. In a trice, he would be lifting her skirts . . .

Appalled, Cassie pulled herself from the heat of his embrace. "Samuel, don't!"

He didn't appear at all vexed by the abrupt end to the kiss. Rather, a devilish smirk played at the corners of his mouth. "There now," he said, running his thumb over her damp, sensitized lips. "That's much better."

Cassie evaded his caress and stood up on shaky legs. With all the dignity she could muster, she moved behind a chair, clinging to the back for support. "I don't care for your methods. Such familiarity has no part in our bargain."

"Perhaps it should. We're married, after all. Indulging our mutual desire for lovemaking would lend authenticity to the ruse."

He had to be jesting. But his torrid gaze spoke otherwise. His outrageous suggestion made her mind go blank to all but the image of herself in bed with him, learning exactly how a man pleased a woman.

Her husband lounged on the chaise, his arms stretched across the back. Watching her intently, he lowered his voice to an alluring pitch. "To be honest, Cassie, I never expected to want you so much. I find you quite irresistible."

A throb of longing robbed her of breath. She was distracted by his profession of desire and daunted by the answering desire inside herself. But rationality prevailed over temptation. She was horrified by how easily he could sway her good judgment. *"No,"* she said. "I won't have an affair with you."

"That's the beauty of it. It wouldn't be an affair." Rising to his feet, Samuel strolled toward her. "We've the blessing of church and state to take our pleasure of each other as often as we like."

The closer he came, the faster her heart raced. "You're speaking nonsense," she said. "Our marriage vows mean nothing to you, else you wouldn't have abandoned me for four years."

He stopped in front of the chair. He had his back to the fire, putting his face partly in shadow. But she could see that a moody frown had replaced the seductiveness. "Abandoned?" he said. "I left you in good hands with a houseful of trusted servants and a guardian to see to all your needs."

"Yes, you'd trapped your prey and locked her in a gilded cage. While you were free to go your merry way."

"I gave you a chance to grow up. You should be thankful I didn't force my attentions on you. Not many husbands would have left you a virgin."

Even as she blushed, she welcomed a surge of anger. It was so much safer than succumbing to impossible yearnings. Her fingers pressing into the brocaded chair, she said, "Should I be grateful that you used me to further your own ambitions? That you caught me in your net before I was old enough to make my own choice?"

All irritated male, he stood with his legs planted apart and his hands on his hips. "Don't be nonsensical. Most women would love to be given carte blanche to buy whatever catches their fancy."

"Then it's a pity you chose *me,* Mr. Firth. I want nothing from you but your signature on the deed of separation."

He regarded her with an icy stare. The fire snapped softly as if to warn her not to push him too far. Belatedly, Cassie remembered he was a dangerous man, a man who would stop at nothing to achieve his goals. If she angered him, he might nullify their bargain.

But she wouldn't back down. She couldn't. Intuition told her that if she showed any weakness he would manipulate her to his will. And she had already displayed a vulnerability to his touch.

The tension gradually eased from his expression. He walked around the chair and stood very close to her, his gaze caressing her mouth. "Mr. Firth, is it? Methinks the lady desires another kiss."

She did. But for self-preservation, she would grant him this one concession. "Don't flatter yourself . . . Samuel."

"You learned your first lesson well," he said with an amused nod. "Let me give you a word of advice. If you cooperate, you'll find me much easier to live with."

Did he expect her to spend the next two months placating him? Cassie swallowed a retort and strove for icy politeness. "It might be simpler if you were to write down all your rules. There's paper and pen over there on the desk. I'll say good night and leave you to the task."

When she turned to go, he snared her hand and brought her around to face him. She recoiled, but he maintained his hold, his thumb caressing the tender skin of her inner wrist. "Patience, darling," he murmured. "I needn't write down what I can sum up in a few words."

"Then do so quickly. I tire of your company."

He chuckled softly. "As you wish. Henceforth, you'll

behave in public as a loving wife. You won't move away when I stand near you. Nor will you flinch when I touch you. If you disobey those rules, I shall have to punish you." His penetrating gaze dropped to her mouth before lifting again to meet her eyes. "And next time, I may not be able to stop."

Cassie felt an involuntary clench of excitement, which she squelched without mercy. "We'll see about that, *Samuel.*"

To this day, I have no memory of swallowing even a bite of my dinner. I spent the time anxiously watching the distant beach for Mr. Montcliff.

"Your guardian is to deliver the ransom himself—a hundred gold sovereigns," Percival Cranditch remarked. "How shall I kill him, m'lady? Shall I slit his throat? Or do you fancy seeing him hang from the yardarm?"

"Spare him," I begged. "He is your brother, your flesh and blood."

"We shall see if his blood is blue—or as red as mine." Grinning, the pirate pointed to the shore. "Ho, there. Our guest has arrived at last."

—The Black Swan

Chapter 9
The Runaway Cask

The next morning, Cassie was on her way out when she discovered an unwelcome visitor in the house. She had risen late after a fitful sleep. Several times during the night she had awakened, warm and restless, keenly aware of her husband's presence in the master's bedchamber. She had dreamed of his kiss—and more. Now she felt sluggish and bleary-eyed and anxious to visit the office of her publisher.

Passing through the hall on her way to the front door, she heard a man talking in the drawing room. A vague familiarity in that derisive voice gave her pause. Then a chill brought her to full alertness.

Postponing her plans for the day, she hastened into the chamber, her skirts rustling. A short, husky man stood over Flora, who cowered on a chaise near the fireplace. Her embroidery hoop in hand, she gazed up at him in palapable fear.

He was Flora's stepson, Charles Woodruff. And he had learned at his father's knee the sadistic joy of brutalizing women.

Cassie went straight to them. "What's going on here?"

"My lady," Woodruff said, stepping back to sweep her a bow. "It's indeed a pleasure to see you again."

Some six years Cassie's senior, he wore a tailored dark green coat that complemented his flaxen hair and pale complexion. Many might be fooled by his genteel manners, but Cassie knew him for a ruffian of the worst ilk. "What were you doing to Flora?"

"I was merely trying to persuade her to summon you. I trow, she's more stubborn than she was in the vicarage."

He shot Flora a resentful glare that made her shrink. It was the way she always looked when faced by Charles Woodruff or his father, Norman.

She clutched her embroidery hoop like a pitiful shield, and Cassie noticed that a tiny red stain marred the white fabric. Another droplet of blood welled on Flora's pale fingertip.

Horrified, Cassie asked, "Did he jab you with the needle?"

Flora's gaze darted to Woodruff. "There's n-no harm done," she stammered. "It's my fault, really."

Enraged, Cassie swung toward Woodruff to find him watching her with the sharp brown eyes of a weasel. "Craven scoundrel. Leave this house immediately."

"All in due time." He removed a small silver box from his pocket, opened it, and inhaled a pinch of snuff. "My stepmama has told me the news. She says your husband has returned from his journey abroad."

"Yes, and if he finds you here, he'll toss you out on your ear."

A superior look on his face, Woodruff took his time tucking the snuffbox back into his pocket. "Flora also said he's left for his office. Such is the fate of commoners, having to labor all day."

Cassie despised men like Charles Woodruff, wasting their lives in idle pursuits. Odd to think that she and Samuel were alike in their desire to work. "*You* would do well to find another occupation aside from bullying women."

"Such a spirited girl you are," he said, eyeing her up and down. "I can't help but envy your husband in the bedchamber."

Her stomach clenched. This wasn't the first time he had hinted of his desire for an affair with her. His lewd reference made her feel sullied, a vastly different reaction from her response to Samuel's kiss. "I've heard enough. If you won't leave of your own accord, I shall summon a footman."

She turned to go, but he stepped into her path, blocking her with his opened arms. The cunning look in his eyes warned her to keep her distance. "Wait," he said. "I haven't yet told my stepmama the purpose of my visit. I'm sure she'll be very interested to know what my father is planning."

"Planning?" Flora said in a frightened whisper.

Charles Woodruff peeled back his lips in a smile, revealing protruding teeth. "He grows weary of paying you a quarterly stipend. He intends to challenge the deed of separation in a court of law."

Flora made a strangled sound in her throat.

Stepping to the chaise, Cassie placed her hand on Flora's small, trembling shoulder. "Don't listen, my dear. The deed is perfectly legal. Andrew Jamison made certain of that."

"There *is* one loophole," Woodruff said. "No judge in the land would uphold the deed if my father can prove that she's cuckolded him—by seducing her own stepson."

The hideous allegation sickened Cassie. She didn't doubt for an instant that Charles Woodruff would tell such a blatant lie. "That is patently false. You'll go to jail for perjuring yourself."

"It's well worth the risk. Father's promised me a hefty increase in my own allowance." He caressed Cassie with his eyes. "However, for the right inducement, I could be persuaded to change my testimony."

His meaning was so reprehensible that it took Cassie a moment to comprehend him. Her skin crawled with revulsion. Did he truly think she would submit to him? And with her refusal, what would happen to poor Flora?

Before she could collect her thoughts, Flora flung aside her embroidery and leapt to her feet. Tears welled in her brown eyes. "No! I'll return to Norman if I must. But please don't involve Cassie in your dastardly plots."

Seeing her friend so overwrought only hardened Cassie's resolve. "It's all right, Flora. We'll let Mr. Woodruff present his vile proposition to my lawyer."

Shaking his head, Charles Woodruff laughed. "Ladies, ladies. I meant no lechery. If Lady Cassandra could but persuade her rich husband to outbid my father's offer, then I'll be happy to tell the truth in court."

Samuel stood on the docks, watching a crew unload casks of rum from his ship. A forest of masts stretched in either direction as far as the eye could see. The air was pungent with the stench of hides, the fumes of tobacco and spirits, and the stink of the river itself. All around him, the babble of foreign tongues mingled with the fractured English of Cockney laborers. Sailors sang boisterous songs to celebrate their liberation from long months at sea. Foremen barked out orders. Chains rattled and ropes splashed as gangs of workers manipulated the cranes, hoisting the barrels over the side of the ship. In the midst of organized chaos, a customs-house officer in his brass-buttoned jacket scribbled entries in his ledger.

Samuel relished it all. The hustle and bustle of the quay,

the cold brisk air, even the smells of the maritime district. The docks represented fortunes to be made in rich cargoes of silk and wine and spices. He had come to oversee the audit of his warehouse, but he had arrived before Hector Babbage and the team of clerks.

Standing near the doorway, Samuel watched as laborers rolled casks of Portuguese rum across the cobblestones and into the huge brick structure. He had to be honest with himself. His sense of satisfaction today had less to do with the vigorous life around him than with a more personal matter.

Cassie desired him.

Given her reserved nature, he hadn't expected her to respond so quickly to his seduction. But from the moment he'd touched his lips to hers, she had been his for the taking. She had melted in his arms with a delightfully innocent passion. The memory of her womanly body, her full breasts, had kept him awake long into the night. He had been sorely tempted to steal into her bed and initiate her before she came fully awake.

As much as she would enjoy his lovemaking, he knew in his gut that she would despise him afterward. Only look at how angry she had been in the aftermath of their kiss. Indulging his lust too soon would earn her hatred and ruin his ultimate plan.

In his experience, women were divided into two categories, those who would lift their skirts on no more than a smile from him, and those who needed coaxing to relax their high moral standards. Cassie, however, would require more than a little coaxing.

Unlike his other women, she was a virgin. She had spent four years without a husband, and in that time, she had grown accustomed to a certain amount of freedom. It would take patience to win her trust. He would have to woo her, cultivate her, learn her secret hopes and dreams. His restraint would be worthwhile in the end, for Cassie was more than just another conquest to him. Henceforth, she would share his life and occupy a place of honor at his side. She would be the mother of his children.

The prospect of impregnating her stirred him in a way that went beyond the sexual. He craved to see her ripen with his seed, to watch her suckle his infant at her breast. Never before had he made love to a woman with any purpose beyond their mutual enjoyment. The anticipation affected him like an aphrodisiac, dominating his thoughts and trapping him in a purgatory of arousal—

A loud crash yanked him from his reverie. An ominous drumroll of noise filled the air. Men shouted warnings. Sailors and workers scattered. Samuel turned on his heel toward the commotion.

A huge cask of rum rolled straight toward him.

In the same instant, a ragged youth flew out of nowhere and gave him a hard shove.

Samuel staggered back against the doorway. Instinctively he seized the lad and yanked him out of harm's way as the barrel collided with the brick wall just inches from them. Having narrowly escaped being crushed, he could only stare in shock. The impact had broken several of the metal staves on the cask, and the sharp smell of rum filled the air.

Men came running to examine the damage. A foreman took charge and summoned a cooper to repair the staves.

Samuel realized he still had a grip on the boy's bony shoulder. He looked down at his savior. The lad was painfully thin and clad in a tattered shirt that may once have been white, but had now turned a dingy shade of gray. A black top hat minus the brim perched on a mat of dark hair. His bare feet were filthy and his face hadn't met a cake of soap in years, perhaps never. Samuel guessed him to be about twelve, the same age Samuel had been when he'd set out to make his fortune.

"Lemme go."

The urchin wriggled in an attempt to slither away, but Samuel held tightly to the back of that grimy shirt. "Wait. You saved my life."

His blue eyes lighting with crafty awareness, the youth stuck out a grubby paw. "I'll take me reward, then. A shillin'."

Samuel felt an ironic amusement. How Cassie would laugh to hear that his life was worth only a single piece of silver. He was reaching into his pocket for a coin when, through the cacophony of voices, he heard a familiar one.

"Dear me!" Hector Babbage squeezed through the crowd of onlookers and blinked at Samuel through a pair of gold-rimmed spectacles. An expression of horror creased his plump face. "Have you been injured, sir? Shall I summon a physician?"

"I'm fine," Samuel said. "How long have you been here?"

"Only a moment. Someone said a runaway cask almost struck you." Clutching a ledger to his rotund chest, Babbage gravely shook his head. "A man was killed that way only last week on the docks. Not one of our men, of course. No such an incident has ever happened here before."

"Go inside. We'll start the audit upstairs."

Babbage's face turned gray. "Upstairs, sir?"

Samuel had forgotten the man's fear of heights. "All right, send your clerks upstairs. Set up an office for yourself on the ground floor."

"Yes, sir." The chief accountant bobbed his balding head and then vanished into the warehouse.

Staring after him, Samuel wondered at the coincidence of Babbage appearing just moments after the accident. Would he stoop to murder if he knew the audit would turn up discrepancies? He was a mild-mannered, almost timid man, but Samuel knew better than to judge by appearances.

"*I* seen wot 'appened, guv'nor."

Samuel looked down at the urchin. A canny intelligence shone in those blue eyes. "Come here, out of the way."

Leaving the hive of busy dockworkers, he marched the boy to a quieter spot by a ship that had already been unloaded. Samuel sat on an upended crate so that he could look him in the face. "Tell me what you saw just now."

The boy crossed his skinny arms over an equally skinny chest. "Wot's in it fer me?"

Samuel produced a guinea from his pocket. His eyes widening, the brat lunged for the gold piece, but Samuel held it out of his reach. "First, your information."

His attention shifting between the coin and Samuel, the boy said rapidly, "I seen a man by the hoist. 'E loosed the chain when the foreman weren't lookin'. 'Tis why the barrel fell."

Samuel frowned. "What man? The one who spoke to me just now by the warehouse?"

The brat shook his head. "'E wore dockman's clothes, wid a cap pulled low over 'is 'ead. But 'e were a toff like ye. I can spot 'em a mile off. 'Tis the way they walk, like they owns the world."

Samuel took only marginal notice of the boy's derisive tone. A gentleman had detached the chain from the hoist. He had caused the cask to drop. The deliberate action had happened close enough to Samuel to put him in the direct path of danger. Was it a prank or a murder attempt?

And if the culprit wasn't Babbage, then who else?

"This is a serious charge. Are you quite certain of your facts?"

In a pose of indignant pride, the boy hitched his thumbs in the waistband of his breeches. "I got sharp eyes, I do. I know what I seen."

"Then describe the man."

"Not so tall as ye. A bit stout in the ribs." The urchin shrugged. "'Appened in a twinklin', it did. Don't know no more'n that."

Samuel scanned the busy quay full of sailors and laborers. "Do you see the fellow anywhere?"

The boy hopped nimbly up on the gangplank of the ship. From the high perch, he surveyed the throng and shook his head. "Cor, 'e'd be a block'ead to 'ang about, eh? T' stay by the scene o' the crime."

"You should heed your own advice." Even as the boy gaped in surprise, Samuel reached up and seized him by the back of the breeches, hauling him down off the gangplank. Maintaining a firm grip, Samuel held out his other hand. "My pocketwatch. If you return it, I won't haul you off to the magistrate."

Goggle-eyed, the urchin stood unmoving. Then he slowly reached inside his shirt and produced the gold timepiece with its dangling fob. "Wot o' the guinea? I earned it, fair 'n' square."

He was so brazen, Samuel had to bite back a grin. His wry humor was born of understanding. He knew what it was like to live on the street, to fight for a crust of bread. Had he not talked his way into a lowly position as a clerk at a shipping company, he might have ended up like this boy.

Instead, after the death of his mother, he had worked long hours, watched and listened and learned. The moment he'd come of age, he had started his own shipping firm. Within a decade, his shrewd business sense and canny investments had made him richer than many aristocrats.

He focused his attention on the boy. "Tell me your name."

"May'ap I don't 'ave one."

"Everyone has a name. Only the truth will secure you this coin."

The boy adjusted his brimless hat and muttered something under his breath.

"Speak up," Samuel commanded.

"Mick," he admitted defiantly. "'Twas what me mam

called me. Said me da was a scurvy Irish sailor spoutin' blarney."

"Well, Mick. If you want honest employment, then report to my office in the Strand tomorrow morning. Ask for Samuel Firth." He gave Mick the address and the coin, and left him clutching the guinea.

Heading to the warehouse, Samuel wondered if Mick would show up. Boys like him tended to look no farther than their next meal. With money lining his pocket, Mick would likely see no need to labor.

Still, he'd had the initiative to push Samuel out of the way of that cask. If not for young Mick, Samuel might have been badly injured, perhaps even killed.

The laborers had resumed their tasks. A crew of men sang as they lowered a keg of rum to the dock. Another team rolled a huge barrel into the warehouse. All appeared normal again.

Nevertheless, Samuel kept a sharp eye peeled for a slightly stout gentleman in the garb of a laborer. And he thought about all the people who would want him dead.

Never have I felt such joy and such despair! My dear Mr. Montcliff stood on the beach, a coffer of gold coins in his hands. There was no hesitation in him as he stepped into a dinghy manned by one of the pirates.

Standing at the rail, Percival Cranditch watched his enemy intently. I knew he would murder my guardian in cold blood. I had but one faint hope to keep Mr. Montcliff out of the clutches of the pirate captain.

While Cranditch observed his half brother being rowed to the ship, I edged away and stepped atop a coil of rope. The makeshift stool raised me high enough to accomplish my purpose.

I clambered atop the side and cried out a warning to Mr. Montcliff. Then I hurled myself into the icy depths of the sea.

—The Black Swan

Chapter 10

Set in Stone

"Mr. Jamison has gone out for a meeting with a client." The secretary, a stooped older man named Barrymore, regarded Cassie with abject apology. "I'm sorry to say, my lady, he isn't due to return for at least another half an hour."

Cassie subdued a groan. After tossing Charles Woodruff out the door, she'd had to spend a good deal of time consoling Flora. Cassie had promised to check the legality of Flora's separation without delay. She had stopped here to consult with Mr. Jamison on the way to her publisher. But it was already the middle of the afternoon, which didn't bode well for accomplishing the urgent errand of revising her book.

Swallowing her impatience, she smiled at Barrymore.

"May I wait, then? And you'll inform me the moment he arrives?"

"Most assuredly, my lady."

He hastened to direct her into the solicitor's office. She knew Barrymore only slightly from the times he had delivered messages for his employer. From his sidelong glances, Cassie presumed he'd heard the news that her husband had dismissed Mr. Jamison's services. Bowing to her, the secretary closed the door and she was left alone.

Too restless to remain seated in one of the leather chairs, Cassie slowly traversed the length of the office with its shelves of legal books and the mahogany desk that gleamed faintly in the light of a tall window. Odd to think she had never been here before today. Although she had known Mr. Jamison for four years, he had always called on her at home. It wasn't proper for a lady to visit any place of business other than the shops, and Mr. Jamison always observed proprieties.

But he would have to make an exception this once. Cassie couldn't take the chance of Samuel finding out that she'd consulted the solicitor. She had enough trouble without inviting more.

If Samuel caught her disobeying him, he might kiss her again.

Her legs turned to jelly. Pausing by the desk, Cassie placed a gloved hand over her bosom and felt the swift beating of her heart. How was it that the mere thought of him had such a weakening effect on her? She quailed at the notion of spending months in his company. Instead, she pictured herself writing at her desk in that cottage in the country, with the chirping of birds outside and a soft breeze blowing through an open window.

That was her fondest dream. To earn enough as an author to pay her own way so that she need never depend on a man for her support.

Or for her happiness.

Cassie renewed her vow to resist his diabolical charm. Now that she knew the extent of her vulnerabilty, she would be on her guard. It would be sheer madness to give in to temptation. Samuel would take control of her life and prevent her from achieving her goal. She would become a mere ornament on his arm rather than an independent woman.

It was far too high a price to pay for pleasure.

Listening for the sound of Mr. Jamison's arrival, she roamed the office, casting a desultory glance at a few paintings of woodland scenes. She had so much to do that her patience was wearing thin. In addition to calling on Mr. Quinnell at the publishing house, she had to find proof that Samuel had committed a crime. Then she could use his misdeed as a bargaining chip.

What had the dowager Lady Stokeford said so long ago? That he sometimes lent money to indebted noblemen and charged them a high rate of interest. That he had amassed his wealth by using questionable business practices.

Cassie had already rejected the notion of writing to the dowager to ask for more information. Samuel's grandmother didn't yet know about the deed of separation, and Cassie was reluctant to tell her, for the dowager would be appalled. There had to be another way to uncover the truth.

She stopped short and turned her gaze to Mr. Jamison's desk. The smooth expanse of polished wood reminded her of the solicitor, pristine and neat and elegant. Not even a pen or ink stand marred the surface.

Would Mr. Jamison keep a record of Samuel's business transactions?

Cassie had always considered herself something of a coward. That was why her heroines were so valiant, so that she could live vicariously through their adventures. She herself could never commit such daring acts as espionage.

But the stakes were extremely high. There wouldn't be very many opportunities like this one.

Quelling her conscience, she darted behind the desk and sat down in Mr. Jamison's big chair. She paused only to cock her head and listen for sounds of his return. Thankfully, the outer office remained quiet.

She pulled on the center drawer only to discover that it was locked. Then she tried the one to her right, and this one slid open without a sound. With trembling fingers, Cassie browsed through the row of files, all neatly labeled with various names. She spied one marked "Mrs. Flora Woodruff," which no doubt contained legal papers. But to her great disappointment, she didn't see a file inscribed with her husband's name.

Had Mr. Jamison already returned any business papers to Samuel? Or were those files kept elsewhere? In Barrymore's desk, perhaps?

The drawer to her left contained only a tidy stack of paper and the accouterments of writing: pens and pencils, a silver inkpot, and a small knife for sharpening quills. There were no other cabinets in the office.

Although the task seemed fruitless, she paged through the files again, one by one, allowing herself only a scant few seconds with each. Most contained dry legal documents such as wills or contracts for people whose names she didn't recognize. Halfway through her search, she stumbled upon something of interest.

The one-page document appeared to be a private trust. It provided for a comfortable monthly allowance to one Hannah Davenport, the funds to be issued by Mr. Andrew Jamison from the account of Samuel Firth. The bold black scrawl of her husband's signature extended across the bottom of the paper.

Cassie stared down at the paper, which was dated over four years earlier. A note showed the woman's address to be in Soho. Why would Samuel authorize the solicitor to send a quarterly stipend to this woman? It was far more than the amount paid to a mere servant. The fact that Samuel had taken the care to make the arrangement legally binding could only point toward a single explanation.

Hannah Davenport was one of his ex-mistresses.

And she must know something incriminating about him, too, for he had been compelled to buy her silence.

Anger and elation warred inside Cassie. But she had no time to sort out her emotional upheaval. In the next moment, she heard the rumble of male voices in the outer office.

Quickly she shoved the file back in its place and shut the drawer. Springing up, she rounded the desk and hastened to the guest chair. She had barely an instant to sit down and arrange her skirts before Andrew Jamison opened the door.

His gray eyes intent, he strode straight to her. He looked unusually agitated from his furrowed brow to his taut mouth. Even his silvered brown hair was mussed. For the space of a heartbeat, she feared he knew that she'd been snooping in his desk.

Taking her gloved hand, Mr. Jamison pressed it between his. "My lady, is something amiss? Has that man done you ill?"

The question startled Cassie. "Samuel?"

"Who else? If he's misused you—"

"No! He hasn't." Remembering Samuel's kiss, she struggled against a blush. "The reason I'm here has nothing at all to do with my husband."

It was on the tip of her tongue to ask Mr. Jamison about Samuel's involvement with Hannah Davenport. But then he would know she was guilty of examining his private files. Andrew Jamison was like a father to her, and she couldn't bear to invite his censure.

"Forgive me," he said rather stiffly, letting go of her hand. "I could think of no other reason for you to come here. You do know that Firth dismissed me yesterday, don't you?"

Biting her lip, she nodded. She had been so wrapped up in

her own worries that she'd forgotten. Jamison was a prosperous man, but the loss of a lucrative account represented the loss of income for him. "I'm sorry that Samuel has treated you so shabbily. It's all my fault, isn't it? You advised against moving into Lord Stokeford's house, but I did so anyway."

The solicitor's face softened. "My dear, you obeyed your heart. If I objected to the move, it was only out of concern for your welfare. After all, Firth had hired an entire staff of servants to care for all your needs."

"I don't need pampering," Cassie said tartly. "I never wanted that."

"You've grown up to be quite independent," Jamison said. A fond smile flickered across his distinguished features as he sat down in the chair beside hers. He looked like the consummate older gentleman in a coat of charcoal gray over black trousers. His gaze sobering, he gave her an intent look. "Will you return to his house to live?"

Cassie ached to spill out all her fears and worries, to ask the solicitor's advice and let him guide her as he'd always done. But she hesitated, knowing it was time she took charge of her own life. Besides, she could never admit her strong sensual attraction to Samuel. It was too private to share with anyone else.

"Samuel has moved into the Stokeford town house for the present," she said. "He's promised to sign the deed of separation once I introduce him to society."

His face darkening, Jamison leaned forward. "Don't believe him, my lady. He told me that he has no intention of letting you go."

The news jolted Cassie. But it was nothing less than she'd surmised already. She could only hope that Hannah Davenport had information that Cassie could use to force Samuel's hand. "He's quite the devious man, my husband," she said, striving for lightness. "But I've resolved to find a way to make him sign the document."

"How? A sheltered young lady like you is no match for a man who grew up on the streets." Jamison ran his fingers through his hair in uncharacteristic agitation. "You should never have married Firth. Had I been consulted on the matter, I would have put a stop to it."

His protectiveness touched Cassie deeply. But it was too late to change the past; she could only determine the future. Patting his arm, she said, "I greatly appreciate all you've done for me. And I have one more favor to ask of you."

"Anything, my lady."

"It isn't for me, but for my dearest friend." She told him about Norman Woodruff's scheme to challenge Flora's deed of separation—without mentioning the lewd advances made by Charles Woodruff.

To her relief, Mr. Jamison was just as incensed as she was. "Tell Mrs. Woodruff not to fret," he said. "I've dealt with many a scoundrel in my time. I'll write a letter to her husband and explain the fate of perjurers. I'll paint so grim a picture he'll drop the suit at once."

A measure of worry lifted from Cassie's shoulders. Now, if only she could deal with Samuel so effectively.

When the hackney cab drew up outside the publisher's office on Albemarle Street, Mr. Quinnell was standing outside, bending over to lock the door. He was a rather short man with a bristly moustache and equally bristly gray hair sticking out from beneath his top hat. He carried a rolled umbrella beneath his arm.

He spied Cassie and scurried to greet her as she alighted. "Ah, my lady," he said, with an exuberant wave of the umbrella. "It's a pleasure to see my favorite author again."

Alarmed, Cassie glanced at the hackney driver, but the sour old man seemed interested only in taking a nip from his flask. Nevertheless, she drew Mr. Quinnell a short distance away to the relative privacy of a hedge. "You mustn't say such things in public," she reminded him in a whisper, glancing up and down the quiet street. "Someone might overhear."

Instantly contrite, he pressed a finger to his lips. "Do accept my sincerest apologies. Of course you're anonymous. If anyone asks me, I have no knowledge of the true Lady Vanderly."

"*Mrs.* Vanderly. That's my pen name."

"It's Lady Vanderly now. Oh, I hope you don't mind. We'll sell so many more copies of *The Black Swan* if readers know the mysterious author is a true lady from the highest circle of society."

Cassie's heart lurched in dismay. "I *do* mind. The book must be published under the pseudonym we agreed upon."

Mr. Quinnell ducked his head in a sheepish look. "It may be too late."

Her throat dry, she asked, "*May* be?"

"It *is* too late, I fear. The covers were imprinted just yesterday at the bindery. But 'pon my word, you'll love the look of it! We used the finest maroon leather with 'Lady Vanderly' and the title written in gold lettering on the spine."

"What of the pages?" Cassie was almost afraid to ask. "There's an important change I simply must make in the text."

"Change?" Mr. Quinnell fairly staggered as if she'd suggested he set fire to a rare copy of the Gutenberg Bible. "Why, the novel is absolutely perfect as it is. The ladies are going to love every last word!"

At any other time, his praise would have gratified her. But she could think only of Percival Cranditch with his uncanny resemblance to Samuel. "Nevertheless," Cassie said firmly, "I must make a few small alterations. They're minor details, but they've been weighing on my mind."

"Er . . . well . . . I'm afraid that's impossible, m'lady. The fact of the matter is, the pages are being printed as we speak.

I was just on my way to the bindery to check on the progress."

Cassie closed her eyes momentarily and prayed to awaken from this nightmare. But another look at Mr. Quinnell's affable face told her the truth. She grasped at one last straw of hope. "Surely a change can still be made. The presses must be stopped. I'll pay the expense myself." She didn't know where she'd find the money, but she'd worry about that later.

"That's out of the question," he said somewhat indignantly. "It's too late for changes. The type may as well be set in stone."

"It can't be," she whispered. "Surely there's a way . . ."

"Now, now, it's only natural to worry about how your first book will be received by the public." Courteously taking her arm, he escorted her back to the hackney. "Please be assured, I'll do everything in my power to make *The Black Swan* a smashing success. Ladies will be queuing up in droves to purchase it. I would stake my reputation on the matter!"

Cassie wished she could share his enthusiasm. "When will the book go on sale?" she asked faintly.

"Within the fortnight, I'm pleased to say." Mr. Quinnell beamed at her. "Wasn't it clever of me to discern that if I rushed the book into print, it would be available during the height of the social season? Only think of how many more copies we will sell!"

The waters closed around me like an icy shroud. I sank down, down, down into the treacherous brine. The shock of my desperate action threatened to overtake my senses. But I clung to one thought, to reach Mr. Montcliff so that I might alert him to the wicked trap set by Captain Cranditch.

—The Black Swan

Chapter 11

Rose Petals

In the gray twilight of early spring, Samuel paced the drawing room at the Stokeford town house. Just moments ago, the footman had lighted a branch of candles to ward off the encroaching darkness. But Cassie, who had departed soon after luncheon, hadn't yet returned.

Her absence disturbed Samuel, and not just because he wanted to pursue his seduction of her. He wanted her *here,* safe with him. London after dark abounded with footpads, thieves, and other riffraff. What was worse, he'd discovered that his obstinate wife hadn't kept the carriage he'd provided for her. She preferred to walk or to take a hackney cab. Which meant that she was out there alone, without even a groom or coachman to protect her.

The little fool!

He peered out the front window of the drawing room. The veil of dusk covered the trees and shrubbery of the square. Lamps glowed here and there in the windows of the neighboring houses. Only a few pedestrians and carriages traversed the cobbled street.

Where had Cassie intended to go today? The Hampton Lending Library. Her tasks there included selecting books to purchase for the use of the subscribers. It was yet another facet of the independent life she had devised for herself. He could admire her for doing useful work.

But not if she endangered her life by staying out after dark.

A sense of disquiet plagued Samuel. After that harrowing episode at the docks, he felt the need to hold Cassie in his arms. The audit had been tedious work, and he had departed early from the warehouse, his mind filled with the anticipation of seeing his wife. It had been a blow to discover that she wasn't waiting here for him.

Was she so damned bent on autonomy that she would ignore the dangers of roaming the city alone? He'd put a stop to that.

Samuel turned abruptly from the window. Unaccustomed to worrying about anyone but himself, he stalked to a sideboard and poured himself a brandy. As he drank it, he prowled the drawing room. The gold and crimson décor was in a style from the previous century, elegant but dated.

Among the scenic watercolors on the walls, a small collection of silhouettes caught his attention. He went over to examine them more closely. The likenesses had to belong to four of Michael's five children, excluding the new baby. They were handsome children, he noted coldly. He would expect no less of the noble Michael Kenyon.

Thinking of his eldest brother, Samuel grimaced. Michael stayed here whenever he came to London, which apparently wasn't often. The house had been passed through three generations of Kenyons, and along with the title of Marquess of Stokeford, Michael had inherited the place from his father.

Samuel's father. The man who had never acknowledged

the existence of his bastard son. The man who had abandoned his mistress upon learning of her pregnancy.

Samuel's jaw tightened. George Kenyon, the old Lord Stokeford, had walked these floors, sat in these gilded chairs, warmed himself by the white marble hearth. If he knew that his by-blow was living here now, albeit temporarily, he would turn over in his grave.

Samuel culled a certain satisfaction from that. Yet he couldn't shake the sense of being an outsider here. In some hidden part of himself, he felt like a penniless boy with his nose pressed to the window of a sweets shop.

Curse it. He had amassed more riches than most aristocrats with their inherited wealth and superior airs. His own house was far grander than this one. He would create his own dynasty to rival that of the Kenyons. The blood of kings and dukes would flow through the veins of his children.

As soon as he seduced his wife.

What the devil was keeping Cassie? If something had happened to her, his plans would be ruined.

He set down his glass with a decisive click, then strode out into the entrance hall, his footsteps echoing on the marble floor. A few candles flickered in sconces on the walls, but he took little notice of his surroundings. By God, he'd had enough of waiting. He'd go out and find her himself.

The footman was opening the front door. A woman's quiet voice spoke a greeting to the servant. The object of Samuel's potent thoughts hastened into the house.

Cassie didn't notice him; her attention was focused on tugging off one of her gloves. In the candlelight, her face looked as exquisite as a cameo. A straw bonnet with a blue ribbon enhanced her freshness of youth, while a form-fitting pelisse delineated her womanly bosom. She was frowning as if something weighed on her mind.

Stabbed by a dagger of relief, Samuel went straight to her. Anxiety gave way to anger. "You're late."

Her gaze narrowed on him; then she glanced down at her hands as she peeled off her other glove. "Good evening," she said with a hint of dignified sarcasm. "I didn't realize we'd set a schedule."

Taking her arm, he pulled her out of earshot of the servant and into the drawing room. He watched moodily while she tucked her gloves in the reticule that dangled from her wrist. The image of her encountering ruffians dogged his mind. "You went out without a groom," he accused. "You're not to do so again. Especially not after dark. Is that clear?"

Her spine visibly stiffened. "We agreed that you wouldn't interfere with my daily activities."

"I will if you endanger yourself. Henceforth, you'll have a carriage at your disposal. I'll expect you to use it."

"More of your rules? Pardon me if I'm too weary to quarrel. It's been a long day, and I'll bid you good night."

Instantly, Samuel stepped into her path. Just as instantly, he recognized his faulty handling of Cassie. Her lips were compressed into a thin line. Her blue eyes flashed with resentment. She had that prim, touch-me-not aura about her again, when he wanted her melting in his arms.

He lowered his voice to a silken murmur. "According to our bargain, we're to spend the evenings together. Dinner will be served in half an hour."

"I'll take a tray in my chamber."

"Then I'll join you. It can be quite pleasant to partake of sustenance in the bedchamber."

Pink misted her cheeks. She gave him a wide-eyed look of shock. And desire, to his immense gratification. Her lips parted slightly as if in anticipation of his kiss.

Then she drew up her chin, as befitting the duke's daughter. "I find your ungentlemanly remarks offensive," she said in her chilliest tone. "As you give me no other choice, I shall come to the dining room at the appointed time." With that, Cassie walked past him and went back out into the hall.

From the doorway of the drawing room, Samuel watched her ascend the staircase. Not once did she falter in her measured pace. Not once did she look back. It was as if he no longer existed.

He had to admire her pluck. His wife had a strength and vitality that approached his own iron will. It would make the challenge of seducing her all the more interesting.

And his victory all the sweeter.

Upon reaching her bedchamber, Cassie threw her reticule onto the bed and wished she'd had the courage to hurl it in Samuel's face. She yanked at the ribbons that tied the bonnet beneath her chin. "Blasted man," she muttered under her breath.

Gladys emerged from the dressing room. "Do have a care, m'lady. You'll tangle the knots." The scrawny, gray-haired maid bustled forward, and her efficient hands had the ribbons unfastened in a twinkling. She took the bonnet and gave Cassie a keen look. "You're a mite late, if I may say. And Mr. Firth has been kept waiting this past hour."

The note of censure in Gladys's tone lit the fuse of Cassie's temper. "Mr. Firth can go to the devil."

The maid's eyes widened. "My lady!"

"Do pardon the language," Cassie forced out as she unbuttoned her pelisse. "But I won't recant the meaning."

"Dear me, you've been lonely without him. But he's come home to you at last. He's a charming man and a good provider." The maid's face took on a worshipful look. "Not to mention, a handsome bloke. A woman could do far worse."

For once, Cassie didn't appreciate the maid's frank advice. Gladys couldn't possibly understand the hopes and dreams that Cassie nurtured in her heart. Dreams that would be ruined if her husband had his way. "Yes," she said bitterly, "Samuel is rich and handsome. But he's also untrustworthy and arrogant and . . ." *Seductive. Far too seductive.*

Cassie clamped her lips shut. She had already overstepped the bounds of her natural reserve. That was the effect Samuel had on her; he rattled her to the point of blurting out her innermost thoughts.

"Ah, well, 'tis only been a day or two since his return," Gladys said as she helped her mistress out of the snug pelisse. "In time, you'll come to appreciate your husband. It's only right."

A retort sprang to Cassie's tongue, but she managed to squelch it. Debating his virtues—or lack thereof—would serve no purpose. She must focus on her aim of evicting Samuel from her life.

As Gladys followed her into the dressing room, Cassie set her mind to the matter. Tomorrow, she would search out Hannah Davenport and question her. Given the amount of her quarterly payments, the woman very likely knew something ruinous about Samuel.

Then Cassie could oust him from this house before she was forced to accompany him into society. A quiver of foreboding shook her. A fortnight! She had but a scant two weeks before Mr. Quinnell would release her book into the hands of avid readers.

Two weeks before everyone would read her novel and speculate on the true identity of the author, Lady Vanderly. Two weeks before anyone connected Samuel to the evil pirate, Percival Cranditch. Two weeks before she brought disgrace and scandal to dear old Lady Stokeford.

". . . to poor Mrs. Woodruff."

The name caught Cassie's attention. Her gaze snapped to Gladys. "I'm sorry, I was woolgathering. What did you say about Flora?"

The maid helped Cassie step out of her plain blue morning gown. "She was feeling poorly, I fear, so I brought her a tisane a short time ago. She took to her bed after that dreadful stepson of hers came to call this morning."

Guiltily, Cassie realized she'd almost forgotten about Charles Woodruff. She had to tell Flora the encouraging outcome of her meeting with Andrew Jamison. "I must go to her at once."

"The poor mite is sleeping now," Gladys said. "And you mustn't go running about the corridor in your shift."

As the maid helped her into a dinner gown of peach silk, Cassie was transfixed by the image of Samuel catching her in dishabille. He would draw her into his arms, clasp her to his hard body, and kiss her until her legs had all the substance of melted butter. His hands would touch her all over . . .

". . . a peculiar letter in the afternoon post."

The voice of her maid caught Cassie's attention again. It was unnerving to realize how Samuel's return had affected her concentration. "I beg your pardon?"

"A letter, m'lady. 'Twas addressed to your unmarried name. I left it on your desk."

The news drove out every other consideration. Leaving Gladys in the dressing room, Cassie went straight to her desk and picked up the letter.

The address bore the name "Lady Cassandra Grey" in the same block lettering as the first one she'd received. It had been two nights ago, the night she'd gone to the theater.

Cassie stared down at the letter clutched tightly in her fingers. In the upheaval of Samuel's return, she had forgotten all about her mysterious admirer. Now, apparently, he'd written to her again.

"What is it, m'lady?"

Gladys hovered a short distance away, inquisitiveness in her sharp brown eyes. "A mistake, I'm sure," Cassie said, summoning a smile. "You may go now."

"But I've yet to do your hair—"

"It's fine. I can tidy it myself."

At her firm tone, the maid curtsied and left the chamber.

Cassie waited until the door closed. Then she turned the letter over and used her fingernail to break the wafer. As she unfolded the paper, dark bits of something cascaded to the floor.

Instinctively, she jumped back. Bending down, she picked up one of the pieces and rubbed her thumb over the velvety texture. It was the petal of a bloodred rose.

She brought the petal to her nose and inhaled the faint fragrance. It wasn't dry yet, which meant the petals had been plucked quite recently.

Most probably this very morning.

With trepidation, she returned her attention to the letter. Only a few words comprised the brief message:

My darling Cassandra,

Red is the color of my love, the heart that throbs for you alone. Whenever you see a red rose, think of me,

Your Devoted Admirer

An eerie foreboding scurried over her skin. Who had sent the note? Was it a prank? Somehow, she couldn't imagine Walt or Bertie or Philip shredding a rose and writing such a cryptic message, disguising their penmanship in block lettering, no less.

Perhaps it was Samuel. The two letters had coincided with his return. But her husband had been candid in his courtship of her. Love had nothing to do with what he wanted from her.

Cassie gathered up the petals that scattered the blue patterned carpet. As if they were tainted, she quickly dropped them back onto the paper and folded it. She couldn't shake a sense of uneasiness. *His* hands had touched these petals, this paper.

The hands of the man who watched her.

• • •

"Tell me about your books," Samuel said.

The remark caught Cassie completely off guard. They were walking out of the dining room and into the hall. He had been the consummate charmer over dinner, entertaining her with more tall tales about his travels abroad. Their conversation had been a welcome distraction from that troubling letter she'd received.

Now, however, she felt a jolt of confused alarm. Had Samuel found out about her writing? Perhaps he'd had her followed. Perhaps she'd been observed speaking to Mr. Quinnell a short while ago.

"Books?" she repeated numbly.

His keen stare drilled into her. "You look puzzled. You did say you intended to spend the day purchasing books for the Hampton Lending Library."

Ah, her *fib*.

Awash with relief, Cassie gave an airy wave of her hand. "Oh, that," she said. "It wasn't very interesting. I won't bore you with all the details."

"I happen to like details." As he stopped her in the hall, his voice lowered to a seductive pitch. "I want to know everything about you, Cassie."

A new turmoil filled her. A more dangerous tumult of desire and resistance. Deeming it best to ignore his insinuation, she said, "There really isn't much to tell. I scanned a few history texts in order to decide which one would suit the needs of our subscribers." Her gaze flitted to the staircase. "The work was long and tiring, so I really must—"

"Have a distraction," Samuel finished smoothly. "Come into the morning room. We'll practice our dancing."

"Dancing! But it's late." What really upset her was the instant image of herself in his arms as they whirled around the floor. She knew intuitively that he had no intention of rehearsing the formality of a country dance or a minuet. He would favor that most scandalous dance of all, the waltz.

As if he'd read her thoughts, his grin flashed at her. "When we go into society, we'll be setting out for parties at this hour. You'd do well to accustom yourself to late nights."

"I've ample time yet. We agreed upon a fortnight. Baron Beasley will be hosting a small dinner party—"

"We'll make our debut at the Duke of Nunwich's ball. It's considered the launch of the social season."

No! "A more gradual approach would better serve your purpose," she argued. "There will be far too many people there. It will be too confusing for you to remember everyone's name."

"Nonsense. I've an excellent memory. And a strong desire to show off my beautiful wife."

Shameless charmer. She was nothing to him but a possession, a means to an end. Yet his words glowed inside her. Did he truly find her beautiful?

The thought vanished as he steered her into the morning room. Cassie stopped short. No longer was the chamber cozy and comfortable.

All the furniture had been shifted against the walls. The carpet had been rolled back, leaving a broad expanse of polished wood floor. A pianoforte had been moved to a place near the door.

She swung toward Samuel. Angry at her vulnerability as well as at his high-handed behavior, she snapped, "This is *not* your house. You have no right to rearrange things as you please."

"It's merely temporary," he said in his most coaxing voice. "It's been four years since I set foot in a ballroom. I can't imagine that you have, either."

"Then I'll hire a dancing master. You may do the same."

"I haven't the time for scheduled lessons. We'll have to make do right here."

Her yearning for his arms mustn't be indulged. Desperately she cast about for a credible excuse. "Flora's asleep. There's no one to play music."

"There's me."

To her astonishment, he sat down at the pianoforte and launched into the most exquisite rendition of a waltz that Cassie had ever heard. The airy notes floated from his fingertips in a magical flurry of sound. She closed her eyes, the better to absorb the spritely melody.

A sense of wonder overtook her. She could feel the music like a living entity, full of heart and fire, and wholly unlike Samuel. It was as if she'd been granted a glimpse into his soul. His dazzling, unexpectedly sensitive soul. All of her cares and objections fell away into the irresistible desire to dance. In utter abandon, she spun in a pirouette around the floor.

The music ceased. She opened her eyes to find Samuel watching her intently. The flare of heat in his eyes made her blush at her lapse of control. "Where did you learn to play so well?" she said quickly. "It's hardly a man's skill."

"Blame my low upbringing. I was raised in the world of the theater."

"I wasn't criticizing." Drawn by his unexpected complexities, Cassie ventured toward him and leaned against the pianoforte. His face had gone hard and remote, as if he regretted revealing his talent. Or perhaps he felt that his past was a source of shame. The novel notion of vulnerability in him caused her voice to soften. "Tell me about your youth. Your mother was an actress, was she not?"

"There's no point to resurrecting the past."

Samuel rose from the bench, but she stepped back, determined not to be intimidated . . . or romanced. She wanted to penetrate his hard mask and find out if he had a true capacity for tender emotion or if his music was simply an exceptional skill. "The past has shaped you. It's made you the man you are. If it hadn't been for your mother's affair—"

"I wouldn't have grown up despising the Kenyons. I wouldn't have made my fortune. And I wouldn't have married you."

"Well, yes, but—"

"You're my wife, Cassie. Nothing else matters." He moved closer, crowding her. "I brought you here to dance, not to talk."

She retreated another step. "It's wonderful that you have such a gift for music," she said to distract him. "Truly, I've never heard anyone play with such power and passion."

"I'm a passionate man. And very skilled with my hands."

The smirk had returned to his face. She regretted the pale skin that surely revealed her blush. "I'll thank you not to turn every remark into an innuendo."

He took her in his arms before she could so much as blink. "Forgive me," he said in that silky tone. "The opportunity was irresistible. Just like you, darling."

"There, that's exactly what I mean. You shouldn't *say* such things—"

He touched his finger to her lips. "No quarreling. Shall we dance?"

He placed his left arm around her and, with his right hand, took firm hold of hers. Her lips still tingled from his brief caress. Her heart stuttering, she protested, "But I can't. If you must know, I've never waltzed before."

"Then let me show you how it's done." Samuel began the steps of the waltz in perfect time as if the notes he'd played still lingered like ghostly music in the air. Far too aware of him as a man, Cassie felt stilted and awkward. She stumbled, but he deftly righted her.

"Look into my eyes," he murmured. "Depend on me to guide you. The music is there if you'll just listen."

His voice bewitched her. His eyes were so intense a blue that she lacked the will to break the spell of his gaze. As he twirled her around the floor, she heard the beautiful melody in her memory. Within moments, her movements became as fluid as his, and she and Samuel danced as one entity.

The fanciful thought seemed a part of the magic. There was no denying the enthralling joy that swelled in her. She was aware only of their graceful movements and Samuel himself, his exotic scent of spice, the chiseled harshness of his face, the taut muscles of his arm against her back.

When he finally brought her to a halt, she felt a deep-seated warmth and a breathlessness that had little to do with exertion. A little dizzy, she clung to his shoulders. "Oh, my. *You* don't need lessons."

"Nor do you." He stood so close she could see the individual dark lashes that framed his eyes. "At least not with me."

He wanted to kiss her; she could see it in the way his gaze skimmed her mouth. A coil of yearning wrung Cassie's willpower. Seizing on a distraction, she babbled, "I confess, I often skipped my dancing instructions as a young lady. There are many places to hide in a ducal palace, and I availed myself of all of them. Even back then, I hadn't the desire to enter into society."

"You were a timid child." Samuel spoke dismissingly, as if that fact no longer mattered.

But he didn't *understand.*

"My reluctance sprang from more than just that," Cassie said with vehemence. "I never wanted to grow up to be like . . ." *My parents.*

"Like whom?"

She hesitated, belatedly reluctant to malign her mother and father to a man she scarcely knew. It was the sort of confidence one might tell a husband—but Samuel was hardly the typical spouse. "I shouldn't have spoken. The past doesn't matter, you said so yourself."

"Ah, but your aversion to society affects our bargain," he said, using twisted male logic designed to suit his purposes. Taking her arm, he guided Cassie to the bench before the pianoforte and sat down beside her. "Tell me. You're referring to your father, I presume."

Her heart wrenched. Of course, he knew about her father's gambling. Maybe if she told Samuel a little more, he would comprehend her distaste for his scheme. "You're wrong," she murmured. "It was *both* of my parents who thrived on social events. The duchess was incredibly beautiful and glamorous. I was quite in awe of her. They spent most of their time here in London, going to parties every night."

"They left you in Lancashire."

"Of course. And whenever my mother was at Chiltern Palace, she could speak only of returning to the city. It was as if being in the country sapped the life out of her." Cassie stared fiercely at her hands, folded in her lap. "It was so hard to believe the news that she'd died."

"How did it happen?"

"She and my father attended a large gathering of friends at Vauxhall Gardens. Somehow, on the boat ride home, Mama fell into the Thames. Several men jumped in to save her, but she drowned. I was thirteen at the time." Cassie didn't add that the grievous message had arrived on the eve of her fourteenth birthday. For once, her parents had promised to come to Chiltern Palace for the occasion, something they rarely did since her birthday occurred during the height of the social season.

"Most likely, she'd been drinking," Samuel said flatly. "I've known women like her, vain and self-indulgent to the extreme."

His harsh denouncement abraded Cassie. "You didn't know *her.* I'll thank you not to speculate about the duchess."

"The duchess? Is that how she wished you to address her?"

"No, it was just . . . the way I viewed her." As a brilliant butterfly drawn to the nectar of society. Cassie had been a shy stick of a child, preferring books to people. It was no wonder her mother had always seemed baffled by her only offspring.

Taking her hand, Samuel massaged her tense fingers. "I dislike the way the aristocracy leave their children for months at a time."

His opinion surprised Cassie. Of course, he had had an entirely different upbringing, living with his mother in the close world of the theater.

She wanted to lean into him, to ask him about his past and to confess her own lonely childhood. But she didn't want his pity. "I've never needed constant attention," she said firmly. "That's why I don't care much for society."

"Or perhaps you fear you can't measure up to your mother."

The sage observation erased her momentary softening. She snatched back her hand. "I shouldn't have expected you to understand."

Seemingly undaunted, Samuel slid his arm around her shoulders, drawing her lightly against him. "Forgive me," he murmured. "But allow me to say, I can't imagine the duchess was any more exquisite than you are."

As before, his compliment caught her off kilter. Why was it that honest praise from other men failed to move her, but Samuel's blatant tribute set her heart aflutter and turned her mind to mush?

As she drew a breath to retort, his head swooped down to feather a kiss across her parted lips. The light contact enervated her body. She intended to push him away—truly it would be foolish to do otherwise—yet her hands settled on his chest instead, absorbing the feel of hard muscles through the layers of his coat and shirt.

He held her as if she were precious to him. His mouth moved with consummate skill, his tongue dipping inside to taste her. With the deepening of his kiss, her insides clenched in a wanton rush of desire.

She twisted on the piano bench and pressed herself closer to him, but it wasn't close enough. His arms tightened, but it wasn't tight enough. His hands moved over her back, her waist, her hips, but it wasn't satisfying enough. She wanted—*needed*—to appease the ache inside herself.

Yet he continued his leisurely exploration of her mouth, nipping at her lower lip, soothing it with his kiss. His embrace somehow displayed both ardor and restraint, the tenderness of a man for his beloved. His breath warm against her lips, he murmured, "Let's go upstairs."

The liquid silk of his voice flowed over her senses. Cassie's eyelids were heavy as she lifted them to look at him. She felt dazed, unsteady, grateful for the support of his arms. "Pardon?"

He rained kisses over her cheeks, her nose, her chin. "I want you, Cassie. Invite me to your bed."

A throb of pure desire heated her belly. Then she noticed the sharpness to his gaze. And the truth behind his command struck sense into her.

Her posture stiffened. With newfound strength, she shoved him back on the bench. "Knave! I'm well aware what you *want*."

"I want to make love to my wife."

He reached for her again, but she stood up and stalked away, whirling to face him. Once again, Samuel had delved past her guard. He wielded tenderness like a sword. He used seduction as a means to override her wishes. All for his own devious purposes.

"You *want* me to forget about that deed of separation," she said with bitter understanding. "Because if you sign it, the Kenyons will know that you failed in your marriage."

In the candlelight, his eyes glittered like hard blue sapphires. But a lazy smile touched his lips. "I gave you my word, Cassie. You'll just have to trust me."

Somehow, I managed to stay afloat until Mr. Montcliff was able to rescue me from certain death. Having overcome the pirate manning the dinghy, he helped me out of the icy water and then swiftly rowed us to shore. There, he respectfully placed his coat around my cold, shivering form. "Belinda," he cried. "My poor Belinda."

My teeth were chattering so that I could not reply. Only then did I notice another skiff setting out from the pirate ship.

At the helm rode the tall, powerful form of Percival Cranditch.

—The Black Swan

Chapter 12

Miss Davenport's Secret

The next day, before Cassie could set out on her quest, she was interrupted at her breakfast by a trio of agitated gentlemen. They brushed past the footman and marched into the dining room like an army of knights rescuing a damsel in distress.

His face livid, the young Duke of Chiltern led the group. Walt was followed closely by Philip Uppingham, in a lilac coat and pale yellow breeches, his dark hair strategically tousled, and Bertie Gunther, whose tall gaunt form towered over his friends.

"What's this about Firth living here?" her cousin demanded without preamble.

Annoyed, Cassie set down a half-eaten piece of toast. She rose to greet her visitors with cool composure. "Good morning to you, too, gentlemen. Had any of you had the manners to notify me ahead of time, I would have set three extra places."

Her sarcasm had varied results. His ears turning scarlet,

Bertie ducked his head. Philip faltered to a stop, his face wary. Both of them looked to her cousin for direction.

Walt elevated his chin in a defensive pose. "Sorry, Cass. But desperate situations call for desperate measures. We had to offer you our protection!"

Cassie refrained from pointing out that just two days ago, he had chastised Samuel for walking in unannounced. But she was loath to add fuel to the fire of her cousin's anger. And it did touch her heart to know that her friends were concerned for her welfare.

Considering what to tell them, Cassie dismissed the footman. She went to the sideboard and fetched three cups, the silver carafe of coffee, and a porcelain pot of tea. The sugar bowl and pitcher of cream already sat near her half-finished plate of food.

"Do sit down, gentlemen. Would you care for coffee or tea?"

Walt eyed her accusingly as he threw himself into the chair beside hers. "Never knew you to serve coffee," he growled. "It's Firth, ain't it? You're catering to the fellow's tastes."

The comment set her teeth on edge. It was the servants who went out of their way to pamper Samuel. But if she choked, she would keep a civil tongue. "Samuel is indeed a guest in this house. And like any guest, his wishes will be accommodated."

A clamor of objections came from her friends.

"A guest?" Philip repeated, slapping his palm on the linen-draped table. "The blackguard deserted you four years ago. How can you welcome him back?"

"He must have coerced you," Bertie said with uncustomary heat in his brown eyes. "If the rogue has harmed you in any way—"

Walt sprang up. "Where is he? By gad, I'll call him out!"

"Samuel has already left for his office," Cassie said, giving her cousin a quelling stare. "And I've told you twice already, you are *not* to challenge my husband to a duel. The scandal of it would only hurt *me*."

That logic had the desired effect. Her cousin slumped back down and regarded her in morose disbelief. "You've forgiven the knave, then? How could you *do* so?"

"I've forgiven him nothing. His stay here is temporary. I intend to introduce him to society." As the three men again protested all at once, Cassie held up her hand to silence them. "Do hear me out. I demand that courtesy."

Bertie stirred his tea as if it were the most fascinating activity in the world. Philip curled his mouth in a sullen expression. Walt drummed his fingers on the side of his cup as an outlet for his impatience.

They didn't know about the deed of separation. Nor did she intend to tell them about her plan to find incriminating evidence against Samuel by interviewing Hannah Davenport. Cassie would brook no interference from them, however well-meaning it might be.

"It has long been Samuel's desire to be accepted by polite society," she said. "However, people must be led to believe we've reconciled. Once his place is established among the *ton*, he's agreed that we shall keep separate houses."

"He's lying," Walt burst out. "The scoundrel only wants to win your trust. He'll—he'll seduce you!"

An awkward silence descended on the dining room. Walt blushed as red as the unfortunate spots on his face. The other two men looked embarrassed as well, although they cast furtive glances at Cassie.

Mortified, she clung to her composure. She knew they were wondering if Samuel already shared her bed. But their curiosity would go unslaked. "In less than a fortnight, the Duke of Nunwich will give a ball to open the social season. I shall attend with Samuel."

"He must be forcing you to do so," Philip declared. "We won't allow it."

"Let us protect you from the villain, my lady," Bertie added earnestly.

Radiating devotion, Walt reached out to grasp her hand. "Firth doesn't deserve you, Cass. He's nothing but a common bastard."

Cassie's stomach knotted. Something in her rebelled at hearing Samuel derided so callously. Samuel, who played the pianoforte with the exquisite skill of a master. Samuel, who kissed with the enticing tenderness of a lover . . .

She withdrew her hand from her cousin's grasp. "Enough," she said in her iciest tone. "I've made my decision, and I expect you—all three of you—to abide by it. Should I hear another word spoken against my husband, I'll consider it an insult to *me*."

Mutters and grumbles met her ultimatum. A range of emotion was reflected on their faces: disbelief, indignation, distress.

And the shock of betrayal.

Dismally, she realized that they viewed her alliance with Samuel as a breach of loyalty. If only they knew it was all a sham. For most of the past four years, they had been her dearest friends and staunchest supporters. But now she wondered if things would ever again be the same.

A short while later, a footman assisted Cassie in stepping out of the carriage in a quiet neighborhood in Soho. The luxurious vehicle had been waiting for her this morning at the Stokeford town house. She resented being forced to use the fancy conveyance. It was yet another symbol of being kept in a gilded cage. But if she'd slipped out alone, Samuel would have questioned her whereabouts.

She smiled brightly at the coachman. "I'm calling on an old acquaintance. I shouldn't be gone above half an hour."

As the burly coachman doffed his top hat and settled in to

wait, Cassie thought guiltily that she was becoming quite an accomplished liar. But she had no choice. Heaven help her if anyone found out she intended to visit Samuel's former mistress.

Her spirits quailed at the prospect. Inside her seethed a mixture of trepidation, determination, and . . . curiosity. As a sheltered lady, she had never had occasion to glimpse a courtesan, let alone speak to one. But she couldn't back out now. There was information to be gained from Hannah Davenport—information that could be used to force Samuel to sign the deed of separation.

Besides, she could consider this an educational experience. An author never knew when she might need to describe such a fallen female.

Cassie marched toward the house, one in a row of brick houses, with a tiny front yard edged by a decorative iron fence. Pots of violets bloomed on the windowsills. The door was painted white with a shiny brass knocker that gleamed in the sunlight.

The cozy residence surprised her. She checked the address again, plainly marked in metal numbers above the door. But there was no mistake. She had expected something tawdry or ill-kept, not this pleasant, cheery home with its freshly scrubbed windows.

Reaching the porch, Cassie hesitated again. Did she truly have the mettle to question Samuel's mistress? Then she scolded herself for cowardice, grasped the knocker, and rapped firmly.

In a moment, the muffled sound of hurrying footsteps approached. The door opened a crack, and Cassie found herself facing a short, plump woman as round as an apple and with ruddy cheeks to match. A mobcap rested on a thatch of tight gray curls. Clearly the housekeeper, she wore a dirt-smudged apron over her drab brown dress. Her efficient manner explained the well-kept state of the dwelling.

The housekeeper bobbed a curtsy. "May I help you, mum?"

Her manner exuded a cheerfulness that instantly set Cassie at ease. She handed the woman a calling card. "Allow me to introduce myself. I'm Lady Cassandra Firth, and I would like to speak to—"

"Mr. Firth's wife! Oh, good gracious me!" As if Cassie were a queen, the woman hastily threw the door open wide. "Come in, come in. This is a wonderful honor!"

Confused by the warm reception, Cassie glanced over the unremarkable furnishings of the tiny entryway. Had Samuel spoken of her to this servant? And why would a gentleman's wife be welcomed with such enthusiasm into the home of his light-skirt?

The housekeeper busied herself with removing her apron. Her florid face beamed with joy. "Forgive me, m'lady. I'm in such a dither! I never expected . . . oh, you must come into the parlor at once."

Without further ado, she fairly bounced toward the adjoining chamber. A young, freckle-faced maid knelt in the corridor, polishing the baseboards while staring with unabashed interest at the visitor.

The housekeeper clapped her hands at the girl. "Suky, bring a tea tray with damson pastries and rum cake and lemon curd. Master Sam's wife has come to call, and she'll have only the best!"

Master Sam?

Cassie felt a knell of mortified distress. Dear heavens, was he on such intimate terms with the members of this household? Did that mean he was still a regular visitor here? That he had already come here since his return to England?

Suky scrambled to her feet, dipped a curtsy, and sprinted toward the back of the house.

Cassie wanted to protest that she didn't need refreshment when her stomach was tied in knots over the impending interview with the housekeeper's employer. But she held her tongue and followed the woman into a snug parlor that clashed with her preconceptions of a courtesan's house. A collection of china dogs decorated the mantelpiece, and the overstuffed chairs appeared comfortable and well used. A basket of knitting sat beside the hearth.

"There, now," said the housekeeper, ushering Cassie to a seat on a blue chaise. "You sit right down and rest your bones. Och, you're even more beautiful than I imagined. Like an angel come down from heaven. The perfect wife for dear Master Sam."

Then the woman did something astonishing. She heaved her considerable bulk into a rocking chair as if settling down for a long chat.

While Cassie believed firmly in the equality of people, she was *not* accustomed to having servants sit with her. Perhaps such rules of proper behavior weren't practiced in the house of a harlot. Nonplussed, she said haltingly, "I've come to speak to your mistress, Miss Hannah Davenport. Is she at home?"

A merry peal of laughter broke from the woman. "Och, I didn't think! Oh, I am a lummox, am I not? 'Tis cleaning day and I'm looking like one of the servants." At Cassie's uncomprehending stare, she added rather proudly, "*I'm* Hannah Davenport, m'lady."

Cassie was struck dumb. *She* was Samuel's mistress? The woman looked ancient enough to be his grandmother! "I . . ."

"Not what you're expecting, eh? P'rhaps you thought I'd be a proper governess like in one of them fancy houses in Mayfair." The woman laughed again as if it were all a great jest. "But I'm a simple nursemaid who's lucky enough to be looked after in me old age. By such a fine man as your dear husband."

Cassie struggled to grasp the incredible news. Hannah Davenport had been Samuel's *nursemaid*? The realization of her mistake struck her like a blow. What a dunce she had been! He wasn't paying bribes to a former mistress. That legal document she'd found merely provided a comfortable living for a former servant. A beloved servant, apparently.

But Samuel was a cold, unfeeling man . . . wasn't he?

Aware of the woman's bright blue gaze, Cassie said, "It's quite . . . admirable of Samuel to give you a quarterly allowance."

"And the house, too. 'Tis mine, free and clear. Bless him for finding me four years ago. He saved me from death and starvation."

"He did?"

"Ah, he didn't tell you the whole tale, did he?" Hannah Davenport wagged her stubby finger. " 'Tis just like him, not to boast of his own good deeds. He was like that as a lad, too, never a braggart like the other boys."

Were they speaking of the same man? Samuel had certainly boasted of his seductive powers over women. Though perhaps not in words. His arrogant manner made it *seem* as if he were flaunting his prowess. Afraid she might blush, Cassie said quickly, "Four years ago . . . that must have been around the time of my marriage."

" 'Twas a few months before then. You see, we'd lost contact with each other for a long time. Then, one day, Master Sam's brother—Lord Joshua Kenyon was his name—came asking questions about him. I showed him where the birth was recorded at St. Martin's Church. Only a few days later, Master Sam himself tracked me down in the tenement where I was living. I'd lost me job, you see, and no one would hire an old woman." As her eyes welled with happy tears, she fumbled for a handkerchief and loudly blew her nose. "Oh, what a moment that was! To see my boy grown up to such a fine man."

Samuel *wasn't* a fine man; he was a devious manipulator who had purchased Cassie's hand in marriage in order to get revenge on the Kenyons. But she couldn't bear to shatter this woman's illusion. "How long had it been since you'd seen him?"

"Not since my dear boy was ten and his mam dismissed me. Said he was too old to be coddled." Hannah Davenport leaned forward, her large bosom resting on her knees. In a confidential manner, she whispered, "But I think she was jealous, I do. He always spent more time with me than with her. And Joanna Firth was one to love the attention."

Interest flared in Cassie. The story captivated her, as did the awareness that there was information to be gained, after all. "Mrs. Davenport—"

"That's *Miss,* m'lady. I never did find me a husband. Me sister used to say 'twas me own fault for talking too much, that I'd chatter the fellow to death within the month." Smiling merrily again, she added, "Though I'll beg you to call me Hannah as Master Sam does."

It was easier to comply than to fret over petty formalities. "Hannah, then. Pardon me for prying. But would you mind telling me about Samuel's mother? I never had the chance to know her."

"Mind? Why, of course not. And don't blame Master Sam for not telling you. Men never talk of important matters. But look, here's our tea."

Suky delivered a large tray piled with pastries and cakes. Hannah poured the tea into china cups and urged Cassie to fill her plate. "Baked every bit of it with my own two hands," Hannah proclaimed. "Try the lemon curd—'twas always Master Sam's favorite."

"It's wonderful," Cassie said, as the tart-sweet confection melted on her tongue.

Teacup in hand, Hannah rocked, the chair creaking rhythmically under her weight. "Now, then, where shall I start? Did you know Joanna Firth was an actress? Never quite the toast of the London stage, though."

"Why was that?"

"Too many fine performers and too few parts to go around. I saw it happen many a time, for an actor or actress to have his hopes dashed. 'Twas an endless round of auditions, living on borrowed funds, and waiting to hear from the directors."

"Were you an actress, too?"

Hannah let out a hoot of laughter. "Now that's kind of you, dearie, but who would pay their precious coin to watch an overblown fool like me prance about the stage? Nay, I labored behind the scenes as a costumer. 'Tis where I met Joanna."

Her mind clamoring with questions, Cassie took a casual sip of tea. "What was she like?"

"Dramatic, flighty, with her head full of dreams. She poured her heart and soul into the theater, but the poor dear never found more than secondary roles. Then she met Lord Stokeford."

"George Kenyon, Samuel's father," Cassie clarified.

Hannah nodded sagely. "Joanna was besotted—he was the first blueblood she'd ever met, and to hear her talk, you'd think he walked on water. I tried to warn her that he was married, and that men like him took their pleasure as they wished, but she wouldn't listen. Claimed to be in love with the drunken sot, but *I* think she was in love with a dream." Sighing, Hannah shook her head. "I declare, that woman lived her life like a stage play. Everything was a drama. And she was always sure that things would turn out right in the end."

The sorrowful tale touched Cassie's heart. "Lord Stokeford abandoned her."

"Aye, when Joanna found herself in the family way. And like many a poor woman in her situation, she was sure his lordship would set her up in her own house." Hannah clucked her tongue. "But when the no-good coward heard the news, he denied his duty. He said the child was just as likely fathered by one of her other lovers."

Cassie's eyes widened. "*Is* that possible?"

"Nay! I'll say this in her favor, she was faithful to the rascal. She wasn't a wicked woman, Joanna. Only foolish and headstrong and bent on having her own way. Why, even after

Master Sam was born, she was sure that his lordship would come back to her. She wrote to him often, but there was never any answer."

Incensed, Cassie put down her teacup. "How terrible of him not to acknowledge his own son . . ." Her voice trailed off as she realized that she could almost understand why Samuel hated the Kenyons. He was absolutely wrong, though, to blame the entire family when the fault lay with one man.

"Aye, and there was Joanna with precious little money, only a pittance to pay me to watch over Master Sam whenever she found a part to play. 'Tis a sad, sad tale." Nibbling on a slice of cake, Hannah rocked at a pensive pace. Then her face brightened again. "But what a fine young lad Master Sam was. So sweet-natured and thoughtful. Whenever he had an extra penny, he would always fetch me a posy from the streetseller even before he'd buy himself a sweet."

Cassie nearly choked on a sip of tea. Sweet-natured? Thoughtful? Was the woman mad? "Surely he wasn't always well behaved."

"Och, all boys have their ways. He had many a scrape with the bullies until he grew big enough to best them. And he could be a rapscallion, too. Why, I remember how he'd sneak out of the rooming house at night, and he'd go to the theater. That's where he learned to play such pretty music."

Cassie sat back and listened as Hannah entertained her with stories about her darling Master Sam. Even if half of it was embellishment by his doting nursemaid, his attributes had outweighed his faults. Despite his lack of fatherly guidance, he'd had a decent upbringing.

Yet he had grown up intent on making himself the equal of the Kenyons. He had made hatred the driving force in his life. She could never forget that.

The clock in the hall bonged the hour, and Cassie started in surprise. "Gracious. I didn't mean to stay so long. I'm keeping you from your work."

"Och, I've all the leisure in the world thanks to Master Sam. 'Tis a rare pleasure to meet you at last." Then Hannah's smile drooped a little. "Though I must say, I do wish he would come back from his travels soon and visit his old nursie. I'm sure *you* wish for him even more."

Surprised, Cassie blurted, "He *is* back. He returned several days ago. I thought you knew."

Hannah's face lit up and she clasped her wrinkled hands to her massive bosom. "Nay, I did not! I've not seen Master Sam since he gave me this house. 'Twas Mr. Jamison who told me of Master Sam's wedding and his travels around the world."

Cassie pursed her lips. It was just like Samuel to believe that money could solve everything. "Well, perhaps he'll come to see you soon."

As the old nurse pushed out of the rocking chair, she shook her head. "He's very busy, I'm sure. Not that I'm ungrateful, you know."

That sorrowful demeanor wrenched Cassie's heart, and purely on impulse, she said, "I'll speak to him about the matter. Don't fret, Hannah, I'll make sure he pays you a visit very soon."

"Do you mean to say that as the daughter of a duke, you won't sit next to me at dinner parties?" Samuel asked.

He sprawled on the chaise and eyed Cassie, who stood in front of him in the drawing room, her posture as stiffly correct as any governess. But there was nothing of the rigid spinster in her shapely figure. His wife had never looked more lovely, with wisps of blond hair curling around the delicate features of her face. He very much doubted she knew that with the fireplace behind her, the pale green skirt of her gown turned semi-transparent, affording him a view of slim, shadowy legs.

Cassie referred to the open book in her hands. "According

to Stockdale, by the order of precedence, the daughter of a duke outranks all women with the exception of duchesses, marchionesses, and royalty. Therefore, I would take my seat nearer the head of the table than you."

"I see." Samuel allowed her to think that information was news to him, although he had known as much already. Long ago, he had made it his business to learn all he could about the nobility. "However, you're my wife and I want you beside me. Isn't there anything that can be done to rectify the situation?"

She pursed her lips, and he could see the indecision in those beautiful blue eyes—should she tell him or not? "If I notify the hostess ahead of time, I suppose," she said reluctantly. "But it would mean giving up my courtesy title. I would no longer be known as Lady Cassandra, but simply Mrs. Firth. I am not willing to do so."

He had to award her a commendation for honesty. She could have easily kept that point from him.

Rising from the chaise, he went to her and stroked his forefinger down her soft cheek. "Is there any way I could convince you?"

Cassie stared up at him, an odd intensity in her eyes. It was the same look she'd given him several times during dinner, as if she were struggling with some inner dilemma.

He hoped to God it was her attraction to him. Because then he'd have a chance to tip the scales in his favor. He could remind her of the power he wielded with his kiss and his caress.

As he bent his head closer, she lifted the book like a shield against his chest. "Kindly keep your distance," she said. "I know all your methods of convincing a woman."

She was delightfully naïve, and he couldn't help but smile. "You know far less than you think."

He took the book from her and tossed it onto a chair. Lifting her hand, he kissed her soft palm, inhaling her faint flowery scent. She took in a swift breath, though to his surprise, she didn't pull away.

"I—I think we've had enough of rules for one night," she said. "I'm sure you're tired. You've been working long hours at your office."

That oblique reference to bedtime startled him. And sent the blood from his head on a downward rush to his groin.

Samuel straightened, holding her hand in a tight grip, studying her candlelit features. "Are you inviting me to your bed?"

Stupid. He instantly regretted his blunt statement. He'd made that same mistake the past two nights. When would he learn?

Just as he'd feared, her eyes widened. She tugged her hand free and stepped back. "*No.* I was simply making a comment, that's all. You were a little late returning home this evening, and . . . I wondered if you were having problems at your business."

"I'm conducting an audit. It's taking up a lot of my time." But he didn't want to think about that now. He wanted to make up for his bumbling by romancing her.

Drawing Cassie close again, he put his arms around her, enclosing all that womanly warmth against him. He wanted nothing more than to lift her skirts and take her on the hearth rug, to brand her as his. But he settled for a kiss.

After an initial stiffness, her lips softened and parted to allow him entry. The hands that had been pressing against him moved upward to circle his neck and play with his hair. Her tongue met his tentatively, with a virginal reluctance to acknowledge her womanly passions. He coaxed her with his mouth and with his touch, keeping his hands above her shoulders so as not to frighten her again. If it killed him, he would seduce her gently but inexorably, each night moving her a little closer to allowing him the rights of a husband.

"I've been thinking about you all day," he murmured against her mouth. "You've become quite a distraction from business matters."

Cassie sighed, a needy sound that threatened his discipline. Drawing back slightly, she moved her fingers over his face as if learning the contours. He reveled in the knowledge that she was growing more comfortable with his embraces. "Samuel, I wondered . . ."

If you'd take me upstairs and make passionate love to me.

But to his disappointment, she concluded, "I wondered if you would show me around your offices. Perhaps tomorrow."

"Impossible. I'll be spending the day at my warehouse near the docks." He nipped her lower lip, then soothed it with his tongue. "Another time, though."

Yes. Maybe by then, she'd be his. He could close his office door and lay her down on his desk. He would sink into her, absorbing her cries of pleasure with his mouth, the chance of discovery adding an edge to their passion. The fantasy pulled him deeper into the throes of desire.

Unable to resist, he bent his head to her bosom, nuzzling the soft mounds that swelled above her bodice, tasting her skin with his tongue. For a few moments Cassie allowed him the liberties, her quick breaths encouraging him. He curled his hand around her breast, and through the barrier of cloth and corset, he could feel the tightening of her nipple . . .

She pushed him away. "Stop! I don't want you doing that."

"Liar," he murmured.

Her cheeks pink, Cassie pursed her lips. For a moment, she looked as if she would argue the point. Then she said in her haughtiest tone, "I've had quite enough of you for one evening. Good night."

In high dudgeon, she turned on her heel, snatched up the book of etiquette, and marched out of the drawing room.

And in spite of his frustration, Samuel chuckled. All in all, he could only be pleased by his progress.

"To my carriage," Mr. Montcliff said. "And make haste!"

He carried the coffer of coins whilst we hurried across the rocky beach to the phaeton that awaited us by the roadside. Mr. Montcliff snapped the ribbons and the fine gray gelding set off at a trot.

I looked back to see that the skiff had just made shore. Percival Cranditch leaped out and shook his fist at us. Had I but known the ordeals to come, I would not have felt the joyous bliss of relief. For that gratifying sight would not be my last encounter with the wicked pirate captain.

—The Black Swan

Chapter 13

The Purloined Letters

"I'm Lady Cassandra Firth, and I'm here to see my husband."

Cassie addressed the brown-haired clerk at the desk in the foyer of Firth Enterprises, a huge brick building off the Strand. After a day spent wracking her brain, she had been able to conceive of only this one way to obtain the necessary incriminating evidence.

The young clerk leaped to his feet as if he'd never before seen a lady, let alone in a place of business. He fumbled with his pencil and dropped it to the floor. He started to reach down, apparently thought better of it, and bowed to her instead. "Mr. Firth?" he said in a squeaky tone. "But he's gone to the warehouse for the day, m'lady."

Although Cassie knew as much already, she put her gloved hand to her mouth and affected an air of flighty surprise. "Oh my, I was *so* certain he'd asked me to come here today. He wishes to give me a tour of his building, you see."

"I—I'd be happy to oblige—"

"Gracious, no. Mr. Firth would be angry if I kept you from your duties." She gave her expression just the right combination of hauteur and helpless female. "Though perhaps I should wait for him a bit, in case he returns. Will you be so kind as to show me to his office?"

The clerk hesitated only a moment. "As you wish."

He hastened to open a nearby door, allowing her to precede him into a long corridor. As they passed several large workrooms, she could see men at their desks like children in a classroom, their faces bent to account books and ledgers. Her escort kept glancing at her in consternation as if he weren't quite certain that he should allow a lady into this male sanctum.

"We'll keep this our little secret, won't we?" Cassie murmured. "If my husband doesn't arrive soon, I'll depart and no one need know I was here. I don't wish to look silly for getting the day wrong." For good measure, she fluttered her lashes at the clerk.

"I shan't tell a soul. You have my word on that."

She graced him with a warm smile that had the desired effect of melting him into a puddle of smitten man. From out of nowhere came the memory of Samuel's voice.

I can't imagine the duchess was any more exquisite than you are.

Was he right? Was she as beautiful as her mother? Did she possess the same power over men?

No, she *didn't* want to be a vain, flirtatious woman who depended on society to make her happy. She needed only a peaceful cottage in the country and the freedom to work on her novels.

But Samuel could stop her from achieving her dream.

Unless *she* could thwart *him* first.

The clerk led the way up a flight of stairs and into a small reception area containing several plain chairs, a Turkish carpet, and an unoccupied oak desk. Samuel was out today, completing an audit of his warehouse near the docks. It was the ideal opportunity to search his office.

Yet worry had kept her awake half the night. What if he changed his plans? What if he returned to his office to fetch something? She had gathered the courage by pretending she was the heroine from *The Black Swan*. If Belinda could survive being held prisoner on a pirate ship, then Cassie could accomplish the more mundane task of espionage.

Besides, after rifling through Mr. Jamison's desk, she was almost a seasoned spy.

The clerk ushered her into an inner office that was nearly as austere as the outer one. He bowed for the third time and backed out as if she were royalty. Once the door was closed, Cassie lost no time examining the chamber.

For a wealthy businessman, Samuel could have afforded the finest furnishings. But his office was clearly designed for work, with a pair of leather guest chairs, a small fireplace, and a desk. The venetian blinds were open to a view of the busy Strand. The only decoration on the wall was a large map of the world.

His desk was piled with ledgers and paperwork. A silver inkwell sat beside a collection of quills in a cup. The pewter branch of unlit candles proved that Samuel worked late at times.

But not *very* late.

In the three days he'd been in the Stokeford town house, he had spent every evening with her. In accordance with their bargain, she had to prepare him to face society at the ball given by the Duke of Nunwich. Last night, she had drilled Samuel on the order of precedence and proper address.

Last night, he had also kissed her breasts.

Her bosom tightened at the memory. Each night he had kissed her, one of those long, slow kisses that set her heart to pounding and scattered her senses. Each night, he had murmured variations on the proposal that they indulge their marital rights in the bedchamber. Each night, she'd managed to deflect him from persuading her.

But the task was becoming increasingly difficult. The visit with Hannah Davenport had altered Cassie's view of him as a ruthless man who cared nothing for people. Well, certainly he *was* ruthless in many ways, but perhaps there was a smidgen of good in him, too. Samuel could have ignored the plight of his old nurse and left her to die in poverty. Instead, he had rescued her and given purpose to her life.

Guilt niggled at Cassie. Although she'd made that rash promise the previous day, she hadn't asked Samuel to visit Hannah. Cassie wanted to chastise him for not sharing his time as well as his money. But there was no way to do so without revealing to Samuel the fact that she was investigating him.

And the sooner she found proof against him, the better.

Aware of the ticking clock on the mantelpiece, Cassie went to the desk and seated herself in the leather chair. The subtle scent of spice conjured up the image of Samuel sitting here, resting his forearms on the blotter, dipping one of the quills into the inkwell, his mind focused on some business matter. Did thoughts of her ever distract him?

Good heavens, *she* was the distracted one.

With renewed resolve, she leafed through the papers on his desk. There were proposals for shipping various goods around the world and letters awaiting his signature. One pile contained nothing but lists of items with a monetary value attached to each. It appeared to be a room-by-room inventory of every object in the building, down to the last pencil and chair.

Nothing criminal in that.

Cassie opened one of the ledgers, a fat volume filled with entries of purchases, salaries, and other expenses. She studied the numbers for a time, trying to grasp a knowledge of his business. To her dismay, she had no notion how to distinguish between legitimate entries and illicit ones. The frustrating task boggled her mind and made her head ache. She longed to be back at her own desk, spinning romantic adventures that had nothing to do with the complex mysteries of accounting.

But she wouldn't give up so easily.

Abandoning the ledger, she opened the top drawer of the desk. A mundane miscellany of items filled the space: pots of ink and extra quills, a sheaf of blank stationery paper imprinted with the company's name and address. There was also a small sack of coins and a half-filled tin of licorice drops.

She sampled one, letting its smoky sweetness dissolve on her tongue. The taste brought the wistful remembrance of childhood. Her father had always kept licorice in his pocket, and she associated it with the rare happiness of having her parents at home in Lancashire. Odd to think that Samuel liked licorice, too.

But his likes and dislikes were of no concern. Bending down slightly, she peered into the back of the drawer. A packet of folded papers, bound by a piece of string, caught her attention. Letters?

Cassie had reached inside and grasped the bundle when a noise from across the chamber froze her. The rattle of the doorknob.

"You there!" Samuel called out. "What are you doing?"

In the dim light of the warehouse, he stalked toward a man in the shadows. The fragrance of coffee and spices filled the air. A ship from Brazil had arrived yesterday, and a crew of laborers had spent the better part of the day piling sacks of goods against the far wall.

A man stood half-hidden in the gloom by one of the piles. There was something furtive about him that had caught

Samuel's attention a moment ago, while he'd been reviewing the results of the audit with his head accountant. He'd left Hector Babbage in mid-sentence and had proceeded straight toward the stranger.

No, not a stranger. With a relaxing of tensed muscles, Samuel recognized the curly ginger hair and stout form of Ellis MacDermot.

The Irishman strolled forward to greet him. "Hullo, Firth. Glad to find you here."

Samuel shook MacDermot's hand. "What the devil are you doing in my warehouse?"

"I was told at your office that you were at the docks. I came to see if you've signed that contract yet. My mill has produced a shipment of tweeds ahead of schedule, and I'd like to send it on its way to Belgium."

"The document is on my desk, but I haven't gone over it yet." His mind turning to another matter, Samuel clamped a hand onto MacDermot's shoulder and steered him toward a corner where they could speak in private. "Now, about the other night at the theater—"

"A jolly good jest, wasn't it?" MacDermot's teeth flashed in a grin. "Imagine, not recognizing your own wife!"

Jest? Samuel had been furious at the time. Now that matters had turned out rather well, however, he could only express a mild annoyance. "A warning would have been better appreciated."

MacDermot hung his head, though his brown eyes glinted with glee. "'Twas too irresistible a moment. I do hope the lady gave you a fine welcome home."

Samuel had no intention of trading ribald quips with MacDermot or anyone else. Cassie was his private pleasure. No one would ever know that he hadn't yet bedded his virgin wife. "We've resolved our differences. We'll be attending Nunwich's ball together at the end of next week."

"Nunwich, eh? You've come up in the world. Only the cream of the *ton* at that one."

Samuel wondered at the note of envy in MacDermot's tone. The Irishman was connected to nobility and often hobnobbed with society, but perhaps he hadn't received an invitation. "I've been neglectful in not signing that contract. Let's go tell Babbage where I'm going. Then we'll head over to my office."

Cassie stared in surprise at the visitor who entered the office. She had been prepared to use her charm on one of the men who worked here. Instead, she found herself gazing at a skinny boy of perhaps twelve.

His unbleached linen shirt and brown breeches looked brand-new and his face was reasonably clean, though his neck and ears were dirty, as if he hadn't thought to wash there. An odd, brimless black hat perched on a haphazard thatch of dark hair. He clutched a broom in his grubby paw.

The astonishment on his face turned quickly to streetwise suspicion. "'Ey!" he cried out. "Don't be pokin' in the master's desk!"

Summoning a breezy smile, Cassie surreptitiously stuffed the bundle of letters into her reticule. She closed the drawer and stood up, the better to show her authority. "I'm Mr. Firth's wife, Lady Cassandra. May I ask your name, please?"

He glowered a moment, then mumbled, "Mick. An' the master's out for the day."

"He promised me he'd be back," she said, artlessly repeating her lie about the appointment to tour the offices. "I can't imagine what's keeping him."

But Mick didn't look convinced of her sincerity. "Ye were lookin' in 'is desk. Ye were stealin' from 'im."

"I needed paper to write a note to my husband," Cassie improvised. "I was going to leave, but I didn't want him to return and think I hadn't come."

"'Ow does I know ye ain't flummoxin' me?"

His cheeky manner amused Cassie more than it ought, considering the circumstances. "I suppose you'll have to take me at my word."

"'Tis what any thief would say." He looked her up and down. "Though I ain't never seen one so fancy as ye."

"A gentleman would not speak so rudely to a lady." She eyed his broom. "And if you've come to do the cleaning, I must ask you to return later."

"Nay, I'll be about me duties 'ere." Mick set himself to sweeping the floor, all the while flashing glances at Cassie.

His blatant distrust dismayed her. How was she to search the office under the scrutiny of those suspicious blue eyes?

Perhaps she could outlast him. To support her ruse, she would pretend to write the note.

Cassie sat back down in the chair, arranged her skirts, and then withdrew a piece of paper from the drawer. She inspected all the quills, found one she liked, and took her time sharpening it with a penknife. Opening the silver inkwell, she dipped the point and then held it poised over the paper as if she were pondering what to say. All the while she was aware of the reticule in her lap, heavy with the purloined letters.

And she was aware of Mick watching her.

She began to write some fabricated nonsense about bettering the working conditions at the company. It was likely that Mick was unlettered and would be unable to read her words should he venture closer. And if she was forced to leave the note here and Samuel found it, hopefully he would think it was a report from one of his employees.

She noticed that Mick was making a pretense of his own. "I should think that corner is quite clean by now," she observed, "since you've been sweeping the same spot for the past five minutes."

Mick moved over to the window and industriously wielded his broom. "If it ain't spic and span, the master'll 'ave me 'ead. 'E'll beat me bloody an' toss me carcass out on the street."

She added a democratic review of all discipline to her fictitious note. "Is Mr. Firth so strict an employer that he would discharge you for missing a single speck of dust?"

"Aye. Got to earn me keep, I do. The master pays me a shillin' a week." Mick paused a moment, then added reflectively, " 'Course 'e paid me considerable more fer savin' 'is life from a turrible murderer."

An increase in salaries went on her list. "So you saved his life, did you?" she said, admiring Mick's vivid imagination. "And from a murderer, no less. How did it happen?"

" 'Twere down at the docks. A man loosed the chain on the 'oist, and a barrel o' rum rolled straight at the master." With great relish, Mick added, "*I* pushed 'im out o' the way, I did."

"Did you apprehend the would-be murderer, too?"

"App-wot?"

"Catch," she clarified. "Did you nab the fellow and turn him over to the magistrate?"

"Nay, 'e got clean away. But the master, 'e were so 'appy t' be alive, 'e give me this job. Sweep and empty rubbish from six to six, an' six days a week."

She dipped the pen in the ink, then included shorter working hours in her note, along with a recommendation against child labor. "How long have you been employed here?" she asked, thinking to trip him up, since Samuel had returned to England only five days ago.

" 'Tis only me second day," Mick said, bending down to apply the broom with enthusiasm beneath a table. "But I'm gonna save me coins an' open me own pub someday. 'Tis 'ow the master got so rich, by hoardin' 'is money. 'E tole me so 'imself."

Cassie still wasn't sure how far to trust Mick's word. Had Samuel really been kind enough to take the urchin under his wing? He had helped Hannah Davenport . . . "Wouldn't you rather be out playing with your friends?"

"Them!" Mick said disdainfully. "Thieves and bullies, the lot o' 'em. *I'm* gonna make somethin' o' meself. The master says 'tis important t' 'ave am . . . am . . ." He paused to scratch his head beneath the brimless hat, then triumphantly concluded, "Ambition!"

"That's good advice and very admirable of you to heed it. But what about your family? Do they mind your working such long hours?"

His expression turned instantly sullen. He turned his back on her and attacked another corner with the broom. Over his shoulder, he muttered, "Ain't got no family."

Cassie's heart turned over. So Mick was one of the many orphaned children who roamed the streets of the city. It had been surprisingly generous of Samuel to give the boy gainful employment.

Did he recognize himself in the urchin? According to Hannah Davenport, Samuel had been about the same age when his mother had died and left him alone in the world.

But she couldn't allow herself to feel sympathy for her husband. Undeserved misfortune was no excuse to make revenge the focus of one's life. Nor to purchase in marriage the naïve fifteen-year-old daughter of a duke.

Abandoning all pretense of writing, she rose and left her reticule on the desk. She walked to Mick and studied his painfully thin form. He wouldn't look at her. She wanted to put a comforting hand on his shoulder, but respected his pride. So to get his attention, she took hold of the broom handle. "If you haven't a family, then where do you live?"

He shrugged evasively. "'Ere an' there."

The poor child probably slept in an alleyway with no protection from the cold or rain. "I'll speak to my husband," she said. "He can find you a place to live. Perhaps you could even stay in one of the servants' chambers at our house—"

"Nay!" His blue eyes rounded in alarm, Mick pulled his broom out of her hand and backed away. "Ye mustn't speak t' the master! 'E'll think I can't take care o' meself."

"I cannot allow you to sleep on the streets," she said firmly. "Safer arrangements must be made."

Mick opened and closed his mouth as if wrestling with a dilemma. "I'm safe right 'ere," he said in a grudging tone. "I got me snug little 'idin' place in the basement. Ain't nobody knows, not even the night watchman."

"But who cares for you? What do you eat?"

"I buy from the pieman. An' I don't steal nothin' from the master. Least not since I snitched 'is pocketwatch—though I did return it."

Another tall tale? No, this one had the ring of truth. "Oh, my. It's a wonder he offered you a job."

Eyeing her, Mick ducked his chin in a beseeching look. "Ye won't tell the master, will ye? 'Bout me 'idin' place, I mean."

Her heart melted. "Your secret is safe with me."

"Ye best keep t' yer word. 'Cause if ye don't, I might 'ave t' tell 'im ye was pokin' in 'is desk."

The wily little blackmailer! How did he know it was crucial that Samuel not find out she'd been snooping? Half amused and half dismayed, Cassie was about to tell Mick what happened to children who threatened adults, when her worst nightmare became reality.

The tramp of footsteps came from the outer office. She heard the voices of two men.

One of them belonged to her husband.

Mr. Montcliff took me to an inn where my maid awaited me. There, I retired to a chamber and refreshed myself with dry clothing. Only then did I join my guardian in a private dining chamber. As we supped, I related the ghastly tidings about the parentage of Percival Cranditch. Mr. Montcliff's face grew grim, but he made little commentary, and at the end, expressed only his concern for me. Although he had taken care to tell no one of my abduction, my reputation would suffer should anyone find out I had spent three days aboard a pirate ship.

"To know he is my baseborn brother makes my duty all the clearer," Mr. Montcliff proclaimed. "I fear, Belinda, we must marry at once."

—The Black Swan

Chapter 14

Samuel's Discovery

For the blink of an eye, Cassie stood frozen. Then she sprang into action, heading to the desk to retrieve her reticule with its cache of stolen letters. Just as she tightened the ribbons to close it, Samuel entered the office.

He looked tall and strikingly handsome in a tailored coat of dark blue worsted, his white cravat enchancing his sunburnished skin. The wind had tousled his black hair, giving him a rakish air. Despite the circumstances, her body responded to his nearness with a surge of softness and heat. To her chagrin, the pounding of her heart had as much to do with desire as alarm.

He stopped and stared at her. His smile died and his brow creased. "What the devil . . . ?"

Cassie fought the impulse to cower. Determined to look at

ease, she summoned her most artless smile. "Hello, Samuel. I was just chatting with your newest employee."

His attention veered to Mick, who had been watching the interchange, but now commenced to sweeping diligently. "Mick, you can finish that later."

The lad opened his mouth as if to protest. Then he glanced at Cassie and scuttled out of the office.

Only then did she notice the man standing behind Samuel.

"Mr. MacDermot!" she said in surprise, recognizing his curly red hair and the impish face of a leprechaun. "I never thought to see *you* here."

Mr. MacDermot ducked his chin rather sheepishly. "I'm afraid I neglected to mention that your husband and I are business associates."

Samuel's face darkened and he flashed them both a quizzical frown. "I didn't realize you two were acquainted."

"We know each other from the lending library," Cassie explained. "I work at the reception desk on Thursdays, when Mr. MacDermot comes in to select his weekly biography." She smiled at the Irishman. "How did you like the book about Julius Caesar?"

"Positively fascinating," Mr. MacDermot said in a hearty tone. "Those Romans were harsh rulers but fond of lavish entertainments. Quite savage, too. Gladiators fighting lions and bears, slaves thrown to the wolves—"

"Save the discussion for another time," Samuel said on a note of impatience. "Cassie, I'd like to know why you're here. Is something amiss?"

His keen gaze seemed to detect her guilt. Foolish thought, for he couldn't know the heaviness of the reticule hanging from her wrist. "Wrong? Why, no. I was hoping you would take me on that tour of the building."

"Tour?"

"Yesterday evening, I mentioned that I'd never seen your offices. Don't you remember?"

"I remember telling you I'd be at my warehouse today. As soon as I'm done here, I'll have to return there."

She looked at him from beneath the screen of her lashes. "I'm sorry, I must have misunderstood. As you appear to be busy, I'll run along and leave you to your business matters."

"Perhaps *I* could escort you on a tour," Mr. MacDermot offered. "I've been here often enough to know the run of the place. If you don't mind waiting, that is."

Cassie wanted only to leave, to escape the strain of lying and examine those letters for evidence. "That's very kind of you, but—"

"But you'd rather *I* take you around," Samuel cut in. "Since you're already here, I'll make room in my schedule. You can wait outside while MacDermot and I review a contract."

There was a coldness to his manner as he strode to his desk and sat down. Did he see through her deception? Or was he merely annoyed that she had interrupted a business meeting and made demands on his time?

She noticed the strain around his mouth and eyes, as if he were weighed down by problems. In the evenings, he spoke little of work. She wished for a moment that he would confide in her so that she might ease his troubles, whatever they were.

"What's this?" he said, scowling at the paper in his hands. "An increase in salaries? Shorter working hours? A condemnation of child labor?"

Horror struck the softness from her. Dear God, it was the note she'd been writing, the imaginative list of complaints about his office. With any luck, he would think it had been left by one of his employees . . .

That desperate hope vanished as he lifted his head, his eyes narrowed on her. "Well, well, Cassie. This is *your* handwriting. And for someone who's never even toured this building, you seem to know quite a lot about running my business."

• • •

The following afternoon, Samuel made a point to investigate the suspicious actions of his wife. Despite the ongoing audit of his company, he had been too distracted to concentrate on his work. So in the middle of the afternoon he returned to the Stokeford town house and headed upstairs to Cassie's bedchamber.

He knew she wasn't there. It was Thursday, the day she volunteered her services at the Hampton Lending Library.

The day MacDermot visited the library.

Anger knotted Samuel's chest. It couldn't be a coincidence that the Irishman made a habit of checking out a book on the day Cassie worked at the reception desk. Damn MacDermot! If the man had designs on Cassie, he was as good as dead.

Samuel forced himself to remain calm. He had issued a warning to MacDermot, and that was that. If he went off half-cocked every time a man engaged in a light flirtation with Cassie, there'd be trouble aplenty when they entered society. He hadn't expected to feel so possessive of his wife.

Her chamber was vacant, but he took a quick look into the adjacent dressing room to make certain. Satisfied, he closed the door and turned the key. He scanned the frilly chamber, and his gaze stopped on her bed with its mounds of pillows. How well he could imagine Cassie lying there naked, a smile on her face and her arms open to welcome him . . .

Hell.

Turning on his heel, Samuel went straight to her desk. He knew exactly what he sought—proof that she was stealing money from his company.

The suspicion consumed him. Though he didn't want to believe it, he could arrive at no other logical explanation for her *il*logical behavior yesterday. Why else would she have come to his office? Why else concoct that harebrained excuse of wanting a tour of his building? Why else write all that nonsense about improving the working conditions of his employees?

He still smarted from *that* jab, too. She had made a lame excuse about being an advocate of the laborer. So he had taken her around the firm, let her see for herself the suitability of the environment and the contentment of his staff. Cassie had pretended interest, yet the entire time, he could tell she was anxious to escape him.

She had looked as beautiful as an angel and as guilty as sin.

Desire and anger burned in Samuel. He should have known Cassie was no different from any other woman. He'd given her everything she'd wanted, but it wasn't enough. She must be squirreling away the extra funds as a hedge against the time when he signed that damned deed. Apparently she didn't trust him to support her.

Or perhaps she was taking the money for someone else. Her cousin, Walt, possibly. Despite his exalted title, the present Duke of Chiltern had about as much ready cash as Mick.

Samuel tightened his jaw. Whatever Cassie's reasons, he intended to stop her. But first, he needed hard proof of her culpability. He had checked with his bank this morning, but the account he'd set up for her four years ago contained only a modest sum. Cassie—or her cousin—had to be keeping the stolen money somewhere else.

He opened the top drawer of the desk. The messy contents included a jumble of quills and pencils and discarded scraps of paper.

Thinking he might find a clue, he examined the pieces more closely. Each one contained odd phrases in abbreviated form, as if the notes had been dashed off in a hurry. They made no sense to him.

Sophia A.—wrings hands, but intrepid! Why?

Remember! Sir D. needs pistol at docks

Y.P. steals jewels from Lady G.

Samuel frowned down at the fragments he'd spread across the desk. Pistol? Jewel theft? Who the hell was Y.P.—and all these other people, for that matter?

As he considered the scrawled notes, an icy knell of alarm struck him. Was Cassie involved in something more sinister than petty thievery? Was she in some sort of trouble?

And what was that reference to the docks? Had she had something to do with the murder attempt on him? Had she hired someone to kill him?

His mind resisted the notion, but it throbbed like a sore tooth. She certainly had a motive. If he were dead, she wouldn't have to bother with a deed of separation. Nor would she need to steal from his firm. His wife would inherit the bulk of his considerable wealth.

God! Until yesterday, he had believed Cassie naïve and innocent. He had thought her unaffected by the seamier side of life. It had been refreshing to converse with a beautiful woman who was trying so hard to resist him. He had delighted in making her blush.

What a fool he had been!

Grimly, he brushed the notes back into the top drawer, taking care to replace them in the same approximate order as he'd found them. Now, more than ever, he had to find proof of her culpability. But the middle drawer contained nothing more damning than a sheaf of blank paper. The bottom drawer revealed more paper—and this had writing on it.

He picked up the stack and examined the topmost page. It was Cassie's penmanship with many scratched-out words and notes written in the margins. By the time he'd read the first paragraph, he realized to his amazement that it was a story.

By the time he reached the bottom of the sheet, he knew the identity of Y.P.—Yves Picard, an evil Frenchman facing Sir Dudley, the dashing hero.

A slow grin rose to Samuel's mouth. Cassie, a writer? That explained the ink stains he'd observed on her fingers and her wariness the time he'd tried to draw her out by talking about the romantic books she liked to read. And it certainly explained those cryptic notes.

He felt somewhat foolish to have misconstrued them, but also immensely relieved—and curious to know her fantasies. Delaying his quest for the moment, he settled back in the chair and scanned several chapters of the unfinished manuscript. The heroine, a brave but hand-wringing lady named Sophia Abernathy, embroiled herself in scrape after scrape as she led the hapless Sir Dudley on a merry chase to save her from the diabolical Yves. There was a highwayman and a crumbling old manor house, stolen jewels and a singularly exciting pursuit through the docks of London.

The vivid scene brought a scowl to Samuel's face. Where had Cassie gained her information? Had she visited the wharves? By God, it was no place for a lady!

One fact was certain, he had underestimated her. Cassie was a multifaceted woman with hidden depths. She could volunteer her time at a lending library or obtain a deed of separation. She could steal from his company or write with great passion. She could melt in his arms like the sweetest of lovers.

But the problem of the missing money still remained. He would find out the truth. If Cassie was guilty, he would deal with her in his own way, without handing her over to the law.

The desire to possess her burned in him. And now that he had discovered her secret—or at least one of them—he knew precisely how to seduce his wife.

Over the following days, I had cause both to rejoice and to despair. While Mr. Montcliff rode to York to make the arrangements, I remained at the inn with my maid under the protection of a stout coachman and groom. A modiste was summoned to stitch my trousseau, and I spent the hours at the happy task of selecting silk and lace for my wedding gown.

Yet a constant thought drew down my spirits. Did Mr. Montcliff feel for me the tender sentiment of love? Or was it merely gallantry that had prompted his offer of marriage?

—The Black Swan

Chapter 15

A Walk to Remember

For the next five days, Cassie lived in fear that Samuel would discover what she'd stolen from his desk. At dusk on the fifth day, she paced in her bedchamber, discussing the problem with Flora, who sat patiently listening while working on her embroidery.

"How stupid of me to have taken that parcel without first ascertaining its value," Cassie said for the umpteenth time. "Who would have thought it was a collection of old playbills?"

"Anyone could have mistaken them for letters," Flora said loyally. "You didn't have time to examine the papers."

"I should have contrived a way. Samuel is bound to notice they're missing." That certainty sat like a cold lump in her stomach, outweighing even the fact that she still lacked any documentation of the shady business dealings necessary to force him to sign the deed of separation.

The ball given by the Duke of Nunwich was a week away. So was the publication date for *The Black Swan*. She had only a matter of days before the ladies of the *ton* would read her book and quite possibly recognize Samuel as the thinly disguised villain, Percival Cranditch. If anyone guessed, the Kenyons would become an object of gossip.

The playbills added another complication to her roster of worries.

Going to her desk, she picked up one of the playbills and unfolded it. The paper was yellowed and tattered. Toward the bottom of the list of actors and actresses was the name "Joanna Firth."

Samuel had kept these playbills in his desk at work. They had been bound by a carefully knotted piece of string. Did they mean something to him? Or had he simply tossed them into his drawer and forgotten them?

Cassie had a dreadful suspicion they were precious mementos. She believed her husband to be a cold, methodical man who thought of nothing but revenge. But she kept discovering evidence to the contrary.

It had been far simpler to despise the mask than the many-layered man beneath it.

"It's commendable of him," Flora ventured, "to keep such a remembrance of his mother. Most men would have thrown them away."

Cassie carefully folded the playbill and tucked it back inside the drawer of her desk. "*I* can't toss them into the rubbish, either. They may be all Samuel has left of his mother." Agitated, she resumed pacing. "Oh, bother my foolishness in taking them!"

Flora cast her a worried look. "You'll replace them, won't you?"

"How can I? If I'm caught at his office again, he'll know I'm up to something."

"Oh, dear. Perhaps you could wrap up the playbills and mail them back."

Cassie shook her head as she roamed the bedchamber. "He would make the connection at once. Who else has been poking inside his office?"

"Then perhaps . . . perhaps you could leave the playbills in his bedchamber. He might think he'd brought them home and forgotten them."

Cassie had already considered and rejected that course of action. "This isn't his house. He's only lived here for a week, so it's highly improbable that he would make such a mistake."

"Hmm, I see what you mean." Flora glanced at the clock on the bedside table, as she had several times already. "What other choice do you have?"

"I wish I knew."

Samuel had looked so very forbidding that day in his office. He had taken her on a tour of his building, introducing her to all of his employees by name. The place had been clean and well lit, with an aura of camaraderie among the personnel, which had only made her feel all the more guilty for writing that thoughtless criticism of the working conditions.

Cassie caught herself wringing her hands like Sophia Abernathy. How had her well-planned life turned into such a gothic novel?

Flora peered at the clock again and set down her sewing. She sprang to her feet. "Let's go for a walk," she said brightly.

"Now?" Cassie glanced outside at the gathering dusk. Samuel would return home very soon. But she didn't want to admit to a desire to fuss over what to wear to dinner tonight. "It's growing dark."

"We'll take a short stroll around the square, that's all,"

Flora replied. "It's rather stuffy in here, is it not? Bless me, it would do us both a world of good to breathe some fresh air."

Cassie wondered at the nervous agitation in Flora. Smoothing her skirt, she fluttered like a little brown wren. Cassie thought perhaps *she* was making Flora anxious with her pacing.

She felt an instant remorse. She had been so caught up in her own problems that she had forgotten to consider her friend's plight. Despite Mr. Jamison's reassurances, Flora was still distraught about the trouble with her estranged husband, and Cassie couldn't blame her. The Reverend Norman Woodruff was even more vile a man than his spawn, Charles.

"I'll be happy to walk with you," Cassie said, reaching for the thin blue shawl that lay across the back of the chair. "Shall we go, then?"

"You'll need your pelisse," Flora said. "It's quite chilly outside."

Cassie wanted to protest that they would be gone for only a few minutes. But if it comforted Flora to mother her, then so be it. While she donned her favorite straw bonnet, Flora scurried off to fetch her own wrap. Then they went downstairs and out the front door.

The shadows of twilight cloaked the dark mounds of shrubbery in the square. Cassie and Flora kept to the walkway nearer the houses where an occasional gas lamp lit the cobbled street. Candles glowed in the neighboring windows, and to the west, the sky wore the deep lavender skirts of sunset. The streets were nearly deserted at this hour; the wealthy were at home, preparing for the evening's various social events.

Cassie tried not to watch for a tall man on horseback. It was the height of foolishness to feel so eager to see her husband. "I do hope Samuel doesn't think I've come out here to wait for him," she confided. "He's already too confident of me for his own good."

Flora darted her a glance. "Oh, dear. Do you still dislike him so much?"

She sounded distressed again, so Cassie resisted the impulse to vilify Samuel in no uncertain terms. "I dislike the reason he married me," she said calmly. "I'm nothing more than a convenient way for him to become the equal of the Kenyons."

"Perhaps he's changed. He does seem a charming man, and he tells so many wonderful stories about his travels. He's almost like one of the heroes in your books."

"Hardly," Cassie scoffed. "Both Mr. Montcliff and Sir Dudley are the epitome of gentlemanly behavior."

"But look at the kind way Mr. Firth helped his old nurse. And that poor little urchin at his office."

Cassie almost wished she hadn't shared that information with her friend. Flora simply couldn't comprehend the depths of his hatred for the Kenyons. "You're overlooking his determination to be accepted by society. I'm merely a pawn in his game."

"Is it so terrible for a man to want to better himself?"

"If he does it at *my* expense, yes. And consider the dowager Lady Stokeford. She deserves his respect and love, not his malice."

"Perhaps you can change him."

"I doubt that. He's too certain of his own righteousness."

They reached the corner and Flora started across the street, heading for the square. Lagging behind, Cassie said, "Shouldn't we stay on this side? It's rather gloomy over there by the park."

"Why, it isn't so dark yet," Flora said with uncharacteristic fortitude. "We'll keep to the pavement alongside the street. Ah, I do enjoy a good, brisk walk."

Cassie lengthened her steps to match the swift pace of her friend. Flora was acting decidedly peculiar tonight. She glanced up and down the street as if expecting a visitor at any moment. Did she fear that her husband or stepson might appear?

"Have you heard from either Mr. Woodruff?" Cassie asked.

In the dim light, Flora cast her a wide-eyed glance. "Why, no, thank heavens. Not since that morning several days ago. You said that Mr. Jamison had taken care of the matter."

"Yes, and you must tell me at once if they contact you, especially your husband. He'll be in violation of the deed of separation."

Flora walked in silence a moment, then said in a musing tone, "Will *you* still seek your own separation from Mr. Firth?"

The startling question brought Cassie to a halt in the shadows beneath a huge plane tree. "Of course! Why wouldn't I?"

Flora stopped, too. "I . . . I thought perhaps you might give yourself a chance to become better acquainted with him. Already you've discovered that he isn't the ogre you believed him to be."

Flora's shift in loyalty wounded Cassie. Why couldn't Flora see beyond his charm? "That's nonsense," Cassie stated, resuming her march down the footpath. "I've seen quite enough of his character. He may display an occasional kindness, but he's ruthless when it comes to getting what he wants."

Flora scurried along at her side. "But he isn't cruel like Norman. In truth, I'd venture to say Mr. Firth cares for you very much."

A disbelieving laugh escaped Cassie. "Samuel cares only for himself. You forget, we hadn't even been introduced when he purchased me as his bride. Immediately after the wedding, he left me for four years."

On their wedding night, no less. That memory still stung.

"But I've seen the way he looks at you. As if you were the

only woman in the world." Clasping her hands to her bosom, Flora sighed. "It's so very romantic."

An involuntary warmth stirred to life inside Cassie. In some foolish part of her, she wanted to believe Flora was right, that Samuel harbored deeper feelings than carnal lust. But Flora had no knowledge of those ardent kisses or his repeated attempts to lure Cassie into the bedchamber.

Cassie held those private moments in her heart.

She inhaled a breath of cold, cleansing air. If Samuel were to return home now, he might guess the unladylike direction of her thoughts. She needed time to clear her mind. "It's growing late. Perhaps we should go back now."

"Not yet! Oh, do walk a bit farther." Flora slipped her hand through Cassie's arm, preventing her from leaving. "It's such a lovely, clear evening. Look, there's a full moon rising."

Like the face of a shy maiden, the pale orb peeked over the rooftops. Its light lent a silvery sheen to the darkened buildings. Then Cassie noticed that Flora wasn't admiring the lunar display. She was staring over her shoulder at the street behind them.

Puzzled, Cassie turned to look. There was nothing out of the ordinary, only the black shape of a coach rounding the corner and heading toward them. The clatter of hooves and the rumble of wheels were the only sounds to disturb the quiet.

Despite Flora's claim to the contrary, she had to be worried about Norman and Charles Woodruff. There was no other explanation for her fidgety behavior. Cassie placed a reassuring hand on her friend's shoulder. "I do hope you aren't hiding something from me."

Flora gave a violent start. "Hiding?" she squeaked. "Why ever would I do that?"

"Because you're trying so hard to be brave. But I wouldn't think less of you for being afraid . . ."

Cassie's voice trailed off as the coach drew up beside them and stopped. Her steps faltered. Her flash of surprise altered swiftly to alarm.

In a single lithe leap, the coachman jumped to the ground. Two steps brought him face to face with Cassie.

He stood like a dark monolith in the shadow of the trees. Clad in a greatcoat, he towered over her. His features were concealed by a black demi-mask, and through the holes his eyes glittered at her.

He held out his gloved hand. "I've come for you, my lady."

That deep, guttural tone struck a faint chord in her. But she was too panicked to think. A scream formed in her throat. Before she could utter a sound, he clapped his hand over her mouth and hauled her up into his arms.

In a frenzy, she squirmed against his iron embrace. His heat enveloped her, as did the leather smell of his glove. She tried to turn her head, to look frantically for Flora.

Flora! Why did she not call for help? Had she swooned? Or run off?

Then she spied her friend standing beside the coach. Flora didn't appear at all distraught. Instead, she opened the door of the coach!

As her captor thrust Cassie inside the dimly lit interior, she reeled from disbelief and horror. He deposited her on the seat, and without another word, shut the door. The sound of a click met her stunned senses.

Cassie scrambled to the door and jiggled the handle. Locked! The other door yielded the same fruitless result.

She pounded on the window, which had been covered on the outside with blacking. "Flora! Let me out!"

Her frantic cries proved to be of no use. The vehicle rocked as the highwayman climbed back on the driver's seat. Then the coach set off at a swift pace that caused her to grab for the support of the hand strap.

Cassie sank back against the seat. Dear God! She'd been abducted!

A small lamp with a glass chimney allowed her a view of the interior of her prison. The walls were lined with crimson silk trimmed in gold, the cushions upholstered in the same rich fabrics. Only a very wealthy man could afford such a luxurious coach.

But who?

Her mind whirled with impressions. His hard muscled body. His scent of leather and spice. His deep voice . . .

Like a thunderclap, his identity shook her.

Samuel!

The day of my wedding dawned bright and clear. At last I would realize my dream of marrying Mr. Montcliff, my guardian and the man I loved with all my heart. But as I happily prepared myself, I had no notion of the dreadful event that would disrupt the ceremony.

—The Black Swan

Chapter 16

Strathmore Castle

As shock gave way to rage, Cassie sprang up from her seat. She flew to the other side of the coach and pounded on the wall beneath the driver's seat. Beneath *her husband.*

"I know it's you, Samuel! Stop this coach at once!"

The vehicle rumbled onward. There was no sign that he'd even heard. The thick padding on the walls muffled her blows. She glanced frantically over the wall and ceiling for a speaking tube, but if there had ever been one, it had been removed. She had no choice but to endure this farce.

If indeed it *was* a farce.

Releasing a huff of breath, she sat back down. Clearly, the abduction had been prearranged. Somehow, Samuel had managed to coax Flora into assisting with the vile scheme.

No wonder Flora had been anxious to go for a walk. No wonder she had been on edge the entire time. And no wonder she had been so eager to convince Cassie of Samuel's worth.

You might give yourself a chance to become better acquainted with him.

Cassie smarted from the betrayal, but she heaped all the blame on Samuel. It wasn't really Flora's fault that she had been hoodwinked by a master manipulator. He must have told Flora that he wanted only to talk to his wife. That he needed to get Cassie alone so they might resolve their differences.

But he had lied. His real purpose could only be . . . seduction.

A shivery warmth coursed over her skin and settled low in her belly. The quickening of her breath made her feel lightheaded. He wouldn't dare ravish her . . . would he?

Yes, he *would*. Hadn't she told Flora he was merciless when it came to getting his own way? He cared nothing for Cassie's wishes.

And deep down, she feared most of all that he wouldn't have to use force to make her fall into his arms. No matter what angry thoughts consumed her mind, her body ached for his.

Foolish, foolish, *foolish*!

The coach rumbled onward to an unknown destination. The covered windows prevented her from peering out to gain a clue as to the direction they were heading. After a time, though, she could tell by the sound of the wheels that they had left the cobblestoned streets of the city and traveled down a hard-packed dirt road.

Were they out in the country? Where was Samuel taking her?

To a place where they would be alone. A place where he would use his considerable skills to wear down her resistance. He would give her no choice in the matter. Warmth pooled within her, but she fought the bodily temptation. She did *not* like being his prisoner. She wanted a separation, not a real marriage!

If she possessed half the courage of her heroines, she

would break the window and throw herself out of the coach. But she wasn't dauntless Belinda of *The Black Swan* or the intrepid Sophia Abernathy of the work-in-progress. Nor did Cassie have a bludgeon handy to shatter the glass. The heels of her shoes were more suited to dancing. She examined every nook and cranny in the sumptuous coach, but could find no suitable weapon.

Blast Samuel! What madness had induced him to don the garb of a highwayman and waylay her?

Then an appalling sense of déjà vu swept over Cassie. The situation was uncannily similar to a scene in her book. The villainous Yves Picard had kidnapped Sophia and spirited her away in a carriage . . .

Had Samuel discovered the unfinished manuscript in the bottom drawer of her desk? Had he uncovered her dearest secret? Good heavens, when *The Black Swan* was published, he would know straightaway that she had written that one, too!

Cassie reined in her runaway fears. It had to be just a horrid coincidence. He was home only in the evenings, so when would he have had the opportunity to go through her desk? And for what reason?

No, another explanation made more sense. Samuel knew that she read ladies' novels, and he must have conceived the pretense on that basis.

How ironic that he had chosen to enact a villain rather than a hero. As if such depraved behavior would appeal to her!

Appeal to her intellect, that is. He needn't know about the little note of excitement that hummed inside of her. Nor that she continually had to divert her thoughts from dwelling on the moment when he would take her into his arms and kiss her senseless.

The coach made a sharp turn, tossing her to one side. The vehicle began to slow, as if they were nearing their destination.

Cassie's heart tripped. She sat up straight and collected her thoughts. She must concentrate on all the reasons why she was furious with Samuel. She must convince him of the futility of his scheme. She must remain cold and think of nothing else but outwitting him.

She must *not* let him kiss her—or she was doomed.

Samuel had a feeling he was in trouble.

As he jumped down from the coachman's seat, he tossed the reins to a waiting groom. A glance at the medieval stone castle with its strategically placed lamps in the windows assured him that his instructions had been obeyed to the letter. Now, if only he could get Cassie to cooperate.

He combed his fingers through his windblown hair. Shortly after taking her captive, he had discarded that idiotic mask. Now he put it back on, intending to continue the charade as highwayman.

He wasn't proud of the fact that he had frightened his wife half out of her wits. Just as he'd anticipated, though, she had ascertained his identity quickly. He had heard her angry pounding inside and the muffled cry of his name. Then all had gone silent.

She would be fuming. She might even come at him with her claws bared. It would take deft handling to calm her, but he would win in the end, as he always did.

He drew the key from his pocket. By the glow of the moon, he twisted it in the lock and cautiously opened the door.

The flickering light of the lamp cast a golden illumination over his wife. Cassie sat straight and ladylike, her hands folded in her lap. A jaunty straw bonnet framed her delicate features. She gazed at him with one eyebrow elevated in an expression of aristocratic disdain.

The ice maiden. He would have almost preferred the spitting wildcat to this frozen scorn.

In keeping with his role of bandit, he bowed deeply to her. "Welcome, my lady. I trust you had a pleasant ride."

"Take the mask off, Samuel," she said coldly. "Though I must add, you look better with it on."

Samuel took the jab in stride. "Allow me to escort you into my lair."

He held out his hand, but she ignored it. "I wish to return home."

"Alas, you're my captive. And should you refuse to cooperate, there will be consequences."

Her eyes widened slightly, though she kept her chin elevated. "I've had enough of your games. I'm staying right here until you come to your senses—"

He leaned inside the coach and caught her up in his arms, hauling her out by judicious force. For a moment she lay soft and warm against him, the pure essence of woman, her face a pale oval in the moonlight. *His wife.* Tonight he would possess her.

Then she stiffened and her fist lashed out at his chest. "Put me down!"

"I think not."

He nodded to the gawking groom, and the bandy-legged man loped up the front steps and opened the massive door. Keeping a firm grip on Cassie, Samuel strode into the house and through an appropriately gloomy hall. Torches flickered in sconces on the walls, and the scrape of his footsteps echoed as he mounted a wide flight of stairs.

But his wife didn't appear to notice the carefully chosen gothic ambiance. While Samuel clutched her close, she squirmed in his arms and continued to flail at him. One blow glanced off his jaw. It knocked his teeth together and reverberated through his skull.

"Dammit, Cass. You'll hurt your hand."

"Villain! You don't care if I'm hurt."

She was wrong. He wanted her safe and unharmed and

aching only with passion. But first he had to ensure that she couldn't run away from him. There would be no escape for her tonight. His blood surged at the thought. It was past time that he made their marriage a reality.

At the end of a murky corridor, he shouldered open a door. Inside, a multitude of candles lit a cavernous bedchamber. He was sorely tempted to take her straight to the four-poster bed. Once she'd had a taste of pleasure, her prickly temperament would improve vastly.

But fool that he was, he wanted her willing, and that would take considerable cajoling. So he let her down in the middle of the room, then strode over to lock the door.

Cassie was there in an instant, grabbing for the key. He was quicker.

Stretching up his arm, he tucked the bit of metal atop the ornately carved doorframe. The height ensured that Cassie couldn't easily retrieve the key. She would be forced to pull over the heavy chair from the fireside, and even if he was asleep, he'd be awakened by the noise.

A small sound of frustration broke from her. She held her gloved hands to her mouth. As she stared at him, her face was stricken with the dread of a trapped creature.

Not even that well-aimed clip to his jaw had struck him with such force.

Unnerved, he removed the black mask. He took her hands and peeled off her gloves, gently stroking the knuckles. "Cassie," he murmured, "don't be afraid. I only want to make you happy."

"Happy?" She yanked back her hand and slapped his face with a stinging blow. "You kidnap me and take me heaven knows where, then lock me in this bedchamber. And you expect me to be *happy*?"

Rubbing his cheek, Samuel felt a nudge of dark humor. "Not yet. But you will be."

"I most certainly will not. I'll only be happy to leave here."

"Give me a chance, and I'll change your mind."

"My mind is my own. I don't need a knave like *you* to make my decisions."

"Yes you do," Samuel said, his temper fraying. "Take off that hat and coat. You may as well accustom yourself to my company tonight."

And for the next six nights, too. Cassie didn't know yet that he'd cleared his schedule and left the crucial audit in untrustworthy hands, all because he craved this long-delayed honeymoon.

He walked away and left her standing by the door. She needed a few moments to absorb the implacability of his command. Acceptance of her fate wouldn't come easily to a woman of her stubborn nature.

Just as he'd expected, though, she wasn't taking off that tightly buttoned pelisse or the sensible straw bonnet on her head. Her fists clenched at her sides, she stood glowering at him. As if he were the diabolical Yves Picard.

Shrugging off his greatcoat, Samuel tossed it over a chair. Then he sat down to remove his boots. Waves of heat came from the wood fire that crackled in the massive grate, but it was nothing to match the heat inside himself. He focused his mind on lust. He'd wanted to be inside her ever since he'd seen her from across the theater. He wanted to be inside her right now, turning all that righteous indignation into wild passion.

Cassie marched toward him. "I knew you were despicable, but not to this degree. You lied to Flora, convinced her to aid your dastardly plan, and trapped me here against my will."

"So I'm a blackguard. What about *your* sins?"

"Mine? What have I done?"

Though she spoke defiantly, a certain wariness entered her demeanor. Guilt. Dammit, she *was* guilty, and it shocked him to see the proof in those beautiful blue eyes.

Although he hadn't intended to bring up the issue, anger overruled his better judgment. He threw his boots aside and stood up, the better to intimidate her. "I know about your thievery," he said curtly. "You lied about the reason you were in my office that day. You were rifling through my desk."

Her gaze wavered. "What do you mean?"

"Don't play the innocent. You were stealing from me."

She drew a deep breath and released it slowly. "Did Mick tell you? I—I didn't think he would."

God! She didn't even attempt to deny her culpability. He took hold of her arms, forcing her to look at him. "Mick didn't say a word. I figured it out myself. But you couldn't have done this alone. Who helped you?"

"No one! Why would you say—"

"I want the truth, dammit. Was it Babbage? Or some young clerk that you could more easily charm?"

"You're speaking nonsense. I had no help."

A hot fury gripped Samuel. Did her co-conspirator mean so much to her? "Tell me. It'll go easier for you if you don't protect him."

"I don't know what you're talking about."

He gave Cassie a shake to stop her lies. "I've given you everything. Are you so greedy that you'd rob my company, too? Or did you act out of spite?"

She blinked as if confused. "I haven't stolen anything—except those playbills. I vow, I didn't know they meant so much to you."

Playbills?

Then a memory stabbed him. A long time ago, when he'd been in the midst of moving from one house to another, he had brought some old papers to the office and shoved them to the back of his drawer. He couldn't explain precisely why he'd kept them. But something in him had balked at throwing the only memento of his mother into a rubbish bin.

Rather than dwell on useless sentiment, he said with

heavy sarcasm, "So that's your excuse. You took a packet of playbills. Why the devil would you do that?"

Her expression anxious, she tentatively touched his chest. "It was a mistake. And I assure you, they're safe. I wouldn't destroy something that belonged to your mother."

Her sympathy had to be a sham designed to distract him. Yet his throat tightened, making his voice harsh. "Then what *did* you mean to take? Information about my bank account?"

"No! I was looking for . . ." Cassie lifted her chin and gave him a steely glare, as if she'd made up her mind about something. "For evidence."

"Evidence of what?"

"Your shady business practices. I wanted to use the proof to force you to sign the deed of separation."

The reason knocked him off balance. It would explain why he had failed to find any proof of her culpability. There had been nothing of interest in her desk but that unfinished manuscript. None of his employees had ever seen her at the firm on any other occasion. His inquiries at the major banks had yielded no secret account held by a woman of her description.

Could he believe her?

God help him, he wanted to trust her. Or maybe he just wanted . . . *her*.

Needing to think clearly, he walked away and pressed his hand to the cold stone wall. Then he swung to face Cassie. "Who told you I'm dishonest? It had to be one of the Kenyons."

"Lady Stokeford thought I should know. She told me exactly the sort of man you are."

He cursed under his breath. "So I have my grandmother to thank for poisoning your mind."

"Are you saying it isn't true? That you're an honest man?"

Cassie wore that disdainful look again. One dainty, upraised eyebrow that almost goaded Samuel into defending himself.

But he was done with quarreling. If he had engaged in acts that bordered on the criminal, he had no regrets. He had harmed no innocent, only those men who had dubious morals themselves. It had been necessary in his pursuit of a fortune, to make himself the equal of the Kenyons.

His wealth had secured him a blue-blooded bride. He reminded himself that he had yet to establish his own dynasty.

But when he gazed at Cassie, none of that seemed to matter anymore. He could think only of his hunger to get her into bed.

No bride could have been happier. As I walked down the aisle with the sunlight streaming through the windows of the chapel, I was filled with the joyous knowledge that soon I would be the wife of Mr. Montcliff. Fair-haired and proud in his wedding raiment, he awaited me at the altar. His smile lent me hope. If indeed he felt only fondness for me, at least now I would have the chance to win his love. Fleetingly, I wondered if Percival Cranditch would ever know the part he had played in my marriage to his half brother.

—The Black Swan

Chapter 17

RAVISHED

The moment Samuel started toward her, Cassie noticed the glint in his eyes and the swagger in his stride. His demeanor had undergone a change from savage to seducer. In the blousy white shirt and tight black breeches, he looked exactly as she had pictured the pirate captain in *The Black Swan.*

Her breathing quickened, and her knees trembled. A telltale warmth bathed her depths. She felt infinitely safer when he was cold and furious. "You haven't answered my question," she said with as much aplomb as she could muster. "Are you dishonest or not?"

"If I said I wasn't, you wouldn't believe me." Those piercing blue eyes dipped to her mouth. "And if I said I was, you wouldn't kiss me."

She thrust her hands between them, but that only had the unfortunate effect of alerting her to the hard muscles of his chest. His heat penetrated his shirt, and she could feel the strong beating of his heart. "I'm not going to kiss you, anyway."

He smiled with entirely too much confidence. "Let's set aside our differences for now," he said in a silken murmur. "The evening would be far better spent in more pleasurable pursuits."

When he bent his head to her mouth, she jerked her face aside. His lips brushed her cheek instead, sending shivers over her skin. To shore up her dwindling sanity, she said forcefully, "If you think I can be seduced, you're mad."

"I'm mad for you, darling. Only for you."

It was a melodramatic statement worthy of her books, yet her toes curled and her heart hastened. She was aware of how alone they were, locked in this chamber that had been designed for her seduction. How exciting it would be to indulge the ardor she felt . . . and how imprudent. "What of what *I* want?" she demanded. "What of the deed of separation?"

"We made a bargain, and I fully intend to keep it. As for what you *want*"—Samuel untied the ribbons beneath her chin and removed her bonnet, tossing it onto a chair—"I can fulfill your every desire."

The declaration held her mesmerized. As he sifted his fingers through her hair, several pins popped out and fell to the floor. The heavy mass of locks tumbled to her shoulders, and he bent closer, inhaling like a wild beast catching the scent of its prey.

Cassie told herself to stop him, but the slow massage of his fingers felt too hypnotic. She should move away from the temptation of his body . . . but she didn't. His mouth trailed over her brow and down her cheek, leaving a path of stinging kisses that weakened her legs. He seduced her with such finesse that surely he must have practiced his techniques on many other women. And probably during the last four years, without sparing a thought for his marriage vows or the virgin bride he'd left behind.

That shouldn't infuriate her; she should be glad that he'd turned elsewhere to satisfy his earthy passions. Yet she angrily thrust his hands away. "Don't. Our bargain didn't call for *this*."

"Then it should. I won't be signing the papers for another two months. Think of all the enjoyment we could be having in the meantime."

Think? Her problem was that she *couldn't* think. He shifted his hands lower, deftly undoing the buttons of her pelisse. "Besides," he continued, "we've waited long enough for our wedding night."

She twisted away and retreated behind a chair. No, not retreat, but rational action. "We *did* have a wedding night."

He had the audacity to grin. "Then why are you still a virgin?"

A blush suffused her cheeks. "If you hadn't married a mere child—"

"We would have already consummated our marriage. We'd have the good sense to be over there in bed."

Without any good sense at all, Cassie glanced at the bed with its crimson hangings, plump white pillows, and thick eiderdown coverlet, turned down invitingly. The prospect of lying there with Samuel made her skin tingle and her breasts tighten. Her all-too-vivid imagination laid waste to her intelligence.

Samuel took advantage of her distraction to lock her in his arms again, drawing her full against him, breasts to chest, hips to hips. The enticement of him surrounded her, allowing no space in which to collect her scattered thoughts. Her eyes closed briefly—until she realized he'd slipped his hands inside her opened pelisse to cup her bosom. The stroke of his thumbs over the peaks ignited sparks . . . of alarm.

She batted his hands away. "Don't *do* that. I wish to go home."

His lean face wore a knowing smirk as if he saw right through her pretense. "No you don't."

He was right, blast him. Her willpower lay in shambles. Yet at the same time Cassie knew she shouldn't trust him—if only she could remember why. "Samuel, please, we mustn't . . ."

"Trust me," he murmured, in an uncanny reading of her thoughts. "I know exactly what we *must* do. It's been inevitable since I saw you across the theater."

His intense blue eyes snared her in the moment before he kissed her. A long, stirring, skillful kiss that dissolved her resistance and sent shivers down her spine. *Her husband.* How fitting that she should desire him in every part of her body and soul. He was right; she could no longer fight the inevitable.

She stood on tiptoes and looped her arms around his neck. At that sign of surrender, his embrace tightened and the slow kiss grew ravenous. He lured her with every thrust of his tongue and with the pressure of his loins against hers. She gave back in bountiful measure, loving the taste of him, the scent of spice and leather that defined Samuel.

Cool air wafted over her back; by some sorcery, he had undone the long row of buttons. He peeled the gown from her shoulders, and Cassie shifted position to allow the unwanted garment to slide to the floor in a puddle around her feet. All the while, she kissed him, and a feverish urgency blotted out all but the need to feel his flesh against hers.

Tugging his shirt out of his breeches, she moved her hands over the smooth muscles of his back. He groaned deep in his throat, a feral sound that caused a rush of excitement through her veins.

"Cassie," he said against her mouth, as if he couldn't

quite believe it was she. They kissed again, with an insatiable passion, and she felt his hands at the fastening of her corset, freeing her from the cage of linen and whalebone. Then she wore only her shift and stockings, but rather than embarrass her, it felt gloriously right.

He took her breasts in his hands, stroking her with a magical combination of the rough and the gentle. He ended the kiss only to apply his lips to her throat as he drew down the neckline of her shift. Then his mouth closed over one nipple, his tongue laving her, creating a shocking burst of pleasure that wrested a moan from her.

She melted completely. Her hands delved into his hair, holding his head while he suckled her. *Samuel.* She couldn't imagine why she had denied him—or why she had denied herself. Nothing else seemed important anymore, only this closeness, this feast of indulgence.

When she was so weak she could no longer stand, he guided her over to the bed, kissing her all the while. He peeled off her shift, leaving her clad in only stockings and garters. "Lie down," he said.

Willingly, she lowered herself to the cool sheets, but when she reached for the covers, he stopped her. "Let me look at you."

And he did, while he shed his shirt and unbuttoned his breeches. His hot scrutiny embarrassed her, but not enough to keep her from watching *him.* Sweet heaven, he was magnificent. The candlelight glowed on the tautly defined contours of his chest. A dark mat of hair narrowed over his abdomen and pointed downward to the part of him that was still covered.

His hands on the waistband of his breeches, he gazed at her, his eyes vigilant. "Are you frightened?"

She knew why he asked. On their first wedding night, when he had removed his robe, she had cried out in fear. When he had touched her, she had flinched. When he had realized her ignorance and explained what he meant to do, she had burst into tears.

She shook her head in answer to his question. "I want this. I want *you*."

It felt strangely liberating to say that aloud, when she had tried so hard to repress her lust for him.

Samuel gave her a crooked smile. Then he pushed off his breeches and kicked them aside. As he turned to open a drawer in the bedside table, she was transfixed by his stark male beauty. The length and thickness of his male member displayed his passion for her, and a heated dampness gathered between her legs. But despite what she had told him, the prospect of taking him into her body stirred fear in the midst of fever.

She could still turn him away. He hadn't forced her on their wedding night, nor would he tonight. If she changed her mind, he would rant and he would coax, but ultimately he would respect her wishes. Although a ruthless man in business and matters of revenge, Samuel had a contradictory core of kindness and generosity, a fascinating depth that he kept well hidden.

He sat down, the mattress dipping beneath his weight. His gaze roved over her, and an awareness of her nudity brought an accompanying shyness. In self-defense, she brought one arm over her breasts and the other to lie across her mound.

He moved her hands aside. "You're too beautiful to be covered."

"I'm not . . ." She halted the automatic protest and amended, "I'm not accustomed to this."

His shrewd eyes studied her. "You were about to say you aren't beautiful."

"But it's *true*." She had been gawky and timid as a child. Even now, when she looked into the mirror, she saw no sign of her mother's vivacious loveliness. "The duchess was the glamorous one. Men flocked to her."

"Men flock to you, too." Samuel grimaced, baring his

white teeth. "Maybe you haven't noticed, but I certainly have."

Cassie laughed softly in disbelief. "Do you mean Walt? He and Philip and Bertie are in my literary group, that's all." She thought briefly of those two letters from a secret admirer, but now was not the time to fret over his identity.

"Don't forget Jamison and MacDermot. They adore you, too." Samuel splayed his hand over her abdomen, where it lay for a moment, hot and heavy. "Not that any of them will ever have you."

She thrilled to his possessiveness, even as her mind rebelled against it. Was he so jealous of her friendships? Didn't he know she had held her marriage vows sacred? Even if *he* had not.

Then she noticed a small blue vial in his other hand. He poured a small measure of liquid into his palm and set the bottle on the bedside table. As he rubbed his hands together, she caught the scent of musk and roses.

"What is that?" she asked.

"Oil. To relax you."

"But I'm not . . . *oh*."

He took hold of her hand and massaged it, then moved along her arm in leisurely strokes that grew increasingly closer to her bosom. Before he reached there, he gave the same attention to her other arm, starting at the tips of her fingers and working a path upward. She felt so limp, she might have been a rag doll. Never had she known that a touch on her arms could be so erotic. He leaned over her, tempting her with the sculpted muscles of his chest.

But he wouldn't let her caress him. "This is for you," he said. "Only you."

The intent look on his face silenced her protest. Then she couldn't think at all as he shifted his focus to her breasts. His hands slick with oil, he lightly kneaded her, his thumbs plying the sensitive peaks and stoking the fire inside of her.

Closing her eyes, she heard herself moan. His ministrations caused the spread of heat through every part of her body. He moved lower in long, unhurried strokes over her belly. She parted her legs in shameless abandon, aware of her swollen and throbbing center, something that would have shocked her had she not lost every vestige of modesty.

"Please . . ."

"Not yet."

He bent his dark head and brushed a consoling kiss against her midsection. Then he unfastened her garters and slowly peeled down her stockings. Oiling his hands again, he devoted himself to her legs, one at a time, until she feared she might die from . . . *something*. "Samuel," she said pleadingly.

"Yes, I know." His voice sounded both soothing and strained, and he lay down beside her, his body so much larger and stronger than hers. He gazed deeply into her eyes, watching her as he reached down to part her intimate folds.

He explored gently at first, then as she responded with soft, insuppressible cries of enjoyment, his touch gradually became harder and faster. She tried to lie still, but her body demanded otherwise. She clutched at him, desperate for a release from the unbearable tension he evoked with one fingertip.

When he removed his hand, she moaned in frustration, and Samuel shifted his body to cover her. His member probed her entrance, and she stiffened in an onrush of fear. He was too large, too thick, too powerful. "I can't—"

"You can." He pressed into her, pushing slowly and deeply, his gaze dark and rapt. The intermingled pain and pleasure wrested a gasp from her. As he stretched her, penetrating completely, something magical happened and the discomfort altered to a wonderful sense of fullness.

He bent his head to her ear and whispered her name again in that thrilling, almost reverent tone. *"Cassie."*

The rasp of his voice induced a response in the place where they were joined. He slowly withdrew to her entrance and thrust inward again. She arched her hips, tightening her muscles in order to savor his possession of her. She found his rhythm and moved with him until they were one being caught up in frantic harmony.

His muttered endearments enhanced her passion. Again, she felt that indescribable *wanting*. And then she found it. Her world splintered, and she tumbled into a pleasure so deep and vast that she was lost.

When awareness returned, Samuel was still embedded deeply in her. His chest heaved as he watched her and his eyes glittered with something like . . . triumph.

He seduced her mouth in a hard, hungry kiss. Then he took several more thrusts, the cords of his neck taut, his head thrown back as he groaned from the force of his completion. His brief fury of movement renewed her own ecstasy, and again the intense ripples of pleasure coursed outward from her womb to flood her body, gradually fading into utter satisfaction.

He sprawled over her, relaxed and heavy. Cassie loved the weight of him, pressing her into the mattress. She loved the way he brushed soft, sleepy kisses to her neck. She loved his scent and his smile and his vitality. She loved . . . *Samuel.*

No. That was impossible. It was only the newness of the experience that made her feel this outpouring of tenderness toward him. They had consummated their marriage, and it was his marvelous body that she loved.

Yet an undeniable warmth wrapped around her heart. Perhaps their intimacy had stripped away her defenses, allowing her to see more clearly to the source of her resistance to him. Perhaps it wasn't lust that she had feared, but love.

Perhaps she had never stopped loving Samuel.

As a fanciful fifteen-year-old, she had accepted the betrothal because she had loved a dream, the hero she had imagined Samuel to be. Now, she found herself fascinated by his complexities, his unexpected kindnesses, his wit and his tenacity. She loved him with a woman's clear vision, in spite of all his faults and frustrating ways. And in spite of his hatred of the Kenyons.

The thought wrenched her. Oh, how could she?

Samuel must have felt the tension in her, for he lifted his head to study her. A smile softened the chiseled planes of his face. With his fingertip, he traced the outline of her lips in a stirring caress. "No regrets."

It was a command, as he always commanded her. And it was based on the mistaken assumption that she mourned her surrender. Nothing could be further from the truth.

He bent his head and took her mouth in a long, lazy kiss that spoke more of affection than lust. Yet Cassie couldn't dupe herself into believing their newfound intimacy had caused any profound change in his emotions. So long as Samuel was driven by hatred and revenge, it was impossible for him to love her.

She didn't *want* him to love her, anyway, Cassie told herself. She wanted his signature on the deed of separation. Didn't she?

"Don't move," he murmured, briefly caressing her cheek. Rolling away from her, he rose from the bed.

Cassie propped herself on her elbow and watched him walk across the chamber. The sight of his loose-limbed male grace stirred her desires. She wondered feverishly if they would make love again, and how soon. She missed him already, that sense of oneness—

Then she noticed his action. Going to the fireplace, he tugged a slender cord that dangled from the ceiling. The bellrope.

She sat up, yanking the covers to her chin. "What are you doing?"

"Ordering dinner," he said casually, returning to the bed. "Afterward, you'll have a bath if you like."

"You've summoned a servant?" Of course there were servants. Who else had lit the candles and stoked the fire?

She threw off the covers and dashed for her shift, which lay in a crumpled heap on the rug beside the bed. Shaking it out, she tugged it over her head. Then she snatched up one stocking and hunted for the other.

"Looking for this?" Samuel held out the length of silk, but deftly moved it out of her reach when she would have grabbed it. Amusement warmed his eyes. "There's no cause for alarm. The servants here are very discreet."

"Discreet or not, I can't—" A thought struck Cassie, causing her to stop and view the chamber with new eyes. A myriad of candles lent a romantic aura to the heavy furnishings and four-poster bed. Rich medieval tapestries hung from the stone walls. If Samuel knew the servants here so well, it must mean he had brought other women here, that she was merely the latest in a long string of lovers. She forced out the unpalatable question. "Is this . . . your love nest?"

"You might call it that."

Though her throat tightened, she held herself with dignity. "Take me home at once. I'm your wife, not your lightskirt."

His smile gentled, and he feathered his fingertips down her arm. "I created this 'love nest' strictly for us, Cassie. It was quite a feat to accomplish in a mere five days."

"Five days?"

"I paid an exorbitant amount to a land agent to find this house, furnished, thank God, and another fee to a lawyer to rush the closing. I signed the papers only this afternoon."

Her mind whirled that he would go through so much

trouble and expense to seduce her. "But . . . five days," she repeated, thinking back. "You were angry with me for coming to your office. So why would you plan such an elaborate scheme? Why didn't you simply . . . ?"

"Force you? I preferred to seduce you, Cassie." One corner of his mouth still curled in a faint smile. His fingers played with a golden lock of hair that had spilled down her shoulder. "And five days ago, I made an interesting discovery about you . . . *ma chérie*."

My dearest.

Even as her insides curled with pleasure, a warning bell clanged in her head. *Ma chérie.*

Then she remembered.

Yves Picard, the villainous Frenchman, had uttered that same endearment to Sophia Abernathy when he had abducted her.

In a haze of happiness, I stood before the altar with my beloved at my side. The cleric read the service from his prayer book. At the moment when the holy man decreed, "Whosoever shall object, speak now or forever hold your peace," a gruff voice rang out from the rear of the chapel.

"I object!"

My heart stopped beating. In shock, I turned to see the powerful figure of Percival Cranditch filling the doorway.

—The Black Swan

Chapter 18

Quibbles

The blood drained from Cassie's face. She told herself there had to be another explanation. But that scene resonated in her mind. Yves had taken Sophia to a crumbling old manor house very much like this one, and Sir Dudley had come heroically to her rescue.

Dear God. Her suspicions in the coach had been right. Samuel must have found her unfinished manuscript and read it!

Now he stood before her in naked, satisfied splendor—and *smirked.*

Shock and fury chased the chill from her veins. Spinning around, she seized the jar of ointment from the bedside table and hurled it at him. "Knave! You had no right to look in my desk."

He deftly caught the vial against his bare chest, though a few drops trickled down that expanse of muscled flesh. "A bold accusation, considering that *you* had already rummaged through *my* desk."

Cassie huffed out a breath. "*I* had good reason."

"As did I."

Before she could challenge that statement, a knock sounded on the door. Cassie glanced wildly around for a hiding place. "Oh, no!"

"Oh, yes." Samuel slid his hand down her thin shift to fondle the curve of her bottom. Then he gave her a gentle push toward an open doorway half hidden in the shadows of a corner. "Wait in there."

She started in that direction, then veered back to snatch her corset and gown from the middle of the rug. It was bad enough that the rumpled bed announced what had so recently transpired. Catching sight of Samuel, still grinning at her in bare-bottomed glory, she snapped, "*You* put some clothes on, too."

"If it pleases you." His chuckle followed her as she fled to the safety of a dimly lit dressing room.

Dratted man! Did he find her modesty so entertaining? Or was it her *book* that amused him?

Anguish gripped Cassie anew. He had probably laughed all the way through reading it. He had taken her months of hard work and reduced it to nothing more than a jest!

Clutching the pile of her clothing, she sank onto the chair in front of the dressing table. She felt mortified, wounded, *violated.* Not in her body, but in her soul. Without a qualm, Samuel had gone into her chamber and read her manuscript. He had rooted out her dearest secret and now he dared to *mock* it . . .

And he had gone to great expense to bring her fantasy to life. On remarkably short notice, he had purchased a house—*a house*—in order to re-create the gloomy atmosphere of that scene in her novel.

When Samuel had carried her up the stairs, her mind had been on other matters. But now she recalled a shadowy hall lit by torches, and a high ceiling that vanished into darkness. This chamber had the same gothic look as the rest of the house, with stone walls and heavy carved furnishings. A table held an assortment of lotions and powders and brushes, all clearly new, provided for her use. A dressing gown hung from a hook on the wall.

Would he go to such elaborate lengths just to ridicule her?

No, to seduce her. And she couldn't fault him for *that.*

In the midst of her pain and anger, Cassie felt a delicious shiver that had nothing to do with the chilly air. The scent of musk and roses reminded her of how he had taken care to arouse her completely. He could have worn down her defenses and seduced her anywhere, at any time. Instead, he had constructed an elaborate ruse, posing as a highwayman and abducting her, transporting her to this medieval manor house.

He had done it to *please* her.

But that didn't excuse him for invading her privacy. She felt battered, exposed to a man she couldn't wholly trust.

What if he let out her secret?

A sick feeling lurked in the pit of her stomach. When *The Black Swan* was published, Samuel might very well realize that she was the author.

If the book was a smashing success as Mr. Quinnell had predicted, all the ladies would be discussing it. When she and Samuel went into society, people would note the similarities between him and the wicked Captain Cranditch. Everyone would whisper that Samuel too was the baseborn son of Lord S——. It would cause a sensation, make him an object of ridicule, and he would know that it was her fault.

She buried her face in her hands. His dream was to be accepted by society. No matter how vile his motive, she could not rejoice to know that she would have a part in dashing his hopes. Samuel had grown up in poverty without a father's guidance. Spurred by the ambition of bettering himself, he had earned a fortune. He had bought an aristocratic bride.

And he had made love to her with such wonderful, tender passion. He had brought her a happiness and fulfillment beyond her wildest imaginings. She had fallen in love with him, for better or for worse, even if she could never admit that truth to him.

Oh, what was she to do?

The muted sounds of servants drifted from the bedchamber. Clad in her shift, Cassie sat clutching the bundle of her clothing. She had come in here intending to dress. But now she looked askance at her plain corset and sensible gown. Then up at the skimpy garment of rose silk that hung from a hook.

She fought a losing battle with anger and pride. Maybe he had searched her desk, but she had done the same to him. That put them on even footing, didn't it? And if she had only this one night with him, she would enjoy it to the fullest.

Removing her shift, she slipped on the robe. The silk felt cool and soft to her sensitized skin. The neckline dipped scandalously low over her breasts. It was the perfect way to seduce a man.

And to punish him first.

Samuel had lifted the silver lid on a plate of cold roasted chicken when Cassie stepped back into the bedchamber.

Though he'd just enjoyed a swallow of an exceptional burgundy, his mouth went dry. He stood riveted by the sight of his wife. She hadn't donned all her clothes as he'd expected, given her fury at him.

Instead, she wore a dark pink gown that clung to her curves like a second skin. She had loosely repinned her hair so that a few golden locks drooped artfully to her shoulders.

As she strolled toward him and the fabric shifted, he caught glimpses of her full breasts. It was obvious that she was naked beneath the gown.

Oh, yes.

All the blood in Samuel's head descended to his loins. He fumbled as he set down the silver lid, hardly noticing that it teetered on the edge of the table.

Cassie had been furious over his discovery of her secret hobby. It had been a foolish admission to make, anyway. He knew from his business dealings never to reveal his tactics. Why hadn't he kept his mouth shut?

He had planned to smooth her ruffled feathers over an intimate dinner, then use all of his charm to coax her back into bed—or perhaps into the tub of steaming water that had been set up by the fireplace.

Now, his feverish appetites altered that course of events, moving rutting to the top of the list.

Wild, uninhibited rutting.

He walked straight to her. His erection strained against the breeches he had donned for the sake of her modesty—though maybe he shouldn't have bothered. In half a second, he'd have his hands inside that erotic pretense of a gown.

But Cassie deftly eluded him, taking up a stance on the other side of the linen-draped table that had been set up for their dinner. She picked up the discarded silver lid and replaced it on the proper dish. Then her clear blue eyes regarded him with a maddening blend of coolness and sensuality.

"I'd like a word with you," she said.

He cudgeled sanity back into his mind. Her manuscript. His prying. "I'm sorry if I upset you," he said quickly. "That wasn't my intention."

She lifted an eyebrow. "I assume you're referring to my book. I'll have you know my writing is a private matter. It shall be kept that way."

The implication affronted him. "Dammit, Cass. Do you think me a tattler?"

"I hardly know what to think of you. It isn't as if you've shared all *your* secrets with me."

Samuel went instantly on guard. Had she guessed his plan to get her with child and make her forget about ending their marriage?

He was tempted to change the subject, but that would only increase her suspicion. It was better to use charm. Despite her coolness, Cassie was as susceptible as any woman.

Going to her side, he took her hand and turned it over, brushing his lips over her smooth palm. "Ask me anything you like, darling."

"All right. Why do you never visit Hannah Davenport?"

He froze with Cassie's hand still held to his mouth. He could smell the scent of musk and roses on her skin. But it was only a peripheral awareness, outweighed by the raw emotions she had stripped open inside him. To hear her divulge that name from his past shook him deeply.

How the hell had she found out about his old nursemaid?

He realized the answer in a flash of anger. "Jamison told you," he said, releasing her hand. "I knew I couldn't trust that bastard."

Cassie's lips tightened. "He never breathed a word. I found out about Hannah myself . . . from a document in Mr. Jamison's desk."

"So you searched his office, too. I'm married to an accomplished spy."

"I stumbled across the file while looking for evidence of *your* misdeeds." As if that statement excused her illicit actions, she hit him with another well-aimed revelation. "Last week, I called on Hannah. I wanted to see what she knew about you."

Once again, Samuel couldn't move. He felt vulnerable and exposed, as if she'd gutted him so that she could view his soul. Why did she bring this up now? Unless it was her way of meting out punishment for reading her manuscript. "Nothing in that document identified her as my old nurse. Who did you think she was, my mistress?"

He'd scored on that guess, for Cassie blushed and looked defensive. She folded her arms in a way that drew the silk robe taut over her bosom. "Better you should ask about Hannah's welfare."

His anger subsided in an instant. "She isn't ill, is she?"

"No, but she's lonely. Oh, Samuel, she loves you like a son—and you've ignored her. You haven't been to visit her since you found her again."

Memory took him back to that tenement in Cheapside, a stinking hole fit only for the rats that scrabbled in the walls. At first, he hadn't even recognized the gray-haired slattern slumped on a broken chair. Then she'd spied him, and the brightness of joy had transformed her face into the Hannah he remembered from his youth . . .

Savagely, he seized his glass of wine from the table and paced the bedchamber. "I've been gone for four years, in case you've forgotten. And Hannah's allowance is more than adequate. She has no cause to complain."

Cassie followed him. "I never said she complained. She's very happy in the house you gave her."

"Then leave the matter be."

"But she misses you. And no wonder—she raised you from infancy. She comforted you when you skinned a knee and she tended you when you were ill. She stayed with you at night when your mother had a performance." Cassie's voice lowered. "She called you her darling Master Sam. And she was terribly grateful when I offered to intercede for her."

Though guilt tightened his throat, he drained his wine. "So it's you I have to thank for putting the idea in her head."

"Is that all you have to say?" Cassie shook her head disapprovingly. "If you troubled yourself to find Hannah and give her a home, then you must love her. Why is it so difficult for you to admit that?"

Because he knew what love did to a person. He had seen what it had done to his mother. She had wasted her life pining for the nobleman who had spurned her. "I owed Hannah a debt, and I've settled it. There's nothing more to be said."

"Money." Her hands on her hips, Cassie glared at him. "People need love and attention and *time* every bit as much as money. And you *will* visit Hannah. I insist upon it."

An unexpected dark humor twisted in Samuel. Grown men didn't dare give him orders, yet this slip of a woman commanded him to do her bidding.

He reached out and pulled Cassie close. Holding her flush against him, he moved his hands on a slow, downward glide that traced her feminine form. Bending his head to her fragrant hair, he murmured, "And if I don't? Will you use your body as a bargaining tool?"

Instead of slapping his hands away, she answered his question with one of her own. "Why must you always try to appear to be such a hard man?"

"I *am* hard." He fitted their bodies together so there could be no doubt about his meaning. "Quite obviously so."

Her eyelids lowered, just enough to betray her arousal. Then she slipped out of his grasp and whirled to face him. "I'm speaking of your obstinate character, as well you know. You would have the world believe you cold and harsh. Yet you treated Hannah with great kindness. And Mick, too. You took him in off the street and gave him work. That isn't the act of an unfeeling man."

"Mick needed a job, and I needed a custodian. It's called a fair trade."

"It's more than that. You gave him good advice about the importance of ambition. And I've been wondering—have you given a thought to his education?"

Samuel wrestled with the impulse to deny it. But she'd

only probe and prod, so he might as well admit the truth. "I've hired a tutor for him. He'll take lessons every morning. But I told him he'll have to repay me someday."

"That's very good of you." She gave him a strange, penetrating look. "I think . . . he reminds you of yourself as a child."

The turn of conversation made Samuel distinctly uneasy. "Don't read too much into it, Cass. Men are not as complicated as women."

Going to the table, he poured himself another glass of wine. The intimate dinner he had planned lay untouched. The fine china dishes held an array of cold meats and cheeses, along with dates and oranges imported from the Mediterranean. Because Cassie didn't seem inclined toward seduction at the moment, he filled a plate with food.

But when he turned around, she was no longer scowling at him. She stood by the brass tub, trailing her fingers through the water. Glancing over her shoulder at him, she said, "But you *are* complicated, Samuel. How can you be two men, one compassionate and the other cruel?"

She was the dichotomy. Alluring and disapproving both at the same time.

He seated himself at the table and broke a piece of bread from the crusty loaf. "I wonder how you can think of so many questions to ask."

"It's my nature. I'm a writer, and even we inferior scribblers like to know *why* people do the things they do." A faint smile touched her lips. "Do you mind if I bathe before I join you for dinner?"

On that scant warning, she untied her sash and let the robe slither to the floor in a dark pink pool.

Leaving her naked.

Samuel almost choked. He watched feverishly as she stepped into the brass tub, giving him a rear view of the most gorgeous female body God had ever created. When she turned to lower herself into the water, he caught a profile glimpse of her tawny mound and perfect breasts.

Then all that voluptuousness sank out of sight as she tilted her head back against the rim of the tub and closed her eyes. "Mmmm. This does feel wonderful."

His plate of food forgotten, Samuel stared at her. Now *that* was an invitation if he'd ever heard one.

Or was it?

Even we inferior scribblers.

Although his brain had taken up residence in his balls, he had enough presence of mind to recognize her pique. She thought he had derided her novel. And she was most definitely torturing him because of it.

But two could play that game.

Cassie was having second thoughts about her boldness. As she lay back in the tub, she concentrated on appearing relaxed. But inside, she was a seething jumble of anxiety and desire.

The warm water enveloped her like a caress. The surface lapped at her chin, and her closed eyelids made her other senses more keenly acute. But she heard nothing at all from Samuel.

Was he still sitting there at the table? Perhaps he thought food more interesting than her at the moment. Perhaps she wasn't supposed to desire him again so soon. Or perhaps she was supposed to wait for him to make the first move.

And why had she so stupidly uttered that petty complaint about inferior scribblers? It had just slipped out somehow. She hadn't even been thinking about her stung pride. She had succeeded only in ruining the moment that had been designed to torment him.

Then her heart beat faster as she detected a hint of spice. She sensed his presence in every pore of her skin, in every soft place within her body.

Something touched her lips.

She opened her eyes to see Samuel kneeling beside the tub, leaning toward her. His broad chest with its superbly sculpted muscles loomed only a few inches away. He held a section of orange to her mouth, and she parted her lips automatically. As he popped the morsel inside, his fingers brushed her sensitive lips, sending a bone-deep quiver straight down to her loins.

It was an incredibly erotic combination, the tang of the orange, the keen blue fire of his eyes, the heated embrace of the water. Heaven be praised, Samuel did intend to make love to her again. *Now.*

"About your book," he said.

"My . . . what . . . ?"

"It appears I've given you the wrong impression. I *did* enjoy reading it. Very much."

Instantly wary, Cassie stiffened. She crossed her arms beneath the water and wished she were fully armored in clothing instead of lounging in a tub like an offering. "Don't lie," she said. "I was present when you laughed at me, remember?"

Seemingly unperturbed, he fed her another segment of orange. "I wasn't laughing, I was smiling. And with good reason. It isn't every day a man discovers his wife's fantasies written down on paper."

"You *did* laugh—when I went into the dressing room."

He chuckled now, and his smile made him so attractive that Cassie nearly forgot her vexation. "That had nothing to do with your book," he said. "It was your reaction to being discovered making love with your husband."

She sank a little deeper and hoped he would think her blush came from the warmth of the bath. Was it truly her modesty that had amused him?

To cover her confusion, she groped for the cake of soap at the bottom of the tub, lathered her palms, and made a show of scrubbing her arms and shoulders. His avid gaze followed her movements, and she was too shy to wash elsewhere while he was watching. "You couldn't possibly like a ladies' novel," she said. "You'd think it a lot of melodramatic nonsense."

He shook his head. "Don't put words in my mouth," he said, silencing *her* mouth with another slice of fruit. "I enjoyed the insight into your dreams—at least for the most part."

"What do you mean?"

"If you must know, I've a quibble or two with your story."

Leaving her in awful suspense, he rose and strolled to the table, drawing her gaze to the snug black breeches that saved him from nudity. But not even a lurch of untimely desire could banish the anxiety that riddled her.

He *would* criticize her book, she knew it. She shouldn't be afraid of hearing what he thought, but she *was*.

After a moment, curiosity overruled her cowardice. "Well? Tell me your *quibbles*."

Taking all the time in the world, Samuel peeled another orange. He was frowning, a fact that truly worried her. "First," he said, "there was that chase through the docks."

Yves Picard had been escaping with the stolen jewels and Sir Dudley had almost captured him. "I worked hard on that scene," she said defensively. "It was very exciting!"

"And entirely too authentic. I'd like to know how you managed to write such vivid descriptions."

With that one crumb of implied praise, her wariness vanished into a glow of delight. "You truly enjoyed it, then?"

"I told you I did, and I meant it. You're an excellent writer. Now answer me. The docks are not a place for ladies."

Too pleased to take offense at his stern look, she admitted,

"I talked Walt and Bertie into taking me there last autumn. I used the excuse that I was curious to see the place."

"So your cousin and your friends don't know about your writing? I'm the only one you've told?"

Samuel's expression had turned entirely too smug. "I didn't *tell* you," she reminded him. "Flora is the only person I've told." And Mr. Quinnell, of course. But she didn't want to think about the imminent publication of *The Black Swan.*

"You're not to go near the wharves again," Samuel stated. "If there's any other research of that sort needed, I'll accompany you."

She hid a twinge of dismay. "I've done perfectly well on my own. I will *not* allow you to interfere with my writing."

"I won't interfere. My sole purpose is to keep you safe from harm." He strode toward her again, that hint of a swagger in his walk.

Watching him, Cassie felt breathless and aching. She was perfectly safe—except from *him.* And oh, how she wanted to experience his ravishment again. "What . . . is your other quibble?"

He knelt beside the tub again and fed her another piece of juicy orange. "Picard abducted Sophia and kept her imprisoned overnight. I couldn't help but wonder what happened between them."

Chewing the fruit, Cassie stared at him uncomprehendingly. Then his implication struck her, and she swallowed and sat up straight. "I beg your pardon," she said indignantly. "I made it quite clear that he locked her in a tower chamber and left her there."

Samuel seemed fascinated by the sight of her breasts, damp and rosy from the heat of the water. But when he touched her, it was only to brush back a stray lock of hair that had fallen onto her shoulder. "And you expect me to believe that the dastardly Picard kept his hands off a beautiful woman?"

Cassie sank back down in the water. "Yes, I do. It can't happen any other way."

"But he called her *ma chérie.* That would indicate an attraction to her." Samuel flashed her his most villainous grin. "I suspect they shared a little tryst in that tower room."

"That's absurd! Sophia would never do something so sordid."

Yet his observation appalled her. In her naïveté, she hadn't spared a second thought to the possibility of Sophia's innocence being compromised. But now that Cassie had experienced passion, she could understand its powerful pull. And Yves was a very charming Frenchman. Yes, it was indeed very possible that he would have ravished Sophia.

And what about Belinda in *The Black Swan*? Belinda had spent *three* nights on the pirate ship with Percival Cranditch, a scoundrel modeled after Samuel himself.

Oh, *blast.* Cassie didn't need to find yet another doubt about the forthcoming publication of her first book.

She immersed herself even deeper into the bathwater and glared up at him. "You're teasing me. No one would think such a thing but you."

A knowing smile crinkled the corners of his eyes and gave him the aspect of a rogue. He used the last bit of orange to trace the outline of her mouth. "Never mind, then, it's just a man's observation. You keep your fantasy, and I'll keep mine."

She parted her lips to accept the fruit, but he ate the piece himself, watching her with piercing blue eyes that seemed to see straight into her soul. Samuel had fantasies, too?

A realization struck her. "So that's why you played the role of villain tonight. That's *your* fantasy."

"How wise you are, *ma chérie.*" Holding her gaze, he reached for the cake of soap in the water. "But for such a clever woman, you aren't very accomplished at washing yourself. You've missed a few places."

Moving behind her, he slid his soapy hands over her breasts. Cassie experienced a shock of liquid fire inside herself. How she loved the glide of his big palms over her bath-warmed skin. Turning her head to look up at him, she said in a sultry voice, "Perhaps I was waiting for your help."

"Ah, I see." He bent his head and touched his mouth to hers, and she could taste the faint tang of oranges on his tongue. The long, slow kiss left her starving for more. Against her mouth, he murmured, "Now, about your book . . ."

"Yes?" Cassie didn't want to talk about her book anymore. She didn't want to talk at all, only *feel*.

"Perhaps at the end," he said, "you should let Sophia run off with Picard."

"You're jesting," she said weakly, as his slick hands worked their slow magic down her body. "He's a scoundrel. Sir Dudley is a *gentleman*—"

"And too tame for the intrepid Sophia. *He'd* never engage in a tryst."

"Certainly not. He respects her. She's a lady."

"Hmm." Underwater, his fingers traced patterns over her belly. "So ladies don't like being seduced. Is that what you're saying?"

"Yes . . . no . . . oh, *do* stop teasing me." With intrepid boldness, she took his hand and moved it lower, right where she craved his touch.

He chuckled, but Cassie could no longer voice anything coherent. His skillful fingers knew exactly how to caress her. The pleasurable sensations rose in her, building to a tidal wave that rushed through her, suffusing her with rapture, leaving her gasping and limp and glowing.

Samuel looked inordinately pleased by her response, although she was aware that he had not taken his own satisfaction. He lifted her out of the bath and proceeded to dry her with a linen towel in front of the fireplace.

Cassie clung weakly to him, pressing kisses to his face,

loving the prickle of his skin. "I'm getting you damp," she murmured, then laughed at the absurdity of her words as she reached for the buttons of his breeches. "Oh, Samuel, I don't want to waste a single moment tonight."

"We've time aplenty. We're staying here at Strathmore Castle until early next week."

Surprised, Cassie stilled her hands. Had he changed his mind? "*Next week* . . . but what of the duke's ball?"

"We'll return the day before the party. That should give you plenty of time to prepare." Samuel's smile held the promise of delights to come. "In the meantime, we'll enjoy our honeymoon for the next six days."

"I've come for your bride," said Captain Cranditch. "You reneged on your promise to pay her ransom."

Mr. Montcliff stepped in front of me. "How dare you! I'll run you through first."

With the ring of steel, my guardian drew his dress sword from the scabbard that hung at his side. The blade glistened in the sunlight.

Percival Cranditch grinned as he pulled forth his own weapon, a wicked rapier that no doubt had caused the demise of many an innocent. "So this is how it is to be. A fight to the death betwixt brothers."

—The Black Swan

Chapter 19
The Diamond Serpent

Seven days later, Samuel drove Cassie back to London in his sporty blue curricle. The bay gelding trotted briskly along the dirt road. The jingle of the harness and the rhythmic clopping of hooves had a lulling effect on Samuel. A soft spring breeze blew, the morning sun shone brightly, and a sense of utter satisfaction relaxed him.

His plan had succeeded astonishingly well. So well that he and Cassie had come to a mutual decision to linger at Strathmore Castle for an extra night. He couldn't even remember who had first made the suggestion, only that they had both been eager to prolong the honeymoon.

But leaving their love nest had caused a subtle change in Cassie. No longer was she pert and laughing, open with her affections. Even before the curricle had departed through the iron gates, a certain reserve had descended upon her.

In a ladylike pose, she kept her gloved hands tucked in her lap. Once again, that straw bonnet hid the glory of her hair. Clad in pelisse and gown, she looked as buttoned up as a prim old maid. Maybe she didn't want him to guess how much she disliked having to return to London.

He transferred the ribbons to one hand and settled the other over hers. "The estate is ours. We can return at any time."

Cassie gave a start of surprise. Then she shook her head slightly, frowning at the road as if anticipating problems to come. "There's the duke's ball tonight. It'll be the start of an endless round of social events."

For the first time, Samuel half wished he hadn't insisted on this scheme. "We needn't attend every party. More often than not, we'll stay home. I'm sure we can find other things to occupy our time."

Her cool blue eyes flirted with his. A small smile, a faint blush, then she looked away again, clearly rebuffing conversation. As he drove, Samuel glanced at her profile, but that composed, aristocratic façade hid her thoughts. Her teeth worried her lower lip, and he wondered what was disturbing her.

Maybe she already regretted giving herself to him.

His mind resisted that notion; certainly Cassie had enjoyed the past seven days as much as he had. They had spent every moment together. He had taken her on picnics and rides in the countryside, always finding some secluded spot in which to make love. They had explored the house and grounds by day and slept in each other's arms by night. He had especially liked the time after he'd played the pianoforte for her, and she had surrendered to him right there, climbing into his lap to ride him. He had guided her down all the myriad paths to pleasure, and she had been an avid adventurer, much to his gratification.

He'd discovered too that it was more than his wife's body that pleased him. He liked her wit and her passion for writing, her boldness in challenging him and her occasional shyness. She had no real notion of her beauty, either, a refreshing change from other women.

And she had a fire in her that belied her aura of ladylike restraint.

This morning, just before dawn, he had awakened to the touch of her mouth and hands. They had spent a long time kissing and caressing, slowly arousing one another, whispering in the darkness, and he had enjoyed the prelude every bit as much as the deed itself. He'd relished the aftermath, too, holding her in complete contentment. That was something new to him; never before had he lingered with a woman.

With absolute certainty, Samuel knew that he had not had enough of Cassie. If anything, he craved his wife even more than he had on the night he had abducted her for the purpose of getting her with child.

A fierce tenderness gripped him. He wanted to see her rounded with his seed, to watch her suckle his baby at her breast. He wanted to hold the son or daughter that they had created together. Considering the vigor and frequency of their lovemaking, there was an excellent chance that she had conceived already.

He glanced at her solemn face again, wondering if she had considered the possibility. Maybe she was struggling with doubts over that deed of separation. Pregnancy would change everything, make her realize that she belonged with her husband.

"We have less than two months together," he said casually. "What if the passion between us is still burning then?"

Startled, she stared at him, her eyes wide in the pale oval of her face. "Is *that* what this week was all about? You thought if you seduced me, I'd change my mind about the deed of separation?"

Hell. So much for that conjecture. "You misunderstand me," he said smoothly. "After the season is over, I'll sign the deed if you like. But will you still let me sleep with you?"

God, that sounded pathetic. As if he were begging for her favors.

She arched an eyebrow. "I can't answer your question, Samuel. We'll have to wait and see."

As if she had more important matters on her mind, Cassie turned her gaze to the fields of wildflowers along the roadside.

He tightened his jaw in dogged determination to probe her thoughts. "What will you do, then? After I sign the deed, I mean."

Her gaze alighted on him, then flitted away again like a cautious butterfly. "I intend to buy a house in the country."

"You can have Strathmore. I bought it for you." The constant reminder of their honeymoon surely would work in his favor.

She shook her head. "I don't want a mansion, I want a cottage. A small, cozy place where I can devote myself to writing."

She did? And clearly, she didn't want her husband there with her, a fact that triggered resentment in him. "You're very serious about your writing, then. I assumed it was merely a hobby."

Cassie blinked warily. "It's something I enjoy, that's all."

"I can help you," Samuel said in sudden inspiration. "When you finish the book, I can use my business connections and find a publisher for you—"

"No!" Her emphatic voice cut him off. Running the tip of her tongue over her lips, she went on. "This is my private project. I won't have you interfering."

"All right," he said, his patience fraying. "So you don't wish to share your dreams with the rest of the world. It's better that way. To be honest, I'd rather we keep your fantasies between the two of us."

His attempt to remind Cassie of their intimacy fell short of reawakening her passions. She pursed her lips and narrowed her eyes, gazing fiercely at her hands as if they were the most fascinating sight in the world.

They *were* fascinating, to him at least. Although he preferred her hands shorn of gloves and exploring his naked body.

Cassie remained silent, returning her attention to the scenery as if she'd completely forgotten his presence. After a time, she addressed him again, and her face wore a look of steely resolve. "Since we're speaking of the future," she said, "I would like your promise on something."

"Name it."

"I want your word that if I should be . . . in a family way, you'll never take my child away from me."

It was a pistol shot from the darkness. The shock of it spread through Samuel's chest. He wanted to throw back his head and howl from the pain. But he didn't, because then she would know how deeply she'd wounded him.

The breeze played with the wisps of her hair that had escaped her bonnet. She watched him, biting her lip, and now he understood that little furrow of worry on her brow. She *had* been thinking about the ramifications of their lovemaking. And she believed him so ruthless, he'd rip their baby from her arms.

He drew a searing breath, turned grim eyes to the road. "It's a bit premature to speak of such matters."

"No it isn't," she insisted. "In cases of legal separation, the father can claim the children and raise them himself. He can forbid the mother any contact with them. It's happened to other women, Samuel. I won't have it happen to me."

His stomach churned. Her low opinion of him was obvious. Brutally obvious. "And what of my rights? Will you deny our son or daughter a father? I won't have *that* happen."

"No, of course not." Her face softened, and she placed

her hand on his sleeve. "I know how it hurt you to grow up without a father—"

He shook off her hand. "You know nothing, Cassie. I'm not like George Kenyon, willing to abandon my child."

"I—I didn't mean to imply you were. You may come to visit us at any time you like."

"How magnanimous. You speak as if the issue has already been decided."

Distress radiated from her. She gripped his arm again and looked up into his face. "Don't be angry, Samuel. I only wish to make certain that if we have a child, I won't be forced to give it away. Surely you can understand that."

The impact of those big blue eyes reached past his fury. He *did* understand, that was his curse. Even now, he wanted to bend his head and kiss her fiercely, to feel her warmth surround him. To give her whatever she asked.

"I will never separate you from our child," he said through clenched teeth. "You have my word on it."

He whipped his gaze back to the road. He had no qualms about making such a promise.

Cassie—along with any children they might have—would stay with him. Whether she liked it or not.

Cassie had never been more glad or more regretful to be home. But as she entered her bedchamber, she had the peculiar sense of viewing it through new eyes.

She stood for a moment and absorbed the familiarity of her surroundings. The pale blue draperies and dainty furnishings had always soothed her. The pens and inkpot sat on her desk as always. The pair of blue-and-yellow-striped chairs were drawn up to the hearth, ready for her to settle down with a good book. But now she found herself missing stone walls and crimson bedhangings—and a lover who had fulfilled all her dreams.

No, a man whom she loved with all her heart. A man who could frustrate her with his hatred of the Kenyons and thrill her with his rakish smile.

Cassie released a pent-up breath. Everything here was the same. It was she herself who had changed.

Slowly, she removed her bonnet and pelisse. Samuel had dropped her off at the house, given her strict orders to rest, and gone straight to his place of business. Flora had greeted her at the door, anxious to know if her part in the abduction had been forgiven. It had taken Cassie considerable time to reassure her friend that the enforced honeymoon had gone well. Pleading a headache, Cassie had begged leave to come up here.

She felt a twinge of guilt at the deception, but she had needed time alone. Time to adjust to the alterations in her life. There was an awareness in her body now, the perception of herself as a woman. And an ache of emptiness that made her long to return to Strathmore Castle and the haven of Samuel's arms.

She wanted to cling to the joy they had shared, yet from the moment they'd walked out the front door and entered the carriage, the weight of the future had descended upon her. She had wrestled with her reluctance to enter society, and her fears about the publication of her book.

But those worries had been eclipsed by a more compelling consideration, something that had lurked at the edge of her mind during their seven days together.

Samuel's seed might have started a baby inside her.

A melting warmth suffused her. She spread her hand over her womb, trying to imagine herself with child. Would Samuel be happy in that event? Or would he gaze at her with that stone-faced coldness?

I'm not like George Kenyon, willing to abandon my child.

He had been so angry with her on the ride home. Furious,

in fact. She had never imagined he would think she was comparing him to his father!

Perhaps she should have avoided the topic altogether.

Cassie sank down on the bed and leaned against the mahogany post. But she had felt compelled to bring her fears out into the open. It would have been negligent of her not to do so. She had *needed* his promise. The very thought of having her baby taken away filled her with horror.

And now she couldn't forget the way Samuel had looked at her. With icy rage in his eyes. His strong reaction had taken her by surprise.

Will you deny our child a father?

She had been thinking only of her own needs, not Samuel's. She hadn't stopped to consider that he might have feelings on the matter, too, that perhaps he might *want* children. And she had feared that the ruthless side to his nature would hold sway once they'd returned to the city. Yes, he had been a tender lover for the past seven days and nights. But Strathmore Castle had been a dreamlike interlude, and London was reality.

London was the ball tonight, Samuel's introduction to the *haut ton*. It meant the fruition of his plan to make himself the equal of the Kenyons. He had demanded that she be at his side as his consort, and he wouldn't relent on that issue.

Cassie shivered, rubbing her arms. She abhorred the notion of entering society, making small talk with strangers and pretending politeness. Another dread weighed on her, one she hadn't mentioned to Samuel.

Nearly six years had passed since the death of her mother. There would be people present who had known the duchess, people who remembered her vividly. They would compare Cassie to the beautiful, polished Duchess of Chiltern and find the daughter lacking.

And they would remember the gossip about Cassie's marriage.

She would far rather spend the evening curled up in her bed and thinking about Samuel. Better yet, to entice him into her bed and make him forget their quarrel.

The thought caused an ache within her. She wanted him with a desperation akin to obsession. Seven days had not been enough. The desire he had awakened in her seemed eternal, a vast, compelling need that had been honed by their lovemaking.

We have less than two months together. What if the passion between us is still burning then?

She had wanted to ask in return, "What if it never ended?"

No. She couldn't let herself fall into that trap, no matter how tempting. Samuel wanted to preserve their marriage solely for the purpose of revenge. It would destroy his pride to be viewed by the Kenyons as a failure.

And it would destroy her soul to stay with a man who didn't return her love.

She must hold fast to her own dream of freedom. It was her only hope of overcoming the wrenching heartache of loving Samuel. A legal separation would ensure that she was unencumbered by a man, able to direct her own life and to pursue her writing in peace.

Feeling the need to hold her manuscript in her hands, Cassie went to her desk and sat down. But even as she reached down to open the bottom drawer, she spied a small parcel atop the desk, tucked alongside the dish of quill pens.

She picked up the package, and her blood turned to ice. Her maiden name was printed in block letters across the top. *"Lady Cassandra Grey."*

Prodded by morbid curiosity, she unwrapped the brown paper to find a small cloisonné box, exquisitely inlaid with blue and black enamel. She opened it warily, remembering the rose petals that had showered out of the last letter.

Inside, Cassie found a folded piece of paper, and beneath it—

She gasped. On a nest of blue velvet lay a dainty diamond brooch in the form of a serpent.

She touched it wonderingly, running her fingertip along the curve of gemstones, a tiny emerald forming the eye of the snake. There was something vaguely familiar about the piece, something that tugged at her memory.

When she unfolded the note and read the message, she trembled with shock. And she knew exactly what had stirred that faint sense of recognition.

My Darling,

This brooch once belonged to your mother. Wear it to Nunwich's ball, and I shall know that you wish me to reveal myself.

Your Most Ardent Admirer

* * *

With only half his attention, Samuel guided the curricle through the busy streets of the business district. It was early afternoon, the Strand was clogged with traffic, and because he was hemmed in by other vehicles, he was forced to lag behind a dray piled high with beer kegs. The vexing slowness enhanced his foul mood.

Hell.

He should be basking in satisfaction after spending seven days in carnal heaven. He had accomplished his purpose in seducing his wife. As a bonus, Cassie had turned out to be every man's dream, insatiable in her desire for him, delightful in her eagerness for more.

Except on the way home.

I want your word that you'll never take my child away.

His hands tightened on the reins. Pain throbbed inside

him. Cassie's request had left a raw wound in his gut.

No, he wasn't injured, he was *furious*. Furious that she could dare to make such a demand of him. Furious that she could lay claim to their child and then so graciously allow him visitation rights.

Most of all, he was furious that she still had her mind set on leaving him. He had thought . . .

Dammit, he had *hoped* that their incredible closeness would have enslaved her, too.

To her defense, perhaps she didn't realize the rarity of their wild passion. But Samuel knew. He felt as randy as a boy chasing after his first girl. He couldn't remember a time when he'd spent a full week with the same woman, yet still desired her a hundredfold more.

In truth, he couldn't recall ever spending an entire night with a lover. He always had his pleasure and then left, never allowing himself to sleep in her arms as he'd done with Cassie. It was impossible that he could be so tied in knots over a woman who could walk away from *him*.

I want your word that you'll never take my child away.

Her ill opinion of him stuck in his craw. Dammit, she wouldn't have the chance to leave him. He wouldn't allow it. He would make her accept his permanent place in her life . . .

The dray turned a corner, and just his ill luck, only a block away from his office. But then Samuel realized there was another reason for his maddeningly slow progress.

A knot of people were gathered in front of the brick building. A watchman in a long greatcoat directed traffic around the scene. Vehicles slowed down so the drivers could gawk.

Frowning at the unusual sight, Samuel inched his way forward, lost patience, and pulled to the side of the road. He snapped his fingers at a passing urchin and flipped him a coin to watch the curricle. Then he pushed through the throng of bystanders. Their hushed mutterings bespoke a disaster.

He reached the inner circle of men. Several gray-faced clerks from his office huddled by the wall of the building and another watchman stood like a guard over something that lay on the pavement.

A body.

A rough horse blanket had been thrown over the corpse, but the plain brown shoes and trouser cuffs that stuck out clearly belonged to a man. A dark stain of blood spread from the area of his head.

"What the hell's going on here?" Samuel demanded.

The grizzled watchman aimed a glower at him. "Stand back, guv'nor. Ye're trespassin' on official business 'ere."

"I'm Samuel Firth. I own this building."

The news wiped the scowl from the old man's face. He snatched off his hat and clapped it to his stout chest. " 'Tis a turrible thing, sir. Turrible, indeed. I was just walkin' about me duties 'alf a block away when I saw it 'appen wid me own two eyes."

"What? Was he struck in the street?"

"Nay, sir. The gent took 'is own life in broad daylight. Jumped, 'e did. Right from up there." The watchman jerked his thumb at the top of the four-story building.

Bile rose in Samuel's throat. He stared in disbelief, trying to make sense of the nightmare. "Who? Who jumped?"

"Ask them." With a shrug, the watchman nodded at the cluster of clerks.

The employees looked at one another and shuffled their feet uneasily, as if they were reluctant to be the bearer of bad tidings.

Then Mick elbowed his way out from behind them. His brimless hat sat askew on his black hair, and his thin face bore a look of fright. He swallowed hard, then said, "I—I'll tell ye, master. 'Twas Mr. Babbage."

Mr. Montcliff requested that the duel take place outside the sanctity of the chapel. But the pirate captain would not be deterred. Clad in black breeches and white shirt, a crimson sash at his waist, he sauntered down the aisle with his rapier at the ready. His ocean-blue eyes flicked over me, then returned to his half brother.

"I'll spill your blood right here," he said. " 'Twill be your funeral, Montcliff, and then my wedding, for your bride shall marry me."

—The Black Swan

Chapter 20

A Novel Sensation

The Duke of Nunwich was a ruddy-cheeked man of thirty with an elevated sense of his own worth. Standing beside him in the receiving line, his young wife had a bovine look to her placid features and a cowlike contentment to let her husband direct the conversation.

As the duke made a courtly bow over Cassie's hand, she could see a bald spot nestled in his thatch of blond hair. "Ah, Chiltern's daughter," he said. " 'Tis a delight that we meet at last. Chiltern and his duchess never missed our parties."

Her stomach lurched, and for a moment Cassie couldn't speak. Her mother and father had been in this very house, gaily greeting Nunwich as bosom friends. It was daunting to think she'd be expected to take their place. "It's a pleasure to meet you, too, Your Grace."

But the duke was no longer listening.

Nunwich cast his haughty gaze on Samuel, lifting a

quizzing glass to his bulbous eye as if to examine an oddity. "And Mr. Firth. You're connected to the Kenyons, I believe. You're Stokeford's half brother."

Cassie feared that Samuel would take offense. But to her amazement, he winked at the duke. "Or so the gossip goes."

The duke froze, his lips pinched; then he elbowed his wife and laughed. "There now, we like a man with a sense of humor, don't we, Theodora?" Returning his attention to Samuel, he said magnanimously, "Do you hunt? Perhaps you'd care to join our shooting party in the autumn."

Samuel inclined his head in a cool nod of acceptance.

He and Cassie left the long receiving line in the foyer and ascended the grand staircase to the ballroom. Marveling at his calm, she clung to his arm. As always, her heart turned over when she looked at him. In a dark blue coat and tan knee breeches, Samuel had a devastating handsomeness that put all the other men here to shame. His black hair, blue eyes, and strong features marked him as a Kenyon, though it surely would anger him were she to tell him so. He even carried himself with an aristocratic air of confidence, as if he belonged among the *haut ton* by right.

Which he did. The blood of the nobility flowed through his veins, but that wasn't why she admired him. He had earned his wealth and stature through hard work. Beneath all his arrogance, he had a sense of honor that he kept hidden lest anyone think him soft. He was more a lord than those who had been born to the privilege.

She was fiercely proud to walk at his side. And she was glad to help him accomplish his objective in gaining acceptance, no matter how misguided his motivation.

"Congratulations," she murmured sincerely. "You've already secured an invitation. And an important one."

Samuel shrugged as if it were his due. "There'll be others."

"But it's a start. I know how much this means to you."

He made no reply, his gaze scanning the crowd, as if

he were plotting his next conquest among the *ton*. As they reached the top of the staircase, Cassie had the frustrating awareness that he had shut her out again. He had been cold and remote ever since she had wrested that promise from him this morning.

Will you deny our child a father?

His words haunted her. Didn't he know her better than that? Her heart ached with unspoken love, the love she didn't dare reveal if ever she hoped to win her freedom from him. But how she yearned to recover their closeness of the past seven days, to see the lighthearted Samuel again, teasing and smiling and thrilling her with his kisses.

He had returned home from his office with barely enough time to change into his evening clothes. She had been downstairs already, waiting for him, after spending hours primping. She had thanked him for the suite of diamond jewelry, a necklace and earbobs that a jeweler had delivered to her. He had complimented her in a formal manner, remarking that the gems looked especially fine with her pale blue gown.

And he had asked her about the diamond serpent.

Warily, Cassie touched the brooch pinned to her bodice. Should she have told Samuel more than the fact that it had belonged to her mother? Should she have mentioned the letters from her unknown admirer? Should she have confessed to her shock at learning the man had known her mother, when his first two letters had mentioned nothing of that?

But Samuel had been so forbidding, so absorbed in his own thoughts, and it had not seemed the right time for such a confidence. It surely would have started another quarrel, for she could well imagine his reaction to her receiving love letters from another man. She didn't know if she could even fully explain to Samuel her desire to meet the man who had befriended the duchess in this glittering world of the *ton*.

As they entered the crowded ballroom, the majordomo announced their names. Heads turned. Ladies raised lorgnettes to peer at them while others whispered behind their fans. Gentlemen stared, craning their necks.

Cassie stood paralyzed, her hand gripping Samuel's arm. All other considerations vanished as the old shyness swept her into a tight grip. Her cheeks felt pale, her head dizzy. She fervently wished for a hole to open in the polished parquet floor and swallow her up.

Many of these people had known her parents. They would compare her to the vivacious duchess. They would also remember the scandal of Samuel paying off her father's debts and purchasing her as his bride.

Samuel's hand settled over hers on his arm. He bent his head close, his gaze intent on her. "Courage," he whispered. "Pretend you're the intrepid Sophia."

The warmth in his deep blue eyes penetrated her numbness. The heat of his hand revived her. She relaxed slowly, the tension draining away. In its place she drew strength not from a fictitious character but from a hidden store inside herself.

She managed a smile, and Samuel smiled back. Keeping his hand over hers, he guided her forward to mingle with the crowd. She glanced up at him, but to her dismay the moment of connection had vanished. As they strolled the perimeter of the ballroom, he resumed that remote expression as if he were preoccupied with fixing his place in society.

Was that why he had encouraged her? Because he wanted her assistance? She would prefer to think that he still desired her, that they could resolve their differences. The thought enabled her to face the evening with hope, for at the end of it, she and Samuel would go home together.

For the first time, she noticed her surroundings, and the fairyland décor of the ballroom enchanted her. The long mirrors on the walls reflected the light of a multitude of candles in the chandeliers and on pedestals around the room. On a balcony overlooking the chamber, an orchestra tuned their instruments. The panorama of ladies' gowns and gentlemen's coats made the place look like a vast spring garden.

One of these men had sent her the diamond serpent.

Cassie's stomach clenched. At that moment, a stout, middle-aged officer in dress uniform stopped in front of her and bowed. "Lady Cassandra, if I may be so bold as to make your acquaintance? I'm Colonel Mainwaring, an old friend of your parents."

For a moment the old nervousness threatened; then she forced a polite smile. "It's a pleasure. Have you been introduced to my husband?"

The two men shook hands. But the colonel's attention remained fixed on her. "You wouldn't remember me, but I visited Chiltern Palace a time or two. Your mother was a superb hostess, a true wit at conversation. I simply had to say, you look very much like her."

His avid brown eyes made Cassie uneasy, especially since he appeared to be staring at the diamond brooch. Was *he* her secret admirer? But when would the colonel have ever seen her before?

With a lack of originality unworthy of her parentage, she murmured, "Thank you."

"May I request the honor of your hand in a country dance? With your husband's permission, of course."

She hesitated, uneasy with the notion of being alone with this stranger. And yet . . . she had only a child's memory of her mother. Perhaps Colonel Mainwaring might help her gain an adult's understanding of the duchess. "I—I would like that—"

"Unfortunately, all of her dances are already spoken for," Samuel said. "If you'll excuse us." His hand at her elbow, he bore her away.

"That was rude and unmannerly," she whispered. "Colonel Mainwaring was only trying to be agreeable."

"Like hell. He was staring at your breasts."

Or at the diamond serpent. "Don't curse. He knew my mother, and I should have danced with him."

"But you wouldn't have enjoyed it." Samuel took two glasses of champagne from the tray of a passing footman and handed one to her. "You really are shy with strangers."

Cassie sipped the bubbly drink and regarded him over the rim of her glass. But there was no censure in his gaze, only interest, and she felt suddenly breathless. "I did warn you. Perhaps you should have chosen your wife more wisely."

He took her gloved hand, his thumb moving in circles over her palm. Bending closer, he murmured, "I chose well. You are the most beautiful woman here. And you don't even realize it."

The evening took on an unprecedented sparkle. Cassie felt giddy, as if the champagne had gone straight to her head. How did he *do* that? How did he turn from cold man to seducer?

As she basked in his admiration, a familiar face appeared beside him. A smile sprang to her lips. "Walt!"

Her cousin wore a pale green coat that complemented his sandy hair. He flashed a wary look at Samuel, then pointedly ignored him, leaning closer to kiss her cheek. "Cass. It's good to see you. You left town without telling me."

"It was unexpected—" Cassie began.

"She needn't report her whereabouts to you," Samuel said in a pleasant tone, splaying his fingers over the small of her back. Graciously, he added, "However, next time we'll make sure you're informed."

Next time. Cassie's womb contracted with a pulsebeat of desire. Did Samuel intend to take her back to Strathmore Castle? Did that mean he'd forgiven her?

She was aware of his hand, warm and possessive, against her waist. Or was he simply staking his claim on her?

Walt looked none too happy. He had the appearance of a resentful lad who had been scolded by his elder.

She stepped away from Samuel, took her cousin's arm, and turned the topic to something less volatile. "Where are Bertie and Philip tonight? I'd hoped to see them, too."

"They're talking with the ladies, trying to secure acceptance for the dances. I'll take you to them—if it's all right with your husband."

Samuel appeared unfazed by that ill-natured tone. "You appear to be in good hands for the moment," he told Cassie, "so I'll excuse myself. I see an old acquaintance."

Surprised, Cassie watched as his tall, handsome form vanished into the throng of guests. "I didn't think he knew anyone here."

"He's not just a businessman, he's a moneylender," Walt said flatly, guiding her through the crowd. "Firth knows more than one gentleman here. Fellows who are down on their luck at the tables and desperately in need of cash. He charges them an exorbitant amount of interest."

Cassie turned a reproachful frown on her cousin. "Have you been investigating my husband?"

Walt's cheeks took on a dull flush that only made his unfortunate spots darker red. "Don't be angry," he said defensively. "I asked around, that's all. Several gentlemen have gone to debtors' prison because Firth refused them an extension on their loans."

Lady Stokeford hadn't told Cassie *that*. But perhaps she shouldn't be surprised. After all, Samuel had lent money to her father, with *her* as collateral.

Pushing away that painful memory, Cassie sipped her champagne. Then an abhorrent thought struck her. Could she use this to get Samuel's signature on the deed of separation? "Is it illegal to lend money to gamblers?"

"Not really," Walt mumbled. "But dash it all, it's ungentlemanly to send a fellow to the dungeon for an unpaid debt."

"Those *gentlemen* were foolish to gamble in the first place. And if Samuel lends them money, then they've an obligation to repay him or suffer the consequences."

"Still, you defend him. You're devoted to the fellow." Walt aimed morose hazel eyes at her. "You didn't talk this way before he returned to England. You had nothing good to say about him at all."

Cassie flushed to remember her prior opinion. "I know Samuel better now. He isn't a monster. He can be a kind, thoughtful man. If you'd take the time to know him, too, you'd realize that." She couldn't tell him about Hannah Davenport or Mick. If Samuel wanted to keep his secrets, it wasn't her place to betray him.

Walt lifted a skeptical sandy brow, but he merely said, "At least you have funds now. Empty pockets can be tiresome."

"Oh, Walt, if you need money, do let me help you—"

"Nay, I'll not be supported by Firth. What sort of fellow do you take me for? But you . . . you deserve all your fancy clothes and fine jewels." Then his gaze alighted on the diamond serpent. "I say, didn't that brooch belong to Aunt Helen?"

Cassie touched it self-consciously, running her fingertip over the curved shape. "You remember it?"

"Dash it, Cass, I'm only a year younger than you. I saw Aunt Helen wear it to church once." He flashed her a boyish grin. "I spent the entire service imagining it coming to life and slithering down to the floor to frighten all the girls."

She laughed. "Shame on you for being so irreverent."

At that moment, a thick-set man in the garb of a gentleman obstructed their path. His bald head was nestled in his stiff white collar like a boiled egg in a cup.

He nodded at Walt. "Your Grace," he said in a gravelly voice. "Do me a good turn and introduce me to the lady."

Walt grudgingly complied. "Lady Cassandra Firth, may I present the Earl of Eastwick."

"So you're the bride that Firth bought," the earl said, looking her up and down as if she were a prime mare on display at Tattersall's. "Your maiden name was Grey, was it not? Lady Cassandra Grey."

Though the ballroom was warm, a chill scurried through her. Was he the one? "Yes, it was."

Lord Eastwick's face settled into a satisfied grin. "Then I've won the wager, by gad. I knew you were Helen's daughter—you look the very spit of her. Come over here and tell Pangborn and Nellingham who you are." He nodded at a group of men who laughed raucously and ogled the women.

Lord Eastwick reached for Cassie's arm, but Walt blocked him. "You should know better than to involve a lady in your wagers."

The big man curled his upper lip. "Namby-pamby schoolboy. When you grow up, mayhap we'll let you in on some of our games."

As he ambled away, Cassie held on to her cousin's arm to keep him from charging after the earl. Walt's red-tipped ears and clenched fists displayed his temper.

"Dash it, leave go of me. I'll plant him a facer for insulting you."

And for insulting Walt's tender pride. "You can't start a brawl in the midst of a party," she said, keeping a firm grip on his arm. "You'll have yourself tossed out."

"Huh. It'd be worth the satisfaction. The fellow's a gamester of the worst ilk. Promise me you'll stay clear of him and his sort."

"That goes without saying." Yet a morbid curiosity overruled her distaste. How well had Lord Eastwick known her mother? Could he tell stories about the duchess's reign as queen of society?

Walt looked ahead, through the hordes of guests. "Oh, there's those two rascals now. Bertie's too shy to speak, but Philip has his sights set on the incomparable Miss Harris."

At one end of the ballroom, gilt chairs had been provided as a gathering place for the chaperones and their charges.

Gentlemen milled around the young ladies like bees to nectar. The older matrons sat and chatted among themselves while keeping a close guard on the girls.

Cassie spied Bertie's gangly form at the rear, while the more verbose Philip stood talking with an uncommonly pretty, dark-haired girl in a white gauze gown that lent her the aspect of a goddess. Beside her, Philip looked like a tulip in a pale pink coat and leaf green breeches, his brown hair artistically rumpled.

"Oh, here's Cassie now," Philip said, waving her over. "She helps out one afternoon a week at the Hampton Lending Library. She'll know the answer to your question."

He introduced the beauteous Miss Harris, and her friend, Lady Alice, a rather plump girl with a mass of shiny brown hair and a cheery smile.

"What will I know?" Cassie asked.

"Dear Alice has been telling me about a new novel for ladies," Miss Harris confided. "She says it's positively delicious. But when I went to the bookstore this afternoon, they'd completely sold out of it."

"I vow, 'tis the best book I've read in years!" Lady Alice said. "There's a dashing pirate and an abduction and lots of exciting adventures."

A lightning bolt struck Cassie, riveting her to the floor. "A new book?" she asked, her throat dry. "What—what is the title?"

Lady Alice giggled. "Oh, how silly of me not to have said. It's called *The Black Swan* and it's by a new author named Lady Vanderly."

The earth shifted beneath Cassie's feet. She gripped her champagne glass and tried not to show her shock. Her book was already on sale? With all the upheaval in her life she had nearly forgotten. And just as Mr. Quinnell had predicted, *The Black Swan* was well on its way to being a success!

A part of her rejoiced with pride to hear praise from a reader, while another part sank with dread at the consequences. If these ladies were already talking about the book, then others would be, as well.

She realized that Miss Harris was speaking to her. "I simply *must* get my hands on my very own copy," the girl said fretfully. "Mr. Uppingham was kind enough to suggest that you might know how to do so."

"I'm—I'm afraid I've been out of town for a few days. But you might try at some other bookstores. Or contact the publisher directly."

"What a brilliant notion," Miss Harris said, awarding Cassie a smile. "I'll do so first thing tomorrow."

"I shall have to read this excellent work myself," Philip said, directing his fervent gaze at Miss Harris. "Perhaps next week, I could call on you. We could discuss it."

Cassie felt a wry amusement in the midst of her anxiety. She knew too well Philip's true opinion of romantic fiction. That was why she had never admitted the truth to the men in her literary group.

A matron with a multitude of chins who was sitting behind the girls leaned forward and said with a sniff, "*I* know of no Lady Vanderly—it must be her pen name. And I, for one, should like to know who she really is. The impertinence of the female, to pretend to be one of us."

"Perhaps she *is* one of us, Mama," Miss Harris said. "Alice said she knew quite a lot about good manners and the *ton.*"

"Oh, I just had a marvelous thought," Lady Alice squealed, clapping her hands. "Perhaps Lady Vanderly is here tonight!"

Miss Harris gasped. Ignoring Philip, she and Lady Alice studied the crowd as if hoping to spot a lady wielding a quill pen and a sheaf of foolscap.

A sense of doom shrouded Cassie, and she curled her fingers into her palm. Her glove hid the ink stains, but she felt exposed nonetheless. She feared it was only a matter of time before she was unmasked.

And if anyone noticed a resemblance between the dashing pirate and Samuel, she might as well dive into the icy brine like Belinda.

"I want a word with you, Jamison."

Samuel cornered the older man in the foyer, where he stood in conversation with several other gentlemen. Suave in dark blue, Andrew Jamison looked none too pleased at the summons. He compressed his lips into a thin line and excused himself from the circle.

His frosty gray eyes speared Samuel. "If I may remind you, Firth, I'm no longer in your employ."

Jamison's aristocratic disdain made Samuel grind his teeth. But he had more important matters on his mind. He had to find out what Jamison knew about the death of Hector Babbage. "We'll speak in private."

He stalked down the corridor, and Jamison had the good sense to accompany him. The solicitor looked perfect as always, his salt-and-pepper hair neatly combed and his stately aura worn like a mantle of nobility. Samuel hadn't been surprised to spot Jamison here. As the second son of a viscount, he'd be invited to these parties, despite his common profession.

The deed of separation had proved Samuel's mistake in trusting Jamison. But had that been a fatal error?

He veered through a doorway and into a sumptuous dining parlor. Two footmen were fussing over the place settings, straightening a glass here and a fork there. At a glower from Samuel, both servants scuttled out and shut the door.

"I trust this matter concerns Lady Cassandra," Jamison said in the reproachful tone of an outraged father. "I understand you took her out of town for a week."

Did everyone know his private business? "It's no damned concern of yours what I do with my wife. And who the hell told you, anyway?"

"I called at the Stokeford house a few days ago. I spoke with her companion, Mrs. Woodruff."

The news fed the furnace of Samuel's temper. "I warned you to stay away from my wife."

"I needed to visit Mrs. Woodruff regarding a legal matter."

Liar. He'd wanted to see Cassie. "You're in love with my wife. Will you deny that?"

Jamison's gaze shifted slightly, betraying the truth.

The tension in Samuel exploded. He seized the solicitor by his perfect white cravat and shoved him against the wall of the dining room. Crystal clinked on a nearby sideboard. "Where were you early this afternoon?"

Jamison's nostrils flared. He twisted, trying in vain to break Samuel's hold. "I wasn't anywhere near your wife."

"Answer my question, dammit."

"I was at my office, then out to luncheon with a client. Leave go of me now."

Samuel tightened his grip. "Who? Will this person testify to that fact?"

"Certainly! But I needn't explain myself to you."

That haughty tone incensed Samuel. "The hell you don't. Did you murder Hector Babbage?"

Jamison stopped struggling and stood paralyzed. His gray eyes widened, then narrowed on Samuel's face. In a tone of disbelief, he said hoarsely, "Babbage . . . dead? How . . . what happened?"

His manner conveyed shock and incredulity, and either he was blameless—or he was an excellent actor.

Samuel slowly loosed his hold and stepped back. The horrifying death scene still resonated in him. He had spent the afternoon interviewing witnesses, but everyone had been just as shocked as he was. No stranger had been seen lurking about the building. Tomorrow, he would finish the interrogations, starting with the night watchman as he came off duty.

After examining the damning results of the audit, he had concluded that only one man could have stolen the money—Babbage himself.

But although all the indicators pointed to suicide, Samuel had reason to believe it had been a setup.

It had to have been.

Intimidation, however, would achieve nothing. Better to convince Jamison he'd been let off the hook and then see if he could be tripped up.

"Babbage fell from the roof of my building," Samuel said tersely. "The watchman called it suicide. But I'm convinced he was pushed."

"Pushed? Good God . . . why?"

"Embezzlement." The word tasted sour, and he controlled another surge of anger. "Over the past fortnight, Babbage conducted an audit, and it proved my suspicions correct. Someone's been stealing from my company."

Jamison adjusted his cravat. "Who's the thief? Look there for your murderer."

"It isn't so simple. There were small amounts taken from every department, spread out over the past two years. It was done very cleverly. In fact, I've every reason to believe Babbage himself stole the money."

"You're making no sense, then. He must have taken his own life, perhaps out of remorse or guilt." Jamison ran his fingers through his hair, mussing the brown and gray strands. "I would never have believed it of him, though. He seemed to be such a quiet, ordinary fellow."

Samuel had thought so, too, and a sense of betrayal gnawed at him. At least the accountant hadn't been married and had left no family to mourn him.

Samuel focused on Jamison, watching him closely. "I

believe he had an accomplice. Someone who pushed him off the building out of fear that Babbage meant to confess the truth to me."

The solicitor stared. "What? Did someone actually *see* him being pushed?"

"No, but he had a deathly fear of heights. He had a ground-floor office. He seldom went upstairs."

That was the crux of the matter. That, and the attempt on Samuel's life. A gentleman in the guise of a dockworker had deliberately loosed that runaway cask at the docks. According to Mick, the perpetrator had not been Babbage.

"Such a fear doesn't prove he had an accomplice," Jamison scoffed. "If a man knows his crime is about to be discovered, he might well act out of character. I've seen enough court cases to know that."

Samuel leaned against the wall, keeping his gaze on Jamison, who paced back and forth. "Then explain why he didn't choose another method—poison perhaps, or hanging himself."

"He may have acted on the spur of the moment. Remorse overcame him, so he chose the most convenient way out of his pain."

If only Samuel could believe that. "Over the past few years, you've spent a good deal of time at my offices."

Jamison stopped to glower at him. "So have a hundred other men. Circumstantial evidence will get you nowhere in a court of law."

His stiff bearing, his reddened cheeks, his steely stare all spoke of offended pride rather than secret guilt. But Samuel had been around enough thespians in his youth to know that reactions could be feigned. And he might do better to keep Jamison off guard. "You're quite right," he said smoothly. "If indeed you're innocent, perhaps you'll agree to help me."

"Help you?"

"You know the men in my office. Have you had any thoughts on who might have helped Babbage steal the money?"

Jamison eyed him coolly for a moment. "No, but give me some time to think about the matter. I'll do what I can to assist—for Babbage's sake, not yours."

The two men stood in the aisle of the church, their rapiers at the ready. But ere the first ringing blow could be struck, the stout vicar rushed at the pirate with his prayer book held out like a shield.

"This is a house of God," he cried. "Begone from here!"

As any man of conscience would do, Mr. Montcliff lowered his sword.

But not Percival Cranditch. Taking swift advantage of the distraction, he struck out with his blade. And while I watched in horror, my bridegroom clutched his chest and sank senseless to the floor.

—The Black Swan

Chapter 21

Rose Among Thorns

Cassie enjoyed the dancing more than she'd expected, considering her state of tension. The men were lined up on one side, the ladies on the other. Concentrating on the graceful, complicated steps kept the problem of her book at bay. With the chandeliers shedding golden light and the orchestra playing, she could even tolerate the company of yet another of her mother's former admirers.

The aging but handsome Sir Lyle Upshaw made the picture of a dandy in a tailored coat of golden brown, undoubtedly designed to match his equally golden brown eyes and golden brown hair. Strong cheekbones and a jutting jaw gave him an air of distinction worthy of a fictitious hero.

He was also a dead bore.

Several times, she had caught him preening in the mirrored walls, watching his own elegant moves. In the occasional moments when the dance steps brought them together, he could speak only of his role as the arbiter of fashion.

But at that moment, he startled her by raising a gold quizzing glass to peer at her bosom. "I say, is that a diamond snake you're wearing?"

Cassie tensed. Did he know the brooch had belonged to her mother? In accordance with the dance, she twirled around him, trying to read that avid expression. "Yes. Why do you ask?"

"I had the most brilliant inspiration. It would look smashing pinned to my crown."

"Your crown." Her imagination conjured a very odd picture of Sir Lyle with the brooch pinned to his head.

"It's my name for this design. It's one of my many original creations." He lovingingly stroked his elaborate neckcloth. "These young pups learn a simple waterfall and think they're all the rage. But *I* know one hundred and twenty-three ways to tie a cravat. Not even Brummel himself could lay that claim."

"Extraordinary," Cassie murmured, swallowing the impulse to laugh. Perhaps she'd include a comic character modeled on Sir Lyle in her next book. Then the dancers switched partners and she found herself paired with a young man too timid to meet her gaze.

So instead she scanned the crowd for Samuel's tall, dark-haired form. He had danced only once with her, leading her in the first waltz with his hand at her waist and his blue eyes alive with fire. But except for the possessive heat in his look, he had been reserved and distant, and he'd frustrated her by immediately going off to speak to another acquaintance.

She couldn't imagine who could be more important than his wife. Especially when he had insisted on their bargain to introduce him to society. Thus far, she had introduced him to no one at all, so apparently he had needed her only to secure the invitation. That realization made her feel neglected—and irked.

Then she spied a man who made her blood run cold.

Charles Woodruff.

The short, husky man stood by a pillar and watched Cassie intently. His curled lip and narrowed gaze radiated resentment. While she and Samuel had been away at Strathmore Castle, Mr. Jamison had called on Flora. He had related the encouraging results of his letter to Charles's father. Apparently the Reverend Norman Woodruff had withdrawn his vile plan to challenge Flora's separation papers.

Was Charles merely disgruntled at losing his bid at blackmail? Or was he hatching some other wicked scheme?

The progress of the dance moved her from his view, and when the music stopped at last, she stood at the opposite end of the ballroom from Charles. She left Sir Lyle to his self-admiration, but instead of returning to the matrons' corner where Walt awaited her, she escaped through the crowd to the staircase hall with only one thought in mind.

To find Samuel.

The casement clock showed half past eleven. It was early yet by standards of the *ton,* but she'd had enough of smiling at strangers and making small talk and enduring stares. She wanted to be home with her husband, to scold him for abandoning her and then coax him to forgive her for their earlier quarrel. She would use all of her wiles, all of the skills he had taught her, to lure him back into her bed . . .

"Lady Cassanda Grey?"

The respectful voice spoke from behind her. Rattled to hear her maiden name, she whirled around, bracing herself for an encounter with another of her mother's old friends. But it was a young footman in blue livery and a white wig.

"I'm Lady Cassandra," she said.

"A gentleman asked me to convey this to you." The footman handed her a single red rose along with a folded piece of expensive stationery sealed with a wafer.

She looked down to see her maiden name printed in familiar block letters. Her heart took a tumble. "What man? Can you tell me—"

But the footman had already walked away, his stiff uniformed figure vanishing into the multitude of guests.

Clutching the note and the flower, she glanced around in the vain hope that her secret admirer stood watching. But she could see no one in particular paying attention to her.

Cassie hurried down a corridor and found a secuded alcove with a Grecian statue on a pedestal. By the light of a flickering wall sconce, she unfolded the paper and scanned the brief message.

My Dearest Lady,

You are a rose among thorns. If you would meet the man who loves you as he loved your mother, come out to the rose garden at midnight.

* * *

Samuel scoured the ballroom for his wife. A confusion of people milled about, the guests pairing off for the supper that was scheduled for midnight. He couldn't see Cassie anywhere in the crowd.

He regretted having neglected her for so long. He had waltzed with her once, then left her in the care of her cousin again. Babbage's murder had been topmost in his mind, and he hadn't been able to forget the attempt on his own life, either. It seemed to point to the fact that Babbage's accomplice bore a grudge against Samuel, too.

Several gentlemen here had owed him debts at one time or another, so he had sought them out and asked discreet questions of them, attempting to assess their guilt. But his efforts had proven fruitless.

Then, while in the drawing room, he'd been pulled into a game of cards by the laconic Earl of Ravenhill and the jovial Lord Manfred Baxter, two old friends of Michael Kenyon.

"So you're Stokeford's long-lost brother," Baxter had said, pumping Samuel's hand in a firm grip. "The damned reprobate told us about you the last time he was in London."

"Reprobate, bah," scoffed Lord Ravenhill. "Vivien might have something to say about that description."

"We've all suffered the leg shackle," Baxter said with a laugh. "You too, Firth. Come and commiserate with us."

To Samuel's guarded surprise, he'd liked the men. He'd enjoyed trading barbs with them, drinking whiskey and smoking cheroots. It was a male camaraderie that he'd missed in his travels and his devotion to work. He'd left with Ravenhill's invitation that he and Cassie join them for dinner next week, along with Baxter and his wife.

Samuel had fit in well with Stokeford's friends. One might say he had stepped right into his elder brother's place. He should feel a sense of triumph. But all he felt was . . .

The need to see Cassie. The desire to hold her in his arms. The hunger to make love to her and blot out the horror of Babbage's death.

Not even that promise she'd extracted from him seemed important anymore. It only made his plan of getting her pregnant more crucial. By God, he'd prove to her that he wasn't like his sire, that he wouldn't walk away from his own child as George Kenyon had done.

Near the arched doorway, he spied her cousin chatting with a plump debutante. Without apology, he interrupted them. "Chiltern. Have you seen Cassie?"

A guilty flush spreading over his pockmarked face, Walt shook his head. "Not since Lyle Upshaw took her off to dance over half an hour ago. I—I suppose I should have looked for her, but . . . I was about to escort Lady Alice in to supper."

His lovelorn glance fell unheeded on Lady Alice, who

had been flirting outrageously with him only a moment ago but now stared at Samuel as if mesmerized. "Sir," she said in an almost reverent tone. "You look so like a pirate . . ." Then she blushed. "Oh, do forgive me, I'm prattling."

Over the years, Samuel had been the recipient of many looks from women, but this was too much. Walt already looked livid, and he didn't want to antagonize the poor lad. "Never mind, I'll find Cassie myself."

He strode away toward the dining room, but failed to locate her in the orderly lines of guests who were filling their china plates with lobster and caviar and other delicacies.

Dammit, where could she have gone? Didn't she have the sense to know that he wouldn't allow any other man to escort her into supper? This wasn't a formal dinner where protocol would require she sit apart from him.

Maybe she'd felt deserted and had slipped off somewhere by herself. It would be just like her to be off in an empty room reading a book. She had been so shy about talking with strangers . . .

Guilt gnawed at him. He hadn't planned on playing cards for so long with Ravenhill and Baxter. But the time had slipped away. Cassie would be miffed, and he'd have to grovel to make up for his neglect. Then he would take her home and entice her into bed.

If only he could find her.

Cassie sat down on a stone bench and reached down to remove her dancing slipper. She gave it a shake, and a pebble struck the graveled pathway with a tiny clink.

Absently rubbing the sole of her foot where the stone had scraped it, she shivered from more than the cool night air. Lanterns had been strung through the tree branches, creating small pools of light in the shadows. The gardens covered quite a large area for a house that was located in the middle of the city. The sound of music and laughter drifted from the house.

She had ventured out here expecting to find other guests strolling the concentric pathways. There would be safety in numbers. But apparently everyone had gone back inside for supper.

There was no one around. At least no one she could *see*.

Keeping her gaze sharp for any movement in the gloom, Cassie replaced the slipper on her foot. She felt uneasy, already regretting her decision to meet the man who had sent her those cryptic letters. But he had given her the diamond serpent, a treasured memento of her mother. She was curious to know how he had acquired it, for surely the duchess wouldn't have given away an expensive piece of jewelry—unless she had loved him.

The thought nauseated Cassie. Was he the reason the duchess had preferred society to her own daughter? Had her mother carried on an affair with him?

The darkness seemed to close in on Cassie. She mustn't wait out here any longer. There was something sinister about a man who had kept his identity so well hidden, who revealed bits of information clearly designed to intrigue her. In his first two letters, he had proclaimed his love for her, and only today had he revealed a relationship with her mother, too.

Rising from the bench, Cassie turned her gaze to the safe haven of the house, the windows glowing. Guests mingled upstairs in the supper room, and she belonged there with them. She had been foolish to come out here alone, to be swayed by her longing to know more about her mother.

Cassie started down the pathway. At the same moment, the tall figure of a man filled the doorway of the porch, a black outline against the golden candlelight.

Her heart lurched. Was it him—her secret admirer?

Then he stepped outside and realization hit her. She knew that confident walk, that broad form. *Samuel.*

Relief poured through her veins and weakened her knees. Anxious for his company, she started toward him. Then a shadow moved.

In the bushes that rimmed the porch, the dark shape of a man rose from a crouching position.

The faint glow from one of the hanging lamps glinted on something metallic in his hand. Something he pointed up at Samuel.

A gun?

She screamed. And three things happened all at once.

A flash of light. A loud report. Samuel fell.

Without a thought to my own safety, I rushed to Mr. Montcliff's side, aghast to see the stain of blood on his wedding raiment. But no sooner had I knelt beside my guardian than Captain Cranditch sheathed his sword and strode forward. Tall and threatening, he towered over me, his fierce features alive with triumph. He held out his black-gloved hand to me.

"Come, my lady. You're mine now."

—The Black Swan

Chapter 22

CONFESSIONS

Instinctively, Samuel dropped to the floor of the porch. His hands met the cold stone paving. The bullet whistled past him, too close for comfort.

From across the darkened gardens, he caught a glimpse of Cassie, scurrying toward him, a slim, pale ghost in the gloom. He shouted, "Stay back!"

He leaped off the porch and onto the graveled path. Right beside the place where he'd spied the man with the gun only seconds ago.

The bushes were empty now. From the corner of his eye, he saw a movement at the corner of the long porch.

The black shape of a man burst out of the shrubbery and raced toward the rear of the garden.

Samuel dashed to the right to cut him off. Pebbles flew from beneath his feet. The man had to be heading for the gate, a dark rectangle in the stone fence. When he glanced over his shoulder at Samuel, he made a hasty left and darted into the stables adjacent to the carriage house.

The place looked as dark as sin. The staff would be out front, socializing with the other coachmen and grooms.

Samuel paused only long enough to seize a lantern from one of the trees. Then he rushed into the building and looked around. He stood at a T, with corridors to his right and left and stalls straight ahead.

A few horses poked out their curious heads. Except for the scrape of hooves and a few snufflings, the place was silent.

The squawk of hinges came from his right. He sped in that direction, down the corridor, going through a doorway that led into the mews behind the property. The stench of rubbish and horse droppings hung in the chilly night air. He caught sight of his quarry running through the shadows at the end of the alley.

That furtive form vanished around the corner.

Samuel lunged in pursuit. When he reached the side street, he met a maze of carriages and coaches, their teams of horses patiently waiting for the end of the ball. Here and there, the coachmen and grooms gathered in groups, chatting and laughing, having their own party. Several men loudly played fiddles and fifes, masking the sound of that shot back in the garden.

Holding up the lantern, Samuel started in the direction the man had gone. But the patter of light footsteps came from behind him.

He turned to see Cassie hastening to his side, her face pale and drawn with anxiety in the light of the lantern. She launched herself at him, her arms going around him, her cheek pressed to his coat. "Samuel!"

For one mad moment, he allowed himself to hold her close and rejoice in her safety. He was acutely aware of her slender form, her vulnerability. That thought made him put her firmly away. "Dammit, I told you to stay behind. You could be hurt."

"*You* could be hurt." She ran her fingers over his arms and up to his face, caressing him as if his welfare mattered to her. A tremor in her voice, she went on. "I saw you fall. I thought you'd been shot!"

"I didn't fall. I ducked." Glancing over his shoulder at the darkened street and the labyrinth of carriages, he battled a fierce frustration. She had ruined any hope he had of tracking his assailant. "Come along. I'll take you home."

"But shouldn't we find the gunman?"

"There's no *we* about it. And I can't go after him now."

He steered her down the street, toward the lights of the front doorway and away from danger. Instead of peppering him with questions, Cassie fell silent, no doubt suffering from the shock of the shooting.

She probably believed the fellow was a ruffian bent on robbery.

It was tempting to allow her that illusion, but he didn't dare. She had to be warned. Horror gripped his gut. If she had been standing closer to him in the garden, she might have taken the bullet meant for him.

He had no choice but to tell her the truth.

As Samuel stepped into their coach and shut the door, Cassie knew she had to tell him the truth. He seated himself opposite her, his face a frosty mask in the dim light of the flickering lamp. He was still furious with her for coming after him. Her presence had prevented him from giving chase to the gunman.

Her secret admirer.

With a gently rocking motion and a familiar clopping of hooves, the coach started off for home. She felt chilled and sickened and in desperate need of Samuel's comfort. But he had shut her out again, and perhaps it was a fitting punishment for her mistake.

She couldn't forget the terrible sight of seeing him fall. Of believing him dead—even if only for a moment.

Cassie squeezed her eyes shut, trying to make sense of

the nightmare. She had been lured out to the garden not for a simple meeting, but for a far more deadly purpose. The man who had written those letters must have guessed that Samuel would come in search of her. All along, he had wanted to kill her husband. Her secret admirer must be a madman who believed he could win her for himself.

And oh, dear God, her rash behavior had almost cost Samuel his life.

Tears threatened, but she held them back, opening her eyes to view his grim features. She laced her fingers together so tightly they hurt. And she forced herself to speak.

"Samuel, I've a confession to make—"

"I've something to tell you—"

They both spoke at the same time. Samuel held up his hand to stop her. "Wait. This is very important. The gunman wasn't intent on robbery. His sole purpose was to kill me."

She stared in confusion. How had Samuel found out? Before going to the garden, she had torn the letter into little bits and stuck the red rose into an arrangement of flowers in the corridor. There was no way he could have known . . .

Unless he'd looked in her desk again. While she was downstairs waiting for him to change his clothes earlier in the evening, he could have gone into her chamber and found the note that had been enclosed with the diamond serpent. But why had he said nothing until now?

"So you know?" she murmured. "About my secret admirer?"

Samuel's sharp blue eyes pinned her. "What are you talking about?"

"The reason I went out to the garden. At the ball, a footman gave me another message from the man who's been writing to me. He asked me to meet him outside." At the raw shock on his face, she felt her stomach clench. "Isn't that what you meant?"

Samuel leaned forward and seized her wrist in a tight

grip. "Do you mean to say that a man has been writing you anonymous love letters? And you went to meet him?"

The savagery of his expression frightened her. "It isn't what it seems," she said quickly. "He knew my mother. He said he'd loved her. And that he loved me, too—he was watching over me."

"Watching you?" he snapped. "Since when?"

"Since the day you returned to England."

"And you didn't see fit to tell me? God!" Samuel released her hand abruptly, as if he couldn't bear to touch her. "Instead, you went out there tonight for a rendezvous with a stranger. *Alone.* How could you be so foolish?"

Cassie's throat tightened and her eyes prickled with incipient tears. She felt naïve and remorseful and utterly stupid. "I—I thought there would be other people around, strolling the gardens. I'm not accustomed to these balls, and I didn't know everyone would go in to supper at once."

"He chose his time well, that's certain. And then he waited in the bushes until I came looking for you. As he knew I would." With a violence that shocked her, Samuel slammed his fist down on the cushion. "Dammit, it *has* to be connected. It *has* to be the same man."

"What man?"

His eyes narrowed on her. The light of the flickering lamp on the wall of the coach cast half of his face in harsh shadow. "Someone has been embezzling money from my company," he said tersely. "That's what I was about to tell you. I ordered an audit a fortnight ago, and today, my chief accountant was found dead. He was murdered."

A chill of disbelief raised the fine hairs at the nape of her neck. Cassie couldn't fully absorb what he was suggesting. "But . . . how could a man who knew my mother . . . who wrote those letters to *me* . . . also be stealing from your firm?"

"I don't know, but I intend to find out. It can't possibly be a coincidence." Blowing out a breath, Samuel bent his head, running his fingers through his hair in an expression of abject frustration. When he looked up again, his expression was harsh, unforgiving. "You kept his letters, I trust. Perhaps I'll recognize the penmanship."

"He disguised it, I'm afraid. All of his notes were printed in block letters as a child might do. As if he were trying to hide his identity because *I* might know his handwriting. Oh, and he addressed them to my maiden name."

Samuel cursed through his teeth. "That means he could very well be someone you know. Were there any clues in the letters? Do you have any idea at all who he might be?"

"No, but I wanted to find out, that's why I went to meet him. I—I wanted to speak to someone who had known the duchess and . . . loved her." Cassie swallowed hard, touched the diamond serpent pinned to her bodice, and confessed, "He gave me this brooch, Samuel. It came by post. It was there on my desk, all wrapped up, when we returned from Strathmore today."

"You're wearing his *jewelry*?" Her husband's rage was palpable, a living entity in the close confines of the coach.

"This piece belonged to my mother, I remember it clearly! He asked me to wear it tonight . . . as a sign that I wished to meet him."

"So you did as he requested. Dammit, Cass! Next time, ask my advice on the matter!"

The cold censure in his voice ripped into her heart. His fury, his disgust, was too much to bear, especially after their quarrel that morning. The tears she'd been repressing spilled freely down her cheeks. "You were so angry at me today. I couldn't tell you. I just *couldn't*."

Her voice caught, and she buried her face in her hands as misery swallowed her. A part of her was appalled at the raw outburst of emotion. She *never* cried, *never* lost control, at least not since Samuel had left her after their wedding. But now, nothing could stop the flood of anguish inside her.

Samuel uttered a groan and moved to her side of the coach. Taking Cassie in his arms, he tucked her against his chest while he stroked her hair. He held her tightly while she sobbed, his embrace fierce—as if he wanted to absorb all her heartache into himself.

His lips brushed her brow. In a rough, strained voice, he muttered, "Cassie . . . darling . . . don't weep. Please don't. I'm sorry—for everything. I shouldn't have spoken so harshly."

"No, *I'm* sorry," she said, burrowing into him and fearing he only meant to be kind. "He could have killed you. And it would have been all my fault." That thought brought a fresh flow of tears, the shame at what she had caused by her own foolishness.

"It would *not* have been your fault." Samuel's voice was stern as he brought out his handkerchief and dabbed her cheeks. "My God, you had no notion of his purpose. How could you? But promise me . . . don't ever, ever do anything like that again."

"I won't, believe me, I won't." She drew a shaky breath, fighting to regain control, yet consumed by anxiety for Samuel.

Who would plan such a terrible scheme to shoot her husband at a party? To write those letters to her, to use her as bait to lure him outside? To attempt murder?

A memory assailed her. Her eyes widened on his rugged features through the dim light from the coach lamp. "Oh, dear heaven," she said faintly. "There was another attempt on your life. Mick told me about it. He said a cask of wine rolled toward you at the docks, but he pushed you out of the way. I thought he was making it all up."

Samuel grimaced. "Mick talks too much. Don't let it worry you."

Sick with dread, Cassie ran her fingers over his cheek,

savoring its roughness and warmth, his vitality. "Not worry? This man . . . he's going to try again. I fear it."

Samuel framed her face with his hands, his thumbs wiping away the last of her tears. "I'm going to find him," he stated confidently. "You may assure yourself of that."

She felt assured of nothing. Both times, the assailant had come close to killing Samuel. And the man *had* succeeded with the accountant at Samuel's office.

Dear God, she couldn't think of that, she must concentrate on uncovering his identity. "If he knew my mother, then you'll need my help."

"Only with information," Samuel clarified. "You're to stay close to home until this is resolved. Is that understood?"

She curled her fingers around his arm. "The threat isn't to me, it's to *you.*"

"And you're close to me, which puts you at risk. You're not to interfere with my investigation. That's final."

Cassie kept her objections to herself. But she fully intended to assist in any way that presented itself. "You'll want to know about all the men I met tonight."

"Particularly if he showed any interest in the brooch. There's Colonel Mainwaring, for one." Samuel's lips formed a flat line of repressed anger. "He was staring at your breasts—but maybe also at the diamond serpent."

"Perhaps you should return to the ball, see if he's still there." Cassie only reluctantly voiced the thought, for she didn't want to let Samuel out of her sight.

Thankfully, he shook his head. "At this point, it wouldn't prove much one way or another. Too much time has passed. He could have departed on a pretext or doubled back and rejoined the party. Now who else?"

"There was the Earl of Eastwick," she said, remembering his oxlike form and coarse nature. "He approached me while I was talking to Walt."

Samuel scowled. "Eastwick! Dammit, he's a reprobate of the worst ilk. What did he say to you?"

"He'd made a wager that I was the duchess's daughter. He wanted me to come and prove it to his friends, but Walt sent him away."

"It seems Walt has a good head on his shoulders, after all. I'll be sure to interview Eastwick."

Cassie dutifully listed a few other men—and some ladies—who had remembered her mother. But none of them had paid any particular attention to the diamond serpent.

"And then there was Sir Lyle Upshaw. He noticed the brooch while we were dancing." Remembering his vanity, she managed a wry smile. "But he's a true coxcomb, and I can't imagine him crouching in a bush and firing a gun. He might ruin his perfect cravat."

Samuel's harsh expression softened subtly. A hot intensity burned in his blue eyes. With his fingertips, he traced her lips in a feather-light caress. "Now there's my girl. You're smiling again."

Just like that, the atmosphere in the coach altered, becoming charged with sensuality. Her hand lay on his chest, and Cassie felt the strong beating of his heart. With every breath, she inhaled the unique scent of him. Their closeness triggered a tingle of desire that spread through every part of her body. It was as if they were back at Strathmore Castle again.

Perhaps all they'd needed to bridge their rift was to touch again. And if an embrace could make him forget their differences, only think of what a kiss could do.

She cupped his face in her palms and brought his head down to hers. He responded at once, penetrating her mouth in a deep, savoring kiss that made the world fall away, leaving only the two of them. His hands cradled her breasts, stroking her through the barrier of her bodice. Passion surged through her veins, giving rise to the desperate need for fulfillment.

"Samuel," she murmured in between kisses. "I need you.

So much." Sliding her hand down his body, she found his engorged length pressed against his breeches. She wanted to take all that heat and hardness inside of herself, to be one with him. With a shiver of pure desire, she reached for his buttons.

He groaned, catching her fingers and staying their action. "Wait . . . we're almost home."

Indeed, the coach turned a corner and brought them to a halt in front of the Stokeford town house. Samuel was breathing hard, as if he'd been running, and she felt the same, starved for air, starved for *him.* He helped her out of the coach, the perfect gentleman except for his eyes, which glittered with fervor. Once inside the house, they hastened upstairs as if a fire nipped at their heels.

"Your room?" she asked.

"No, yours."

Samuel knew it had to be her bed. He wanted her to have memories of wild lovemaking that would keep him uppermost in her thoughts. He wanted her to realize how impossible it would be for her to walk away from him.

A candle burned on the bedside table. As they entered the chamber, he shut the door. They were kissing and touching, already shedding their clothing. Cassie shared his fever, pushing off his coat and letting it fall to the floor, then unbuttoning his waistcoat and breeches. Her lips met whatever spot was handy, his shoulder, his jaw, his chest. He did likewise, kissing her throat and face as he worked at the fastenings of her gown.

He ordered himself to slow down. If it killed him, he would make this a memorable experience for her. He'd always prided himself on his skill with women. He always made it last, built the tension gradually to ensure her full and complete satisfaction.

But tonight his self-control had gone up in smoke. The events of the day had awakened a reckless, driving need in him. He wanted to be inside Cassie *now.*

Stripping off gown and corset and shift, he kissed her

again, a deep, ravenous kiss as he walked her backward to the bed. He kicked off his shoes and breeches, and then tumbled her down onto the edge of the mattress. She lay beneath him like an offering from heaven, her skin flushed with arousal, her breasts full and peaked. She still had her garters and stockings on, and he reached to unfasten them.

But Cassie wouldn't let him. Bracing her feet on the floor, she took him in her hand and guided him to her center. She was hot and wet and ready, and in one strong thrust, he delved inside her, as deeply as he could go. In the next, she was crying out in rapture, clutching at him, her neck arching and her body quivering. Her swift response sent him over the brink himself, a plunge into unending pleasure.

But it did end, and he drifted back to awareness, too sated to move. She sprawled beneath him in utter relaxation, her eyes at half-mast and her arms lying limply at her sides. The soft smile on her face caused a tightness in his chest, a richness of emotion that he didn't care to examine.

He knew only that he wanted to stay right here inside her for the rest of his life. He had no intention of letting her go, regardless of their bargain.

Which meant keeping her in a state of bliss.

He bent down to kiss her lightly, first her lips, then her cheeks, letting his mouth glide over satiny skin. "That was over far too quickly. We'll take it slower next time."

"Mmm." Cassie moved her hips as if enjoying the feel of him inside her. Her hands went on a stimulating trek over his backside. "We have the rest of the night."

He chuckled at her obvious relish. "You're an astonishing woman, did you know that?"

She shook her head, as naïvely unaware of her appeal as ever. "No . . . don't other women enjoy this?"

"Not all of them, I hear. But that isn't what I mean. You should be angry at me for shouting at you. And for deserting you at the party."

Fool. Why had he reminded her of that?

Cassie scooted up on the bed, forcing him to slide out of her. Her face solemn, she picked up a pillow and hugged it. Her hair had come undone, the golden mass cascading around her bare shoulders. "I understand now. You were preoccupied, thinking about that man who'd been murdered. Why didn't you tell me?"

"And ruin your evening? It's not a topic fit for a lady, anyway."

"I don't care about conventions. Someone has threatened your life, and I want to know *everything*. I demand it."

With her chin up and her eyebrow elevated, Cassie looked fiercely autocratic, a lady who knew her power over him. And curse him, he was too susceptible to her to refuse. So he told her about the audit and the embezzlement, and why Hector Babbage must have had an accomplice. At the end, he felt somehow lighter to have shared the burden.

"And you thought *I* was involved," she chided. "That's why you searched my desk."

His mistaken belief seemed foolish now, and he covered his remorse with a shrug. "I didn't know what else to think when I found you in my office."

He braced himself for recriminations, but Cassie let the point drop. She stroked the back of his hand absentmindedly. "Tonight at the ball, you were investigating some men there, weren't you? That's why you deserted me."

"Yes, but don't ask me to elaborate. I won't."

"You didn't know about my secret admirer then. So why would you think Mr. Babbage's accomplice was someone from society? Could he be a man you've sent to debtors' prison?"

He tensed. "Who told you about that?"

"Walt found out. But never mind getting angry at him. If it's the truth, then you mustn't hide it from me."

He fought a battle less against temper than a sense of

reluctance. Moneylending was no cause for shame, and he'd always made certain the man had some means of repayment, usually in the form of property. With her father, the collateral had been Cassie herself.

"Yes," he said curtly, "I did speak to several men. For one reason or another, I had to discount them as suspects. However . . ."

"Yes?"

He didn't want to destroy her illusions, no matter how ill conceived. Nor did he want to turn her against him. Yet for her own protection, he had to reveal the truth. "You're not going to like hearing this, Cass. I also spoke to Andrew Jamison."

"Mr. Jamison? I didn't even realize he was there tonight." She caught her breath in a little gasp. "Does *he* owe you money?"

"No. He doesn't gamble, either. He's a damn model of respectability."

She bristled. "Then why would you suspect him?"

The hot blade of jealousy sank into Samuel. Dammit, he had to make her understand. "He's had extensive dealings with my firm over the years. He knew Babbage and could easily be his accomplice. And he has a powerful reason to want me dead." He paused, aware of a burning resentment in his gut. "He's in love with you, Cassie."

Her face paled. "That's ridiculous. It can't be true."

"Believe it." Wanting both to soothe her and to remind her to whom she belonged, Samuel sifted his fingers through the golden silk of her hair. "Tonight, I asked him straightout, and he didn't deny it."

Cassie gazed at him with shocked blue eyes. Then she let out a breath, gripping the pillow to her middle. "I—I don't know what to say. I haven't encouraged him. He's been . . . like a father to me these past four years."

She looked so distraught that he gave her a brief, tender kiss of penitence. "I won't have him in this house. You won't have any contact with him at all, not until I have the chance to investigate further. Is that clear?"

She bit her lip and slowly nodded. "But he wouldn't kill anyone, Samuel. I just can't see it."

Samuel refrained from arguing the point, keeping his contradictory opinion to himself. Cassie had never experienced the seamier side of the world, and she couldn't know how adeptly a clever criminal could conceal his true nature. "Where are those letters? I want to have a look at them."

Setting the pillow away, Cassie rolled onto her side and pulled open the drawer of the bedside table. The beauty of her lissome form distracted Samuel, and he relished the sight of her slim, bare body stretched out as she reached into the drawer. He couldn't resist gliding his hand up over the curve of her hip and the indentation of her waist, to the feast of her unfettered breasts. The tips beaded to his touch, and she glanced over her shoulder at him, her lips parted and her eyes smoky with desire.

"Samuel?"

That breathy tone tempted him almost beyond hope. With great regret, he pulled his hand back. "The letters first."

She drew out a plain wooden box, opened it, and then handed him three folded papers. By the light of the candle, he read them, each one intensifying the heat of emotion in him. Alarm. Fear. Fury.

Dried rose petals fell out of one, showering the sheets.

" 'The heart that throbs for you.' " His stomach twisted, and with a slap of his palm, he thrust the petals onto the floor. "Dammit, if Jamison wrote this drivel, I'll kill him."

Cassie placed her hands on his arm and held tightly. "He was my guardian for the past four years. Surely if he'd known my mother he would have mentioned it to me."

"And the first letter says this fellow is watching you. It's too perfect a fit to be a coincidence."

She frowned at him, making her disapproval clear. "You're

making up your mind without any real evidence. You've resented Mr. Jamison ever since he drew up the deed of separation. But you mustn't let that color your judgment."

Samuel set the box and the letters on the nightstand. "I'll tell you what colors my judgment. When other men lust after my wife."

He pressed her back against the pillows, covering her with his body. But Cassie put up her hands to keep him from kissing her. "Why are you so jealous? I could never, ever want Mr. Jamison, not like *this*."

A primitive rush of exultation filled Samuel. Slowly, erotically, he moved his hips against hers, determined to make her think only of him. "You'll never want any other man, Cassie."

Her lashes lowered slightly, giving her that mysterious look that enticed and frustrated him. "Then keep me happy," she murmured. "Make me yours."

His body responded instantly to the invitation. But despite his primal urges, he wouldn't hurry, not this time. He kissed her again, a slow, tender kiss that made her sigh. As they stroked and caressed in the semi-darkness, they whispered to each other, light banter that he enjoyed as much as the touching.

Something soft and powerful stirred inside his chest. It wasn't love, it couldn't be. He loved her scent, her smile, her eagerness to explore. But he couldn't love *her*. He wouldn't let himself become like his mother. Love was an obsession, and only a fool would risk that pain.

So he concentrated on the physical, controlling himself and prolonging the passion, even when he was once again buried deeply inside of Cassie. They made love looking into each other's eyes, with an unparalleled pleasure that went on and on.

Afterward, she slept in his arms, her head pillowed on his shoulder and her hair like tumbled strands of gold.

But despite the complete satisfaction of his body, he

couldn't sleep. His mind refused to settle. He couldn't shake the irrational fear that Cassie was in grave danger.

Maybe it wasn't so irrational.

As the candle guttered and died in a pool of wax, Samuel stared into the darkness and thought about who wanted to kill him. There was something about the situation that eluded him, something that lurked at the edge of his consciousness. He couldn't rest until he'd examined the facts from every angle.

The gunman must have had some hold over Babbage. He had found out about the audit and murdered Babbage to keep him from talking. That same man had written those letters to Cassie.

He had known her mother, too. Somehow, he had acquired a piece of the duchess's jewelry.

Samuel kept gnawing at that thought. Had the man stolen the diamond serpent? Or had the duchess given it to him? Had he been her lover?

Had he been with her on the night she had died?

The notion gripped Samuel. As if privy to his racing thoughts, Cassie sighed in her sleep and snuggled closer. Aching with tenderness and dread, he bent down and kissed her hair, holding her close to him and trying to recall exactly what she had told him about the death.

Her mother had been returning late at night from Vauxhall Gardens, on a barge filled with a party of revelers. The duchess had fallen overboard, and although several men had jumped in to save her, she had drowned.

Perhaps the tragedy had not been an accident.

The thought jolted him. His blood turned to ice. God! The duchess might have been murdered.

By the same man who now wrote love letters to Cassie.

"Villain!" I cried. "I will never leave Mr. Montcliff."

A fearsome scowl descended over the face of the pirate captain. He motioned to the vicar, who hovered nearby. "You will marry us at once by special license." He withdrew a paper from inside his coat and shoved it at the cleric.

"It must be a forgery," I said. "No bishop would issue such a document to a man of your ilk."

Even as I challenged him, a noise came from the doors of the church. To my vast relief, the magistrate and a group of village men appeared to save me. Seeing that he was outnumbered, Percival Cranditch roared out his frustration and fled through the door behind the altar.

—The Black Swan

Chapter 23

Reviving Cranditch

The next day, after thinking hard on the matter, Cassie wrote a note to the only man she knew who was despicable enough to commit murder.

Now, she rose gracefully from the chaise in the drawing room, hiding her trepidation behind a polite mask. "Good afternoon, Mr. Woodruff. Thank you for responding so quickly to my invitation."

Charles Woodruff looked the picture of fashion in a blue coat tailored to fit his stocky form and gray breeches that hugged short, thick legs. He removed the top hat from his perfectly groomed flaxen hair. To her disgust, he also wore an oily grin.

"Watched me last night at the ball, did you?" he said,

ogling her now. "I had my eye on you, too, but you disappeared."

When he would have kissed her hand, Cassie folded her arms. She could be courteous for the sake of the investigation, but she drew the line at tolerating his touch. "Do sit down," she said, gesturing at an arrangement of chairs near the fireplace. "As I said in my letter, we never had the chance to talk last night."

"Bother the talk. Let's go upstairs straightaway."

He attempted to slide his arm around her, but she stepped quickly to a chair and sat down. "I'm afraid you've misconstrued my message."

"Why else would you ask me here? Your husband's away at his office, and you want to have an affair with me."

"No, I do not." Cassie spoke firmly and bluntly, knowing that subtlety was wasted on him. The very thought of sharing the private act of love with this man—or any man other than Samuel—filled her with disgust. "And I would like to know how you can be so certain of my husband's whereabouts."

Charles Woodruff cast a furtive, alarmed look at the doorway, as if expecting Samuel to come striding inside at any moment. "*Is* he here?"

Rather than lie, Cassie let him stew. "Sit down," she said again. "I've a few questions I'd like you to answer."

As he took the seat opposite her, his expression turned nasty. "If this has to do with my stepmama, then where the devil is she? Afraid to face me after she ruined my plans? Probably counting the quarterly payments my father is forced to send her."

"This has nothing to do with Flora. And you won't be seeing her." Cassie had given Flora strict orders to remain upstairs. She'd had to tell her friend the bare bones of what had happened, and Flora had been worried and fretful despite Cassie's promise to be careful.

"What is it, then?" Woodruff asked with ill-concealed annoyance. "You're keeping me from a dice game at White's."

He drummed his fingers on the arm of the chair. He didn't look like a man who would write her love letters.

But he had attended the ball last night. He hailed from Lancashire; his father, Norman Woodruff, was vicar of St. Edmund's Church near Chiltern Palace. Which meant Charles had known her mother—at least by sight.

Last night, after the shock of the shooting, she had forgotten about that one brief glimpse she'd had of him at the ball. Had he hidden in the bushes and taken a shot at Samuel?

"I'm curious," she said. "Have you ever met my husband?"

Charles warily shook his head. "Someone pointed him out to me last night. Tall chap with black hair. Stokeford's bastard brother."

"Who pointed him out to you?"

"A friend of mine—what matter is it? I know you're just trying to frighten me." He held his chin high, though his beady eyes shifted to the open doorway every now and then.

"My husband *is* a frightening man," she said on inspiration. "Not toward me, of course. *He* has the utmost respect for women. But with other men . . . well, he was raised on the streets, so he can be brutal and ruthless. That's why he's so successful in business." She paused, then added, "What do you know of his firm?"

"Shipping, isn't it? And he's a moneylender, too. I hear that's how he acquired you, as payment for the duke's debts."

Cassie wanted to slap that sneer off his face. Was his remark due to his innate cruelty, or was there a deeper cause? "Have you ever visited his place of business?"

"Nay, why would I?" Charles inspected his nails. "These hands have never been soiled by common labor. One would think you'd prefer them to your husband's."

The notion was so ridiculous Cassie had to suppress a retort. For a moment, she had a fierce longing to be safe in Samuel's embrace again, the two of them hidden from a world that held knaves like Charles Woodruff.

Could she believe that he'd never been near Firth Enterprises? Since she was getting nowhere, she decided to change her line of questioning. "You're from a good family in Lancashire. Your grandfather was a baron, was he not?"

"And my father a third son, blast the luck. Forced to go into the church or starve. I'd have more money if not for my stepmama's pension."

He'd have more money if he worked for it, as Samuel did. "My parents attended St. Edmund's Church whenever they were at Chiltern Palace," she said with forced politeness. "Do you remember them?"

"'Course I do. Your father was that haughty old curmudgeon who never had a kind word for anyone. And the duchess . . . ah, there was a fine figure of a woman."

At the open lechery on his face, Cassie's stomach twisted. Charles would have been about twenty years old when the duchess had died, certainly old enough to have loved her from afar. Or perhaps even to have had an affair . . . if it weren't so abhorrent to think of her mother as being unfaithful.

And with such a man as Charles Woodruff.

She forced herself to ask, "How well did you know her?"

"She flirted with me a time or two. Does that disturb you?" He curled back his lips in a loathsome smirk. "I always thought the duke was too old to please such a beautiful young woman."

Her father had married late in life. He *had* been sour, especially after the duchess's death, but Cassie didn't want to hear her parents' marriage dissected by this man. "You'll not speak disrespectfully of the duke and duchess," she snapped.

His face avid, Charles leaned forward. "You're as pretty

as your mother, you know. You've all her fire, too. And you can't fool me with all this chitchat."

"Fool you?" Out of the corner of her eye, she gauged the distance to the fireplace poker. There were servants within earshot, too; she had made certain of that.

"Ladies always like to talk," Charles said. "I've never understood why, but it puts them in the mood for bedsport. However, I've had enough of your games." He rose and stood over her, holding out his hand. "Your husband isn't here, or you wouldn't be tempting me like this."

Tempting? What had she done but ask questions of him? "I don't play games, Mr. Woodruff," she said coldly. "I'm married to a fine, upstanding gentleman. I can't imagine why you'd think I would bother with *you*."

In a swift move, he grabbed Cassie and yanked her to her feet. His fingers dug painfully into her arms as he slammed her against him. His breath hot on her face, he said, "Come now, don't be so stingy with your favors. Give your friend Charles a little taste. You'll find my manly parts far more satisfying than Firth's."

She brought her heel down hard on his instep. He yelped in pain and loosened his hold.

Wrenching free, she seized the poker and held it like a pike. Her heart pounded with fear, but she forced sternness into her voice. "Come any closer, and I'll give you *this* in your manly parts."

Charles glowered, his face ugly with rage and his fists clenched. "Bitch! I've had enough of your hoity-toity ways. You need a man to take a stick to you." Snatching up his hat, he jammed it onto his thatch of flaxen curls. "Mayhap I'll do so—when you're least expecting it."

Samuel mounted the steps to a modest row house in Soho, not far from where Hannah Davenport lived. Remembering his old nursemaid, he stifled a twinge of guilt. He didn't like that Cassie could stir such a useless emotion in him, or remind him that he had a heart. He didn't like that she saw right through to his soul. Yes, he'd do as she demanded—but not today.

Today he had no time for social calls.

The door was draped in black crepe. He knocked, and after a moment, a thin, middle-aged housekeeper in a mobcap answered the summons.

He gave her his card. "I'm Samuel Firth. I was Hector Babbage's employer. If I may, I'd like to look for some papers he left here."

Tears welled in her hazel eyes. "Do forgive me, sir, but 'tis hard to believe he's gone," she said, wiping her eyes with a corner of her apron. "You'll want his study. 'Twas his favorite room. If you'll follow me."

Samuel walked at her side down a narrow corridor that led toward the rear of the house. "May I ask your name?"

"Mrs. Phipps. Seventeen years I worked for him, ever since he bought this house."

Her sorrow touched him, reminded him of his own sickness and anger at the senseless death. "You were fond of him?"

"Goodness, yes, he was an excellent employer," she said. "Never complained, always ate whatever was set out before him, always kept to an exact schedule."

Samuel wondered how well she'd really known Babbage. He'd certainly fooled Samuel. "Can you tell me about his friends?"

"He seldom socialized, I'm afraid. He spent most of his time in his study and didn't wish to be disturbed. I always hoped he'd meet a nice lady, but now it's too late."

Her chin wobbled as if she were about to weep again, so he said quickly, "Did a man named Andrew Jamison ever visit him?"

Mrs. Phipps shook her head doubtfully. "Not that I ever met. The name isn't familiar to me."

She showed him into a gloomy, book-lined study, then bustled around, opening the venetian blinds so that daylight poured into the chamber. "This room was also his bedchamber. Perhaps you'll find that odd, but he had a fear of heights, and he seldom ventured upstairs." She wiped her eyes again. "I can't imagine why he went to the top of that building."

Nor could Samuel. He nodded curtly, then she took her leave and closed the door.

He walked around, eyeing the plain furnishings and the textbooks on topics like mathematics and economics. The room was as fussily neat as Babbage himself had been. The narrow bedstead in the corner looked more suited for a servant than a properous man in a well-paying position who had also been stealing from his employer.

An outside door led to the garden, a fact that interested Samuel. So it would have been possible for Babbage to admit a visitor without Mrs. Phipps knowing about it.

Sitting down at the desk, he methodically examined the contents of the drawers. There was nothing out of the ordinary, nothing to prove him a thief. Receipts for bills paid. A deed to the house. A will leaving a tidy legacy to Mrs. Phipps and the rest to various charities. But there was no handy book of addresses with Andrew Jamison's name in it. Even the will had been prepared by another solicitor.

Cassie was right; he couldn't let his resentment of Jamison sway his judgment. Keeping that in mind, he reviewed the case. Babbage had undoubtedly been the embezzler, but there was no indication of where the money had gone. Judging by the house in which he'd lived and the clothes he'd worn, he'd been a man of modest tastes.

That only pointed toward one conclusion. He had stolen the money for someone else. And Samuel suspected blackmail.

But what had a man who led such a dull, dreary life done that he feared exposure? It would have to be something reprehensible for him to be coerced into theft, to risk his job, his good name, his very life.

Maybe he'd brought whores here, but so what? Many men discreetly used the services of such women.

Maybe Babbage had preferred men.

Samuel grimaced. Yes, that was a possibility to keep in mind. If someone had discovered his predilections and threatened to turn him in to the law, he could have been arrested for sodomy.

Samuel roamed around the chamber, looked for a wall safe behind the pictures, but found nothing. When he tried the drawer in the bedside table, he found it locked. He had brought along a small ring of keys he'd found in the accountant's desk at work, and the third one he tried turned easily.

Upon opening the drawer, he discovered the reason for blackmail.

There were several oversized, leather-bound books filled with explicit drawings of men with other men, and men with animals in a disgusting display of perversion. Having seen more than enough, Samuel closed the topmost book. So the meek, mundane accountant had had a secret life. And someone had found out about it.

Someone who had used the information to twist his arm.

Samuel grimly turned his mind to his next task. He must find out who had gone to Vauxhall Gardens on the night the duchess had died.

Cassie was pacing in her bedchamber, relating to Flora what had transpired with Charles Woodruff, when the footman announced that another visitor awaited her downstairs. This one shocked her completely.

"Dear heavens," Cassie moaned, checking her appearance

in the mirror in her bedchamber. "I told Mr. Quinnell never to come here."

"It must be something extremely important," Flora said, her hands going still on her embroidery. "Perhaps he's come to say that *The Black Swan* has gone on sale."

"It *has*—I forgot in all the other madness. Some ladies were talking about it at the ball last night. I'll tell you everything after I speak to him."

Leaving her friend in the bedchamber, Cassie hastened down to the drawing room to find her publisher pacing before the fireplace. A short man with a bristly gray moustache, Mr. Quinnell gave her a broad smile, his arms open in welcome.

"Ah, Lady Vanderly," he said in his booming voice. "How good it is to see you!"

Alarmed, she glanced over her shoulder, but thankfully the corridor was empty. She closed the double doors, then turned to face him. "You mustn't call me that. I've told you, no one must connect that pen name with me."

His expression contrite, he clapped his hand over his mouth. "Oh, do forgive me. I keep forgetting."

"And you shouldn't have come here," she added sternly. "If you need to see me, send a note and I'll come to your office at my earliest convenience."

"My lady, pray don't be angry. Allow me to make restitution by presenting you with this—your very own copy of *The Black Swan*." He plucked a slim volume from the table beside him and proudly placed it in her hands.

Nothing could have banished her vexation more quickly. Her breath caught, and she reverently touched the maroon leather binding, her pen name and the title written in gold on the spine. Opening the book, she turned the crisp new pages. An indescribable joy filled her at seeing her words, her story set in print for the first time.

"Thank you . . . oh, *thank you.*" Her throat was so tight, she couldn't think of anything else to say.

Mr. Quinnell beamed, rocking back and forth on his heels. "I must tell you, it was no easy task to keep my hands on a copy. The book is selling like pork pies at Bartholomew Fair! The first printing has already sold out, and it's gone back to the presses for more. We'll have the additional copies in the stores by week's end. Not even I expected such a smashing success!"

The news evoked a jumble of emotions in Cassie. Delight that so many ladies desired to read her story. Dismay that its popularity would heighten the chance that someone would notice the similarity between Samuel and Percival Cranditch. And most of all, dread that her husband would become the object of vicious gossip.

She managed a smile. "If you're pleased, then so am I."

Mr. Quinnell walked back and forth, rubbing his palms together. "I'm more than pleased, I'm making plans. That's why I came to see you."

"Plans?"

"We must think of your future as a novelist. The ladies will be clamoring for more stories from your marvelous pen. And I am most anxious to purchase your next novel."

In spite of all her worries, Cassie felt the thrill of elation. Was her book truly so successful that he would beg for another? It brought her dream of having that cottage in the country so much closer.

A pang struck her breast as she thought of living there without Samuel. But she couldn't attach her hopes to him. She *mustn't.* It would break her heart to stay with a man who didn't love her, who had made revenge and hatred the purpose of his life.

She took a deep breath. "As a matter of fact, I *am* writing another book. It's about a lady named Sophia Abernathy who falls in love with a gentleman named Sir Dudley, but the evil Yves Picard also has his eye on her—"

"Oh, no, no, *no,* we can't have that," Mr. Quinnell interrupted, his shaggy gray brows rising in alarm. "Do pardon me, but I was hoping for something else entirely."

Struck by consternation, she stammered, "Y-you were?"

"Quite. I was at the Hampton Lending Library this afternoon—"

"Good heavens," Cassie said faintly, sinking into a chair and clutching the book to her bosom. "What were you doing *there*?"

"Why, listening to the ladies' conversations." He ducked his head in a sheepish look. "Pray don't think ill of me for eavesdropping. I've found it quite helpful to know what books excite the interest of the public. And from what I overheard, all the ladies are mad for that pirate fellow."

"Percival Cranditch," she said half-heartedly. "But . . . I don't understand what you're saying."

"It's quite obvious, my lady. There's only one course of action to take. You must write another book featuring this Cranditch!"

For a moment, Cassie thought she'd heard wrong. A dizzy wave of shock swept over her. "That's—that's impossible. He dies at the end of *The Black Swan.* His pirate ship is burned."

"Bah! Perhaps you could explain that Cranditch jumped overboard in the nick of time." Mr. Quinnell rubbed his hands together again. "Yes, that's the ticket! You must resurrect Cranditch and make him your next hero."

By the grace of God, Mr. Montcliff had not expired from the blow inflicted by his villainous half brother. Having suffered a sword thrust through his side, my bridegroom had lost consciousness briefly from the shock and pain of the wound. The village men carried him back to the inn. Rejoicing that he lived, I set myself to the task of nursing him back to health. And I prayed that we would never again encounter Percival Cranditch.

—The Black Swan

Chapter 24

LIAISON AT THE LIBRARY

"Are you ill?" Samuel asked, keeping his arm around Cassie's slim waist on their way to the drawing room. "You scarcely ate a bite of your dinner. And Flora and I did all the talking."

Cassie bit her lip and glanced away. A faint pink flush stained her fair skin, enhancing the natural beauty that took his breath away. Her scent wrapped around him, filled him with the need to take her upstairs and lose himself in her heat.

He knew he was a selfish cad for entertaining such thoughts when something was troubling her. But his balls had a mind of their own.

Her clear blue eyes met his. "I couldn't ask you in front of Flora, but I've been worried . . . about identifying the gunman. What did you find out today?"

Samuel had a feeling that wasn't the only concern on her mind. But he'd answer her question, try to figure out her mood. Maybe then he could coax the truth out of her.

He veered to the chaise and sat down with her, drawing

her close to his side, keenly aware of the softness of her breasts pressed against him. "I went to Babbage's house and searched his study. I found out why he'd been blackmailed. He . . . had a taste for obscene drawings."

"Obscene—?"

He made his tone hard, uncompromising. "Don't ask me to elaborate, Cass. I won't."

With pursed lips and curious eyes, she looked up at him. "What else? Did you find any clue as to who his accomplice might have been?"

"No. Nothing. He was extremely meticulous about keeping no records." That, or the accomplice had already gone through Babbage's papers. If he'd possessed a key to the back door, the housekeeper would never have known . . .

Cassie curled her small fingers around his and held tightly. "Samuel, there's another man we should consider. But I'll have to explain something first." She paused, then added, "I'm afraid I haven't been honest with you about Flora."

"Flora?" He couldn't imagine what Cassie's mousy companion could have to do with shootings and blackmail. But Cassie had a determined look on her face, so he refrained from scoffing.

"She isn't a widow, as I led you to believe. She has a husband back in Lancashire. And I helped her to obtain a deed of separation from him."

If he hadn't been sitting down, he would have staggered. And not from the fact that she'd lied to him. It was *what* she had lied about.

He pulled his hand out of hers. He shouldn't feel this raw, irrational resentment. "What do you mean, you helped her? Are you in the business of separating husbands from their wives?"

"Don't be ridiculous. You haven't heard the whole story."

"Then tell me. What reason did *she* have for rejecting her husband?"

Cassie frowned at him. "He beat her, that's what. She came to my doorstep with a broken arm and bruises all over her body. He'd struck her and thrown her against the wall because he thought the beef they'd had for dinner was undercooked."

His bitterness vanished beneath a wave of cold anger. "My God. Who is the blackguard?"

"That's the irony of it. He's the Reverend Norman Woodruff, vicar of St. Edmund's Church near Chiltern Palace. When Flora came to me, I contacted Mr. Jamison immediately. He arranged a legal separation and a generous quarterly allowance in exchange for her silence." She touched his arm. "Please understand, I couldn't tell you. I'd promised Flora."

When Cassie turned that appealing look on him, he'd forgive her anything. Well, perhaps not her plan to leave him. "So why are you telling me now? Are you saying Woodruff is a suspect?"

She shook her head. "Not him, his son—Flora's stepson. Charles Woodruff is just as vicious as his father. And he was at the ball last night. I saw him for only a moment, from across the chamber, which is why I forgot to mention him to you."

Samuel's interest was piqued. "If he hails from Lancashire, he knew the duchess. I'll have to interview him, find out what he knows."

Cassie lifted her chin. "I already did so this afternoon. And don't you dare get angry at me about it."

The news hit him like a bolt of lightning. He surged to his feet and stared down at her. "You say he's as vicious as his father? A man who would beat a woman? And you went to see him?"

"I most certainly did not. I invited him here. There were servants nearby." She pursed her lips as if he were the one in the wrong. "And rather than quarrel, shouldn't you be asking me what I found out?"

Samuel paced to the hearth. If only she knew, his anger was rooted in fear for her. "Then tell me," he said testily.

"He did know the duchess—he admitted to flirting with her. He hinted . . . that he'd had an affair with her."

Samuel felt the sharp nudge of suspicion. Had Charles Woodruff gone to Vauxhall Gardens that night nearly six years ago?

But he couldn't pose that question to Cassie, not until he had more solid evidence. She looked pale, distraught, and so he sat back down beside her, reaching out to caress her cheek. It couldn't be easy for her to learn that her mother had been unfaithful. As a child, he hadn't found it easy to accept his own mother's affair. "Don't let it disturb you. It's possible he's lying."

She shook her head, clearly unconvinced. "I don't like to think the duchess could have carried on with such a man. He's vulgar and vile and believes every woman needs the life thrashed out of her."

Something in her tone stirred a dark suspicion in Samuel. Taking firm hold of her chin, he tilted her face up to his, so that she couldn't look away. His voice tight and controlled, he asked, "Did he try to seduce you, Cassie? Did he threaten you?"

Her eyes widened slightly, telling him everything he needed to know.

He cursed under his breath. He shot to his feet again. "I'll kill him. No, first I'll break both of his arms and make him suffer. And then I'll cut off his ballocks and stuff them up his—"

He realized that Cassie was sitting on the chaise with her hand over her mouth. "Have you gone *mad*?" she said, springing up to face him. "You can't kill Charles Woodruff. You'd go to prison."

He'd condemn himself to hell if it meant keeping her safe. But dammit, she was right. He wouldn't be of much use locked behind bars. "He can't be allowed to get away with brutalizing women."

"I quite agree. But I can't condone more violence, either."

"Men like him don't understand any other language, Cass." Even as he spoke, he knew it was better to let her think she'd won. Then he'd discreetly take care of Woodruff so that he never again bothered any woman. He'd be singing soprano in the choir at his father's church.

And once he'd solved the mystery of Babbage's murder, then Samuel would contrive a clever scheme to ruin the father.

To allay her suspicions, he massaged her shoulders. "All right, then, if it pleases you, I'll just find out what I can about him."

Cassie pursed her lips as if she didn't quite trust him. "I'm beginning to think you should hire a Bow Street Runner. There are far too many suspects for just one man to interview."

"No," he said instantly. "You'd be dragged into the matter. We'd have to tell them about the letters, the brooch, the references to your mother. The information would get out, and people would gossip about you."

"Bother my reputation. We're speaking of your *life*."

And hers.

Reluctant to face an unavoidable decision, Samuel stroked her hair. He wanted to hold her close and never let her go. But what other choice did he have? "This business with Woodruff puts you in grave danger, Cassie. You can't stay here in London any longer."

"I beg your pardon?"

"You're returning to Strathmore Castle at once," he said in an uncompromising tone. "You'll leave in the morning. And I won't hear any arguments about it."

With complete disregard, she argued, "*You're* the one in danger, not me. I won't be banished while you're back here in London. I'm perfectly safe in this house."

"Cassie, think. This man tried to kill me in the middle of a huge party. He's diabolical enough to come up with some scheme to attack me right here in this house. You could be hurt." *Or killed.* His gut twisted at the thought.

"He could also attack *me* at Strathmore. He could abduct me—as a means to lure you to him."

Damn her vivid imagination. "I intend to hire guards to patrol the grounds. Believe me, you'll be safe." He took her face in his hands and resorted to shameless manipulation. "Do it for me, darling. I can't concentrate when you're around. All I can think about is keeping you out of harm's way." He lowered his voice to a husky murmur. "And making love to you. You're a distraction that could cost me my life."

Her face softening, she leaned closer to him, placing her hand on his coat. Her expressive blue eyes revealed a turmoil of emotions: fear, acceptance, desire. How had he ever thought her difficult to read?

She caressed his jaw, running her fingers lightly over his face as if to memorize him for their separation. "All right, then," she said to his great relief. "I'll agree to leave under three conditions."

"Name them."

"First, I want you to escort me."

He had already planned on doing just that. His lustful body leaped at the thought. He would allow himself to stay the night with her at Strathmore, one last interlude in which to brand himself on her memory. "Done."

"Second, I'll need more than a few hours' notice to pack my things for an extended trip. Besides, tomorrow's Thursday, and I wish to work at the lending library in the afternoon."

Objections leaped to his tongue. He wanted her to stay in the relative safety of this house. But when he eyed the resolute look on her face, he hardened his jaw. "As you wish. We'll depart Friday morning."

She nodded regally. "Third, I won't stay alone somewhere without friends or family with me."

"So bring Flora along. She can keep you company."

"I will, but I also had something else in mind." Eyeing him through the screen of her eyelashes, Cassie dropped a bombshell that he cursed himself later for not anticipating. "I'll agree to leave London only if I can go to Stokeford Abbey to stay with your grandmother."

Cassie sat behind the desk at the Hampton Lending Library as an aging gentleman with palsy laboriously signed his name in the withdrawal ledger. Normally, she enjoyed her time here; she relished talking to the patrons who had become friends to her. But today she felt too nervous to take solace in the tranquil scene.

Cloud-softened daylight poured through the tall windows of the rotunda that formed the entrance to the library. People sat reading at tables while others browsed the shelves of books. The scent of leather bindings mixed with the beeswax used to shine her desk, and she could hear the shuffle of footsteps, the turning of pages, the murmurings of conversation. But those peaceful sounds couldn't banish the restless anticipation in her.

Samuel was sending her away. He had agreed—very reluctantly—to accompany her to Stokeford Abbey in Devon. But little did he know, she intended to convince him to stay there with her for a long visit. Let him hire a whole team of Bow Street Runners to solve the mystery. Not only would it keep him out of danger, but he also needed to spend time with his brothers and with his grandmother.

Cassie hadn't yet told him, but she had formulated a new plan for her life. If he could bring himself to forgive his family, to banish the hatred and revenge that had ruled his life, then she would not have him sign the deed of separation. She would happily stay with him, loving him for the rest of her life.

Her heart ached with hope and need—and most of all with fear. The fear that it was too late to change him.

As the old man shakily set down the pen and picked

up his two books, she summoned a smile. "Thank you, Mr. Ackerman. Oh, I should tell you, I shan't be here next week. I'm going on holiday."

"I may not be here, either. At my age, one never knows." Cackling at his own jest, he doffed his cap. "Cheerio, my lady."

As he tottered off toward the front door, two young ladies scurried inside, spied Cassie, and waved. Dressed in the height of fashion, they brought a flash of recognition that made her heart sink.

It was plump Lady Alice and the beauteous Miss Harris.

Cassie groaned inwardly, unwilling to have yet another conversation about *The Black Swan*. Already, several ladies had asked for the book, and she had had to inform them that all five copies were loaned out at present. Perhaps Miss Harris had come to add her name to the waiting list that was two pages long already.

The popularity of the novel reminded her of Mr. Quinnell's outrageous suggestion the previous day. How *could* she write another book about Percival Cranditch, thereby prolonging the chance that someone would recognize the villain as Samuel? But her publisher had shrugged away every objection she had posed. She had put him off with a promise to consider the matter, and still she had not arrived at a solution to her dilemma.

A waft of French perfume preceded Miss Harris. "Oh, my lady, I was hoping we'd find you here," she said, her brown eyes sparkling. "I wanted to thank you for your excellent suggestion. You'll be happy to know that I've managed to purchase a copy of *The Black Swan*, after all."

"From the publisher himself," Lady Alice added, her blue eyes alight. "A very kind gentleman named Mr. Quinnell."

The hairs on the nape of Cassie's neck lifted. Oh, why had she given out such thoughtless advice? She hid her alarm behind a polite expression. "I'm pleased to hear it.

Now, we've several more new books in stock that may be of interest to you, if you'll look on the shelf at the beginning of the novel section. That area is to the right."

The girls didn't take the hint. Instead, they exchanged a secretive glance. "My lady," Miss Harris ventured, "pray don't think me presumptuous, but . . ."

"But we must point out the most amazing resemblance," Lady Alice continued for her friend. She lowered her voice to a confidential whisper. "When I met Mr. Firth at the duke's ball two nights ago—"

"You've met my husband?" Cassie blurted in dismay.

Lady Alice nodded. "And he's such a handsome man," she said, her face awestruck. "I couldn't help but notice that he looks exactly like . . . well, like the pirate in *The Black Swan*."

Cassie sat frozen. Her heart beat so swiftly she feared she might swoon for the first time in her life. She struggled for cool disdain. "Oh? You have quite the imagination."

"That isn't all," Miss Harris said, her dainty features flushed with excitement. "Tell her the rest, Alice."

"I was in the company of your cousin, the Duke of Chiltern," Lady Alice confided. "When I made the observation to him, he said that Mr. Firth was also the baseborn son of a Lord S——."

"Which is the same as the pirate, Percival Cranditch," Miss Harris added triumphantly.

Blast Walt! Cassie wanted to crawl under the desk and hide. Her smile felt so brittle she was certain it would crack at any moment. "How fascinating. I'll have to read the book myself and see if I agree."

"*Must* you read it?" Lady Alice asked with a sly expression.

"Yes, we were wondering if you . . ." Miss Harris paused, her eyes fervent. "If you might possibly be . . .?"

With frantic relief, Cassie spied another familiar face behind them. "I'm sorry, I can't chat any longer. I've a patron waiting."

The girls reluctantly walked away, whispering to one another, glancing over their shoulders at Cassie in a manner she found unnerving. Dear God, they suspected she was the author! Had Mr. Quinnell dropped some telltale hint? She couldn't trust him not to have done so.

Thank heavens she and Samuel were going out of town tomorrow. With any luck, the scandal would blow over before they returned to London.

The short, stocky figure of Mr. Ellis MacDermot strolled up to the desk. "You look as though you've seen a banshee, m'lady," he observed, his freckled face wearing the impish grin of a leprechaun. "What were you three whispering about over here? Is there some exciting gossip I should know?"

"Oh, no . . . we were discussing a book, that's all." Cassie collected her scattered thoughts and focused her mind on the Irishman. "Have you found a good biography for this week?"

He placed a thick volume on the desk. "Old Queen Bess. Now there was a strong, admirable woman. I look forward to many hours of reading pleasure."

"I hope you enjoy it." To cover her rattled state, she wrote the title in the ledger, then handed the quill to him.

He dipped the nib into the inkwell. "By the by, an old friend of mine met you at Nunwich's ball the other night," he said casually. "Colonel Mainwaring is his name."

Cassie's mind sprang to alertness. How incredible to have this opportunity land in her lap. She must use it to full advantage. "I had no idea you knew him, too."

Mr. MacDermot signed his name with a flourish. "I do attend some society events, you know. Back in Ireland, my cousin is the Earl of Killarney. It gets me into a few parties here and there, but nothing so high stare as Nunwich's ball."

The trace of rancor in his tone caught her off guard. Had she offended him? "Forgive me," she murmured sincerely. "I didn't mean to imply that you have no connection to the *ton*.

It's a lot of nonsense, anyway, one group of people setting themselves above all others."

He handed the quill back to her. "Apparently that isn't what your mother thought."

Dumbfounded, she stared up at him, the pen frozen in the air. "My mother? Did *you* know her?"

Mr. MacDermot chuckled, his brown eyes twinkling. "Now how would a humble Irishman like meself know a grand English duchess? Nay, 'twas Colonel Mainwaring who mentioned her to me. He quite admired her, you know. He called her the queen of society."

Cassie calmed the wild beating of her heart and replaced the quill in its stand. "What did he say about her?" she whispered, so that none of the other patrons could overhear. "If you don't mind my asking, that is."

"Of course not. 'Tis only natural to want to hear stories about your late mother. Let me see if I can recall Mainwaring's exact words." Tapping his chin, Mr. MacDermot frowned. "Ah, yes. He mentioned something rather odd about a brooch you were wearing . . . 'twas a diamond serpent, I believe."

"Odd?" She leaned closer, bracing her elbows on the desk. "I don't understand."

"He said it had belonged to your mother. He believed she'd been wearing it on the night she . . ." Mr. MacDermot paused, his reddish brows lowered in a concerned frown. "Perhaps I shouldn't be telling you this."

"I *must* know. Please. It's very important to me."

The Irishman hesitated, then said heavily, "I'm afraid the duchess was wearing that very same brooch on the night she drowned."

As the days passed, I fell more deeply in love with my dear Mr. Montcliff. He bore his pain with fortitude; I read him books to pass the time of his recuperation and made sure he had every comfort. Yet despite his outward cheerfulness, I sensed a grim determination in him. He would not speak of his baseborn brother, but I feared he planned to go after Percival Cranditch.

—The Black Swan

Chapter 25

A Birthday Celebration

Reining in his horse, Samuel gazed at the magnificence of Stokeford Abbey for the first time in his life and felt his gut tighten into a knot.

The stately mansion stretched out in both directions as a monument to noble decadence. The light of the setting sun added warmth to the ivy-covered gray stone and made the vaulted windows gleam like polished mirrors. Huge pillars held up the roof over an extensive porch that led to the oversized oak doors. The house had been built around the ruins of an old monastery, Samuel knew, and its ancient façade reeked of heritage and privilege, everything that had been denied him.

Had he been George Kenyon's legitimate son, he would have grown up here. He would have studied with the best tutors instead of attending a charity school. He would have explored the surrounding countryside, Stokeford land as far as the eye could see. On inclement days, he would have stayed indoors, running down the antiquated corridors and playing games with his brothers.

He would have had a real family.

Yes, with a father who had been a drunken, cowardly lecher. And a grandmother who was an aristocratic tyrant.

His jaw set, he rode up to the coach that had stopped by the massive portico. He'd been better off raised by Hannah Davenport and his own mother, despite her melancholy obsession with a worthless nobleman. He was damn proud of the fact that he had earned his fortune instead of having it handed to him on a silver platter. He'd form his own dynasty apart from the Kenyons.

But not even the reminder of his goal could make his tension abate.

He swung down from his horse. A white-wigged footman opened the door of the coach, and Cassie stepped out. She looked straight at Samuel and smiled.

Samuel's heart stopped beating. Then it took off racing like a two-year-old colt at Newmarket. He wanted nothing more than to bundle his wife back into that coach and take her somewhere private, where he could strip off her clothes and spend the rest of his life in bed with her.

But he'd felt compelled to see her here safely. To accomplish that purpose, he'd tolerate even the odious company of his grandmother and brother. At least he wasn't staying long. By tomorrow at dawn, he'd be back on the road, alone, returning to London to track down a killer.

Leaving Cassie here.

Damn, he didn't want to think about *that*.

He went to Cassie's side. Perhaps it was the soft light of evening, but she looked fragile, her skin pale and her eyes too impossibly blue to be real, her delicate features framed by a straw bonnet. He slid his arm around her slender waist, leaned down to breathe in her scent and relish her warmth. "How was your afternoon?"

"Perhaps I should have ridden on horseback like you," she said with a laugh. "Amazing, how tiring it can be to ride in a luxurious coach, doing absolutely nothing for two straight days."

"And with several stops each day," Flora said as she descended from the coach. She was a plain brown sparrow who faded into the background, but ever since Samuel had heard her dire story, he had taken a private vow to protect her, too. Much to his frustration, however, her stepson Charles had left London, returning to Lancashire before Samuel had had the chance to trounce him.

He offered her his other arm. "Mrs. Woodruff, may I escort you, too?"

She blushed and accepted, and the smile he earned from Cassie was worth the trouble.

As they started up the steps, the front door opened and three elderly ladies hurried outside onto the porch. The famous Rosebuds, Samuel thought disparagingly. They had been friends for well over fifty years, ever since they had ruled society at their debut.

Two women brought up the rear: Olivia, Lady Faversham, a tall, dignified woman who walked with a cane, and Lady Enid, a plump matron who wore a yellow dress with a matching turban on her head.

But Samuel had eyes only for their leader.

Lucy, the dowager Lady Stokeford, had a crown of white hair and a regal demeanor undiminished by advanced age. Thin and insubstantial in a gown of pale blue, she stopped at the top of the stairs and gazed down at him, and his insides clenched with loathing.

His grandmother.

Over four years ago, when she had first learned of his existence, she had tried to drag him into the family. She had ordered him to attend her here at the abbey, but he had ignored the summons. She had expected that a grown man in his thirties, a man who had been abandoned at birth by her craven son, would leap at the chance to become a part of the exalted Kenyon clan.

Now her eyes were bright, her mouth smiling. And no wonder.

Cassie had posted a letter to alert the family of their impending visit. He had forbidden her to mention anything about the embezzlement or the murder, and clearly the dowager believed that she'd won at last, that he'd lost all pride and had traveled here to become one of her adoring grandsons.

Nothing could be further from the truth.

The moment they reached the top of the stairs, Cassie flew into the dowager's arms. "Grandmama, it's so wonderful to see you again."

The old woman hugged her back. "Cassie, darling. It's been far too long."

This wasn't Cassie's first stay at Stokeford Abbey, Samuel knew grimly. Andrew Jamison had admitted as much upon Samuel's return to England. In defiance of her husband's wishes and without his knowledge, she had been permitted to visit the Kenyons on several occasions.

He had Jamison to blame for Cassie's devotion to the family.

"He only returned to England three weeks ago," she was telling the dowager. "Samuel, won't you come and kiss your grandmother?"

He stood frozen, every nerve and muscle of his body rebelling. *Hell.* He'd sooner embrace a cobra. But Cassie looked so beseeching and so anxious, that he found himself walking stiffly forward, bending down to brush his lips across that papery skin. The dowager smelled faintly of lavender, and the shoulders he touched for a brief moment felt frail and bony.

But he wouldn't feel any sympathy. Undoubtedly, her nature was as domineering and haughty as ever.

As he drew back, he felt a shock, for her blue eyes were filled with tears. She reached out to him, her hand wrinkled and blue-veined. "Welcome home, Samuel. Welcome to Stokeford Abbey."

Bloody hell. "I'm only here to escort my wife," he said curtly. "I'll be leaving in the morning."

The dowager's smile faded, and her hand dropped to her side. He hated her for making him feel petty and mean. Which of course he was. She was an old woman, and no matter how much he disliked her, he could have broken the news more gently.

The other ladies rallied around her, twittering sympathetic phrases. And Cassie flashed him a look of disappointment and disapproval that cut straight into him. Her cool stare made him wonder if he'd get that last night with her, after all.

But dammit, he wouldn't apologize. He had only spoken the truth.

Nevertheless, as the women proceeded inside, he trailed after them, feeling as if he'd kicked a kitten.

As if *that* weren't the most ludicrous way to describe the old tigress.

At dinner, Cassie sat beside the dowager as laughter and conversation swirled around her, echoing off the high, vaulted ceiling. Candlelight cast a soft glow over the linen-draped table and sparkled on the china and crystal. Two footmen were clearing away the plates. Despite the formality of the immense chamber, she basked in a sense of homecoming.

How she had missed being here, in the company of family. When she had been frightened and confused after Samuel's abandonment four years ago, the dowager had come to fetch her from Lancashire, where Cassie had fled.

She had fallen in love with the Rosebuds, wise old Lady Stokeford, merry Lady Enid Quinton, and dour Lady Faversham. They had brought her back here, where Michael and his wife, Vivien, had welcomed her as one of the family. Today they had welcomed Flora, too, and she sat chatting happily with Lady Enid.

In truth, Cassie felt more at home here at Stokeford Abbey than she ever had at Chiltern Palace, where she had been alone except for her governess and tutors and servants, her parents visiting only twice a year, in the summer and at Christmas. All of her childhood she had longed for the warmth of such a family as the Kenyons.

If only Samuel felt the same.

For the umpteenth time, her gaze strayed to the opposite end of the long table, where he occupied a place to the right of his brother Michael Kenyon, the Marquess of Stokeford. They were speaking civilly, at least. They had found common ground in discussing the economy, the shipping industry, and Samuel's journeys.

It made her throat catch to see how much alike they looked. The same blue eyes, the same chiseled features, the same muscular build.

But there were differences, too. Silver threaded Michael Kenyon's black hair. Samuel's skin was burnished to a teak hue from his years abroad. His face was somewhat broader, his jawline more squared. And while Michael had the autocratic air of a nobleman born to rule, Samuel had the keen eyes and distrustful manner of a man raised on the streets.

The memory of his coldness toward the dowager entangled her breast. How could he have been so blunt, so cruel?

In the privacy of his bedchamber, she had scolded him, and he had borne her rebuke with stone-faced inflexibility.

"You expect too much," he had stated coolly. *"I can't pretend an affection that simply isn't there."*

Perhaps her grand hope of fostering a reconciliation

between him and his family was a fool's mission. She might do better to wish for a pot of gold at the end of a rainbow. And yet . . . he *was* talking with his brother, and also with Nathaniel Babcock, a courtly, white-haired gentleman who was the dowager's devoted companion.

She realized that the elderly lady was smiling at her. "My dear, I don't believe you've attended to a word we've said all evening," the dowager gently chided. "Nor have you eaten a single bite of your strawberries and cream."

Instantly contrite, Cassie picked up her spoon and sampled the delicacy. "I'm just a bit tired after the journey. But the strawberries are wonderful."

"They're from our own greenhouses," said Michael's wife, Vivien, a pretty, dark-haired lady who sat across from Cassie. "The children helped me pick them this morning."

"I fear they ate more than they added to the basket," the dowager said with a laugh. "You should have seen the red stains on their faces."

Lady Faversham leaned closer, her austere features relaxing in a smile. "I do believe great-grandchildren—and grandchildren—are so much more enjoyable than one's own children."

Lady Enid twittered with agreement. A plump woman with a cheery face beneath her yellow turban, she said, "Cassie, did you hear that my granddaughter Charlotte is expecting again? The little one will be her third."

"With thanks to *my* grandson Brandon," Lady Faversham added proudly. "Marriage to Charlotte has tamed that rogue quite admirably."

"Indeed, the right wife does have a way of domesticating a man," Lady Stokeford murmured, looking pointedly at Cassie.

The twinkle in those blue eyes surprised her. Had the dowager already forgiven Samuel for his rudeness? And how could she think him domesticated? "I fear some men are too cold and arrogant ever to be tamed," Cassie replied softly.

"The Kenyon men do have an overabundance of pride," Vivien said, her brown eyes sympathetic and insightful. "But they also have an overabundance of devotion, which makes the end result worth the struggle."

Cassie ached to believe that could happen for her. Yet perhaps they didn't fully understand the hatred that had guided Samuel for his whole life. He had hardened his heart against them, and she feared he might never come to love them as she did.

She also feared that if he left here, he'd never return. This visit was her one and only chance to save her marriage.

For a moment, Cassie let herself dream of being with Samuel forever, bearing his children, seeing him relaxed and happy and full of love. He was a difficult, complicated man who had known much tribulation in his life. Those trials had shaped his strong, determined nature in a way that made him unique among his brothers. Yet underneath his flinty exterior, he was kind, tender, honorable. She loved him with all her heart, and she'd gladly burn that deed of separation—if only he'd let go of his aversion to his family.

She would do all she could to keep Samuel here, to give him his chance. But she didn't have the power to change him. Ultimately, he had to find his own way.

"What are you women whispering about down there?" Michael called from the other end of the table. "You're clucking like a flock of hens."

"We're complaining about the roosters," Vivien retorted.

Everyone laughed, except for Samuel.

He looked straight at Cassie, and her heart flipped over, as it always did when he fixed her with those blue eyes. Kenyon eyes.

But tonight his gaze was guarded, watchful, cool. Because he loathed being here, she knew, and he could scarcely wait to depart.

The elder Lady Stokeford rose to her feet and clapped her hands. "As matriarch of this family, I've an announcement to make."

Conversation died. The attention of the diners veered to her. The only sounds were the discreet clinking of dishes that the footmen bore away to the sideboard.

"We've a very important occasion coming up next week," the dowager said, directing a fond smile at Cassie. "Cassie will be twenty years old on Wednesday."

Cassie blinked in surprise. In all the upheaval of the past few weeks, she had completely forgotten about the approach of her birthday. Judging by the arrested frown on Samuel's face, he was even more thunderstruck.

Perhaps he hadn't even *known* her birthdate.

"I've planned a small party," the dowager went on. "The moment I learned Cassie and Samuel were coming here to visit, I sent two footmen to notify Joshua and Gabriel. I'm happy to say, my other two grandsons will be arriving on Monday with their families to stay for a fortnight."

"*Small* party, Grandmama?" Michael said. "There are twelve children among us, and the house will be in an absolute uproar." But he was smiling as if the prospect pleased him mightily.

"Fourteen children," Lady Enid corrected. "Brandon and Charlotte will be here, too, don't forget."

"All the more excellent," the dowager declared. Despite the frailty of her body, she emanated an iron strength as she turned her gaze to Samuel. "For once, we'll be here together, all of us. There is nothing more important than family."

Samuel's first instinct was to cut his losses and run. He could borrow a mount from the stables and be on his way back to London inside twenty minutes.

Leaving Cassie here. Without anyone knowing the danger she faced.

He couldn't do it. He couldn't abandon her. Again.

So while the ladies and Nathaniel Babcock retired to the drawing room, Samuel walked with Michael to the library through a maze of dimly lit corridors. Entering the huge, medieval chamber didn't improve his ill humor. The library had two stories of books and a balcony that circled the perimeter to give access to the upper level. With its ancient stone walls and Gothic archways, the room exuded an aura of birthright and aristocracy.

From the moment he'd stepped into this damned house, Samuel had felt as if he were being asphyxiated. He wanted nothing more than to be gone from here.

But his grandmother had drawn the battle lines. He had expected her to oppose his departure, to use tears, bark out orders, play on his sympathies. Yet her well-aimed cannon blast had hit him by surprise. She had pinned him in a corner with his one weakness.

Cassie.

Damn his grandmother! *He* should be the one giving his wife a party. But he hadn't even bloody *known* her birthdate.

Michael went to a table to pour them glasses of brandy from a crystal decanter. Over his shoulder, he said, "There are two absolutes in marriage. You can't forget your wedding anniversary or your wife's birthday."

"I've skipped them both for the last four years," Samuel growled.

"All the more reason to stay for this one."

He gave Samuel the drink, and Samuel was annoyed to see that his toplofty brother appeared sympathetic rather than gloating. But he rejected male camaraderie with this man. "I'm not one of the dowager's devoted grandsons. She has no bloody right to tell me what to do."

"Are you sure it's her edict that bothers you, or your own conscience?"

Leaving Samuel speechless, Michael motioned him to a pair of leather chairs by the hearth. A fire burned on the grate to ward off the chill in the huge chamber.

Blistered by anger and frustration, Samuel sat down and moodily drank his brandy. Hell, it *was* his conscience that prodded him. He had left Cassie for most of their married life. Henceforth, he didn't want to miss any special occasion—or any ordinary occasion, either.

God, he was a wretched fool for her.

He didn't want to admit that aloud, so as Michael took the opposite seat, Samuel snapped, "How the hell do you put up with the dowager's manipulating?"

Michael shrugged. "Grandmama can be domineering at times. But once you come to know her, you'll realize that everything she does, she does out of love."

"I don't want . . ." *Her love.* Damn, he couldn't even say the phrase. Despite the chill in the library, he was sweating. He amended, "I don't want to know her. I came here for the sole purpose of ensuring Cassie's safety. And I need to get back to London." But he couldn't. Not now. Not until after the party on Wednesday.

Michael lifted an eyebrow. "Perhaps you'd better tell me what trouble you're facing."

Samuel launched into a grim recital of the audit, the embezzlement, and the odd circumstances surrounding Babbage's death. He related every detail of the letters Cassie had received, the two thwarted attempts on his own life, and his suspicions about her mother's death. He listed the suspects, starting with Andrew Jamison and including Colonel Mainwaring.

The night before they'd set out for Stokeford Abbey, Cassie had told Samuel about what Ellis MacDermot had reported, that according to Mainwaring, the duchess had been wearing the diamond serpent on the night she died. But it had been too late for Samuel to interrogate the colonel; that task would have to wait for his return to London.

And he'd question MacDermot, too. The Irishman admired Cassie, and that fact alone incited Samuel's suspicions. MacDermot knew her from the lending library, and if he were the secret admirer, perhaps she'd seen his handwriting there, which would force him to disguise it in those letters.

Setting aside those thoughts for the moment, Samuel ended the tale with Charles Woodruff and his father, Norman.

During the long discourse, Michael had brought over the brandy decanter and refilled their glasses. He had offered comments and questions now and then, but mostly he'd just listened. His face had grown darker and darker, but at the description of Norman Woodruff's brutality toward Flora, he let loose with a succinct curse. "And the knave got away with battering a woman?"

"I intend to take care of him," Samuel said tightly. "Both of them."

"I'd like to help—"

"It's something I need to do myself." Dammit, he wanted to put Charles Woodruff six feet under for threatening Cassie. Barring that, he'd settle for beating him bloody. "Unfortunately, Charles left town before I could question him."

"You think he could be your murderer, then?" Michael asked.

"It's entirely possible. He knew Cassie's mother."

"So did I," Michael said, his face hard. "Before I married Vivien, I spent quite a lot of time in London society."

The unexpected boon startled Samuel. He leaned forward, resting his elbows on his knees, the brandy glass in his hands. "Tell me about the duchess, then. What was she like?"

"Vain. Self-absorbed. And a chronic flirt who enjoyed the game of cuckolding her husband and playing two suitors against each other." Michael paused, eyeing Samuel. "I've never told that to Cassie, though. I didn't want to speak ill of her mother."

Samuel nodded, but the words of thanks stuck in his throat. "Do you know anything about the night the duchess died? Who might have been in her party at Vauxhall?"

Michael shook his head. "I wasn't a member of her circle. I could write some letters, though, make some inquiries."

Samuel balked at accepting his brother's assistance. But hell, if it meant keeping Cassie safe . . . "All right. I especially need to find out who was on that barge."

"I'll take care of it at once." Michael sipped his brandy thoughtfully. "But I must point out, in light of all you've said, I'm surprised you'd bring Cassie here at all."

"Why?"

"*I* should be number one on your list of suspects."

Michael's keen stare made Samuel restless and defensive. Why *had* he never entertained that suspicion? It was a difficult question to answer. "Murder and theft aren't your techniques," he said finally. "If you wanted to punish me, you'd use your fists. Or you'd get your lawyers working to end my marriage."

"I did try that," his brother admitted with a faint grin.

"I know." Although irritated and resentful, Samuel realized that he really couldn't fault his oldest brother for endeavoring to help a fifteen-year-old girl who had been sold into marriage. It was not one of Samuel's finer moments.

Draining his glass, he set it on a side table and stood up. "I need your promise that you'll watch over Cassie."

Michael rose, as well. "Of course. I'll alert the gatekeeper and the groundsmen. I can assign men to patrol day and night. No one will come onto the estate without my permission. You have my word on that."

He put out his hand, and everything in Samuel opposed the friendly gesture. But dammit, he'd shaken hands on business deals many times over the years, so what the hell difference did it make?

Gritting his teeth, he shook his brother's hand for the first time in his life. "Thank you," he forced out. "If you'll excuse me now, I'll see if Cassie is ready to retire."

"I'll go with you. Vivien needs her rest since she often gets up during the night to feed the baby." Without waiting for Samuel's assent, Michael walked him to the doorway. "By the by, if you're still intending to leave in the morning, you may as well head out to the kennels to sleep."

Maybe it was the relaxing effects of the brandy. Or the unburdening of his troubles. But Samuel cracked a smile. Yes, he could imagine Cassie's reaction if he said he'd have to miss her birthday party.

Like it or not, he would stay at Stokeford Abbey for a few more days.

At last Mr. Montcliff was recovered enough to travel, so we departed for his estate in Northumberland. We would marry there at the chapel, and start our new life in a place that held no dreadful memories. As the coach rumbled up the drive, I was enchanted by the sight of the stately house, an ivy-grown mansion built upon the ruins of an old abbey.

But no sooner had I remarked on its beauty than a familiar terror chilled my blood. A shot rang out and the horses reared.

—The Black Swan

Chapter 26

UNEXPECTED VISITORS

As the open landau carrying the Rosebuds approached the lake, Lucy anxiously scanned the party of adults and children for her long-lost grandson.

It was Tuesday, everyone had arrived, and the soft breeze carried the sound of their merry laughter. The previous day, Joshua and Anne had come from Wakebridge Hall in Hampshire with their brood of three, while Gabriel and Kate had traveled from Fairfield Park in Cornwall with their four children. Even Brandon and Charlotte were here with their two little ones, from the neighboring estate of Villiers Hall, the seat of the earls of Faversham.

Since the day had dawned unseasonally mild and sunny for April, Michael had suggested a picnic, and most of the party had set out on a brisk walk to the lake, with a few of the smaller children traveling in a ponycart driven by Gabriel. As befitting their advanced age, the Rosebuds arrived late and in grand style, riding in the open landau.

Nathaniel Babcock sat beside Lucy, with Enid and Olivia facing them. Enid's furry brown dog, Fancy, sat at their feet, tail wagging.

But for once, Lucy paid her dearest friends no heed. She couldn't see Samuel among the party. The men were making an arrangement of chairs for their wives, while Amy, at fourteen the eldest of the great-grandchildren, was organizing games for the younger ones. Several footmen were setting up tables beneath the trees for luncheon.

Olivia leaned forward, her clawlike hands curled about the knob of her cane and her gray eyes on Lucy. "He's over there," she said sagely, nodding at a cluster of willow trees that edged the lake.

Lucy turned her head, spied Samuel, and felt a swell of happiness.

Her youngest grandson strolled arm in arm with his wife along the grassy bank a short distance from the rest of the party. Seeing Samuel here on Stokeford land, a part of the family, was Lucy's dearest dream come true. Yet distress lurked in the midst of her joy. "I do hope that today goes well," she said fretfully. "There's so little time left. I fear he'll leave directly after the birthday party tomorrow."

Nathaniel took her hand and kissed the back. "Now, dearest, don't despair. The lad'll come to love you. How could he not? He'll be dancing at our wedding someday, you mark my words."

In spite of her worries, Lucy smiled at Nathaniel, his beloved features as old and worn as hers, his hair white and his blue eyes faded. Yet she could see the handsome young rogue he had once been. Long ago, his reckless ways had ended their romance and parted them for almost fifty years. But in the eight years since he had returned to her life, he had become her devoted companion, offering to marry her so many times, it had become something of a private jest between them.

But perhaps . . . perhaps once this was all over she would shock him by accepting.

"Samuel certainly appears devoted to Cassie," Olivia mused. " 'Tis a welcome relief after how badly their marriage began."

"Happiness in the bedchamber can mend quite a lot of rifts," Enid said, a twinkle in her hazel eyes. "There can be no doubt that he's madly in love with his wife."

Lucy wanted to agree. And yet . . . what if it was merely an infatuation? He'd been back in England for less than a month. "I'm not so certain Samuel can set aside his hatred of me for her sake. He's made it quite clear that he resents being trapped by my scheme."

"*You* didn't determine Cassie's birthdate," Olivia said with a sniff, as the coachman slowly guided the open carriage toward a thicket of trees. "Besides, it's only right and good that he visit you at last."

"I do believe he's fitting in quite well," Enid said brightly. "He's certainly charmed all the ladies—and the children, too."

Lucy had witnessed those small, encouraging signs that he was relaxing his guard. William, her oldest great-grandson, had tagged after his newfound uncle quite a lot these past few days, and Samuel appeared to enjoy the company. "But he's remained cool toward me and toward his brothers."

"There *is* a deep-seated reserve in him," Olivia agreed. "But one can hardly blame him. To be raised in poverty, his mother an actress . . ."

"And to grow up knowing that his own father had deserted him." Lucy forced herself to voice the painful fact of her son's callous, irresponsible act. George had been too cowed by that pious wife of his to dare bring home a bastard son. "Oh, dear, if only I could turn back time."

Nathaniel kissed her hand. "The past can't be changed," he said. "Only the future."

As the carriage drew to a halt in the shade of the trees, she noticed Cassie speaking earnestly to Samuel—and he was frowning now. Abruptly, he left his wife and strode toward the landau.

Nathaniel started to rise, to help the ladies out, but Lucy placed her hand on his arm to stop him. He spied Samuel's approach and flashed a wry grin. "Ah, Cassie's set him on a mission. Do be kind to the poor boy, Lucy."

"Poor boy, indeed!" she whispered, laughing in spite of herself. "Your sympathy should be with me."

There was no time to say more as Samuel opened the half-door of the carriage. "May I offer my assistance, ladies?" he said in a formal tone.

Fancy hopped down past him, preceding Enid and Olivia, their movements slow with age. Only then did Lucy allow herself the pleasure of leaning on her grandson's arm.

Although a part of her resented the fact that he had to be forced to approach her, she was determined to seize the opportunity. "May I speak to you for a moment, Samuel?"

His face was cool, expressionless. "I doubt we've much to say to one another, madam."

Lucy had a lot to say to *him*. But she bit her tart tongue and voiced the one topic designed to capture his attention. "It concerns Cassie."

A muscle tightened in his jaw. "As you wish, then."

He led her down the footpath to the lake. For a few moments, they strolled in silence, and she considered how to express her thoughts without further alienating him. Despite the wisdom of her seventy-eight years, she didn't know quite how to break through his antipathy.

Deep in thought, she stumbled over a stone, and Samuel placed his arm around her back to steady her. His instinctive aid buoyed her spirits, prompting her to speak. "I've been wondering why you brought Cassie here. You're in some sort of trouble, I'll warrant."

Samuel muttered a curse. "Blast Michael! He told you."

"Michael said nothing—not even when I questioned him quite mercilessly. In truth, he urged me not to interfere."

"Then don't. It's nothing that involves you."

"Bah, I may be old, but I'm not witless. I've noticed the guards patrolling the grounds. There are two of them among the servants over there, and I happen to know that Pitson and Hammerly usually work in the stables. Now, will you kindly tell me why?" She paused, then added, "I only wish to help you keep Cassie safe."

Samuel fixed her with a stare. Lucy stared straight back. By heaven, he was a stubborn man, but she could be just as obstinate. She sensed the battle in him; then he led her to a stone bench and seated her.

He remained standing, leaning against the thick trunk of an oak tree. "All right," he said tightly. "I'll tell you. But don't interrupt."

She listened in mingled shock, dismay, and alarm as he related a frightening tale about mysterious letters sent to Cassie, two attempts on his life, a murder at his firm, and his suspicions about the death of the Duchess of Chiltern.

When he was done, Lucy released a shaky breath. She shivered and drew her shawl closer, feeling cold and afraid. Dear God, if he returned to London . . . "You must hire a Bow Street Runner, Samuel. This villain is far too clever, and I won't allow you to walk straight into danger."

She had phrased that wrong; Lucy knew so at once by the angry look on his face. Her other three grandsons had grown up with her high-handed orders, but Samuel had not.

"I don't recall asking your permission," he said curtly. "I'm leaving at dawn on Thursday."

"I don't mean to sound domineering," she said quickly. "But I'm worried about you—"

"Save your worry for someone who wants it. I'll handle the matter as I see fit."

He held out his arm, a clear indication that he considered the meeting finished. Rising to her feet, Lucy wrapped her hand firmly around the crook of his arm. But when he started to walk, she held him in place. There were things that must be said, whether he wanted to hear them or not.

He was as tall as her other grandsons, and she had to tilt her head back to gaze at him. His remote expression made her throat ache. "My dear boy," she murmured. "Please believe I would have been proud to raise you with your brothers—if only I had known of your existence."

Beneath her hand, the muscles of his arm tensed. "I was better off where I was. I didn't need you then. Nor do I now."

The jab hurt. Unable to hide her pain, Lucy said softly, "But *I* need *you.*"

After luncheon, all the men headed down to the other end of the lake to fish for trout. They took several of the older boys with them, including Michael's eldest son, William, the Earl of Hempwood, who had borne that courtesy title since birth. He was a precocious lad of eight with a thatch of dark hair and blue eyes that made him a miniature version of his father. From the moment he'd learned that his uncle Samuel had traveled around the world, he'd attached himself to Samuel's side.

Samuel found himself enjoying the company of his nephew. Over the past few days, they had exhausted the topics of Japan and China and Ceylon, and had moved on to India.

Now, as they lagged behind the rest of the group, William said earnestly, "Are there really snakes that you can charm by playing a flute?"

Samuel nodded. "They're called king cobras, and they're kept in a straw basket with a lid. For a penny, the charmer will play his blow horn, moving it back and forth, and the snake will rise from the basket, with its hood spread, following the movements of the charmer."

"What hood?"

"It's a mass of skin around the cobra's neck. He fans it out to frighten off predators—or to impress the lady snakes with his handsomeness."

"Huh," William said, picking up a stone and throwing it into the reeds. "If I was a cobra, I wouldn't bother with girls. They're too boring."

Samuel grinned. "You might change your mind as you get older."

"I suppose I shall be obliged to take a wife," William said distastefully. "I'm the heir, you know. It's expected of me. I shall have five children, just like Papa."

He looked so dejected by the prospect that Samuel felt an unexpected lurch of sympathy. Maybe he himself was lucky not to have had the obligations of the nobility. He had been free to choose his own life, to follow his inclinations. Odd, to consider his upbringing from that perspective.

As they reached the group gathered on the banks, Michael sauntered toward them. He'd shed his coat and rolled up his sleeves, looking relaxed, yet still the lord of the manor. "William, I believe you've pestered your uncle enough for the moment."

"But I was about to ask him about tigers," the boy protested.

"I'll show you a tiger's tooth later," Samuel said. "It's my good-luck charm, and it's in my chamber."

The boy's eyes goggled. "Truly? Can we go now?"

"No," Michael said firmly. "You may help me teach the younger ones how to bait the hook." Flashing Samuel a wry smile, he led his son away.

Samuel found himself smiling, too, a fact that disturbed him. He was keenly aware that over the past few days, he had forged an irreversible connection with his brothers. He had tried not to like them, tried to convince himself they were haughty and snobbish, but . . . they simply weren't. They were friendly, amusing, and hard-working, each with his own area of interest.

Michael had the huge estate to manage with all its myriad duties. Joshua was a physician, having studied in Edinburgh and trained during his service as a captain in the cavalry. Gabriel was an artist as well as an expert in antiquities; he and his wife Kate had collaborated on several scholarly books.

Samuel had to admit he could almost admire his brothers. They were good, honorable men who had welcomed him into their midst without the slightest hint of rancor. For that reason alone, he was tempted to walk away into the woods, to be alone so that he could remind himself of his purpose.

To found his own dynasty. To exact revenge by becoming their equal.

But who was he taking revenge upon? George Kenyon was long dead. Samuel's brothers couldn't be blamed for their luck of birth. And his grandmother hadn't been aware of her son's abandonment of Joanna Firth.

I would have been proud to raise you with your brothers—if only I had known of your existence.

He tightened his jaw. Devil take the dowager! She was a prime meddler and should have known of her son's cowardly deed. Yet Samuel was aware of a treacherous softening inside himself. He'd witnessed how she loved her family, reading to the children, organizing activities, giving eternal advice to her legitimate grandsons, who bore her interference with teasing and patience.

I need you.

His palms felt damp, his stomach in a knot. Dammit, he didn't need *her*. He would do as he'd planned, leave on Thursday morning, after the party. Once he was away from here, he would recover his equilibrium. He would build a life for himself and Cassie without the interference of the Kenyons.

"Hey, Sam! You'll miss out on the competition."

Gabriel motioned him down to the shore. A dark-haired man with a fondness for informality, he held out a fishing pole to Samuel.

Samuel went down the slope to join the other men, and took the rod from the youngest of his brothers. "Competition, eh? Biggest or most?"

"Biggest," Gabriel said. "Josh caught a ten-pounder here last year."

"At least we think it was that big," Joshua said over his shoulder, casting his line with military precision into the water. "He got away, but I'm aiming to catch the old fellow again today."

"Winner gets a guinea per pound," said Brand Villiers. The Earl of Faversham sprawled lazily on a tuft of grass, his line drifting in the water. A dangerous-looking character with a half-moon scar alongside his mouth, he had been friends with the Kenyon brothers since childhood.

Samuel baited the hook and cast his line into the water, where it landed with a plop. The breeze blew gentle ripples over the crystal blue of the lake. Marsh marigolds bloomed along the edge, and a pair of mallard ducks paddled among the reeds. The beauty of the place clutched at his chest, reminding him that he too might have grown up here if his father had acknowledged his paternity.

I would have been proud to raise you with your brothers—if only I had known of your existence.

Dammit, he wouldn't let himself think about how frail and forlorn the dowager had looked. And he especially wouldn't let himself believe she really did care. He was nothing to her but an obligation and a duty. He was another grandson for her to keep under her thumb.

Standing on the embankment, his brothers flanked him.

Deliberately Samuel turned his mind to fishing. "Do you catch the bigger ones in this spot?" he asked.

Joshua grinned, his white teeth gleaming in the sunlight. "Actually, we only come here to get away from the ladies. If we'd stayed, they'd've had us holding babies and untangling embroidery threads."

"And chattering nonstop about children and the trials of pregnancy," Gabriel added.

"And morning sickness," Brand said with a groan. "Charlotte's been plagued by it for the past month."

Gabriel and Joshua chuckled knowingly.

"Don't forget the cravings," Joshua said. "With our last one, Anne had me going down to the kitchen for pickles and cheese in the middle of the night."

"With Kate, it's slumbering endlessly for the first three months," Gabriel said. "I vow, she'd fall asleep in the middle of a sentence. Just you wait, Sam. You'll have your turn."

Samuel grinned at their good-natured ribbing. But he didn't say anything, because he was struck by the fact that Cassie had already exhibited at least one of the signs of incipient motherhood. These past few days, she'd been more weary than usual, taking naps, retiring early, and falling asleep in his arms. He had attributed it to the country air and all the activities here.

He hadn't realized that it might be a symptom of pregnancy.

Come to think of it, she hadn't had her menses, either, in the fortnight since they'd become lovers.

Samuel reined in a leaping surge of triumph—and a dark uneasiness. Dammit, he hadn't planned on their being here at Stokeford Abbey for so important a moment. He'd wanted them to be alone, building their own family apart from the Kenyons. He couldn't let her start thinking they'd be coming back here often, bringing their children . . .

He felt a tug on his line. Burying all other considerations, he applied his attention to reeling in the fish. Within moments, he landed a large, glistening trout, and it lay flopping on the grass.

While everyone gathered around, laying bets as to its weight, Michael appeared behind Samuel. His grim expression put Samuel on the alert. "What is it?"

"You'd better come with me," Michael said in a low tone that no one else could hear. "I've just spoken with one of my men. It seems your wife has some visitors at the front gate."

Summoned back to the abbey ahead of the others, Cassie hastened into the drawing room to find five men awaiting her.

Michael and Samuel stood at either end of the hearth, their grim expressions and dark handsomeness making them look like matching bookends. On three chairs in front of them sat her cousin, Walt, along with Philip Uppingham and Bertie Gunther.

Caught up by surprise and delight, she took only peripheral notice of the tension in the air. She hurried straight to her cousin, who sprang to his feet, looking somewhat travel-worn in his buckskin breeches and nut-brown coat, his cravat drooping.

"Walt, how wonderful to see you," she said, throwing her arms around him and kissing his cheek. She turned to greet Philip and Bertie, taking hold of a hand of each. They looked just as weary, as if they'd ridden hard, Philip in a claret coat over butternut breeches and Bertie in drab but sensible dark brown. "This is such an unexpected pleasure."

"Tell that to your husband. He's kept us cooling our heels for the past two hours." Walt flashed a resentful look at Samuel. "He's been questioning us as if we were criminals."

"We came to talk to *you,* Cassie, not him," Philip said, slumped in his chair and looking grumpy. "But he's accused us of murder and mayhem."

"We'd never do anything to hurt you," Bertie added, his gaunt face aghast. "Pray, tell him not to summon the magistrate."

Michael placed his hands on his lean hips, looking every inch the Marquess of Stokeford. "*I* am the magistrate in this area," he said. "I can arrest all three of you if you don't answer my brother's questions."

"You can't arrest me," Walt said, although he looked young and frightened. "I'm a duke of the realm."

"I don't care if you're the king himself," Samuel snapped. "You'll be spending the night in the dungeons."

Cassie huffed out a breath. Did he truly suspect one of her friends of being the murderer?

They were all at the ball that night, a little voice inside her head whispered. *Any one of them had had the opportunity to shoot Samuel.*

To silence her disloyal thoughts, she turned on Samuel. "Stop this at once. You can't treat my friends so rudely. To make these accusations is absurd."

"Is it?" he countered. "They've refused to say why they're here."

"I'll be happy to tell Cassie," Walt said in his most ducal manner. "But I'll speak with her alone."

Bertie and Philip muttered their support.

Samuel fixed Walt with an arrogant stare. "None of you will be alone with my wife. Whatever you have to say can be said in front of me."

He came forward and slid his arm around Cassie's waist, gently guiding her to a chair near the fireplace so that she could sit facing her friends. Like a guard dog, he took up a stance beside her. "Now talk," he ordered Walt.

Cassie wanted to protest his high-handed manner. But she knew Samuel was only trying to protect her. He was taking precautions, and he would soon realize that her cousin and friends posed no threat.

Unless one of them really *was* her secret admirer . . .

Walt looked oddly uneasy, shifting in his chair, frowning at Samuel, then at Cassie. "Dash it all, Cass. I didn't want to be the one to tell you this, but—"

"But we had to warn you," Philip said fervently, leaning forward, an artful brown curl tumbling onto his brow. "The gossip has spread through the *ton* like wildfire."

Bertie nodded in earnest agreement. "You see, everyone is talking about Lady Vanderly and *The Black Swan*!"

Once again I found myself in the clutches of Captain Cranditch. With the aid of two vile cronies, he commandeered the coach and made me his captive, along with Mr. Montcliff, who sat bound and gagged by my side.

As the coach veered toward the coast, to the place where his ship lay anchored, Percival Cranditch related his plan to Mr. Montcliff. "You'll watch me wed to the fair Belinda," he said, his face dark and fearsome beside that of his fair-featured half brother. "And then you shall take a dive to the bottom of the sea."

—The Black Swan

Chapter 27

A Deathbed Request

Cassie gripped the gilt arms of the chair and felt the dizzying sense of being trapped in a bad dream. She had put her book out of her mind these past few days. Stokeford Abbey had been a haven from the world, a peaceful interlude with the family she treasured.

Now all that was over.

She was keenly aware of Samuel standing beside her. *This* was not the secret that she'd wanted to confide to him. There was a happier one she held dear to her heart, one she had only just realized today.

But now Cassie couldn't bear to look up at his face, to see his reaction. She wanted to close her eyes and pray this nightmare would go away.

"A black swan?" Samuel asked. "And who the devil is Lady Vanderly?"

Walt, Philip, and Bertie stared beseechingly at Cassie. It

was obvious that none of them wanted to expose her as the author. Knowing it was too late to hide the truth, she took a deep breath and released it slowly. "I'm Lady Vanderly. It's my pen name. I wrote a novel called *The Black Swan*."

Michael uttered an exclamation of surprise.

Samuel didn't move, but she could sense his stunned attention on her. She could see him out of the corner of her eye, his posture stiff and motionless. Then he dropped down to his haunches beside her chair and gathered her hand in his. Amazement shone on the sculpted contours of his face.

"You've *sold* your book?"

"Not the one about Sophia Abernathy. A different one." And oh, dear God, he didn't know everything yet.

"Why didn't you tell me?" Looking more puzzled than angry, he stroked her hand reassuringly. "Did you think I'd be displeased?"

"I—I wasn't certain," she said lamely. "I sold it before you returned to England."

"Don't feel bad, Firth," Walt said. "She didn't tell any of us, either."

"*We* found out from Miss Harris," Philip added indignantly. "I never realized the chit was such a scandalmonger."

"So is her friend, Lady Alice," Bertie chimed in. "They've been telling everyone that the villainous pirate bears a striking resemblance to—" He clamped his mouth shut, his big ears turning red.

The three seated men exchanged a worried glance.

Samuel looked sharply at them, then back at Cassie. His intense blue eyes bored into her. "A resemblance to whom, Cassie?"

Her throat felt too dry to speak. He suspected already; she could see it in his eyes and in his dark frown. "To you, Samuel," she whispered. "I modeled the villain after you."

• • •

Cassie awakened to the soft light of sunset streaming into her bedchamber at Stokeford Abbey. Her drowsy gaze drifted over the canopied bed with its blue hangings, then alighted on Samuel, who sat in a comfortable stuffed chair by the window.

The last rays of the sun glistened on his ebony hair, and his bare feet were propped on an ottoman. His white shirt was open at the throat, revealing the crisply curling mat on his chest. A deep throb of desire tightened her womb. Then she noticed he was engrossed in reading a book.

Her book.

The realization jolted her to full awareness. All of her alarm and mortification returned to swamp her senses. He had been cool downstairs, saying little in response to her awkward explanations. He'd insisted upon seeing the book and determining for himself the closeness of the similarity. Cassie had given him her own copy, which she had secreted at the bottom of her traveling trunk, for she had been too proud of her accomplishment to leave it behind in London. Samuel had disappeared into his connecting chamber to read. He must have come back in here while she'd napped.

In spite of her distress, she hadn't been able to keep her eyes open. She had lain down on the bed and fallen fast asleep. And Cassie knew why.

While listening to her sisters-in-law today discuss their pregnancies, she'd realized the cause of her weariness of late, the tenderness of her breasts, the fact that she was three days late in starting her menses. Those signs all pointed at the stunning, wonderful certainty that Samuel's baby grew inside her. She had planned to share that happy news with him today, not the appalling truth of her book.

Gazing at him, she tried to gauge his mood, but his inscrutable face revealed nothing of his reaction to the story.

Was he waiting for her to awaken so that he could berate her? She had the childish urge to close her eyes again and pretend slumber, to postpone the moment of confrontation.

Instead, she sat up slowly, swinging her legs off the bed and straightening her lavender gown. "Samuel, if I could explain—"

"Wait." Without taking his gaze from the page, he held up his hand, palm out. "I wish to finish."

How had he read the book so fast? Did he find her story interesting? Or was he skimming to find the comparisons between Captain Cranditch and himself?

Fraught with uncertainty, Cassie went to the mirror to re-pin her tousled hair. As she did so, she anxiously watched Samuel in the mirror. He was intent on the book, turning a page every now and then.

She finished with her hair and wandered around the bedchamber, the Persian rug soft beneath her stocking feet. She straightened the quill pens on the small writing desk and alphabetized the books on a shelf. The waiting unnerved her, so she went to the casement window and gazed out at the rose gardens, where a young man methodically pulled weeds.

She turned her mind to the past three days. Their time here at Stokeford Abbey had been more than worthwhile. She could see signs that Samuel was beginning to feel more at ease, although he'd adamantly refused to discuss his family. Nevertheless, she had prodded him when the opportunity presented itself while refraining from pushing him too hard. Forming bonds with his brothers and grandmother was a slow process that simply couldn't be rushed.

But the hope in her heart had grown by leaps and bounds. Even more so now because of the new life inside her. If Samuel could forgive his family and learn to love them, she would happily burn the deed of separation and stay with him. She wanted him to remain here with her, getting to know his family by day and making tender love to her at night.

But if he was furious about *The Black Swan,* perhaps he'd leave for London that much sooner. Perhaps he'd even skip her birthday party on the morrow. She couldn't bear the suspense any longer.

As she walked toward him, he closed the book and lifted his gaze to her. And her spirits sank at the coolness she saw there. " 'The baseborn son of Lord S——,' " he stated. "Could you have been any more explicit?"

Though a part of her wanted to quail, Cassie faced him squarely. "I didn't know you very well when I wrote that book," she said. "You'd left me on our wedding night, and I was still angry."

"So this was some sort of revenge?"

The question flabbergasted her. "I didn't *mean* it that way. It was simply . . . a way for me to give vent to my feelings. And I never intended to sell the manuscript. Flora put the idea in my head, so I submitted the book. I was astonished when it was accepted."

"It would have taken very little effort to change the relevent descriptions."

His sharp tone hurt. "At first, I didn't think it mattered. You were gone, and no one would have noticed the similarities. Then you returned and wanted to go into society, so I went to Mr. Quinnell, my publisher. But it was too late. The book had already gone to the printer."

To her chagrin, Cassie felt wretchedly close to weeping. Crossing her arms, she hugged herself, willing away the lump in her throat. It was the changes in her body that made her emotions so unbalanced of late, for she had never been a watering pot. She had always scorned women who used tears to garner sympathy.

During her speech, Samuel had listened gravely as if weighing her sincerity. Now he placed the book on the table beside him. "All right, then, I'll believe you meant no ill," he said with a hint of formality. "And you shouldn't worry about the gossip. It will die down eventually."

"But it *won't,*" she blurted out. "Not if I do as Mr. Quinnell wishes me to do."

"Do?"

Her legs weak, Cassie sank down on the window seat beside Samuel's chair. "Because *The Black Swan* is so popular, he asked me to resurrect Percival Cranditch. To write another book about him."

A shadow crossed Samuel's face. "Have you already signed the contract, then?"

"No, not yet." Miserable and torn, she said, "Oh, Samuel, if I write a second book, it will only invite more comparisons to your past. What's worse, Mr. Quinnell wants me to make Captain Cranditch the hero. But Cranditch can't be a hero unless he makes peace with his half brother."

"Ah. I see."

That clipped statement held a wealth of meaning. With all her heart, Cassie wanted Samuel to say that he would make peace with his brothers, too, that he would be her hero.

But in the deepening dusk, he appeared as implacable as ever. The prideful set of his jaw, the coldness in his eyes, chipped away at her hopes and dreams. Was she foolish to think he could learn to see the light instead of the darkness? That he could change the beliefs that had been formed in childhood?

Fighting anguish, Cassie murmured, "What did she say to make you despise them so?"

"Who?"

"Your mother, Joanna." She leaned toward him, reaching out to touch his arm, his muscles tense beneath his shirt-sleeve. "You never speak of her. What did she say to turn you against the Kenyons?"

His guarded gaze met hers. "Nothing. She had nothing but praise for George Kenyon. Her love for him was an obsession that outweighed even her feelings for me. With her last dying breath, she begged me to go to my father here at Stokeford Abbey. She said I looked like him, and he'd know the truth, then, that I was his son."

Cassie's heart twisted. "But you never did go."

"Hell, no." Samuel sprang up as if the anger in him demanded release. "Why would I seek out the coward who had done that to her? The knave who had disowned me before I was born? He cared more for the dogs in his kennel than for me."

The depth of his pain knotted her breast. No wonder he'd had such a difficult time accepting his rightful place in the Kenyon family. He had been gripped not simply by hatred, but by a yearning for love and acceptance.

She rose from the window seat and slid her arms around him, holding him tightly, kissing his cheek and aching to erase the pain of the past. "Oh, my dearest, you *are* worthy of love. *I* love you. With all my heart and soul."

His gaze pierced her. But he neither acknowledged her confession nor returned it. Instead, his hand slid downward to rest lightly over her belly in a gesture of possessiveness. "You're all that matters to me, Cassie. You and our child."

Stunned, she covered his hand with hers. "You know? I just realized it myself today."

"So did I." He moved his hand to her hip, tracing her curves in an enticing caress. "I'm extremely pleased, too. I've wanted nothing more than for us to start our own family."

Our own family. His tone seemed to exclude all others, and although Cassie wanted only to lose herself in his embrace, she drew back slightly. "But we'll still come here to visit," she clarified. "I want our child to know his cousins, his aunts and uncles, his great-grandmother."

Samuel's gaze shifted slightly, as if to hide his thoughts. "There's no need to worry about that now. We'll discuss it later."

His evasion struck a knell of alarm in her. "No. I want the truth, Samuel. We'll return here, won't we? With a baby on the way, surely you can see the value of accepting your place among the Kenyons."

His jaw tightened, and he held tightly to her as his gaze probed hers with determined sensuality. "We only need each other, Cassie. You and I and our children, we'll form our own family. With your antecedents, our children will be accepted by the best circles. We don't need the Kenyons."

His answer was a stab to her heart, and Cassie shuddered from the pain of it. Samuel wouldn't change, not for her, not even for their baby.

A life without revenge had been her dream, not his.

She stepped back, out of his arms. "That was your plan all along, wasn't it? You wanted to get me with child so that you could establish your own dynasty to rival the Kenyons."

He didn't even bother to deny it. His face dark and moody, he stood in front of her. "There's nothing wrong with ambition. It's taken me far in the world. I've done it on my own, without help from anyone."

"It isn't a sign of weakness to need love. It takes far more strength to open your heart than to close it."

He said nothing to that; he merely tightened his lips.

Tears swam in her eyes, blurring his image, so that he appeared as a mystical figure, luring her into the prison of his dreams. She voiced the thought that ached inside her. "Will you make me choose, then, between you and the Kenyons?"

He clenched his teeth. "Don't be ridiculous. Come to Stokeford Abbey if you must. I won't stop you."

"But you won't be with me." Cassie couldn't remain with a man who held such hatred inside himself, a man who harbored animosity to a family that she considered as dear as her own. Though her heart was breaking, she forced herself to say, "It *is* a choice, Samuel. And I choose them."

At dusk, we were taken aboard the pirate ship. Mr. Montcliff was tied to the rail, whilst I found myself facing a frightened cleric who had been ordered to preside over the makeshift nuptials. The night grew dark and cold, and lanterns cast a flickering light over the proceedings. With the wicked Captain Cranditch at my side and a gang of gruesome corsairs gathered on deck, I could only gaze helplessly at Mr. Montcliff, memorizing his noble features and dreading his imminent death.

Then I noticed a tiny gleam in his tied hands. Praise God, my guardian held a penknife which he employed to cut his bonds.

—The Black Swan

Chapter 28

An Unwelcome Gift

The following morning, a folded document gripped in his hand, Samuel headed downstairs on a grim mission. He had to locate any two of his brothers. He required a few minutes of their time to act as witnesses.

It was Cassie's twentieth birthday. As his gift to her, he intended to give her what she'd wanted from the very start—his signature on the deed of separation.

The prospect made Samuel sweat. As he neared the bottom of the stairs, his knees almost locked. But he wouldn't let himself turn back. He had to make this sacrifice. He had to release Cassie from her unwitting role in his scheme to found a dynasty. He had to allow her to follow her own dream, to move into that cottage in the country, to have the freedom to pursue her writing, to make her own choices.

I choose them.

The agony of her words ripped into him anew. Even now,

his chest hurt so badly he could scarcely breathe. God, he couldn't lose her. He couldn't lose Cassie.

But he *had* lost her.

Unless he could prove to her that he'd abandoned his long-held hatreds. Not in promises, but in actions. He'd swallow his pride and make every effort to accept his brothers and his grandmother. Rather than offer empty vows, he'd *show* Cassie that he'd changed.

And he'd pray that she would come back to him of her own free will. She'd said she loved him, and he'd been stupid enough to try to force her to accept his scheme. The possibility that he had destroyed her love sat like an icy rock in his gut.

Unfortunately, he had to return to London and track the murderer. Maybe once he was back in familiar surroundings, the iron band around his chest would loosen. Maybe he'd stop feeling as if his heart had been torn out.

Maybe he'd grow wings, too.

It isn't a sign of weakness to need love. It takes far more strength to open your heart than to close it.

Was Cassie right? Had he thrived on hatred all these years because it had been easier than coming here to Stokeford Abbey and risking the pain of love? One fact was certain, he already missed Cassie grievously. He had never depended on anyone, but now he needed her as he needed air to breathe. It had taken no soul-searching for him to realize that he loved Cassie.

Boundlessly. Mindlessly. Endlessly.

But he had to release her. *He had to.*

He strode into the dining chamber to find Michael alone, finishing his breakfast. His brother set down the London newspaper and lifted his coffee cup. "We missed you and Cassie at dinner last night."

Samuel went to the sideboard and poured himself a cup.

He sat down, took a scalding gulp, and forced himself to admit, "We quarreled."

"Ah." Michael gave him a commiserating look. "By the way, Vivien read *The Black Swan* yesterday evening. Chiltern lent her his copy."

God, Samuel didn't want to have this discussion. He didn't want to remember how much he deserved to be portrayed as a scoundrel. "Then Vivien told you. About how closely it mirrors my situation."

Leaning back in his chair, Michael nodded. "I have to say, I thought it your just deserts."

The old animosity stirred in Samuel, but he fought it back. His brother only spoke the truth. Samuel had wed Cassie for all the wrong reasons; he had earned the label of villain. And like Cranditch, he couldn't be transformed into a hero unless he let go of past hatreds.

But first he had to let Cassie go.

Despite all his tough business dealings, Samuel had never been more unwilling to broach a topic. He coerced himself into unfolding the paper and sliding it across the table to his brother. "I'd like you to witness my signature to this."

Michael picked up the document and scanned it, his face darkening. "What the devil? Isn't this a bit drastic?"

"It's what Cassie wants. What she's always wanted." Samuel's throat felt tight, but he continued. "She had the deed drawn up while I was abroad, and posted it to me. I came straight home."

"Good God. I would have, too. And I'd have done my damnedest to talk her out of it."

Samuel grimaced. "I tried, but she wouldn't relent. So I made a bargain with her. If she'd introduce me to London society, I'd sign the deed at the end of the season."

"To buy yourself time to convince her. Very clever. But the season isn't over."

"It is for me." He no longer had any ambition to be accepted by the *ton.* What did it matter without Cassie at his side?

"Are you certain this deed is still what she wants?" Michael asked.

"If it isn't, she can burn it. I forced her to marry me. Now, the choice of keeping me in her life will be entirely hers."

"I see." Giving Samuel a keen look, Michael pushed back his chair. "Very well, then. Shall we go to my study? I'll ring for Joshua to join us."

They left the dining chamber and headed through the maze of medieval corridors. As they entered the cavernous great hall, Walt came trudging down the curving staircase. He wore a pale blue coat that only served to intensify the pitiful spots on his young face. When he spied Samuel, he flashed an angry glare.

"Firth," he said as if the name were a curse. "I want a word with you."

"Come with us, then," Samuel said. "You may as well be my second witness."

In short order, they sat around the large desk in Michael's study. The walls held shelves of books and ledgers, and green draperies lined the tall windows. Sunlight laid a dappled pattern over the crimson-and-gold carpet.

After signing his name beneath the other two signatures, Walt stuck the quill pen back into its holder. His face still bore a look of dazed shock. "Dash it, Firth. I was going to demand that you either treat Cassie with more respect or get out of her life. But you've stolen my thunder."

"My apologies." It was all Samuel could work out past the tangle of his emotions. Staring down at the deed, he felt a sting of heat in his eyes. Lord, it would be the worst disgrace to shed tears in front of these men. Gritting his teeth, he sprinkled a fine dusting of sand over the wet ink.

It was done. Having been witnessed by the Marquess of

Stokeford and the Duke of Chiltern, the private deed of separation would stand up in any court of law.

Now, Cassie alone could change the state of their marriage. He couldn't dictate to her anymore. She had the freedom to choose her own life.

I choose them.

God. Oh, God.

Michael went to a glass-fronted cabinet and brought over a decanter and a glass. He poured a brandy and handed it to Samuel. "You look as though you could use this, old fellow."

As Samuel took a gulp, a footman in Kenyon livery entered the study and bowed to Michael. "There are two gentlemen at the door, m'lord. They asked to see Mrs. Woodruff."

Cassie was already dressed for the party when she heard the tapping on her door.

After Samuel had left her chamber the previous night, she had wept her heart out. Now, sluggish and dispirited after a restless sleep, she sat at the small writing desk and attempted to distract herself by jotting notes for a new book about Percival Cranditch.

Thus far, she had written *Percival = Samuel.*

The tapping sounded again, but Cassie didn't rise from the chair to answer. She had no desire for company this morning. The mere thought of joining the family downstairs distressed her.

Somehow, she must find the strength, though. Today was her birthday, and the celebration was scheduled for the afternoon. She couldn't bear to disappoint everyone, especially the children, who had been planning a surprise, judging by their gathering in small groups these past three days, whispering and giggling, hushing one another whenever she drew near.

So she would smile and laugh. She would show a happy

face to the Kenyons. Although her heart was breaking, she would enjoy her birthday.

But not now. Not yet.

Then the door opened and Flora peered inside. Seeing Cassie at the desk, she came scurrying into the chamber like a little brown mouse fleeing a hawk. Her eyes were red-rimmed and she was visibly shaking. "I—I'm sorry to disturb you. But—but you must come quickly!"

Cassie rose to her feet at once, concern for her friend overriding all other considerations. "What is it?"

Flora's hands trembled as she reached out to Cassie. "The most terrible thing has happened! I saw them from out of my window."

"Saw whom?"

"Norman and Charles. Oh, Cassie, I fear they've come for me!"

Samuel was spoiling for a fight. It was exactly the outlet he needed for his pent-up emotions. But first he wanted some answers.

On Michael's instructions, the two visitors had been brought straight to his study, where they sat in front of the desk. Walt had moved to a wing chair by the fireplace, having been ordered by Michael to remain silent. Michael perched on one edge of the desk, Samuel on the other.

The Reverend Norman Woodruff was a red-faced man with pale blue eyes and a protruding belly that strained at the seams of his clerical blacks. Sitting beside him, Charles Woodruff was a younger version of his father, short, thickset, with weaselly features. He fancied himself a gentleman, judging by his tailored green coat and tan breeches.

At present, he was gloating while the elder Woodruff did the orating.

"I demand to take my wife home with me," Norman said,

bristling with outrage. "I traveled all the way from Lancashire to London to look for her, only to find that you'd spirited her away. 'Twas a long, difficult ride for a man of my delicate constitution."

He looked about as delicate as a crocodile on the hunt.

"You won't be seeing Flora," Samuel said. "She's under my protection now."

"Protection!" Norman said, his face apoplectic with fury. "My son tells me you want my wife as your mistress, and I shall not tolerate it!"

"Charles can spin quite a tale," Samuel said, noting the smirk on the younger man's face.

The reverend shook his fist. "Cad! Dare you deny your culpability? A man of your ill repute and dubious patrimony?"

"You're speaking of my brother," Michael said sharply.

His swift response was gratifying. But Samuel didn't need his defense. "Your son is a liar," he said flatly. "He's trying to deflect attention from his own lechery toward *my* wife."

Charles glowered. "I beg your pardon! That's a challenge to my honor—"

"I accept," Samuel said instantly.

Charles's jaw dropped. "I—I didn't mean . . . I won't fight a man who isn't a gentleman."

Samuel ignored his blustering. He had one simple test to perform before he proceeded. Looking at Michael, he said, "Have you any paper?"

Michael obligingly reached into a drawer of the desk and handed him a blank sheet of stationery embossed with the Stokeford crest. Samuel shoved it in front of the two visitors, along with a quill and a silver inkwell.

"Print your name, both of you."

Norman frowned suspiciously. "I won't," he said. "You could write any drivel above it, and it would appear that I'd signed it."

"I'm not asking for your signature. I'm ordering you to print your letters as a child would do."

Charles appeared just as disconcerted as his father. "It's some sort of trick. Don't do it, Papa."

"You'll both do it," Samuel said. "Or I'll break all your fingers."

Norman seized the pen and hastily printed his name. Charles did likewise, snatching the writing implement out of his father's hand.

Samuel took up the paper and studied it. Norman wrote with flourishes and curlicues. Charles was left-handed, with a spidery quality to his back-tilted letters. Neither sample matched the firm, bold hand of Cassie's secret admirer.

It wasn't proof positive, but it satisfied Samuel. He removed his coat and rolled up his sleeves.

Michael did likewise. "Which one do you want?" he asked.

"The one who threatened my wife," Samuel said. "But I'll gladly take them both on myself."

"Nonsense. I'd enjoy the practice. I once trained with champion pugilists, but it's been a decade since I gave anyone a thorough drubbing."

"What?" Norman lumbered to his feet, looking like an overblown bully who'd been backed into a corner. "What are you saying?"

Charles slid out of his chair and edged toward the door, but Samuel deftly blocked his exit. "I—I've something to do," Charles began.

"So do I." With that, Samuel let his fist fly. He hit the younger man's jaw with a loud crack. Charles went staggering backward. He crashed into a chair and thumped down on the carpet, shaking his head in a daze.

Norman gaped at his son, then at Michael who strolled toward him. "Stand back, Stokeford. Dare you threaten me, a man of God?"

"Say your prayers, Reverend." With obvious relish,

Michael swung a blow to the face that sent the older man stumbling into the unlit fireplace. His arms wheeling, he landed in a heap at Walt's feet.

Walt sprang up from the leather wing chair and stared with widened eyes. "What the devil's going on? He's the vicar of St. Edmund's!"

"He's also a wife beater," Michael said. "He threw her against a wall, hit her with his fist, and broke her arm."

Walt looked incredulous. "Flora? He hurt *Flora*?"

"It happened last year," Samuel said, flexing his stinging knuckles. "He agreed to a separation in exchange for her silence. Only Cassie knew."

"His craven act has never been avenged," Michael added. "Stand up now, Reverend. Let's see you fight a man for a change."

As Norman cowered, his son made a dash for the door.

Samuel caught Charles by his coat and yanked him around for another swift uppercut. The younger man's teeth snapped together. Charles fought back with tricks unbecoming to a gentleman. Street tricks that Samuel knew from his childhood.

Charles jabbed his fingers at Samuel's eyes, but Samuel dodged him, sinking his fist into Charles's soft belly.

Next, Charles went for the groin, bringing up his knee. Samuel twisted to the side and knocked him off balance. While he was reeling, Samuel caught him with a jab to the nose.

Charles teetered into a potted fern on a pedestal. The plant crashed to the floor, and earthenware shattered. Charles landed on a shard and yowled. He rolled over, clutching his backside.

Across the chamber, Michael finished off Norman with a series of well-aimed punches.

Samuel heard a gasp from the doorway of the study. Spinning around, he spied Cassie standing with Vivien and Flora.

A jolt more powerful than any physical blow struck Samuel. His blood lust altered to fierce need. In his agitated state, he took an involuntary step toward his wife.

Then he remembered the deed in his pocket. He had no right to hold Cassie in his arms. Not anymore.

Vivien ran toward her husband. "What is going on here?" she demanded. "This is a house, not a boxing ring."

Blood streaming from his nose, Norman sat moaning on the floor, clutching his arm. "H-he tried to kill me, m'lady," the vicar blubbered in a nasally tone. "He broke my arm. S-summon a physician at once."

"That would be my brother Joshua," Michael said, rubbing his knuckles. "Unfortunately for you, he shares my distaste for wife abusers."

Vivien examined his hand, turning it over and clucking. "You should have taken your quarrel outdoors," she chided. "As for you, Reverend, you'll leave this house at once. Else *I* shall take a whip to you."

"Wait," Walt said suddenly. He'd been standing back, watching the proceedings, but now he marched forward to stand over the cleric. "I have authority over St. Edmund's Church. You will pack your belongings and leave the vicarage. I'll make certain that you never again occupy a post of such honor."

Norman Woodruff sputtered half-heartedly, clearly recognizing the futility of dissuading the angry duke.

"Bravo," Michael said, putting his hand on Walt's shoulder. "I'll help you spread the word."

As the two Woodruffs clambered to their feet, Samuel instinctively started toward Cassie, intending to shield her as the defeated pair left. He didn't want either Cassie or Flora to face so vile a pair of villains.

But as he approached, her gaze met his. Her eyes were cool and inscrutable, clearly rebuffing him. Then she turned her back and led Flora out of the study.

• • •

As the birthday festivities came to a close, Cassie slipped out of the drawing room and headed for the staircase. Her cheeks felt stiff from forcing a smile for so many hours. Her head ached from the effort of appearing lively and cheerful. Now, she could think only of escaping to her bedchamber.

Despite the pain in her heart, the celebration had been a marvelous one, with cake and presents and laughter. The children had put on an amateur theatrical with each child performing a talent. Fourteen-year-old Amy had sung with beautiful clarity, five-year-old Susan had lisped her alphabet, and eight-year-old William had played a flute while a papier-mâché snake rose from a basket. Controlled by one of the younger cousins hidden under the table, the creature had accidentally flopped over at the most dramatic moment, much to the amusement of the audience.

Although Cassie had laughed along with everyone else, true joy eluded her. The happiness of everyone around her had only served to underscore her own misery. As dearly as she loved the Kenyons, she was keenly aware that they possessed in bountiful measure everything she had just realized she desired for herself: a husband, children, a family.

How could she have ever thought she'd be happy living alone in a cottage? Without Samuel, the future stretched out like a bleak gray mist.

When she reached the top of the stairs, Cassie gently settled her hand over her womb. No, not bleak. She would have her son or daughter to love.

Samuel's child.

Throughout the party, she had been aware of Samuel across the drawing room, talking with his brothers and their wives. He'd played the pianoforte, much to everyone's astonished delight. Even from a distance she had seen that his knuckles were skinned from the fight. How she had wanted to kiss him, to thank him for defending Flora, to fuss over him and tend to his wounds.

But Cassie couldn't. Nor could she let herself hope that he'd reversed the hatred of a lifetime. Samuel had stayed for the celebration only because he'd promised to do so, and in his own way he was an honorable man. In the morning, he would be departing for London.

Never to return.

Cassie drew a shaky breath. Foolishly, she had hoped for a small gift from him, some trinket she could treasure. But among all the gaily wrapped packages of books and shawls and jewelry, she had discovered nothing at all from her husband. It only served to emphasize how little she meant to him.

She had never been more to Samuel than a pawn to exact revenge.

Even yesterday, when she had opened her heart and admitted her love for him, his response had been to state his wish to start his own dynasty.

With your antecedents, our children will be accepted by the best circles. We don't need the Kenyons.

But she *did* need them. And so did Samuel, though he was too blinded by ambition to realize the pricelessness of love and family.

The late afternoon sun slanted into her bedchamber, lighting the patterned rug with deep jewel tones of blue and gold. Her head throbbed from the weight of her wretchedness, and she couldn't think beyond falling into bed, closing her eyes, forgetting her troubles.

As she went straight to the four-poster, Cassie spied something lying on her pillow. It was a rolled parchment tied with a bit of pink ribbon.

She picked it up, half fearing to see "Lady Cassandra Grey" written in block letters. But no name was inscribed on the outside. Mystified, she unrolled the paper and examined it.

Her knees collapsed. In anguished disbelief, she sank

down onto the edge of the bed. It wasn't a message from her secret admirer. It was the deed of separation.

And at the bottom, Samuel had signed his name in a bold black scrawl.

A short while later, Cassie caught Walt out in the corridor before he could join the other adults who were playing cards in the drawing room, the children having gone back up to the nursery. She motioned him into a small antechamber and closed the door.

In a daze of despair, she showed the deed to Walt. "You witnessed this. How *could* you?"

"Stokeford signed, too," her cousin said defensively. "And Firth said you'd had it drawn up yourself."

"That was before I . . . before I fell in love with him."

Her voice broke, and Cassie wilted into the nearest chair. The gloom of utter hopelessness swamped her. She rolled up the deed to hide the legal words that granted her the freedom she'd once thought vital to her happiness.

Now, she couldn't imagine being happy without Samuel. But he didn't want her anymore. He had lost no time in ridding himself of a wife who had defied his wishes.

Walt pulled up a footstool and sat down, propping his elbows on his knees and his chin in his palms. "Dash it all, Cass, I didn't mean to make you sad on your birthday. If it helps, Firth looked down in the dumps about the matter, too."

Her foolish heart fluttered, but she firmly crushed the flicker of hope. "Of course he'd be reluctant," she choked out. "Samuel doesn't like to lose. And this deed makes him look like a failure to the Kenyons."

Walt frowned. "Then why did he sign it? Is he so angry about your book?"

"No . . . that's only a small part of it."

He had signed because she had chosen the Kenyons over him. Oh, why had she lost patience and forced the issue?

She should have given him more time to form attachments to his family. It was unreasonable to think a few days were sufficient to change the beliefs of a lifetime. She had pushed him because she'd been so hurt by the discovery of his intention to further his ambitions by using not only her but also their *child*.

Cassie took several shallow breaths and willed herself not to burst into tears again. Yet her eyes filled nonetheless, the hot moisture spilling down her cheeks. "Oh, pray forgive me. I can't talk about this."

Walt looked as helpless as any man faced by a weeping woman. He fumbled in his pocket, then passed his folded handkerchief to her. "If you wish it, I'll call him out. I'll—I'll say I was misled into signing the deed!"

Cassie started in shock. "No! Good heavens, no. You'd only make matters worse."

"Then what can I do? Shall I talk to him? I'll tell him he can't treat you so shabbily!"

And then Samuel would seek her out. They'd have another quarrel.

Oh, dear God, she couldn't face him again, to look at him and know that he no longer wanted her. Another thought occurred to her. Surely there was no avoiding a confrontation with Samuel, anyway. He'd very likely come to say goodbye to her before he left for London.

The horror of that struck Cassie. Everything in her quailed at the notion of seeing Samuel again, knowing that he valued his hatred more than her, even more than their baby.

In desperation, she seized Walt's hands. "I can't stay here at Stokeford Abbey. I must leave. *Now*."

Walt blinked in surprise. "Leave? But . . . where would you go?"

"I—I don't know. Not back to London, though. It's too

dangerous. And not to Strathmore Castle, either." She didn't want to go anywhere that held memories of Samuel.

Then Cassie knew exactly where she could find the solitude that she so craved, the one place where she could heal her wounds and adjust to life alone. "Please, Walt. You must take me to Chiltern Palace at once."

As the minister made a quavering recital of the marriage ceremony, I stood stiffly beside my unwanted bridegroom. Percival Cranditch hadn't noticed that his imprisoned brother had quite nearly sliced through the ropes that bound him. The captain kept his covetous attention on me.

I struggled not to show the fear and dread in my heart. Even with Mr. Montcliff's release, how was one man to conquer a host of wicked pirates?

—The Black Swan

Chapter 29

The Mysterious Coach

"That's the last hand for me," Samuel told his brothers as they sat together playing cards in the drawing room. "I've a few matters to attend to before I leave in the morning."

The truth was, he couldn't sit here any longer, knowing that Cassie had gone upstairs well over an hour ago. She must have found the deed by now.

He burned to see if she appreciated his sacrifice and realized that he'd granted her the freedom to choose. God willing, maybe he'd see love shining in her eyes again.

"You'll give her the deed?" Michael asked, his face serious.

Samuel's throat tightened. "I already left it in her chamber."

His brothers exchanged a glance. "I trust you wrote her a letter," Joshua said. "You explained your reasons."

"Actually, no . . ." Noting their worried expressions,

Samuel felt a jab of uneasiness. "But it's what she wants. It's what she's always wanted."

Gabriel raised a dark eyebrow. "Wives say a lot, and it's seldom what they really want."

"Men are forthright, but women . . . God only knows what they're thinking," Michael said wryly. "There are always hidden meanings that we're expected to understand."

Joshua nodded. "Quite. I know I'd get bloody hell from Anne if I did something so drastic without a word of explanation."

Alarmed, Samuel thrust back his chair. "I'd better find her, then."

Leaving his brothers, he hurried up the grand staircase, his footsteps echoing in the vast hall with its tapestried stone walls. He half ran down the long, twisting corridors to their suite of rooms. Cassie wouldn't have misinterpreted his action, would she? What else would she think he'd meant by signing the deed?

That he'd cast her off. That he no longer desired her. That he'd chosen hatred instead of love.

God, he'd been a stupid fool! But surely he could fix matters. He could explain. It wasn't too late.

At her door, he reached for the handle, then thought better of barging in unannounced. He rapped hard on the thick oak panel, heedless of the soreness in his knuckles. He could no longer walk in on her. With his signature on that deed, he had relinquished all the privileges of a husband.

There was no answer. Unable to bear the suspense, he opened the door and strode inside the chamber. But Cassie wasn't napping. Nor was she in the dressing room.

The purple light of dusk fell upon the empty bed where they had made love during their first three nights here at the abbey. Those tender memories only intensified the pain in his chest. Where was Cassie?

Then he spied a folded note lying on the pillow. Occupying the same spot where he'd left the deed of separation.

"We should have waited till morning," Walt fretted as he drove the curricle down the narrow country road. Like a darkening veil, dusk settled over the hills and hedgerows. "I shouldn't have let you talk me into this harebrained scheme. We've scarce gone ten miles and it'll be full dark soon."

Heartsore, Cassie huddled beside him in the open carriage, the bitter breeze making her shiver despite the shelter of her cloak. With the lowering of the sun below the horizon, the air had grown decidedly chilly. But she had already felt cold inside and out. "I couldn't bear to stay at the abbey a moment longer," she murmured dispiritedly. "I couldn't bear to see Samuel."

Or any other of the happy families. Although the Kenyons would be kind and sympathetic, Cassie felt too devastated to be with them.

"Firth will skin me alive if I don't keep you safe from harm." Her cousin glanced over his shoulder as if expecting him to come riding in pursuit. "Dash it all, if he hadn't sent Bertie and Philip back to London, they could've come along to help guard you."

Fraught with misery, she leaned against Walt's arm and sniffled. "I don't want the company of anyone else but you."

"Aw, Cass, don't turn on the spigot again. I'll take you wherever you want to go—tomorrow."

"Tomorrow?"

Walt pointed with his whip. "There's an inn ahead, at the crossroads. I mean to engage two rooms for us."

Cassie spied the pinprick of light far ahead. "*Must* we stop so soon? There's still enough light to see."

Walt gravely shook his head. "I don't mean to alarm you, but there's been a coach following us since just outside the gates of the abbey. With all Firth's talk of murder and mayhem, I'd feel better if we stopped."

Cassie looked over her shoulder at the gentle slope they had just descended. She saw only the narrow ribbon of the empty road; then the coach rumbled over the hill, a black shape outlined against the purple sky.

For a moment her errant mind fancied it was Samuel coming after her, as he had on the night he'd abducted her. She imagined him a penitent knight in shining armor, rushing after her to beg her forgiveness . . .

But the coach wasn't rushing. It trundled along at a steady pace, another traveler intent on reaching some unknown destination.

Besides, Samuel likely didn't even know yet that she was gone. Gladys, her maid, would find the note at bedtime. She'd give it to Samuel then. It would be too late for him to set out, even if he wished to do so.

And why was she even thinking about her husband? He didn't want her anymore; he'd made that plain enough when he'd signed the deed of separation. She had left the document behind at the abbey, for she never wanted to lay eyes on it again.

Walt deftly guided the curricle into the yard of the inn. A hostler ran forward to hold the horse. Walt hopped down, then lent a hand to Cassie. "Come inside," he said. "A hot cup of tea will restore your spirits."

Cassie doubted that anything could restore her. But she let Walt believe it because he'd been a darling to depart on the spur of the moment for a trip halfway across the country. "I'll—I'll be there shortly. I'll get my—my bandbox."

Truth be told, Cassie couldn't bear to greet strangers in her present state of melancholy. Even that small effort overwhelmed her. She wanted only to go straight to bed and burrow beneath the covers, to forget her heartache in sleep.

As they stood there, the other coach continued on past the

inn, the team of horses trotting smartly. Walt watched it go; then his worried expression eased and he patted her shoulder. "I'll be back in a moment."

He strode into the inn, and the door closed behind him. The hostler unloaded their small bags—there had been no time to pack a trunk—and then led the horse and curricle back to the stables.

Forlorn and lonely, Cassie picked up the circular bandbox and felt the darkness close around her. The cold wind tugged at her bonnet. What was Samuel doing right now? Was he still playing cards with his brothers? Had he even noticed her absence?

She mustn't think about him. Yet his smile, his touch, had become so vital to her that she couldn't block him out. At least in their son or daughter, she would always have a part of Samuel. And he would visit them, for he had promised he'd never abandon his child.

Perhaps by then she would have accustomed herself to living without a husband. What seemed impossible now in her anguish might become more bearable with the passage of time. But oh, how she wished he'd come for her!

The thud of hooves and rattle of wheels caught her attention, and a coach entered the innyard. It stopped a short distance away, the driver a huddled dark lump. Was it the same coach that had just gone past? Had its occupants turned back to seek shelter here for the night?

The door opened and out stepped the black figure of a man. A man whose features lay in shadow.

Oddly, he stooped down as if to set something on the ground. A dark shape in the gloom, he stood up again and surveyed the yard. His gaze seemed to stop on her.

Cassie's heart tripped over a beat. Her mind leaped with impossible hopes. Gasping, she took a step toward him. *"Samuel?"*

Captain Cranditch's voice rang out as he made his eternal vow to me. "Aye, at last the fair Belinda is mine."

When it came my turn to do likewise, I knew that it was my one, my only chance to create a diversion. "No," I cried. "A thousand times no!"

In desperation, I sprang for one of the lanterns and dashed it to the deck.

—The Black Swan

Chapter 30
The Black Swan

"She's gone to Chiltern Palace with Walt," Samuel grimly told the family gathered in the drawing room. Unable to contain his fear, he paced back and forth. "As if that young pup can protect her! Dammit, she was supposed to stay right here!"

Guilt rode him hard. It was his fault that Cassie had left. His fault that he'd given her the deed of separation without a word of explanation. His fault because he'd been too much the coward to present it to her in person. He hadn't wanted to admit to her face that he'd been wrong to make hatred the focal point of his life.

Michael shot to his feet. "We'll organize a search party. They can't have gone far."

"I'll go to the stables," Joshua offered. "We'll need horses saddled."

"You'll also need provisions," Vivien said. "I'll fetch something quickly from the kitchen." She and Anne and Kate hurried out of the chamber.

Gabriel and Brand left with Joshua. Samuel was intensely grateful for their willingness to depart on a moment's notice. They hadn't hesitated, even though dusk gathered outside and they'd likely ride long into the night.

Her face pale, his grandmother hastened toward him, stopping to regard him anxiously. "Find her, Samuel. Bring her back to us."

The dowager could have berated him for his stupidity. But her delicate, age-seamed features held only worry and fear and love.

Those same sentiments battered his own heart. On impulse, he put his arms around her frail form. "I'll do my best . . . Grandmama."

As Cassie stepped closer to the man, she realized to her horror that she'd made a dreadful mistake.

In contrast to Samuel's tall, muscled body, this man had a broader, stocky form. He lunged, seizing her in his iron embrace.

Screaming, she swung the bandbox at his head. It thudded against him, and he cursed, though he didn't relax his firm hold. He thrust her inside the coach, jumped in after her, and pulled the door shut. No sooner had he done so than the vehicle set off at a brisk pace.

Jerked off balance by the abrupt departure, Cassie grabbed for the hand strap to steady herself. No lamp illuminated the black interior, and the man was a menacing shadow right beside her. In desperation, she sprang for the door, but her captor moved quicker.

"'Tis sorry I am to do this, m'lady," he muttered.

She knew that voice. Before Cassie could fully form his name in her mind, he clamped a cloth over her mouth and nose, filling her lungs with an acrid stench that sent her spiraling down into darkness.

• • •

As the party of men rode swiftly out of the stables at Stokeford Abbey, Michael reviewed the plan. They would follow the main road to Exeter, then fan out to ensure that Walt and Cassie hadn't taken a back route toward Chiltern Palace. They would make inquiries at every inn and in every village along the way.

Samuel grimly told himself she'd be safe with her cousin. Surely Walt had the sense not to travel after dark. Yet Samuel couldn't shake a deep-seated fear. He gripped the butt of the dueling pistol in his pocket. He wouldn't rest easily until he knew she was back at the abbey, well guarded by his brothers.

The two-story stone structure of the gatehouse loomed through the darkness. At the clatter of their approach, a middle-aged man stepped out to greet them. As he unlatched the huge iron gates, the balding servant looked up at Michael.

"M'lord," he said respectfully, "a man in a black coach asked entry this afternoon, whilst you were busy at the party. When I told him I'd have to seek your permission, he went away without leaving his name."

Shaken, Samuel drew his horse up close. "Describe him."

As the gatekeeper complied, a fury of recognition struck Samuel. God! He should have guessed the identity of Cassie's secret admirer.

And if that villain had been here only a short time ago, then he might have lain in wait for Cassie.

The awareness of sensations lured Cassie on a slow, upward trek to consciousness. Her temples throbbed with dull regularity. Her cheek lay against a pillow that smelled dank and musty. A gentle rocking motion stirred queasiness in her belly.

Her eyelids felt heavy, as if weighed down by stones. She felt an urgency to open them, a fear that something dreadful would happen if she didn't make the effort. So she did.

Her vision was blurry at first. The soft yellow light of a lantern cast a glow over a small chamber with one tiny, round, uncurtained window that showed the darkness of night. The furnishings were few and sturdy: a chair, a wooden chest, the bunk on which she lay.

Painful memories flooded her. Samuel's name on the deed of separation. Her flight with Walt. The black coach . . .

The door opened and her abductor walked in, a stocky man with reddish hair and the freckled, impish face of a leprechaun.

Cassie stared at him in stupefied shock. Through dry lips, she whispered his name. "Mr. MacDermot."

"Aye," he said, his grin both charming and ominous. "'Tis happy I am to reveal myself to you at last. I've been planning this moment for a long time."

"Where am I?"

"Aboard *The Black Swan*. I christened her after I found out about your book." He shook his finger at her. "You're a sly one, concealing your talents behind a pen name."

He was the sly one, hiding his identity, pretending to be her friend . . .

She sat up slowly, her head spinning. Her thoughts were still scattered from the aftereffects of the potion he'd used on her. "I—I wish to go home."

Ellis MacDermot seated himself on the chair. "I'm afraid that's impossible, m'lady. We'll be sailing in a few hours with the dawn tide."

Panic clutched at her. "Sailing? Where are you taking me?"

"Why, home to Ireland to be my wife. 'Tis what I wished for the duchess, but she refused me."

The duchess . . . her mother.

Her mind whirled as she tried to grasp his words. He had wanted her mother to *marry* him? And now he wanted Cassie?

He must be a madman.

An icy chill tiptoed up her spine. Mr. MacDermot was her secret admirer. He had written those letters. He had disguised his handwriting because she would have recognized it from his signature in the ledger at the lending library.

That meant he was the one who had enticed her out into the garden that night. He had fired a pistol at Samuel . . .

Her heart trembled and her palms felt damp. Cassie took several deep breaths to ward off terror. She must stay calm. She must keep him talking, give herself time to figure out a means to escape.

But he sat squarely between her and the door.

"*You* sent me the diamond serpent," she murmured. "At the library, you told me . . . that Colonel Mainwaring said the duchess was wearing it on the night she died. But was it really *you* who was there with her? On that barge returning from Vauxhall Gardens?"

"Aye, that I was," MacDermot said, shaking his head sorrowfully. " 'Twas a tragedy, to be sure. Six years ago, almost to this very day."

"What happened? Did . . . did you push her?"

He pursed his lips as if annoyed by her question. " 'Twas her fault, not mine, for making me angry. She wouldn't forsake the duke, you see. When I tried to convince her, she backed away and fell over the railing. I grabbed for her, but all I could save was the diamond serpent."

Cassie could picture the scene, MacDermot pressing his lewd attentions on the duchess, forcing her backward until she'd fallen into the dark waters.

Dear God. He really *had* killed her mother. And Cassie herself could be next.

Fighting dread, she moved slowly to the edge of the bed

and lowered her feet to the floor. "You asked me to wear the diamond serpent. But I never saw you at Nunwich's ball." *Except outside in the garden.*

"I wasn't invited." Resentment darkened his features, giving him a sinister cast. "I had to climb the fence—unlike Firth."

"You despise my husband," she murmured, throat tight. "Is that why you stole the money from his firm?"

MacDermot shook his fist. "The common bastard stole *you,* that's why. You shouldn't be using his name. As daughter of the Duchess of Chiltern, you belong to me."

"You killed . . . Hector Babbage."

"'Twas an accident, I vow! The little weasel wanted to confess. He wouldn't listen to reason, so I dragged him up to the roof, just to frighten him. He panicked and fell to his death."

Cassie thought it far more likely that he'd given the accountant a push. But MacDermot seemed intent on deluding himself, and she feared to infuriate him by arguing.

Before she could manage a response, MacDermot's gaze narrowed on her. "You weren't supposed to accept Firth that night at the theater when I sent him over to you."

"*You* sent him?"

"Aye. I'd made it a habit to watch for his return aboard one of his ships. And I knew where you were going that night. You'd told me yourself at the library a few days before."

Cassie had thought little of their polite conversations. But he had been watching her the whole time, seeking information about her schedule. And now there was a smoldering anger in his gaze, for he clearly resented the fact that she had reconciled with Samuel.

She eyed the door. If only she could get past him, find something with which to strike him over the head and knock him out . . .

On inspiration, she crossed her arms as if her stomach

hurt. "Please, I'm feeling rather queasy, and I need some fresh air. Will you be so kind as to take me above deck?"

MacDermot rose to his feet. Reaching to the back of his waistband, he drew forth a gun. "Aye, 'tis time we went up and waited for him."

Cassie quailed at the sight of the long-barreled pistol. "Him?"

"Firth, of course. I expect he'll be showing up very soon."

Her heart leaped, but she crushed her fledgling hopes. MacDermot was lost in his own illusions. Even if Samuel went searching for her, he'd never find her on board a ship. "Perhaps we should go ashore, then. I'll help you look for him." On land, she'd have a better chance to escape.

The Irishman grinned slyly. "He'll be here, m'lady. You see, I left him a message."

His brothers having gone off down other roads, Samuel rode alone into the innyard to find Walt standing beside his saddled horse, talking to a stout man who held a lighted lantern. Walt was obviously upset, his sandy hair wildly windblown and his gestures agitated.

Upon spying Samuel, he came running. "Cassie's gone!" he cried. "She's been abducted! I've been all over the countryside looking for that damned coach, and she's nowhere to be found!"

The news hit Samuel like a sword thrust in his gut. He dismounted quickly. "What coach? When?"

"The one that was following us. I—I went into the inn to engage rooms for us and I heard her scream. I rushed outside, but the coach was already gone. The hostler had unhitched the horse from my carriage, so I was delayed going after her and—oh, dash it! It's been two hours and I don't know where to find her."

Samuel mastered his leaping panic. The trail grew colder

with each passing moment. But he needed more information. "Do you know which direction the coach took?"

"That way." Walt pointed toward the south. "At—at least I think so." His face crumpled, making him look painfully young. "It's all my fault. I should never have left her alone. I *knew* better."

"Blame *me,* dammit," Samuel snapped. "And I'll find her. By God, I will!"

He stalked to the avid-eyed innkeeper and grabbed his lantern. With any luck, he'd see fresh wheel tracks in the dirt and get a clue to the coach's direction.

Tracks where a dozen vehicles had passed. But what else could he do?

He hastened to the verge of the yard—and spied a flutter of paper beneath a rock. Snatching it up, he examined it by the light of the lantern.

Upon seeing the familiar block lettering, he felt his blood turn to ice.

Standing on the deck of the yacht, Cassie shivered from more than the bite of the cold wind off the darkened sea. Ellis MacDermot had tied her hands. He'd hung the lantern on a hook so that it would act as a beacon. He stood beside her, the pistol in hand, still babbling his deluded nonsense.

"Soon I'll be invited to all the best parties," he was saying. "I'm heir to my cousin, Lord Killarney. But once he suffers a tragic accident, I'll be the earl. I'll be eminently worthy of you, m'lady."

Dear God. MacDermot meant to murder his cousin, as well.

Her teeth chattering, Cassie kept her desperate gaze trained on the black shoreline. A faint lightness to the east presaged the dawn. In conjunction with her fear, the swaying of the boat nauseated her.

MacDermot seemed to believe Samuel would come after her, but she wasn't so certain. Even if he did search for her, the chances were slim that he'd find that note MacDermot had left at the inn.

More likely, Walt would discover it and come dashing to his death. MacDermot would shoot her hot-headed young cousin. Unless she could stop him somehow.

The Irishman sidled closer, his expression ghoulish in the light of the lantern. "Lady Cassandra Grey, will you do me the great honor of becoming my countess?"

Cassie controlled a shudder. He had to be a lunatic to believe she'd accept so heinous an offer. It was on the tip of her tongue to say that she had a husband already. But she didn't want to remind Mr. MacDermot of his plan to murder Samuel.

Placate him, she told herself. *Let him think he's won.* "That's very generous of you. I—I would be happy to accept."

"And just in the nick of time." Grinning, MacDermot pointed to the shore. "Look. Our guest has arrived at last."

Flames shot up, and in the ensuing panic, I lost sight of Mr. Montcliff. Then I spied him through the smoke, engaged in a sword battle with Percival Cranditch.

Caught by surprise, Cranditch fought back mightily. But Mr. Montcliff was lighter and quicker, and the pirate captain went down under a rapid thrust of the rapier.

My guardian seized me in his arms and helped me down into a skiff. As he swiftly rowed me to safety, I had one last view of the burning pirate ship against the blackness of night.

—The Black Swan

Chapter 31
Cranditch Redeemed

Her heart pounding, Cassie strained to see through the darkness. Then she saw it—a shadowy figure in the dinghy that MacDermot had left on the beach. The lantern on the yacht would guide the visitor to them.

Dear God. Was it Walt—or Samuel?

Ellis MacDermot seized her from behind and yanked her in front of him. " 'How shall I kill him, m'lady? Shall I cut his throat? Or do you fancy seeing him hang from the yardarm?' " He chortled. "That's what Captain Cranditch said. But *I* intend to shoot your husband."

Her stomach twisted. The situation had an eerie similarity to the scene in *The Black Swan,* when Mr. Montcliff had come to ransom Belinda. But reality proved no match for fiction, for Cassie lacked the courage to dive into the icy brine.

"Unhand me," Cassie said unsteadily. "Captain Cranditch never used Belinda as a shield."

"So right you are. But Montcliff didn't have a pistol as Firth might. This way, I'll get off the first shot."

Not if Cassie could stop him. She had a plan, a tenuous one. But she daren't put it into action yet.

The dinghy drew nearer. Occasionally, she could hear the whisk of the oars over the sounds of the wind and the sea. MacDermot's ragged breathing felt hot against her ear. Out of the corner of her eye, she could see the pistol in his hand. Every muscle tensed, she peered into the darkness. All the while, she wrestled in vain with the tight bonds around her wrists.

The dinghy entered the pale circle of light cast by the lantern. She braced herself to knock MacDermot off balance and spoil his aim.

But except for a greatcoat lying in a heap, the dinghy was empty.

The icy water shocked his senses. Clenching his jaw, Samuel swam beneath the yacht to the opposite side from the lantern. His muscles threatened to lock as he surfaced beside the long black shape of the boat. By force of will, he hoisted himself up to the railing.

Though it was a fair spring night, the cold wind hit him like a frigid wintry blast. MacDermot held Cassie as they peered over the side.

At the shifting of the yacht, the Irishman turned to look back, bringing the pistol around. At the same moment, Samuel sprang.

He went straight for MacDermot's arm, twisting it, causing the gun to discharge harmlessly into the air. Cassie wrenched free and backed away.

Having been forced to leave his own pistol in the dinghy, he pummeled MacDermot with his fists. The Irishman was a wily fighter, strong and quick and determined. He fought back, returning punches, ducking blows, holding his own.

Cassie appeared behind MacDermot, the lantern in her bound hands. Realizing her intent, Samuel drew a breath to shout at her. Too late.

She hurled the lantern onto the deck and scuttled backward.

Glass shattered. Flames spewed up, catching MacDermot's clothing, transforming him into a living pillar of fire.

MacDermot yowled. He clawed at himself in a futile attempt to douse the blaze.

Shielding her view, Samuel pulled Cassie to the railing and clambered down into the dinghy. He untied her bonds, picked up the oars, and rowed for shore, his driving thought to protect Cassie.

She sat frozen, staring back at the burning yacht. Then she threw her arms around him, kissing him frantically, touching his wet clothes as if to seek an injury. "Samuel! Are you all right?"

She reached for his greatcoat and wrapped it around him. But he couldn't forget the terrible moment of seeing her throw the lantern. "A damned foolish trick!" he growled. "You could have set yourself on fire."

"I had to help you. Oh, Samuel, he could have killed you."

"Or *you*." With a vibrancy of emotion, he abandoned the oars to hug her fiercely, speaking from the depths of his unfrozen heart. "My God, Cassie, I love you. I love you so much."

In the bright light of morning, they arrived back at Stokeford Abbey, where Cassie found herself the recipient of much joy and gladness. Samuel insisted upon carrying her inside the house. Though he could scarcely take his eyes from her, she was struck by the fact that he smiled at his grandmother when she thanked him for bringing Cassie back safely.

"With your permission," he said to the dowager, "I'll take her upstairs straightaway and put her to bed."

His grandmother beamed. "She's your wife. You may certainly do as you will."

Cassie wanted to retort that he should ask *her* permission, but for once, she enjoyed his masterful manner. Her head tucked into the hard cradle of his shoulder, she tightened her arms around his neck. "Hurry, Samuel. I'm eager to know what you'll do."

A round of laughter swept the gathering, his brothers standing beside their wives. Michael, Joshua, and Gabriel had met them on the road, having heard the story from her cousin. Walt had been abjectly sorry for his negligence, and she had promptly absolved him of guilt.

Samuel carried her up the grand staircase, taking the steps two at a time. She hadn't let go of him since he'd rescued her like a true hero. Riding with him, she had related everything that had happened with Ellis MacDermot, and in turn, Samuel had described his horror at discovering her gone.

"I love you. I love you so much."

Her heart melted as she remembered his impassioned declaration. He had begged forgiveness for not explaining his purpose behind signing the deed. He had meant only to release her from her unwitting role in his scheme, to allow her the freedom to make her own decisions. Sometime during his third apology, she had fallen asleep in his arms, awakening only upon their arrival home.

Home. Yes, Stokeford Abbey was a home to her, but she also wanted her own home . . . with Samuel and their children.

When they reached her chamber, he set her down carefully on the bed as if she were made of fine porcelain. His eyes were hungry, but he gave her only a chaste peck on the cheek. "You're weary," he murmured. "I'll help you undress." His touch impersonal, he reached for the buttons on her gown.

She reached for the buttons of his breeches.

He stayed her hand, bringing it to his lips to kiss the back. "Later," he said hoarsely. "You need to sleep, darling."

"We'll sleep together." His clothing had dried, and his shirt was stiff with brine as she dragged it out of his breeches. "But wait, I've just remembered. I believe we've something else to do first."

His mouth tilted into a rakish angle. She knew what that smile meant, and she returned it with a laugh.

"Yes, there's that," she said. "But I mean something else entirely."

Hopping off the bed, Cassie went to the desk and found the deed of separation where she'd left it in a drawer. She carried the document to the hearth and tossed it onto the flames, watching it burn. Remembering the fire on the yacht, she couldn't help a shudder.

Samuel slid his arm around her, drawing her close. "Regrets?"

"None." She burrowed into him and let his warmth heal her. "Oh, Samuel, after being abducted myself, I've a great admiration for Belinda. *I* could never have jumped into the sea as she did."

"Good God, I should hope not!" Samuel tipped up her chin so that she could drown more safely in his blue Kenyon eyes. "And I trust I've proven that Cranditch can be redeemed. He does cut a more dashing figure than Mr. Montcliff."

Half irked and half in agreement, she sent him a mock glower. "Perhaps Cranditch *is* the more fascinating of the two. But Mr. Montcliff is the hero of *The Black Swan*. He rescues Belinda time and again."

"She rescues herself by jumping off the pirate ship. And in that scene in the church, when Cranditch nicked him with the sword, Montcliff swooned like a pansy."

"He was *injured,* that's why. And he did save her in the end like a true hero." In the midst of her pique, Cassie noticed the faint smirk that creased Samuel's chiseled features. Instantly, the warmth of desire bathed her insides. With his open white shirt and dark breeches he looked every bit as wicked as Percival Cranditch.

He ran his finger down the bridge of her nose. "But Cranditch is far more popular with the ladies," he said. "Because you based him on your villainously handsome husband."

The truth of that enveloped Cassie in happiness. Henceforth, she'd make her heroes as darkly appealing as her husband. "You're a conceited wretch, that's what."

Samuel nuzzled her throat, sending delicious shivers over her skin. "I'm a wretch for you, my love. Only for you."

THE END

I awakened to find myself lying in a rowboat, my cheek pressed to the damp wood hull. Beside me rested my companion, Mrs. Mason, her wrinkled features composed in slumber. For a moment, I could not imagine what had happened to bring us to so unusual a circumstance. Then the memory of the fearsome storm washed over me, and I sat up with a gasp.

I found myself facing the roughly handsome face of Cap-

tain Percival Cranditch. Plying the oars, he rowed steadily. "Awake at last, Lady Pamela? Look there, and see our new home."

A stretch of green land loomed on the horizon. Palm trees waved along the sandy beach. "Why, 'tis merely an island. I wish to go home to England."

"You shall. With any luck, we'll be rescued in a few weeks."

"Weeks!" I cried out. "But that is impossible. I cannot stay here with you—a pirate captain."

"Indeed," he replied, his grin undaunted. "Then it is lucky for you that I have reformed my wicked ways. You've nothing to fear from me."

I doubted his avowal, for despite the dire circumstances, his ocean-blue eyes twinkled at me, causing my foolish heart to flutter.

—The Further Adventures of The Black Swan

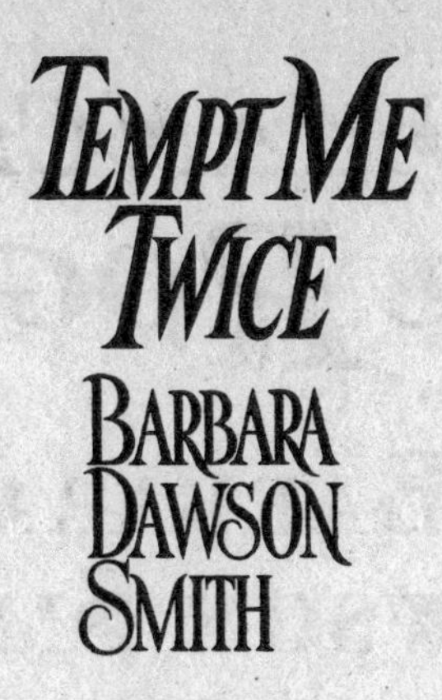

New York Times Bestselling Author of
ROMANCING THE ROGUE

A rogue shrouded in mystery, Lord Gabriel Kenyon returns from abroad to find himself guardian of Kate Talisford, the girl he had betrayed four years earlier. Now sworn to protect her, he fights his attraction to the spirited young woman. Although Kate wants nothing to do with the scoundrel who had once scorned her, Gabriel is the only man who can help her recover a priceless artifact stolen from her late father. On a quest to outwit a murderous villain, she soon discovers her true adventure lies with Gabriel himself, a seducer whose tempting embrace offers an irresistible challenge—to uncover his secrets and claim his heart forever…

"Barbara Dawson Smith is wonderful!"
—Affaire de Coeur

"Barbara Dawson Smith makes magic."
—Romantic Times

ISBN: 0-312-99891-0

ROMANCING THE ROGUE

BARBARA DAWSON SMITH

When Michael Kenyon, the Marquess of Stokeford, finds his grandmother having her palm read by a gypsy beauty, he's convinced that Vivien Thorne is a fortune hunter. The Marquess is determined to expose her as a fraud—and Vivien is equally determined to claim her rightful heritage. Yet neither the spirited gypsy nor the notorious rogue foresee the white-hot desire that turns their battle into a daring game where to surrender is unthinkable . . . impossible . . . and altogether irresistible.

"Barbara Dawson Smith is wonderful!"
—Affaire de Coeur

"Barbara Dawson Smith makes magic."
—Romantic Times

ISBN: 0-312-97511-2